More Praise for *Honeymooners*

"Chuck Kinder is one of th[e] [...] American fiction ... *Honeymoon[ers]* [...] loud humor on every page and [...] pain and follies of the artist's life. This is a splendid book."
—Scott Turow

"Brisk and lacerating, like vintage Albee."
—Walter Kirn, *GQ*

"Hilarious, heartbreaking."
—*Time Out New York*

"*Honeymooners* is, like a hangover, painful and shot through with stinging remorse; and yet the long dark night of the soul it chronicles is so rich with tall tale, funny episodes, and unforgettable incident—as well as unexpected moments of genuine lyrical grace—that one finishes this mythic morning-after story feeling ready at once to sally forth in the estimable company of Chuck Kinder, the mighty Sasquatch of American fiction, and do it all over again."
—Michael Chabon

"*Honeymooners* possesses that 'magical old-timey light,' the light of Kesey, McClanahan, R. Crumb, and the youthful Kerouac. Kinder's *very* funny novel is an homage to a raffish, boozy, disconnect-swagger-life teeming below the surface of the settled old middle-class properness the rest of us cling to. With his wonderful ear for the culture, his mock-sorcerer's pointy hat, a rather startlingly clear vision of human frailty, and by not putting too fine a point on, really, anything, Kinder has illuminated a seam of American longing and celebrated it—even made it lovable."
—Richard Ford

"Garishly funny ... *Honeymooners* shines a dark light on our literary cellars and lower depths. Chuck Kinder's angle of attack is all his own."
—Larry McMurtry

CHUCK KINDER, a native of West Virginia, is the author of two previous novels, *Snakehunter* and *The Silver Ghost.* He teaches fiction writing at the University of Pittsburgh.

By Chuck Kinder

Snakehunter

The Silver Ghost

Honeymooners

A CAUTIONARY TALE

Chuck Kinder

A PLUME BOOK

PLUME
Published by the Penguin Group
Penguin Putnam Inc., 375 Hudson Street, New York, New York 10014, U.S.A.
Penguin Books Ltd, 80 Strand, London WC2R 0RL, England
Penguin Books Australia Ltd, Ringwood, Victoria, Australia
Penguin Books Canada Ltd, 10 Alcorn Avenue, Toronto, Ontario, Canada M4V 3B2
Penguin Books (N.Z.) Ltd, 182–190 Wairau Road, Auckland 10, New Zealand

Penguin Books Ltd, Registered Offices:
Harmondsworth, Middlesex, England

Published by Plume, a member of Penguin Putnam Inc.
This is an authorized reprint of a hardcover edition published by Farrar, Straus and
Giroux. For information address Farrar, Straus and Giroux, 19 Union Square West,
New York, New York 10003.

First Plume Printing, June 2002
10 9 8 7 6 5 4 3 2 1

 REGISTERED TRADEMARK—MARCA REGISTRADA

The Library of Congress has catalogued the hardcover edition as follows:

Kinder, Chuck.
    Honeymooners : a cautionary tale / Chuck Kinder.
        p.   cm.
    ISBN 0-374-17258-7 (hc.)
    ISBN 0-452-28325-6 (pbk.)
    1. Male friendship—Fiction. 2. Married people—Fiction.
3. West (U.S.)—Fiction. 4. Authors—Fiction. I. Title.
PS3561.I426 H66 2001
    813'.54—dc21   00-063616

Printed in the United States of America
Original hardcover design by Jonathan D. Lippincott

PUBLISHER'S NOTE
This is a work of fiction. Names, characters, places, and incidents either are the products of
the author's imagination or are used fictitiously, and any resemblance to actual persons, living or dead, business establishments, events, or locales is entirely coincidental.

This book goes out for

my old coach

Richard Scowcroft

Diane, always Diane

Contents

Honeymooners

Blue Brontosaurus

1

Ralph and Alice Ann had been mere kids and mostly innocent of any adult sense of dire consequences when they first met, fell head over heels in love, and married, using the pressures of pregnancy only as an excuse.

Ralph was eighteen, fresh out of high school, and working in a sawmill to save college money, when one summer evening, after an afternoon of driving around drinking beer, he and some pals pulled into a thunderbeast theme park on a whim. They sat there for a time in the gravel parking lot in Ralph's old rattletrap Ford polishing off their beers and lying about babes. Ralph sipped his suds and stared up at the blue face of a brontosaurus looming above the trees like some strange, low moon with unfathomable yellow eyes.

Ralph and his pals lurched along the park's gravel paths among plants and trees strangely tropical for the Northwest and totally unknown to Ralph. Ralph picked leaves shaped like birds or bats in flight, and he sniffed them and held them up in the evening light. Ralph and his pals climbed great blue backs, swung from blue necks, took leaks on legs like blue tree trunks. Playing monster movie, Ralph and his pals split up, stumbling among the narrow paths grunting like goofy Godzillas.

Deep into the park, Ralph rounded a bend in a gravel path to discover the most beautiful blond girl he had seen in his life. She stood in a small clearing, hosing down a dinosaur, the dusk a haze of light about her as she sprayed prismatic mists of water over the beast's blue back. She wore red short-shorts and a white halter top, and the ends of her long blond hair were darkened with water. Her tanned shoulders and long legs were wet and shining. The leaves of the trees and bushes about the clearing dripped, and water dripped from beneath the blue dinosaur, and the air smelled as rich as any rain in Ralph's memory. Ralph could hear the soft hiss of the hose and from somewhere in the tropical trees around him muffled laughter, as though from another life. Small, bright rainbows glistened over the blue beast, and through the glowing bell of mist and light the girl's long, lovely, tan face floated before Ralph, and the air captured in his chest was like an ancient caged breath. Ralph could imagine this beast the girl watered moving off in the next moments under the dripping trees to disappear.

2

When Alice Ann was ten her mother died after a stroke, and Alice Ann hated her for doing it, for leaving her like that, leaving Alice Ann and her half sister, Erin, to live with Alice Ann's crummy stepdaddy in his hot, cramped trailer at the edge of her stepdaddy's dinosaur park.

Alice Ann would grow more and more to look like her mother, tall and slender, with small, delicate breasts, boyish hips, that cascade of blond hair, even the voice, deep without resonance, a voice screaming would destroy for hours.

One afternoon soon after the memorial service, Alice Ann's crummy stepdaddy picked Alice Ann and Erin up after school. Lookit in the backseat, he told them. Your momma's riding in the backseat, he said, and snickered. Alice Ann looked in the backseat, where she saw a silvery canister with her mother's name and dates of birth and death etched on its shiny side.

Alice Ann thought Ralph looked like a young Abraham Lincoln. Ralph was the smartest boy she had ever met. Ralph wrote poems and he had big plans in which that sawmill played no part. Ralph had dark brown eyes that widened and flashed when he talked about a future to be fished like shining, deep water. The first time Ralph kissed her, Alice Ann thought about how fateful it felt, the way their bodies, both tall and lean, seemed to fit like pieces of a puzzle, bone against soft place, convex against concave, the perfection of dark hairs on the back of Ralph's huge, gentle hands as they caressed Alice Ann's small blond breasts. Alice Ann's stepdaddy hated the sight of Ralph.

Late one summer night, a month after they met, Alice Ann and Ralph made love for the first time in the darkness beneath the blue brontosaurus. When Ralph opened his eyes finally, he said, Holy moly, I'm in love. Alice Ann did not move. A faint breath in her throat told Ralph that she knew what he meant. Ralph had been a virgin. When Alice Ann skipped her period, Ralph bought her a tiny diamond ring. Years later, when Alice Ann finally broke down and told Ralph who had done it to her before him, Ralph told Alice Ann it no longer really ate his heart out that she hadn't been a virgin, too. Besides, her rotten, lowlife stepdaddy was by that time dead as a doornail.

3

When they were first married, Ralph and Alice Ann did not have the proverbial pot to pee in, so they could not set sail like some lucky honeymooners to exotic spots to launch their life together. Forget any thoughts of Hawaii, Niagara Falls, any Caribbean cruise under a yellow, tropical moon and countless stars to romantic ports of call, forget Disneyland. No, Ralph and Alice Ann had to launch their life together at the Dixie Court Cabins and Trailer Park at the southern edge of town. Their cabin had a tiny black-and-white TV set which worked well enough, though, and there was a tiny swimming pool out front, and down the road there was a discount liquor store with an adjoining lounge, and they had enough money for two nights alone before they would move into the small back bedroom of Ralph's mom's trailer.

On their second and last evening there, Ralph had splurged on a bottle of high-class Scotch, and as he walked back to the cabins from the liquor store, he had felt enormously happy. He was looking forward to another long night of abandoned love-making. *Abandoned*, a word he liked the sound and taste of and said over and over to himself, rolling it over his tongue like a cherry-flavored LifeSaver; *abandoned*, the only word to describe what it had been like, throwing caution to the wind, and good manners, making all the noise they wanted, making juicy sounds during sex that were, well, so *abandoned* they were downright animal. Alice Ann, Ralph had gasped at one point while they were taking a breather, this business sure is, you know, abandoned. Alice Ann, Ralph had said, let's always be abandoned.

As the Dixie Court came into view, Ralph saw that Alice Ann was standing beside the little pool in front. She was wearing her new red bikini and she was wrapping her wet hair into a white towel. The early-evening light seemed to shine off her beautiful brown skin, and Ralph felt a flutter in his stomach. There she was, he thought with pride and wonder and lust, his new wife, his bride, the new Mrs. Crawford. Alice Ann was motionless except for her lifted slender arms and her hands folding her hair into that towel. It seemed to Ralph that even from this distance he could catch the scent of her flesh. She was standing slightly on tiptoe, so that the sleek muscles of her long, tanned legs were flexed and lovely-looking. Ralph felt his weenie wiggle.

Alice Ann seemed to be staring at something in the distance, something in the line of pine trees at the darkening edge of the woods maybe. Ralph looked past her, in the direction of her intent gaze, but he couldn't see a thing of interest. When he looked back at her, he noticed for the first time that the two men who were staying in the cabin next to theirs were sitting out front in metal lawn chairs. These men were on a fishing trip, and Ralph and Alice Ann had spoken with them briefly the night before and then again this morning, when they had run into each other at breakfast in the little diner down the road. Ralph had given them a tip about a spot he knew on a nearby creek good for brown trout, and then he and Alice Ann had chowed down on a breakfast of a half-dozen pancakes and three over-easy eggs with extra bacon each, before they had raced back to their cabin to make lots more abandoned love, their fingers and mouths still sweet and sticky with maple syrup.

Both the men were bareback, and they were sitting there in the metal lawn chairs sipping from cans of beer and staring at Alice Ann, and Ralph wondered suddenly if Alice Ann knew this. Although Alice Ann was but a few feet from Ralph, he had the weird feeling that he was observing an image of Alice Ann that had been in some way magnified from far away, as though he were watching her from the wrong end of a telescope. As though it was not the real Alice Ann standing there but some sort of aura of her. The more intently Ralph stared, the more rarefied with clarity and sharpness her features became, yet always with that sense of magnified distance. Who is she? Ralph wondered. Who is she?

Ralph had stood there, frozen to the spot, as he wondered if Alice Ann was posing for those perfect strangers, and the intense, peculiar desire he felt for her gripped his groin and made him both giddy and sick to his stomach. It was as though some beautiful but terrifying image of great portent were being projected before his eyes, the sort of image a story might turn upon.

The one thing Ralph knew for certain was that, in the story he planned to write, this dramatic, frozen moment would set the narrative off in a direction full of utterly unexpected danger and possibly disaster. *Yes,* Ralph had thought, the wife in that story would have made juicy abandoned love the night before with her new husband. And they would have held one another tenderly while they pledged to preserve forever the excitement and mystery of their love and marriage. And then that wife would turn right around and betray that husband in the story. She might not want to do it, but she would have no choice. Ralph would bend that wife in the story to his will. He might even make the wife in the story sleep with both those bareback strangers, if that would make things more interesting. And maybe the husband in the story would betray the wife, too, in order to stir even more trouble into the plot. Even if the husband, too, didn't want to do it. He might have to, for the sake of the story.

Sperm Count

1

In college Jim Stark's first wife, Judy, a very pretty, perfectly nice, sensible young woman who everybody declared was a dead ringer for that American television sweetheart Mary Tyler Moore, had been a cheerleader, vice president of her sorority, and, in her senior year, Homecoming Queen. Judy had made good grades as a math major and planned on teaching high school four years before starting her family of two boys and two girls, about what her own mother had accomplished, in the baby department anyway. When her old boyfriend, a handsome, hell-raising halfback, lost his athletic scholarship due to academic difficulties and dropped out of college his senior year to drive a beer truck for his father's beer-distributing company and drink beer a lot, Judy studied the Dean's List late into the night. Jim Stark was no football star, and he was supposedly something of a moody James Dean loner type, but she had seen him around campus, and he was a pretty big guy and dark, her type, and pretty cute in a hoody, sideburned kind of way; also, he wrote a column for the college newspaper, and most important, he was on the Dean's List in pre-law. There were rumors about Jim Stark, true: that he worked nights as a bartender-bouncer at that forbidden Big Al's place across the river and that as a teenager he had been in some serious trouble with the law. Somebody even told Judy that this Jim Stark guy wrote poems, but he sure didn't look like any fairy to Judy. And who believes every rumor, anyway?

Judy's new husband's law school idea was a joke, of course, and by default, for lack of something better to do, besides enter adult life, Jim eventually earned an M.A. in English literature at West Virginia University, his thesis a Jungian analysis of the poetry of Matthew Arnold (another joke). Which was not necessarily a bad turn of events, however, since Jim was lucky enough to secure a teaching position at a small private college in southern Pennsylvania. College instructors certainly didn't pull in the loot like lawyers, but there was adequate prestige in it back home with family and former boyfriends. Things could have been worse was the way Judy looked at it. She could have ended up married to the driver of a beer truck, which was a job Jim, frankly, would have traded up for.

After a couple of years teaching at the small college, Jim applied to and was accepted by a prestigious Ph.D. program in Victorian Studies, where he rather jokingly planned to explore and catalogue every dark sexual archetype that informed the Victorian imagination. Jim requested a leave of absence from his teaching job to begin his studies, and that June he and Judy traveled to the university town, where they put a deposit down on a lovely first-floor flat with a working fireplace. Judy had already secured a teaching position at a good local high school, and she enrolled to attend evening classes to continue her work toward an M.A. in Guidance and Counseling. Judy began sewing curtains for the new apartment, and they splurged from their meager savings to buy two pole lamps, a wood-tone cuckoo clock for the mantel, and several framed Keene prints of children with enormous, concentration-camp eyes, which Judy had always considered decorative.

But then, in early August, Jim suddenly withdrew half their remaining savings and boarded a bus for San Francisco. In San Francisco Jim moved into a commune of expatriate, doper West

Virginians, and in a letter of explanation to Judy announced that the sick, dark sexual longings of the Victorians meant little to him really, and that he had been a closet flower child all along and he could no longer live a lie. Judy suspected that her husband was deranged from drugs, which was more or less true. Clearly, in the selection of one's lifemate department, Judy had really dropped the ball. Divorce was the only answer, Judy decided, especially after she had secured the word of her loverboy, a junior high school football coach named Doc, that he would forsake his wife and retarded baby daughter for a new life with Judy, after all.

It astonished Judy when Jim wrote her that he had won a writing fellowship to Stanford University (she hadn't even known Jim had applied). At the end of the two-year-fellowship period he would have an M.A. in creative writing under his belt, which was a terminal degree and in some ways more marketable than a Ph.D. in something goofy like Victorian Studies. Maybe there was something to this writing goofiness, after all, Judy speculated. What if her goofy husband actually wrote some old book and sold the thing to the movies?

Because her loverboy coach was balking about abandoning his retarded baby daughter, Judy told him to just forget it, and somewhat relieved, she joined her husband in California to launch a new life.

At the end of his fellowship period, Jim was offered a three-year appointment as a Jones Lecturer, which did not pay beans, true, he acknowledged to Judy, but the prestige of teaching at Stanford would enable him to secure very promising teaching positions in the future, he assured Judy. Jim's first novel, a sort of revenge upon his childhood, had been published by then to generally good reviews, but had sold less than a thousand copies. For months after the novel was published, the first thing Judy would ask Jim when she arrived home each evening from work at the end of her rope was were there any calls about the book? Nope, Jim would inform Judy, nope, no phone calls, no big paperback sales, no calls from tinsel town.

Then one evening at dinner Judy informed Jim that it was time they started planning their family. She hated her job as a sportswear buyer, hated traveling, hated flying in airplanes. She wanted to be at home with babies, like most of her college girl friends were. She wanted a brick house. She wanted furniture of her own. Their rented life had run its course with her. Jim's dog-gone dream of becoming a famous writer was dragging her down. Jim had been a Stanford lecturer two years and had published a novel, so if he got off his butt he could surely secure some promising teaching position for the following fall and begin supporting his family like the husbands of her college girl friends did. Meanwhile, they should take advantage of their insurance benefits and the facilities at Stanford. Stanford had an advanced medical program in artificial insemination techniques, Judy informed Jim, and she announced that she had talked with a doctor at the clinic on campus that very day.

They were sitting at the kitchen table talking after a dinner of squabs stuffed with liver, bacon, and wild rice, a side dish of French stringbeans, Belgian endive salad, and ambrosia served in scooped and scalloped lemon halves. From earlier phone-call comments, Jim had suspected some relationship shit was going to hit the fan that evening, and Jim, a henpecked former tough guy, had slaved over dinner in a tizzy. Now Judy took several pamphlets from her purse and pushed them across the table in front of Jim. Then she handed Jim a small plastic jar.

Well, how was dinner, honeybunch? Jim asked Judy. —Do you think that stuffing was too dry? What about that currant jelly, did that hit the spot? Judy told Jim dinner was dandy and she was stuffed to the gills, and then she told him to read this literature on artificial insemination before the doctor's appointment she had scheduled for him the following Tuesday. He's a real nice doctor, Judy had told Jim. —You'll like him. He makes you feel real relaxed, she said. The little plastic jar had Jim's name typed on a label taped to its side. It was for a sample of Jim's sperm, which would be analyzed to determine his sperm count, Judy explained. Jim would have to time things right, because he had to get his sperm sample to the clinic by a certain deadline after he did it. It? Jim had asked Judy. *It*, Judy said, and wiggled her eyebrows suggestively. Judy told Jim she would accompany him her-self, except she would be out of town next Tuesday. You'll like this doctor, she repeated. —I told him, she said, that we had sex about twice a week. I read in *Cosmopolitan* that sex twice a week is about average for a normal couple our age. In case he asks you, too, so we'll have our stories straight.

Sex! Jim hooted and hopped up from the kitchen table. —Twice a week! Who says that's any of that bastard's business in the first place? Jim inquired as he snapped open a beer he had grabbed from the refrigerator; it foamed over his hand onto the floor and he tossed it into the kitchen sink. —Our stories straight! Christ, we're not applying for a fucken loan. That sumbitch better not ask me nothing like that if he knows what's good for him! Jim informed Judy as with shaky hands he filled his Mickey Mouse Club collectible glass to the brim with vodka. Normal couple! Jim said. —What's that supposed to mean? And how can you spring something like this on me, anyway?

You're the so-called writer around here, Judy reminded Jim. —You know what *normal* is supposed to mean, all right. And if you don't, well, buddy, go look it up in your hundred-dollar *Webster's Dictionary.* And you're a fine one to talk about some-body springing something on somebody. You owe me, buster, Judy reminded Jim. You better do this, she said.

2

So that next Tuesday found Jim flopped naked as the day he was born in his darkened bedroom with his sorry member in his hand, watching the soundless television's blue light flicker on the ceiling. Jim thought of light escaping from our world off into cold space, reaching someplace new forever. Jim wagged his limp, sore penis like a little fishing pole. He looked over at the clock's glowing face on the table beside the bed: 10:32. His doctor's appointment wasn't until one o'clock. Jim still had plenty of time. He pulled halfheartedly on his poor penis. He took a sip of his third screwdriver of the morning. He still had some hope.

Don't give up the jackoff! Jim admonished himself. Never say die! I have not yet begun to jack off, Jim told himself resolutely.

After dropping Judy off at the airport the day before, Jim had made trial runs all afternoon. The first trial run, he had parked in the lot of the campus clinic and for a half hour or so simply stared at the building's front doors, again and again imagining himself walking up to them. He then drove to the Oasis on El Camino for a pitcher of beer. The second trial run, Jim had walked up to the doors and almost entered. The third trial run, after spending an hour at the Red Lion downtown drinking among buddies, mostly outpatients from the Veterans Hospital, one of whom sucked his vodka-tonic through a straw he inserted in a hole in his neck, Jim had entered the doors and sat in the vast lobby on a couch between potted plants and watched people walk by with what appeared to be purpose, and he envied them bitterly. Whenever somebody glanced in his direction, Jim looked at his watch impatiently, as though he were waiting for his wife, say, who could be at that very moment entertaining a test for pregnancy, or having a biopsy, and he would sigh audibly and gaze up at the high ceiling of relentless fluorescent lights, affecting the attitude of a fellow bracing to accept any news.

Jim did owe Judy. Who had to tell him that? And he was the last person in the world to complain about somebody springing things. Judy had been a technical virgin when she and Jim were married, hence her experience was not immense in the male-equipment department, so what could she really know about normal scrotums? Not until nearly a year after they were married did Jim's mother, a nurse and well-meaning woman, let the cat out of the bag, so to speak, when she mentioned to Judy that there were astounding advances being made in medical science every single day, especially in areas such as artificial insemination, so couples like them always had hope. Hope? Judy had asked Jim. Medical science? What in the dickens does that all mean, anyhow?

Only then had Jim tearfully informed Judy, his bride, who had not even seen an ocean until their weekend honeymoon at Virginia Beach, that having her family of two boys and two girls might need a little help in the miracle department from medical science, due to this little disability he had been born with, through no fault of his own. Disability? Judy had said. What daggone disability? You never told me anything about any daggone disability. I have testicles, Jim assured Judy. It's just that those little rascals aren't all the way down where they should be is all, undescended, so to speak. You can say that again, buster, Judy had agreed wholeheartedly. Listen, Jim said, I've fought in the Golden Gloves, I've battled with switchblades, I've driven a stolen car crazily toward a cliff's deadly edge for no better reason than romance, I've pulled seven armed robberies, lived on the lam, and survived to write about it all.

What in the world does any of that bullstool have to do with my two boys and two girls? Judy had been real curious to know.

Eleven thirty-eight, the clock by the bed read, the faint sweep of its second hand luminous as it spun around insanely in the darkened bedroom. Jim had held his limp, sore, sad member in his hand befuddledly. What sexy thing between him and his wife had Jim not tried to conjure? He should be thinking about his wife while he jacked off, shouldn't he? This whole ordeal was for them, wasn't it? For their little baby-to-be, their son, for their future. But Jim found there was nothing, no memory, no imagined thing between them that would do the trick.

At high noon Jim had let himself imagine his wife cavorting with her loverboy coach back home. He permitted himself to imagine his wife and Doc at that motel where they met nights when his wife was supposedly chaperoning sock hops. Jim imagined them in the shower, his wife's hair wet, her slick skin smelling sweetly of soap. When his wife soaped Doc's enormous dick, it hardened in her tiny hand. Then his wife soaped the fingertips of her free hand, and she commenced to run them slowly up and down the tight crack of Doc's muscular coachy ass. At some point Jim's wife inserted her middle finger in Doc's anus and rotated it resolutely. Then Jim's wife joyfully soaped Doc's enormous balls. She knelt down on the slick tile floor then, Jim's wife, the shower water like a warm summer rain over her fresh, pretty petal of a face, and she took her loverboy's coachy coconuts, one at a time, into her mouth. Still upon her knees, Jim's wife moved around Doc, kissing and licking and nibbling the wet skin of his hard thighs as she went. When Jim's wife had finally arrived at her boyfriend's rump, and they were cheek to cheek, so to speak, she had spread Doc's muscular coachy buttocks with her slender fingers, at which point Jim's wife had buried her sweet, moist, pink little tongue into that hairy abyss.

The Seven Warning Signs
of Love

I

When Ralph Crawford and Jim Stark first met and became fast friends as young writers, they were both sappy with expectation. The future seemed to loom before them like a stupendous dream. Soon they were congratulating themselves mightily for living like bold outlaw authors on the lam from that gloomy tedium called ordinary life. They were both daring, larger-than-life characters living legendary as they engaged in high drama and hilarity, the stuff of great stories, they were convinced, and not simply drunken, stoned stumblebums and barroom yahoos.

The stupendous dream Ralph and Jim shared was for fame. They were hungry for it (and who could have guessed how famous old Ralph would become!). And nobody is above taking shortcuts to the rewards of fame, such as enjoying sexual congress with comely strangers. That time, for instance, when Ralph, in the heat of a roadhouse romance, tried to impress a beautiful barmaid by telling her he was none other than Philip Roth, the professor of passion, the doctor of desire. The barmaid had never heard of this Philip Roth. And Jim Stark had once told a beer-joint beauty at a crucial moment that he was Norman

Mailer, that lionized lover and mayor of American letters. Norman who?

2

Jim found Ralph's front door wide open as usual. Ralph's house was a rambling, one-story, ranch-style in a cul-de-sac of solid middle-class homes in Menlo Park. He and Alice Ann had purchased it a few years earlier after a surprise inheritance from Alice Ann's natural father. It had fallen on hard times since then. But nothing a dozen good coats of paint couldn't cure, and maybe a few months of professional yard work, plus an army of good roofers, and it would have been beneficial in the beautification department to have had Ralph's criminal son haul away the heap he had balanced on cinder blocks in the driveway, a vehicle he worked on at all hours with stolen parts.

Besides their criminal children, the bane of Ralph and Alice Ann's lives were the neighbors, who complained haughtily about the frequent midnight howls heard from that hard-luck house, so unlike any sounds ever issuing from other houses on that quiet, residential, tree-lined street. Not to mention the occasional police patrol car's flashing lights, which drew the nosy neighbors like moths to their windows, on their moral high horses, as they observed the events of Ralph and Alice Ann Crawford's family life unfold before them in that losing battle of good intentions against unfortunate circumstances running amok and human nature.

As Jim passed back through the house, he found Ralph's young nephews, Ralph's sister-in-law Erin's twin boys, slumped slack-jawed and drooling before the television in the game room, and they couldn't return to consciousness enough to answer when Jim asked where he could find their uncle Ralph. So Jim clomped on across the flagstoned floor through the French doors that opened onto the enclosed back yard of burnt grass and scraggly orange trees. The humid air was damp with the fallen oranges' odor and so thick with flies Jim had to bury his face in his hands as he stumbled across the yard like a blind man whose seeing-eye dog has run off.

Jim found Ralph in his office, which was the end room of a wing the Crawfords often rented out as a student apartment. Ralph was standing on a chair, shading his eyes with his hands, his face pressed flat against the inner wall of his office, and Jim could see only the back of Ralph's dark, woolly head. Jim leaned in the open doorway and took a sip from a pint of the cheapest vodka. When Jim asked Ralph if he would like a little drink, Ralph gasped and clutched his throat and tumbled backward off the chair.

Oh Jesus, don't do that! Ralph wailed from the floor. —Don't ever sneak up on a fella like that. Jesus, I broke my arm! I did! Ralph whined and huddled on the floor hugging his right arm. —I bet I broke it in two, maybe three places.

Jim walked over to the wall, picked up the chair, and stood on it to take a look himself. Jim shaded his eyes and peered through the tiny hole drilled high on the wall.

She's not home right now, Ralph said. —I was just checking. I really busted my arm. I'm not fooling.

Is that same gorgeous blond coed renting the place? Jim was curious to know.

You bet, Ralph said.

You have any mix? Jim asked Ralph, and stepped down from the chair.

I bet I could scare some up, Ralph said, and pushed himself up off the floor. He was still rubbing his arm. —In the kitchen. Tonic, juice, Coke, you name it. You know, you shouldn't come up on a fellow like that, old Jim. You don't know the harm you could cause. You about scared me to death. I could have had a heart attack. Her boyfriend is a Vietnam vet. He was a killer Ranger or Green Beret or something. He's got these evil tattoos.

One of these days you're going to deservedly eat hot lead, old Ralph. Or get sent up the river.

Well, you'll probably be my cellmate. I didn't drill that little hole in the wall, by the way. I just happened to come across it. By accident. Somebody else drilled that little hole. So don't try to lay that one at my doorstep. And I hardly ever take a peek, anyway. Really, I don't. Just now and then. Only when I absolutely have to. Only when I think my life depends on it. But I've seen some things, let me tell you.

Ralph rehung the framed *Life* magazine–cover photograph of Ernest Hemingway over the tiny hole.

Jim took a gander at the sheet of paper in Ralph's typewriter on his desk. He rolled it and read.

Hey there, that's nothing, Ralph exclaimed, waving his paws at Jim. —I was just working on my correspondence. I'm sucking up to some editor.

Doesn't look like any letter to some editor to me, Jim told Ralph. —What's this I-dream-of-sucking-your-breasts business?

There are editors with breasts, Ralph said.

Come on, Ralph, tell me who it's to. I'd tell you, old dog.

Okay, Ralph said. —Okay. It's to my friend in Montana. The woman Buffalo Bill introduced me to when I was up there. You know. Lindsay. She's coming down for a little visit. Now you keep that quiet. I shouldn't have told you that. Boy, was I dumb to tell you that.

Don't get so paranoid, Ralph. Who in the fuck am I going to tell? Who cares, anyway? Anyway, you can trust me. You know that. So, when is your squeeze coming down?

Pretty soon, Ralph said. —If we can get everything figured out. We'll stay at the apartment in Berkeley. I'm going to run off that kid I've been sharing the dump with. That student. I promised him an A for his trouble. And he'll get it, too. I'm a fellow who keeps his word about such matters.

3

Back in the kitchen Ralph placed a carton of orange juice and a bottle of tonic on the table. Cats roamed about everywhere on the counters. They took turns jumping in and out of the room through a tear at the bottom of the screen door. Jim shooed a couple of the flea-infested creatures off the table and placed the pint in its center and sat down wearily.

What are Erin's boys doing here? Jim asked Ralph. —Where's Alice Ann?

Who knows, Ralph said. —Alice Ann and Erin are off some-where. Erin dumped the twins on me. Shopping, they said. That was hours ago. Maybe it was yesterday. I can't remember. They're probably off in some hot tub smoking dope. Erin has these hipper-than-thou friends. I can't let myself worry about it.

What time do you have, Ralph? Jim asked.

Ralph looked at his watch and then shook his wrist. —This sorry thing never keeps good time.

At least you have a watch that works. So what does it say?

About two o'clock. Which means that's only the ballpark. Give or take ten, fifteen minutes. I don't know. It could be a half hour off, for all I know. Why? Do you have a heavy date or something?

I've got a doc appointment at three. Get some ice, Ralph.

A doc appointment? Are you okay? Is something wrong with you? Ralph said. He held an ice tray under water at the sink.

I had an appointment set for earlier today. For one o'clock. But things came up. Or things didn't come up is what I should say.

What? Ralph said, and shook ice cubes from the tray into a bowl. —What in the world are you talking about, old Jim?

They just happened to have a cancellation at three. Lucky for me, I guess. If I don't make it at three, I'll have to wait two weeks for another opening. I hate the fucken medical profession.

Well, what's wrong with you, old Jim? Ralph put the bowl of ice cubes on the table. He emptied the cold contents from a couple of coffee cups into the sink, then rinsed them out and sat down. —You have a little dose of something? You been sticking your thing in places you shouldn't?

You're the one to talk, you dog, Jim told Ralph. Jim poured vodka over ice he put in one of the cups and added a splash of orange juice. —Ralph, if I tell you, you have to promise to keep quiet. You have to take this information to your grave with you. I'd have to have your word of honor on it. Which is pretty much a joke, I know. But this is really private business.

Sure, old Jim, Ralph said. He cocked his head and bent for-ward, his elbows almost to the middle of the table. There was a slight squint in one eye, like a man taking aim. —Mum's the word, old Jim. Honest to God. What? What is it, old Jim?

Ralph, I just can't tell you.

Jesus, old Jim, you have my word on it. Hey, if you can't tell me, who can you tell? Is it really a dose of something? Something like that? I was just fooling when I said that, but is that it? Who you been pumping, anyway, old Jim?

I found this lump, Jim told Ralph. —On my, you know, testicles.

Jesus, old Jim! Oh no! You did? Really? That's awful. That's awful, old Jim. A lump, you say? Hey, listen, it's probably nothing at all. An infection. An ingrown hair. Something like that. That's my best bet. Hey, listen, what we need is a real drink. Some good stuff, that's the ticket. I've got some good Scotch stashed in my bedroom closet. I hope I have, anyway. If those damn thieving kids haven't found it yet. What do you think, old Jim?

That's all right, Ralph. This stuff is okay with me, Jim told him, and fixed another drink.

Have you had any symptoms? Ralph said. — You know, any of those seven warning signs. How big is the lump?

About the size of a fucken coconut. What warning signs?

A coconut? Holy moly, Jim! Signs, you know. Like coughing.

I cough my head off.

Moles that change shape or color?

You want to see? Jim said and began unbuttoning his shirt.

No! Ralph said. —No, that's all right. I'll take your word about a thing like that. What about weight loss? Any weight loss?

Can't you tell?

So you've lost a few pounds?

A few. So, old dog, your little honey is hitting town.

Holy moly, Jim. Not so loud. People could walk in the door any moment. The walls around this place have ears, I'm here to tell you. I'm not kidding. There's no such thing as personal privacy around this place.

Do you love Alice Ann, Ralph?

What? Ralph said. —Do I love Alice Ann? Is that the question? What is that, some kind of trick question? Do I love Alice Ann? Well, what do you think? Sure I love her. Sure. She's my wife of almost seventeen years, isn't she? We've got these two kids, haven't we? Criminal children, true. But they're ours. Living proof, I guess. Of our enduring love, I guess.

Do you love the lovely lady in Montana, too, Ralph?

Holy moly, Ralph said. —I don't know. I don't have all the answers. You've never heard me claim I have all the answers, have you? Things just happen. You know that. You know. A fellow can just get caught up in events. Just swept along with the tide, as it were. Through no real fault or design of his own. I don't know what I'm doing half the time. Much less have any real sense of direction, or purpose, for that matter. One sorry foot in front of the other is about the best I can manage.

Ralph, do you tell the lovely lady in Montana that you love her?

That's not a word I, for one, use lightly. Love is not a word I, for one, throw around.

Is she a great piece of ass, Ralph? Your lovely lady in Montana.

My lips are sealed.

Does she bang like a screen door, Ralph?

You better believe it.

Does she go down like a submarine, Ralph?

She doesn't even come up for air, Ralph said, and laughed.

You really are a romantic rat, aren't you, old Ralph?

I try.

On those special tender occasions, Ralph, do you?

Do I what?

Do you tell her you love her truly? That you love her more than your wife of nearly seventeen years, who also happens to be the mother of your two criminal children.

I already told you, love is not a word I toss around.

Do you make her promises, Ralph? At those tender times.

I never make promises, Ralph said haughtily, that I can't keep.

What about in your letters, Ralph? Do you put it down in black and white? Do you write to her about the nature of your everlasting true love?

Mostly, Ralph said, if it's any of your beeswax, I write about the weather.

The weather, Ralph? What about that I-dream-of-sucking-your-breasts business, Ralph? Ralph, does your lovely lady in Montana have those sort of magical breasts that like great mountains create their own weather? Do those wondrous breasts create their own rainstorms and springtimes and months of summer?

I'll say. She's got these breasts that won't quit. Hey, you've been smoking dope already today, haven't you? I don't suppose you have any joints on you, do you? I don't suppose you'd be inclined to share, would you? Alice Ann and Erin put a big dent in my stash last night. And then those criminal kids found what was left sometime this morning and cleaned it out. I hardly got a pull off that last poke of dooby. So what else is new.

So your girlfriend has a pair of the world's most amazing breasts, eh, Ralph? Poor old, rotten, Running Dog Ralph, on the ropes of romance.

What's a poor fellow to do? Actually, I don't write about the weather when I write to her. Actually, I hardly even give the weather a second thought. Unless I'm getting rained on or trying to light a cigarette in the wind. Actually, the weather is just something I mostly try to stay out of. Actually, if the truth be told, old Jim, I do tell Lindsay that I, you know, love her. I do make promises that I have no idea if I mean to keep. I do toss that word around, old Jim. That awful four-letter word. *Love*. Old Jim, this is between you and me and the four walls, but boy, I'm in a real pickle.

Romance, old Ralph, is a fucken rat hole.

Hey, Ralph said, what does this business have to do with lumps, anyway? We were discussing your lump, the last I remember.

Love is like a lump, Ralph.

That's one for the books.

Think about it, Ralph.

I don't want to think about it.

Love can consume you, can it not? Just like cancer. And doesn't love have its own seven warning signs?

What warning signs?

All right, Ralph. What about jerking off? Have you been jerking off more than usual? Even a little more? Say, six or seven times a day? Now that's a sure warning sign of love.

I'm the first one to admit I jerk off like a monkey, Ralph said. —But I've been choking my chicken six or seven times a day since I was about eight. That has nothing to do with love.

Ralph, you're the kind of poor sap whose brains are in his dick.

I'd talk if I were you.

Jim picked up the nearly empty pint bottle of vodka and killed it. A huge yellow cat jumped on the table and began sniffing around. Ralph scooped it up and tossed it back over his shoulder, and it hit the floor running.

Ralph, let me ask you something. When you drink a lot, do you, you know, ever have trouble getting the old horse out of the barn?

You mean get a hard-on? Ralph said. Ralph laughed and covered his mouth with his hand. —Who me? No. Never. Not me. Jesus Christ. What are you talking about, anyway?

Never? Not once?

Jesus Christ, Ralph said. —Nope. Never. Nada.

Jim took the empty sperm-sample jar out of his shirt pocket and placed it beside the empty pint bottle on the table. Ralph lit a cigarette and squinted through the rising smoke at the little plastic jar. He reached out and picked the jar up and turned it around in his hands. He read the label. —What in the world is this? This has your name on it?

I want to ask you for a favor, Jim said to Ralph.

Listen, old Jim, I hardly have two nickels to rub together, Ralph said, and put the jar down on the table.

It's not money, Jim told Ralph.

In that case it's yours, Ralph said, and laughed and picked up the sperm jar again to look at. —Name it. Within reason, of course. Hey, take my criminal kids. Take my wretched dog. Take my wife. If she ever comes home again. Take her, she's mine. Or whatever that old joke is. Why does this have your name on it, old Jim?

I've always thought of you like a brother, Jim told Ralph.

—Like we're really somehow related, you know? Like we're blood brothers or something who somehow got separated at birth.

Do you want me to drive you to your doc's appointment? Is that it? Give you some moral support. I know how docs freak you out.

Actually, that might not be a bad idea.

Hey, I'll do it. I'll do it. It's as good as done. But, hey, I'll have to wait in the car. You know me. I get edgy. Docs, they give me the willies, too.

Do you love your kids, old Ralph? If you could do it all over again, would you have kids?

Those criminal kids steal me blind, Ralph said. —I've got those kids dead to rights. I've caught them red-handed time and again.

But would you want kids, if you could go back and do it all over again?

Alice Ann was knocked up when we got married, Ralph said. —But you know that.

That doesn't answer my question, Jim said. —This is important to me, old dog. Would you?

Well, I'll tell you, then. You don't know what helpless frustration is until you have kids. Frustration and unrelieved responsibility and permanent distraction that can make a grown man want to jump off a building. Does that answer your question?

Ralph, let me ask you this: When you jerk off like a monkey, who do you think about?

You are stoned, aren't you?

Come on, Ralph, tell me. I told you about my lump, which is probably the most personal thing I've ever shared with anybody in my life. My wife doesn't even know about my lump yet.

Oh, I don't know, Ralph said. —I think about the usual sort of women, I guess. I'm just a regular guy. Marilyn Monroe. You know. I like Candy Bergen. Ann-Margret. Hanoi Jane. Sometimes Jackie O. Susan Sontag.

What about your lovely ladyfriend?

Sure, I think about her. I think about Lindsay. I think about her a lot.

Do you have a picture of your lovely lady in Montana, Ralph?

Sure.

Could I see it?

Well, I guess so. Sure, why not? Ralph said. He went to the door and looked up and down the hallway, then looked out the kitchen window into the driveway. He slipped his wallet out of his back pocket and then fumbled around opening flaps and folds. —I've got me a secret compartment, Ralph said, and chuckled. He glanced out the kitchen window once again, then slid out a snapshot and handed it to Jim.

Jim couldn't believe his eyes. Ralph's girlfriend was beautiful. The old Running Dog! This Lindsay person was an absolutely lovely woman, with smoky gray eyes set sort of far apart and long, dark, thick hair, and a wide mouth, full lips, full moist-looking lips. Jim permitted himself to picture her going down on old, rotten Running Dog Ralph like a submarine.

So, what do you think, old Jim? Ralph said, stepping around behind Jim, looking over his shoulder. —She's something, huh?

Not bad, Jim said, and then he said, Ralph, I don't really have a lump. I just told you that. Don't ask me why.

Jesus, why would you tell me something like that?

I said don't ask me why, Ralph. I'm not myself today.

You really had me going. You really did.

I'm sorry. There's no excuse for it. I was being an asshole. I do have to go to the doc's, though. That much is true. Routine stuff. And I don't really need a ride. But thanks for offering.

You had me going, old Jim. I was rattled.

I owe you, buddy. Here, buddy, Jim said, and took a couple of joints from his shirt pocket and handed them to Ralph.

Well, thanks, old Jim. Hey, you hungry at all? Ralph said. He stepped over to the refrigerator and opened it and peered in. —I could go for a sandwich myself. I got a big load of deli stuff just last night. Ham. Cheese. You name it.

No. Thanks, though. I've got to make that doc appointment somehow.

Damn it to hell! Ralph exclaimed as he rummaged through the refrigerator. —Gone! Everything is gone! Gone! Not a bite left. Not a sad morsel. There's no end to it. Ever. I don't believe those kids. Those criminal kids. There's never anything left over for me. Never, Ralph said as he opened and closed drawers.

I need to hit your head, old Ralph. Before I take off. I feel a serious number two coming on, Jim said, and slipped the snapshot of Ralph's girlfriend into his shirt pocket.

Help yourself, Ralph said. —You better take some newspaper with you. We're out of toilet paper as usual.

Okeydokey, Jim said, picked up the little plastic sperm-sample jar, and rushed from the room.

Secret Sons

1

So there Jim sat, wearing dark glasses and a raincoat and that beat-up old fedora he affected back in those days pulled low over his eyes on a lovely, clear California day, in a campus clinic at 2:46. Under the flap of his long coat Jim held a tightly wrapped paper sack which contained a small plastic jar that in turn held a single, tiny tear of sperm he had masturbated himself bloody to obtain in Ralph's disaster of a bathroom, while gazing into the gray eyes of Ralph's lovely girlfriend and kicking at cats. Jim stared helplessly at the large round clock on the wall above the desk of what was surely the world's most beautiful nurse. How lovely her blond hair looked piled high like that under her cute white dove of a cap. Such a long, graceful neck. Such soft-looking, delicate breasts pressed into the cupped white starchness of that uniform. The speed of the second hand on the clock above her desk was insane. Jim rubbed his bloodshot eyes beneath his shades and remembered vividly watching another pretty blond nurse, who looked like the twin of that beautiful nurse behind the desk, walk slowly toward him carrying a syringe with a needle the approximate size of a harpoon, intent upon pumping his blood full of the raging hormones of a normal boy.

What Jim remembered then with a sudden and intense vividness was the darkening blue winter light of that Midwestern afternoon sky when he was nine and in Rochester, Minnesota, walking with his parents from their hotel three blocks away to the Mayo Clinic to be made as good as new. Jim was also going to get to meet some real interesting kids who had come from the four corners of the earth to be made as good as new, his folks had assured him. Dirty snow was piled beside the walks higher than his head. When he talked, his teeth hurt in the frigid wind blowing down the high, narrow alleys of dirty snow, but there were so many questions he needed to ask that day.

Will I get a shot today? Jim had asked his mom, and walked into the frozen cracked cloud of his own words. I don't think you'll be getting any shots today, Jim's mom said. Jim said, If I do get a shot, will it be in my arm or in my behind? Will I have to pull my pants down in front of a nurse? How would I know a thing like that ahead of time? his mom said; then she said, Now, don't go to worrying yourself sick, honey. Everyone here is going to be real nice to you. Nobody here wants to hurt you, not if they can help it. That's right, soldier boy, Jim's dad had piped up. That's how come the nice doctor is getting paid a goddamn arm and a leg, to know what the hell he's doing.

The three of them had sat for what seemed like hours in a huge, hot, stuffed, windowless waiting room, where other grim-faced parents sat silently with their own deformed children, everyone thinking about the same thing, thinking that any amount of pain, suffering, and humiliation was worth gimped kids being made good as new. Jim had stared helplessly at a girl with no face until his turn was called, and his dad had admonished him to be a brave soldier boy when that pretty blond nurse jabbed that enormous needle into his cold, shivery, bare, little-boy butt, and even his supportive folks had laughed nervously out loud when his fart had exploded from the cave of his pain and embarrassment like the croak of some fabled, monstrous frog.

So years later Jim had sat in the campus clinic's waiting room and watched the insanely speeding second hand of the large round clock on the wall above the desk of the world's most beautiful blond nurse. The pudgy pervert with the long brown hair who had sat down beside Jim on the couch and the thin, effeminate black man wearing a single silver earring shaped like a tiny fish, who had sat down in the chair opposite, both obviously only half through some sort of sex change in one direction or the other, kept giving Jim looks, this big bozo wearing a fedora, shades, and raincoat on this hot, perfectly sunny California day and going in God only knows what direction. I'm here to stick up the sperm bank, you deformed fuckers, is what Jim screamed at them in his mind. The speed of the clock's second hand was simply insane. Will it hurt? Will I have to pull my pants down in front of people? The brown paper bag hidden under Jim's coat seemed to pulse in his sweaty palms.

What Jim could imagine then was the tiny sour-cream-colored tear of sperm pressing against the clear plastic sides of the jar as though it were trying to push its way through to freedom. That tiny tear wanted to escape; it wanted to make a clean getaway, which was a sentiment Jim could understand. What Jim could imagine vividly was a faint smudge of flesh, of scales, of wet fur, and of infinitely tiny feathers against the clear plastic. What Jim could imagine were absolutely lusterless eyes bulging from a tiny fish face, and wildly fluttering flipper feet, and tiny stunted hands, webbed and with little pearly pinpoint fingernails, gripping the plastic sides, opening and shutting, the swimming shape of their grasp and release a pure movement in membrane, pulling finally through the plastic as though it were the most transparent of tissue and landing on the floor at Jim's feet like a goldfish flipping out of its bowl: Jim's own boy, his own little tadpole of a secret son.

And then Jim had entertained a horrific thought. What exactly would he say to the world's most beautiful blond nurse when his time was up in exactly six minutes and nine seconds and he had to hand her the mysterious brown paper bag warm now to the touch? Here, this is for you. Here, you were expecting this, I believe. Here, you dropped this in the parking lot. Here, you forgot your lunch.

2

Judy had returned to town the following evening, and she had been unusually quiet during dinner, and lucky for Jim, she had not even asked question one about how things had gone at the clinic the day before. Lucky for Jim, because he had no good story for his shameful getaway. How could he ever explain anything, or even describe the startled look on the face of the world's most beautiful blond nurse when only seconds before his scheduled appointment Jim had simply jumped up and torn out of that place like a bat out of hell, his raincoat flapping behind him like crazy wings?

Judy had simply told Jim she was bushed when at last he asked her why she was so quiet. The buying trip had been busy and she had ironing piled up to do after dinner. No, she told Jim, of course the Côtes du Porc Charcutière that he had slaved over all afternoon didn't suck. She just wasn't hungry, and why did Jim have to make World War III out of it? Jim had scraped her virtually untouched Côtes du Porc Charcutière into the garbage and piled the dishes in the sink. She didn't feel so hot either, Judy told Jim as she set up the ironing board. Maybe she was getting her period early, she speculated, for she was all sore and swollen in her privates, and she was feeling as moody as a sore-tail cat. And then when Judy turned the kitchen-counter TV on, she asked why the screen was all sticky. Did you have all your drunken lout buddies over here while I was gone? Did you all go and spray the TV with beer again? Well, Jim and his drunken lout buddies had, but he told her huffily, No way, José, and pretended to sulk at the sink while he did the dishes, and Judy hadn't made an issue of it. Somehow Jim felt that he was off the hook about the clinic, about the sticky TV, about everything. Somehow Jim even felt that he had the upper hand for the moment, a rare occurrence, but he didn't know why, and that is what gave him a sudden case of the willies.

Judy started to iron and Jim did the dishes while they silently watched an old *I Love Lucy* rerun. The half tab of acid Jim had popped just before dinner on a defiant impulse started to kick in quicker and more exciting than he had anticipated, and when he began to giggle uncontrollably at that scene where Lucy and Ethel, who have taken jobs in a candy factory, go bonkers trying to keep up with a conveyor belt run amok, Judy fired up a cigarette and, regarding Jim through the rising smoke with squinted eyes, asked him if he was on controlled substances at that point in time. Jim turned around from the sink flabbergasted and took Judy by her little hand and, although he was slobbering and rubbery-faced with laughter by then, proclaimed his innocence. You've gone and fried your brain again, haven't you? Judy said, and jerked her hand away. She put a blue blouse she had just ironed on a hanger and hung it with some others on the handle of the kitchen door. God how Jim had always loved the starched, outdoorsy smell of freshly ironed clothes when his brain was fried!

We better have us a real long talk, Judy said with a sigh, and she turned off the iron and sat down at the kitchen table. I'm sorry, honey, Judy said to Jim out of the blue, as she flipped ashes into an ashtray and regarded him with those squinty eyes that always made Jim extremely nervous. *She* was sorry, Jim thought. *She* was sorry? At first Jim was absolutely elated at this turn of the tables, but utterly clueless, and then Jim began to get really scared.

Whereupon Judy had informed Jim that she had been with a man. Just like that, out of left field. Say what? Jim inquired. *With?* Jim inquired. You know, Judy said, and wiggled her eyebrows suggestively, *with*. I'm sorry, she said, it just happened. *It?* Jim inquired. *It*, Judy affirmed. —It did. When? Jim was curious to know. On the buying trip, Judy said. Oh, Jim said, on the buying trip. Yes, on the buying trip, Judy said. —It just happened. Who? Jim was curious to know. You don't know him, Judy assured Jim. —He's a new buyer at the store. Well, what exactly fucken happened? Jim was curious to know. If you don't fucken mind telling me. Well, Judy said, and tapped her cigarette out slowly in the seashell-shaped ashtray Jim had given her for their third anniversary, and then she immediately lit another, we happened to be staying at the same hotel and we just went to dinner together after a hard day. Then we danced a few times. He walked me back to my room. So I said, Why don't you come in for a nightcap. He'd been so nice and all. Of course, all I had in the room was a warm can of Pepsi. We laughed about that. We had had a few toddies earlier, I'll have to admit. So, I don't know, nature just took its course, I guess. So he kissed me. Then things just got lovey-dovey.

So just which of the three nights you were gone did it, you know, happen? Jim was curious to know. It happened on the first night, Judy informed Jim. What about the other two nights? Jim inquired. Well, to tell you the truth, it happened on those nights, too, Judy informed Jim. Every single night? Jim said, and then Jim said, You fucked him every single fucken night? So, Jim said, just how many times did you fuck him in three nights, if you don't mind my asking? Whereupon Judy said, Who knows? Who can remember something like that. What difference does it make, anyway? she said. Jim said, What fucken difference does it make? Jesus-fucken-Christ. Okay. Okay. So, Jim said, what happens if you get knocked up, did you even think about that little possibility? Judy said, I won't. The first night, she explained, her friend had practiced withdrawal every time. Then the next day he went right out and bought a box of Trojans. Please, Judy said, honey, honey, please, she said as Jim jumped up and attempted to deck the kitchen door with a swinging back kick.

I was so happy to see you tonight when you came home, Jim told Judy as he collapsed back down at the table and put his head in his hands. —I've been thinking hard about things while you've been gone this time. I thought about how we could make a fresh start. And I didn't just loaf around with my lout buddies and drink beer while you were gone. I slaved over fiction is what I did. My time in the sun is just around the corner, and you better believe it. And I hardly had a drink while you were gone, and I lifted weights and I lost six or seven pounds, and I'm beginning to feel like my old self. And I went to that clinic like you told me to do, and they said we can probably get you pregnant real easy. Sure my sperm count is a little low, they said, but hey, they've sure seen lower sperm counts, they said. Hey, why are you telling me this shit, anyway? You never told me about your last loverboy. I had to figure that shameful business out for myself. You kept your last loverboy a dark, sordid secret. You lied to me about him until I confronted you with the undeniable evidence in hand. And here I am tonight half deranged from drugs and you expect me to deal with this shit about your new boyfriend.

See, I knew it, Judy said, and stabbed out her cigarette. —I just knew you were on controlled substances. I can always tell by your eyes, Jim. They get wide as saucers and sort of runny. I'm telling you because my conscience is guilty, I guess. I guess I just don't want to sneak around.

Are you trying to tell me you and this guy are going to be an item in the romance department? Jim said, as he attempted to surreptitiously check out his eyes in a windowpane.

I want to see him again. And I don't want to sneak around.

Is he single or what?

Melvin is married, but he and his wife have been talking about a separation.

Melvin! My wife is fucking some clown named Melvin! And a married Melvin to boot! Too much, I say. So the bottom line is you want to keep sleeping with this Melvin clown, is that it?

I want to see him. I don't want to sneak around, Jim. Jim, when was the last time we made love?

Hey, don't try to turn the tables! Don't dump all this on my doorstep. I don't turn you on. You think I'm too fat and smell like beer. Don't deny it. Do you want a divorce, is that it?

I can't recall the last time we made love. Yes, you could lose a few pounds and quit drinking beer. But I haven't thought about any divorce.

So you think that because we haven't slept together much lately . . .

Lately? Are you kidding me?

You think I shouldn't mind if you have a sordid affair, is that it?

I haven't thought much about anything. Things just happened, that's all, like I told you.

Just like with your last loverboy? Swept away with desire and passion and hot, uncontrollable, animal lust?

I guess so.

Oh, Lordy. So you want an open marriage, is that it?

What in the world does that mean?

It's what they call it out here in hip, decadent, trendy California when a husband and wife agree that they can both fuck and suck anything cute that scoots.

That sounds downright disgusting. All I want to do is see Melvin sometimes. Until we figure out what's what.

All right. All right. I get the picture, Jim told Judy, and filled his Mickey Mouse Club glass with vodka. Then Jim told Judy that his bottom line was, he didn't want them to break up over this. They had survived her other loverboy, and they could survive this one, too. Get it out of your system, that's what Jim told Judy. —Christ, enjoy yourself. There's no reason for you to feel guilty even. You're just, you know, a normal woman, Jim told Judy, trying to be big about everything, but, also, he would have to admit, entertaining a chubby. —Just do some things for me. Do some things for my sake. One, please don't, for God's sake, get pregnant. I will absolutely draw the line when it comes to raising any little Melvins around here. I absolutely will not abide the sound of any little fucken webbed feet running around here. Two, be discreet. This is nobody's business but ours. The last time you blabbed to all your goddamn girl friends and I was a laughingstock. And, three, I want to know everything. You owe me this. I want to know when you've been with this so-called Melvin. Or when you plan on seeing him. There has to be absolute honesty between us about this sordid business. It's like we're taking a brand-new vow of honesty. If we want our marriage to work under these trying new circumstances, we have to tell each other the whole truth and nothing but the truth.

You mean you want me to tell you the lovey-dovey details?

I don't want anything left to my imagination, that's right. Leaving things to my imagination would be ten times worse than knowing the truth. If I know what's going on, I can just accept it after a certain period of anger and pain and general anguish, and then hopefully forget it. If I have to sit around imagining things, I could easily go crazy. If you don't want to hurt me unnecessarily, you'll tell me the things I need to know in order not to go crazy with wondering. For instance, did you and Melvin, when you all were shacked up night after night on the buying trip, did you all have a lot of, you know, oral sex?

What exactly do you mean by a lot, Jim? Judy asked, and then she reached across the kitchen table and grabbed Jim by his arm and said, Honey, please, don't go banging your head on the table like that.

Later, Jim couldn't really recall much else about what he and Judy had talked about at the kitchen table that early evening. He could recall whining around pitifully for a time, and probably promising to do better, and begging for another chance. He was sure he begged for another chance until he was blue in the face. It seemed to him as though he had told Judy that what he had thought about while he was masturbating in order to fill the sample jar with his so-called seed was how he used to watch her when she was a cheerleader back in college. She was the cutest cheerleader Jim had ever seen, he told her, and he would sit up in the stands and watch her out on that blinding green grass, under those blazing lights, her little hands on her sweet, wagging ass, while she did all those cute little steps and jumps, and the way her cheerleader skirt swirled up above her sweet, Man-Tanned, shaved legs. And then Jim had reminded Judy that she had once been a Homecoming Queen, and that homecoming queens sort of represent a code of proper behavior for women, not unlike Miss America in many ways, and that there are responsibilities that former Homecoming Queens have to consider over the course of their lifetimes. And those responsibilities didn't include giving goddamn sportswear buyers blow jobs, Jim suddenly sobbed out, but then quickly regained his composure. You were the Homecoming Queen of my heart, Jim could recall finally informing Judy, as that insipid line of whimpering sort of petered out.

Judy had said something like: You've sure got a funny way of showing it, Jim. And then she told Jim sadly how unhappy she had been for such a long time, and Jim could understand that. And then Judy asked Jim not to get himself worked up into a dither and wreck the house, but that she'd like to see Melvin that night for a little while. That if he could get away Melvin was going to call her. And that she didn't want to make up some sneaky lie to tell Jim. And when Jim asked, Judy said that just because she and Melvin might see each other tonight didn't necessarily mean they'd get lovey-dovey, but if they did she'd try to remember all the dirty details to relay to Jim, and for Jim not to worry about her getting in a family way either, because surely Melvin had a couple of Trojans left over from the buying trip. And then Judy told Jim that she didn't mean to hurt him, she really didn't. But she had been so sad for so long. And so lonely. And Jim could understand that.

3

In those days Judy and Jim lived in a redwood-shingled bungalow back in a stand of trees across a short, narrow, private bridge over Matadero Creek just south of Palo Alto. The little bungalow had been lovingly hand-built nearly fifty years earlier by an old salt returned from a dangerous life at sea who had lived in it until his death at ninety only a year earlier, when he had been struck by lightning from a clear summer sky while sailing alone on a small mountain lake. Jim and Judy, such a nice, stable-appearing young couple, had been the first people the old salt's aged niece had trusted enough to rent the bungalow to. Jim had loved that little house like no other he had ever lived in, and he had rubbed his fingers over every smooth board in the place. Night after night, Jim would sit out in the kitchen smoking dope and drinking alone, long after Judy had wandered off to bed and his drunken lout buddies had staggered out the door, and in the soft light of the brass wall lamps he would simply gaze around the room, at the thin, vertical redwood boards of the walls that seemed to glow from some inner source of light, and the low, dark ceiling of redwood boards so warm and rich with golden light and shadow. The bungalow's redwood walls were dark with age and the ceilings of the rooms curved gently toward the walls like the inner hull of a boat, which is what the whole house resembled vaguely, a boat, an old sailing vessel of some kind, as though after all those years upon the high seas the old salt could live only in a place that at least resembled something you could sail away in. Jim would look at the grains in the old boards and imagine giant redwoods aging in sunlight and fog a thousand years ago. He would follow a thin, dark, curving grain with his fingertips down a board slick as bone and think of those cross-section cuts of ancient redwoods in California state parks, their dark rings tagged with time and events, the Battle of Hastings, the rise and fall of the Roman Empire, the birth of Christ, the end of love as we know it.

In return for yard work, the old salt had permitted several generations of neighborhood boys to construct and maintain elaborate electric-train sets out in the redwood-shingled garage by the creek (the old salt had ridden a bike everywhere he went, or a bus, and never owned a car), where around walls shaped into miniature mountains wove at least a dozen tracks, circling through forests of tiny trees, through dozens of tunnels, along a running stream with a working waterfall and a little lake, and through two tiny towns with working lights. In return for secret places in the garage where Jim could hide his drugs where Judy would never think to search, he bought the current generation of neighborhood boys beer and slipped them joints.

Early on the night Jim's first wife forsook him, he had gone out to the garage and pulled the switch that set the tiny towns ablaze. He took a fat joint hidden in a bright red caboose and fired it up. He put a couple of the electric trains in motion, aimed in opposite directions on different tracks, and he sat there in the dim light smoking and watching the little trains as they rolled around and around as though they were going someplace in particular. From the open garage doors Jim could see Judy through a kitchen window at her ironing board. As Judy leaned slightly forward, her soft brown hair fell over her face and Jim could see the lovely curve of her neck. She was wearing a sleeveless blouse, and

Jim watched the firm muscle in her brown upper arm flex as she ironed. Once when Judy had raised her arm as she brushed back her hair, Jim could glimpse the delicate whiter flesh of a shaved underarm. When the phone in the kitchen rang, Judy rushed to it. Judging from the brightness of her smile, it was the call she had been waiting for. Judy sat down at the kitchen table to talk. At one point Judy threw her head back laughing, and Jim could see her teeth shine.

The air was sweet that evening with the aromas of the flowering bushes along the creek bank and of bread baking somewhere and of both clean and old oil on the cement garage floor. The lights of the tiny towns had looked somehow so sad to Jim, and fragile and beautiful, and the tiny trains made him remember lying in bed as a boy and being rocked gently by the faint rumble of an endless freight or coal train passing through the little coal town at night, headed someplace special and new and infinitely distant in the mysterious, adult dark. Jim could hear the flow of the shallow water in Matadero Creek, and the croaks of frogs, and crickets, and from beyond the trees the faint sounds of El Camino Real traffic, and he knew that his life there in that beloved little bungalow with that beautiful woman talking on the phone to her new loverboy was lost to him. Even distant sirens sounded like sad echoes from a whole life Jim could imagine someday only faintly remembering.

Jim had watched his first wife talk on the phone and laugh as he hadn't seen her laugh in ages. Judy looked so happy Jim couldn't help but be happy for her. From inside the mouth of one of the tunnels through the miniature mountains, stuck back deep enough so that the trains wouldn't bump against it as they rolled by, Jim fished out the sample jar with its tiny tear of sperm. He tossed it from hand to hand, as he might have a baseball, and then held it up in the dim light, tilting it this way and that, watching the tiny tear glisten as it slid about. Jim let himself imagine tiny eyes, a tiny mouth, teeth like tiny tombstones.

The next time one of the little electric trains swung out of a tunnel onto the straight stretch of track near him, Jim placed the jar in an empty boxcar and watched it ride around. Presently Jim heard the screen door bang and Judy's footsteps come across the brick driveway. Then she was a shadow in the doorway of the garage. Jim could smell her perfume. I'll be back in a little bit, honey, Judy said quietly, and Jim said okeydokey. Jim watched his wife walk to her vehicle in the soft glow from the kitchen lights through the windows. Judy had combed her hair and pulled it back behind her ears with little silver barrettes. She had changed into a short red-and-white-checked sundress. Jim noticed that Judy had a little lift to her step. Jim watched as Judy studied her face in the rearview mirror for a moment, before she pulled her station wagon on out across the narrow wooden bridge to go do it with her new boyfriend, Melvin.

In the hot darkness of the garage Jim had bawled for a while. Then he had plucked the plastic jar from the boxcar when it swung near him. He closed his runny eyes, and with a startling vividness he pictured his pretty first wife naked in her new boyfriend's arms. Whereupon Jim had started bawling again. He started jerking off, too. And this time Jim had no trouble filling that sperm sample jar halfway to its brim in about a half-dozen furious whacks.

Holding to the shadows, Jim had walked out onto the little bridge over Matadero Creek. Years later, when he would attempt to resurrect those moments in his memory, Jim would recall thinking, Is this my real life? Is this it? Jim had stood in the shadows in the center of the bridge blubbering some more and hating himself for it, and finally he quit it. He listened to the shallow water flowing below. He listened to the frogs and the faint sounds of El Camino Real traffic and laughter from a yard up the street. He watched as street light coming through the leaves of the trees along the creek bank was gathered and released on the shining, tremulous current.

In the darkness two hundred yards ahead, Matadero Creek disappeared into the entrance of a tunnel that ran under El Camino Real and most of Palo Alto, to empty finally into the waters of the East Bay, a perilous passage, full of rats starved insane, rabid fish, snakes glowing in the dark, crawdads that dined on the living and the dead: a passage full of danger at every turn, spiritual fatigue, failures of will, a daily ton of turds floating to the Bay, along with Jim's jar of secret sons.

Even in the enveloping darkness Jim could see the tiny sparkle of the splash when he had tossed it, that plastic jar with his name on its label containing his so-called seed, and he had watched that tiny arc of lost, secret sons float in the creek's shallow, shimmering current out of his life for good.

The Wife in the Story

1

Although it was against the terms of the fellowship, Ralph Crawford had retained his part-time teaching position at Berkeley while he was a Stegner Writing Fellow at Stanford (and this on top of illegally collecting unemployment). On one occasion when Lindsay had flown down from Montana for a romantic rendezvous with Ralph at his Berkeley apartment, she had gone along with him to the Tuesday-afternoon writing workshop at Stanford, where Ralph was scheduled to read a story that day.

Lindsay was thrilled with the lovely, sunny day and the silly ride down the East Bay, laughing their heads off, singing along with golden oldies on the radio, windows wide open, the hillside houses and downtown buildings of San Francisco shining white as bones in the distance against a glorious blue cloudless sky, sailboats blowing about the green water of the bay. In the intense clarity of the light that day shapes were luminous, surfaces seemed to swell. Then they strolled across a campus of stone colonnades like caves full of Spanish sunlight and shadow, sprinklers lifting blue bells of light above fiercely green lawns, dogs romping in fountains, woodpeckers pounding high in palms, hordes of absolutely beautiful, blond, sun-browned people pedaling bikes everywhere, pictures of such perfect health and happiness and confident hope they made Lindsay want to barf. Lindsay and Ralph stopped at a plaza display table loaded with turquoise and silver jewelry, where Ralph helped Lindsay select a tiny ring of silver fish, which Ralph pledged he would return to purchase as soon as his next ship came in.

In the second-floor library rooms where the writing workshop met, Ralph had introduced Lindsay around to a blur of faces. She was his fiancée flown down from Montana, where she worked as a cowgirl, to witness his literary lionization is what Ralph told everybody. (Then it must be true, Lindsay had thought, her heart soaring. Ralph really had separated from Alice Ann.) Lindsay had loved the two high-ceilinged rooms the writing class met in, with their book-lined walls and comfortably shabby couches and stuffed chairs, and the huge, oblong table in one room the writers sat around as they listened intently to Ralph read in his soft, almost whispery voice between long drags on a cigarette. Lindsay loved Ralph's looks, a large, shambling man with dark, woolly hair and dark eyes, who had such a sensitive, shy, gentle nature, yet radiated an inner strength she found comforting, compelling. Ralph smoked continuously as he read the story, and he often laughed out loud at lines that cracked everybody else up, too, and Lindsay felt like his wife.

The story Ralph read that day was the one that became so famous in years to come, about a couple on the verge of bankruptcy who had to unload their Cadillac convertible before some creditor could slap a lien on it. The wife in the story, who was smart and had personality and business sense, would have to do it. The wife in the story was gone for hours before the half-drunk, stir-crazy husband got call one. The wife was making the deal over dinner, she said. Returning home finally near dawn, drunk and disheveled, the wife called her husband a worthless bankrupt and dared him to do anything about her being out all night doing God-knows-what with some greasy used-car salesman, and then she had stumbled on off to bed and collapsed. After one sad thing and another, the story ended with the husband tracing his fingertips over the stretch marks on the backs of his naked wife's legs and hips while thinking about how those blue lines looked like dozens, perhaps hundreds, countless really, roads running through the flesh of the wife in the story. The story was a great hit with the other writers that day.

Lindsay had listened to Ralph read his story that day and she had thought about how Ralph's hands had felt on her own flesh the night before while they had made love, how warm they had been, and gentle. Could Lindsay go out and unload a Cadillac convertible in a hurry like the wife in the story? If Lindsay had been the wife in the story, what would have had to have happened to drive her to such desperation and betrayal? The backs of Ralph's huge hands were so hairy, those huge, gentle hands.

When Ralph finished reading his story, the other writers in the class applauded, which Ralph told Lindsay later had never happened before, at least not since he had been there. Ralph's best friend, Jim Stark, had not been in the workshop that day, and this had disappointed Ralph. Wonder where that old dog Jim is, Ralph had speculated. Old Jim never misses workshops. Well, Ralph concluded, Jim had probably been afraid Ralph's story would be the hit it was and Jim just couldn't handle the envy.

(Actually, Jim hadn't been there that day because he was staking out the entrance to where his first wife worked, sitting across the street in his vehicle with his old film-noir fedora pulled low over his steely eyes, while he sipped from a pint of whiskey and waited, hoping to catch his first wife and her loverboy leaving together, arm in arm, or holding hands, whereupon Jim planned on displaying his displeasure by pounding his first wife's boyfriend to a pulp.)

Lindsay and Ralph had driven up in the hills west of Palo Alto with several writers from the workshop to a roadhouse called the Alpine Inn, where they had all downed pitchers of beer until dark, and then later, when the other writers had one after another drunkenly departed, Lindsay and Ralph had pigged out on greasy cheeseburgers whose juice made their fingers shine. Ralph had licked Lindsay's fingers clean, as they sat off alone at a picnic table under the trees by the creek bank. Looking deeply into his eyes,

Lindsay had taken Ralph's huge, hairy fingers into her mouth, one at a time, and Ralph had suggested in a quiet but urgent voice that they employ Lindsay's plastic and grab a motel room down there for the night instead of driving all the way back to Berkeley.

2

In the motel room that night, after Ralph had fallen asleep, Lindsay had tilted the dresser's lampshade and in the slant of light looked in the mirror at her hips. She jiggled her fleshy hips. The wife in Ralph's story had given birth to two children, and yet, except for those blue highways in her flesh, she had been slim and firm. Lindsay had found a copy of the story in Ralph's briefcase. She had noticed Ralph's wallet on the dresser.

Lindsay locked the bathroom door. She lit a cigarette and sat on the toilet seat, flipping her ashes now and then into the sink. Lindsay flipped back through the story Ralph had read that day. In the story the wife had had a boy and a girl barely a year apart before she was nineteen. In the story the wife had been tall and slim, with blond hair that she wore very long and straight. Except for a couple of Ralph and Alice Ann, and one of Alice Ann and their two kids when they were very young, the pictures in Ralph's wallet were mostly of Alice Ann. Alice Ann had a long, thin, beautiful face, and in some of the pictures her long blond hair was almost white. Ralph looked so large and dark beside Alice Ann, a dark, hairy hand clasping a thin waist, a heavy arm hugging her slender shoulders. The picture of Alice Ann and the kids was taken on some beach, some ocean in the background. The kids were building a sand castle whose wet wall stretched to the ocean's edge. The boy was as blond as Alice Ann, but his face was Ralph's; the girl had dark brown eyes like Ralph's, but the nose, mouth, and long, thin face of Alice Ann. Had Ralph snapped that picture of his little happy family at the seaside? Adults had obviously helped those kids build their elaborate sand castle with its many towers. Alice Ann was wearing a red bikini in that picture. She was smiling and shading her eyes with her hands, and she had her left hip stuck out so sassy and sexy. Lindsay held the picture up to the light above the sink. She turned the picture in the bright light and looked closely at the firm, tanned flesh of Alice Ann's upper legs and flat stomach. Just who was the real wife in the story? And the wives in all those other stories Ralph had written over the years? Stories Ralph had sent Lindsay to read over this past year and a half, which at that moment she wished she had never set eyes on— over this year and a half of whispery, late-night, long-distance phone calls, who were the real wives in all those stories? The wife who worked as a waitress to make ends meet, that student's wife, now this wife with looks and personality and drive who could unload a Cadillac convertible in a hurry, who was desperate and angry and who had stretch marks running like roads through the flesh of her legs and hips because of bearing her worthless, bankrupt husband's babies.

Lindsay had brushed her teeth until she tasted blood. She examined her bleeding gums in the mirror, for all it mattered. Lindsay hated her wide mouth and big buck teeth. She had the big mouth of a horse. Trigger was one of her nicknames she hated. Table Legs, Fat Farm, Pimple Plantation were other childhood nicknames that broke her heart. Lindsay tore the seaside picture of Alice Ann and the kids in two and tossed it to float among the cigarette butts in the toilet. Alice Ann floated face up, and Lindsay's hand had hesitated at the toilet's handle. With a thumb and forefinger, Lindsay fished Alice Ann out. She shook this part of the picture over the sink and patted it dry with a towel and put it into her leather cigarette case. She washed her face and hands and rinsed her sore mouth with warm water. When Lindsay flushed the toilet, it sounded like thunder.

But it didn't wake Ralph. Ralph was knotted up in the center of the bed, the covers bunched over his shoulders, his head half under the pillow. He looked desperate in his heavy sleep, his jaws clenched, his arm flung out across Lindsay's side of the bed. Lindsay nestled back in bed with her bottom next to Ralph's. There was a sound coming from inside Ralph's nose when he breathed. Lindsay tried to regulate her breathing to Ralph's, but she couldn't catch his jagged rhythm. She could hear traffic from

El Camino Real up the street, and through the motel's thin walls sudden laughter from the next room. She was afraid to turn off the soundless television set and be plunged into total darkness in this strange room. And then Lindsay had the thought that in all the motel rooms of her memory the television was always on. Why should questions of happiness make Lindsay always suffer?

Lindsay lay there wide-awake in the half-light and listened to the sounds of sex from the next room. She then had an idea of her life as just a long deflowering. She would never have another husband, or give birth, she realized. In her imagination motel rooms opened endlessly onto more motel rooms, like grains of sand in some kids' castle at an ocean's edge, countless cells of sex. Through the papery walls came moans that could wake the dead. Lindsay covered her ears and shut her eyes. Now I lay me down to sleep, Lindsay said to herself. If I should die before I wake, I pray the Lord my soul to take. God bless Daddy and Mommy. God bless Ralph.

Lindsay opened her eyes. If she fell asleep her soul would leave her body. Lindsay uncovered her ears and placed her hand palm flat against the thin wall and let her memory work. Stale smoke filled the motel rooms of her memory, ashtrays of butts, plastic cups of bourbon, greasy boxes of leftover pepperoni pizza, and across the motel room that night was a barely touched family-pack bucket of Kentucky fried chicken on the dresser which Ralph had insisted they pick up for when they would surely be ravenous at midnight. Beside it was the Bible Ralph had found in a drawer, and from which after they had made love the first time this night he had read the Song of Solomon, his voice sonorous, now pitched low and somber, now rising, now thrilling, a voice even richer than when he had read his own story earlier this day about that desperate wife with veins like roads in her flesh.

The toilet flushed in the next room, and when it flushed immediately again, Ralph sat up in bed. Ralph stared at the television set, his eyes wide and bright as a bird's. He clutched the covers to his chest and looked wildly around the room. Ralph looked at Lindsay as though she were some vegetable he would not eat as a child. Are you okay, honey? Lindsay asked him. Ralph lay back down without answering and pulled the twisted covers over his head. Ralph's red pajamas, which he had had stuffed in his briefcase, clearly planning all along on not driving back to Berkeley, and which he put back on after each time they made love, were covered with tiny blue sailboats. Perhaps his mother had given them to him. For Christmas. For his birthday, maybe. Would any wife buy her husband, her lover, red pajamas with tiny blue sailboats on them? Let him kiss me with the kisses of his mouth, for thy love is better than wine, were lines Lindsay ran through her mind as she lay there in the half-light. She heard more moans from the next room. O thou fairest among women. O thou whom my soul loveth. By night I sought him who my soul loveth. I sought him, but I found him not. A cry came from the next room.

Lindsay paced the room smoking. As though grains of light flowed from the room into the television set, surfaces seemed deflated. Lindsay's flesh felt like foam. She shivered violently. She put on Ralph's shirt and sat in the chair before the dresser. She drew her feet up underneath the shirt. On the television were shots from news helicopters of a freeway pileup, police cars' flashing red lights far below, bleeding flares. Then a cut to a toothpaste commercial and a zoom-shot kiss. Behold thou are fair, my love. Thou has dove's eyes within thy locks. Thy breasts are like two young roes that are twins, which feed among the lilies.

The next room's door opened and shut. Lindsay hurried to the window and pulled back the curtains. The parking lot below was full. Up the side street a red light blinked on the corner of El Camino Real, and liquefied traffic in the bluish, mercury-vapor lights shone sleek and mysterious, and Lindsay recalled her girlhood feeling that the night held some great adult secret she would never come to know.

In the parking lot below a man kissed a woman passionately. She was a pretty woman, wearing a checked sundress, and there were silver barrettes in her short brown hair. They held each other for a few moments, and then the woman unlocked the driver's-side door of a small station wagon parked next to Ralph's car. The man was wearing a white belt and white shoes, and he waved to the pretty woman playfully the whole time she backed her station wagon from its slot and drove onto the side street toward El Camino Real and her home just blocks away on Matadero Road. The man cut across the pool area toward the side street. He walked around the pool's deep end and then stopped and stared into the shivery water, where bluish lights bobbed like bright birds about to break the surface into the night air. The man stared across the small pool as though he were studying some distant shore of lights. The man glanced around him and then pulled out his penis and began urinating into the pool. Ralph made a sound in his sleep and then talked in what sounded for all the world like tongues. Lindsay was afraid to turn away from the window. She felt that if she turned from the window, turned around and looked at Ralph, she would fall out of the state of love forever.

The phone's busy signals were like the sounds of some lost race, an electric language Lindsay could learn over time. She sat with her back to Ralph's sleeping form. He mumbled again and again in his desperate sleep. In its reflection in the mirror above the dresser the bed was a maw and Ralph was twisted in its covers like some huge blue-spotted tongue. The television light was as cold and startling as a refrigerator's opened in the middle of the night. When Lindsay dialed Alice Ann's number the next time, only moments later, it was too late, for Alice Ann was already out the door.

Alice Ann was on her way to meet somebody for a drink and a long talk. Jim, namely. Alice Ann had called Jim to see if he had any idea where in the fuck her so-called husband, old rotten, *Running Dog* Ralph might be. Jim had told her he didn't have a clue. Jim had told Alice Ann he didn't even know the whereabouts of his own wife that night when flaws in time kept them, all the sundry players, locked relentlessly in parallel planes.

Lindsay let the phone ring off the wall. There was a comfort in the ringing, the ringing and ringing only Lindsay could hear. Chicken bones in an ashtray looked blue.

You Are Not Your Characters

I

To celebrate their seventeenth wedding anniversary Alice Ann had made reservations for her and Ralph at a restaurant in one of those little, chic shopping malls full of import shoppes, expensive boutiques, and Dalton bookstores, so popular on the peninsula south of San Francisco, and she had invited Jim and Judy to join them. At some point, during a weak, sentimental moment, Jim had crossed his heart and hoped to die while promising Judy not to beat her new boyfriend to a pulp, and as they were more or less on speaking terms then, they agreed to go.

The restaurant Alice Ann had selected for the joyous occasion featured Greek cuisine, and it was obviously a place she was familiar with, the way she raved around about the food. Ralph hated it, of course, oily, smelly, foreigner's fare. The joyous, celebratory evening was off to a flying start by the time Ralph inquired about who Alice Ann had been in this wretched establishment with before. For it sure hadn't been him. Not in this lifetime, anyway. Some of Alice Ann's new hipper-than-thou chums probably was what Ralph speculated out loud. He was already about half drunk. So was Jim, and they all had smoked a couple of killer doobies in the parking lot. Rather, Ralph, Alice Ann, and Jim had, for, as usual, Judy was the designated driver.

That cute remark is in reference to my est group, Alice Ann had smilingly informed Jim and Judy, slowly twisting the ends of her long blond hair around in her fingers as she talked. Alice Ann really was a good-looking woman, and Jim had always thought her hands were especially lovely, with long, slender, expressive fingers that always flashed with rings.

That's the crowd you pay an arm and a leg to, to tell you you're a turd, Ralph had said.

Cute, dearest, Alice Ann said.

First it was those meditation classes, Ralph said. —Then that yoga farm where she went on that suspicious retreat. Wonder what in the world you grow on a yoga farm?

Isn't our anniversary boy amazing? Alice Ann said. —To criticize me for trying to broaden my horizons. Ralph takes pleasure in making light of me trying to expand my consciousness.

Do you plant little yoga seeds? Ralph said. —What's a yoga taste like, anyway? To the best of my knowledge, I, for one, have never personally eaten a yoga. Is it anything like a carrot? Okay, okay, I'll admit I'm not much of a, you know, connoisseur, but there are things in this world I wouldn't put in my mouth if you paid me. Why does it have to be so dark in here, anyway? Ralph said, and held his hand up before his face. —You can hardly see your hand in here.

Ambience, hon, Alice Ann said.

It is pretty dark in here, Judy piped up. She'd been sitting there with a faraway, dreamy look in her lovely brown eyes, probably missing, Jim had reflected, Melvin's member. Judy really was a good-looking woman, too, Jim had to admit, his little blow-job queen, while Jim, on the other hand, looked like a heavy, hirsute, lowlife rider of Harleys.

You can say that again, Ralph said. Ralph picked up a small candle-lantern from the center of the table and held it above his menu. He frowned and shook his old, woolly head. —This is all Greek to me, he said, and chuckled.

I think it's très romantic, Alice Ann said. —Where's your sense of romance, Ralph?

What's this? Ralph said, and pointed to an item on the menu. —Number six. Under the dinners. I can't even pronounce it.

That's *pastitsio*, hon, Alice Ann said. —Which is layers of macaroni, grated cheese, and sautéed ground beef. It's topped with a rich cream sauce and baked. It's yummy, but you ought to try their *souvlakia*.

You don't say? Ralph said, and looked up at Alice Ann with a frown. —Well, maybe I can just order me a nice sirloin burnt to a crisp, the way I like it. And a good old American baked potato. Slavered with sour cream and chives.

Oh Christ, Ralph! Alice Ann said. —It's our fucking anniversary! If you love me, Ralph, you won't act like a horse's ass, and you'll get into the spirit of an anniversary evening. If you don't love me, then you won't.

I know it's our anniversary, Alice Ann, Ralph said. —You don't have to remind me of our seventeen years together for a minute. We have those criminal, thieving kids at home to do that every miserable waking moment.

Ralph hides goodies from his own kids, Alice Ann said. —He keeps a stash of chocolate-chip cookies in his underwear drawer so he won't have to share with his own kids. That's why they are reduced to thievery.

Those criminal kids can get plenty of goodies of their own, Ralph said. —All they do is stuff their greedy little ferret faces with goodies. Then who pays when their pointy little teeth rot out? Tell me that. And that boy has taken to stealing my, you know, Trojans. Right from my underwear drawer, after he's helped himself to my chocolate-chip cookies. I know it. I'm a man who keeps count of what's his. I have that criminal boy dead to rights. A boy stealing his own old dad's Trojans, can you imagine? Is nothing sacred? But, Jesus, what can I do about it? Ralph said. —I can't even beat the boy to a pulp, which, in my book anyway, is the sort of discipline he sorely needs. That boy is bigger than me.

Ralph, Alice Ann said, is the one who could use some discipline. If Ralph had a little more discipline, he'd pay a little more attention to the quality of women he's eating out. And then maybe he wouldn't always be getting those little, runny sores around his mouth.

Jesus, Alice Ann! Ralph croaked. (But he covered his mouth with one of his paws like a reflex.) —Why do you always have to go too far, Alice Ann? Ralph mumbled through his fingers.

Hey, gosh, come on, you guys, Judy chirped. —Hey, I know. Somebody should make a toast to something. To something, you know, romantic, in honor of the occasion.

How about toasting romantic, albeit sordid, buying trips? Jim suggested, which was about the first thing he had had to say that evening, for he'd been basically just parked there feeling real broody and mean and reconsidering seriously his promise not to pound the crap out of his first wife's latest boyfriend.

Say what? Ralph said, his own old, furry ears perking up. —What in the world does that mean, old Jim?

Come on, Jim, Judy said, eyes like daggers. —Don't you start up, too, buster.

I know something très romantic we can toast, Alice Ann said, and raised her glass. —Here's to Ralph's rubbers.

Holy moly, Ralph lamented, and shook his head.

Or, Jim said, to love and marriage. Some fool songster said they go together like a horse and carriage. So come on, everybody, let's all ironically bubble up, Jim said, and tipped his glass against Alice Ann's.

Oh, why not? Judy said, and tipped her glass against Jim's and Alice Ann's glasses, and then she uncharacteristically guzzled her drink down. —I just love champagne to death, Jim's first wife informed everybody.

Count me out, Ralph mumbled through his fingers, which were cupped around his festering mouth and chin again.

By the way, Alice Ann, Judy said, refilling her glass with the cheap-ass bubbly, what did your hubby give you for an anniversary present, anyhow?

A mercy fuck, Alice Ann said, and threw back her own glass of bubbly. —But since Ralph was out of his romantic rubbers, he had to practice withdrawal after about, oh, six or seven seconds.

Let's all drink a romantic toast to the honorable practice of withdrawal, Jim suggested, and lifted his refilled glass.

Okay, buster, Judy had hissed, and if looks could kill . . .

A mercy fuck, Alice Ann? Ralph said. —Are you trying to be funny? Are you? he said, and picked up the little candle-lantern from the middle of the table and held it in front of Alice Ann. He waved it slowly back and forth before her face. —It's so dark in this wretched cave I can't even see the expression on your face, Alice Ann. Alice Ann?

2

Spanakopita, troops, Alice Ann said as she exuberantly fed her face. —God, thin yummy layers of pastry filled with spinach and feta cheese baked to a golden brown. A perfect description of manna. Forgive me, please. It's not my fault. Greek food always does this to me. It drives me crazy hungry, and I know this will sound crazy, but it makes me horny as hell.

Feta cheese? Judy said. —You mean that stuff is in here? Ugh. I didn't know that. Feta cheese, ugh. Feta cheese always makes me think of toe jam.

I agree with you wholeheartedly on that matter, Ralph said to Judy. —That spana-whatever-you-call-it is just so much smelly crud in my book. Let my wife fill herself to the brim with toe jam. Far be it from me to stop my wife from eating anything she has her heart set on eating.

Later, after the waitress had cleared the table and everybody had decided against dessert, but Alice Ann had ordered a final round of drinks, Alice Ann smiled at Ralph and announced that what she had her heart set on doing was footing the bill for this whole night of fucking revelry. Ralph was flabbergasted. Ralph dropped his jaw and fork. Jim raised a toast to Alice Ann's amazing generosity of spirit and good taste and the lovely way she looked that evening. Ralph spluttered and gasped that if they even pulled their way-beyond-their-credit-limit bandit plastic out in public, they could well find themselves thrown under a jailhouse. No fooling, Ralph had lamented, this is no joke. At the very least, Ralph lamented, as sincere as Jim had ever seen him, that worthless, pathetic piece of plastic could well be returned to them on a tray cut into quarters, which would not be the first time for that singular humiliation. Like that shameful, wretched time in Iowa City.

God, what a riot! Alice Ann had laughed.

No, don't even talk about it, Ralph said. —I shouldn't have even brought it up. Jesus. Talk about stupid. That's my middle name, all right. Stupid. Just call me Mister Stupid. That's one sleeping, flea-bitten dog we should just let lie.

Ralph was a student at Iowa then, Alice Ann said. —And he was in John Cheever's writing class. Ralph just adored John Cheever. We had noticed that John seemed distracted and sort of lonely at a faculty cocktail party one Friday afternoon. You know, sort of quiet and sad and off to himself, lonely, yes, if you can believe a famous man like that being lonely. So we just said to ourselves, Why not take John Cheever out on the town? Buy John Cheever a big dinner and show him a high old time. Shoot the works in the John Cheever department was our motto that night.

Who is this John Cheever guy, anyhow? Judy asked.

He's a pretty famous writer, hon, Alice Ann said. —So anyway, we took John to the best restaurant in town. Or was it to that swanky place at the edge of town? Whatever. So we ordered champagne, and not this cheap stuff Ralph insisted upon tonight. I did the ordering that night, so we were drinking nothing but Mumm's no less. Two, maybe three bottles. Who remembers. Shoot the works for John Cheever was our motto that night.

What was old Cheever like? Jim asked Ralph.

You know, Ralph said, the first thing I remember Cheever saying to me about writing was that you aren't your characters but your characters are you. The man took me seriously enough to sit down with me and go over a story and move words around until they fit perfectly.

He must have thought you were cute, Jim said.

I was, Ralph said. —Back in my youth.

So everything was going to be on us that night, Alice Ann said. —John Cheever's money was no good in Iowa City that night. So we ate high off the old proverbial hog, and when the check was presented, we offered up our dubious plastic.

Cheever told me to trust a story's accidents, Ralph said. —Its accidental revelations. The way things you never suspected could emerge in your story. Unlike your life, of course.

Then the old proverbial shit hit the fan, Alice Ann said, and laughed. —Every month or so, Bank of America issues a hit list of bad cards, you know. Well, for some reason the asshole maître d' checked out our card.

He checked it, Ralph said, because you had bounced a check there for lunch a couple of weeks earlier.

Actually, I had bounced two checks there before, Alice Ann said, and laughed. —Anyway, the asshole maître d' checked our card. God, were we ever over our credit limit. Bank of America had been sending us nasty letters for weeks begging us to be responsible American citizen adult types and please quit playing with our poor plastic. We had become your basic B-of-A bandits.

We hadn't always been like that, Ralph said. —Things had just gotten out of hand. We'd gotten so far behind the eight ball, we just sort of threw up our hands.

Well, if you're going to sink, sink with style, Alice Ann said. She blew thin streams of smoke through her elegant nostrils. —Anyway, the asshole maître d' brought the little card back to our table personally. He put the fucking little tray on the table and just stood there smirking. And, sure enough, there was our poor little precious, plastic baby. Mutilated. Cut into quarters. It was hilarious.

It was not either, Ralph said.

What in the world did you-all do? Judy asked.

Alice Ann asked if they would take a check, Ralph said, and laughed, the big slope of his shoulders shaking with mirth.

You're kidding! Jim said, in genuine appreciation.

Honest to God, Ralph said. —Alice Ann didn't bat an eye.

Très true, Alice Ann said. —I didn't give an inch.

They almost called the police, Ralph said. —They were not amused. They made threats.

Well, Christ, what was Cheever doing all this time? Jim asked.

John simply sat there through all this humiliation and smiled, Ralph said. —A sad smile, though, is how I would characterize it. Kindly, but really sort of sad. And his eyes held that same expression, too. As though he had seen people like us going down that old road before and he knew what was in store for them. For us. He was somehow serene about it all. All the yelling and screaming in the ensuing scene. He was drunk, John was, sure. Weren't we all! But he was somehow serene as a Buddha. That's the word that comes to mind. Serene. He was that night, anyway. I had the feeling this really was an old story for John and he knew its ending by heart.

That's not the way I remember it happening, Alice Ann said. —John started yelling at that fucking maître d', too. That's what happened. He was as irate as I was at our treatment. Then they wouldn't even touch his plastic either. They wouldn't even consider it. And of course the assholes wouldn't take a check.

Well, my lands, what really did happen? Judy asked.

Oh, Alice Ann said, John spotted some university people he recognized across the room. So he stumbled over and borrowed the necessary funds from them. One of them was a bigshot dean. No, I think two of them were deans.

That's not what happened, Ralph said.

How would you know, you motherfucking smarty-pants, Alice Ann said. —You were ripped.

Well, so were you.

But you, as usual, were more ripped.

I know what happened that sorry night, Ralph said. —No one has to tell me what happened that wretched night of my life.

We should have walked that fucking check, Alice Ann said. —It was a failure of imagination not to walk that check. Cheever was drunk enough. He would have done it in a second. What a character that wonderful man is. What a story that would have made.

But what in the daggone world really happened? Judy asked.

Not much really, Ralph said. —When all was said and done. John just shelled out. He got stuck with the tab that night. Which was embarrassment enough, let me tell you.

Did you ever pay him back, old dog? Jim asked Ralph.

Not yet, Ralph said. —But I intend to. Any day now.

Shoot fire, Judy said. —I'm going to have to visit the little girls' room pretty soon. Where is it, anyhow?

Go back through the bar, Alice Ann said. —Turn left.

Sounds like you really do know this place like the back of your hand, Ralph said.

Oh, come on, hon, Alice Ann said, and put her cigarette out. She stood up from the table and tossed her napkin on the table. —Let's go powder our twats.

3

When the wives had walked away, Ralph said to Jim, okay, just what all has Alice Ann told you?

Say what? Jim said. —What has Alice Ann told me? Nothing. What would Alice Ann tell me?

She's always airing our dirty laundry for you. Don't try and tell me she doesn't.

Well, you're just being paranoid, as usual. She hasn't told me a thing. Why, what's up?

Alice Ann found the letters.

What letters? You're talking in code, old Ralph.

My girlfriend's letters, that's what letters. Alice Ann found them. God knows how. Jesus. She must have torn the house apart. She must have rooted around like crazy. I had those babies hid, really hid, I'm telling you. If I had buried them like bones in the back yard I couldn't have hid them any better.

So where were they hid?

Oh, they were hid, all right. I've got my places. My secret places not even those criminal kids have found yet. I thought the place where I hid those letters was my best secret place, too. Jesus. Nothing is sacred. Nothing.

Right, especially your girlfriend's love letters. So what happened? What did she do?

You really don't know? Alice Ann hasn't already told you her side of the story, really?

No, Ralph, I told you.

She did plenty, that's what. She sprung them on me. She caught me off guard. Listen to this, old Jim. She waited until today. She saved everything up. Then this morning the, you know, so-called shit hit the fan. Breakfast in bed for the anniversary boy is what she said. She was all smiles. Good-morning kisses for the anniversary boy is what she said. I should have known the jig was up. So she brings me this tray. It's got all my favorite breakfast treats on it. Three eggs sunny-side up. Scratch biscuits with orange marmalade. Those tasty little link sausages done to a turn. Home fries. Cinnamon rolls hot from the oven. Fresh-squeezed orange juice. Coffee. You name it. I should have known. The handwriting was on the wall. So I'm sitting there in bed stuffing my face, happy as a clam. Then she says, I'll bring the paper and the mail in to the anniversary boy, sweetie-pie. No bills, I say. Bury the bills today. I'll deep-six the bills, sweetie-pie, she says. So she brings me the paper and it's turned to the funny page. I like to read the funny page first thing. Then she says, Hey, big anniversary boy, I've got a bright idea. How would you like to play a little post office with your anniversary girl? And she's winking and blinking at me to beat the band. Well, you can guess what I thought she meant by that. So I said, Sure, why not. I mean, I was sort of looking forward to finishing that swell breakfast while it was hot, but when duty calls . . . So I put on my best bedroom look, all sappy with smiles and bug-eyed with feigned desire. And then she says . . . Through rain and snow, through sleet or hail, we never fail to deliver the United States mail, motherfucker, and then she tossed this fat pack of letters, Lindsay's letters, smack in the middle of the goddamn tray. Food went flying everywhere. Eggs. Those tasty little sausages. Home fries all over the funny page. Jesus. Where's it all going to end?

Damn, Jim said. —So then what?

◐ ◑

Oh, screaming, Ralph said. —Yelling. Snarls. Lefts and rights. Some bloodletting. Although minor so far, all things considered. You know, just the usual heated discussion.

Oh boy, Jim said.

But it's only the beginning, Ralph said. —She's saving her best, or worst, I should say, for later. Whenever that's going to take place. Take my word for it. This affair is far from over. What's more, she has suspicions about this cute student of mine.

Are they true?

Well, sort of. But nothing serious. Just a, you know, student. An A student, I might add.

So you got those runny sores around your mouth from eating out some A student, huh?

No! Ralph gasped, clomping a paw over his mouth. —No way! he mumbled. —These are, you know, fever blisters. Plain and simple. She's a nice, clean girl, an A student, like I told you. Please don't breathe a word of this. Please, old Jim.

You can count on me, old dog. This business about you eating out your nice, clean A student is buried. I'll take this little conversation with me to my grave.

And on top of everything else, we're going belly-up again, Ralph said.

Belly-up? What's that mean, old Ralph?

We're on the verge of bankruptcy again. No fooling. Belly-up. Broke. Busted flat. Just like seven years ago, when we declared bankruptcy before. Jesus. It has become a way of life. I read this article recently. It was that kids' Science Made Simple column in the Sunday paper. You know. And it told about how at the end of seven years all the cells of your body have changed over. They're all new, see? It's sort of like at the end of every seven years you're sort of this totally transformed human being. Somebody new, in terms of cells, anyway. Well, I'll tell you this. I'm not a brand-new human being from seven years ago. Maybe my so-called cells are new, but I'm the same old sorry human being belly-up again. In California, after you declare bankruptcy, you have to wait seven years before you can declare it again. That's the way I know seven years of my life have gone by. It's time to belly-up again. You know something? Ralph said, and looked over at Jim and shook his old, woolly head. —You're the best friend I have on the face of this earth.

Hey, listen, old dog, Jim said, I love you, too, and I really wish I could give you a hand, but I only have about fifty fucking bucks to my name.

No, Ralph said. —That's not what I'm talking about.

So, Jim said, what's your point?

I don't know, Ralph said, and shrugged. —I don't know, I guess. Food for thought. Wonder whatever happened to our waitress with that last round of drinks? You know, there's this passage in Dostoevsky. It's about this fellow who is given the choice to die or to stand on this ledge throughout all eternity.

So what's your point, Ralph? Jim asked. —You're sure being a cryptic fuck tonight. So how wide is the ledge?

I don't know, Ralph said. —Some choice. Here comes your wife.

4

Where's Alice Ann? Ralph asked when Judy sat down at the table.

She's still in the little girls' room, Judy said.

She must be doing one of her marathon number twos, Ralph said. —Did she leave her cigarettes? he said, and slid the little lantern around looking. —Holy moly, she must be drunk. She left her bag on the chair, he said, and placed the lantern on the table's edge while he rummaged through the handbag. Ralph looked up quickly when the waitress approached the table carrying a tray of drinks.

Here you go, folks, the waitress said, and placed the drinks around. —Are you sure there won't be anything else tonight, folks? she asked.

No. No, thank you, Ralph said. —I believe that will be the last round, like my wife said. Thank you. Everything was nice. Very nice.

Cool, the waitress said, and placed a small tray with the bill on the table.

Ralph picked the bill up and looked it over. He held it up to the lantern and looked it over again carefully. He returned the bill to the tray and then after a moment picked it up and studied it again, his lips moving as he read it over.

Jaysus, Ralph said, and placed the bill back onto the tray.

Steep? Jim asked him.

Oh, just another nail in my coffin, Ralph said, and gulped his drink, which was a double bourbon.

Hey, old dog, let me grab the tip, Jim suggested. —Here goes, Jim said, and took out the little spiral notebook and pen he always carried in his shirt pocket in those days. He wrote on a page and then tore it out and placed it on the tray. —There you go, old dog, Jim told Ralph. —The tip is covered.

Ralph reached over and picked the notepaper up and read it out loud: *Plant corn early.*

That there's a valuable tip, Jim told Ralph. —My old redneck daddy gave me that tip, and one year it saved the farm.

Ralph rolled up the tip and tossed it over his shoulder. He tapped his coffee spoon lightly on the tabletop and gazed around the dark room.

You wouldn't recognize a good tip if somebody stuck it up your ass, Jim said. —Stay in school, now that's a good tip.

Ralph rolled his eyes and picked up the last of his drink and shook ice loose in the glass. He tossed the ice into his mouth and began to crunch it slowly. He began to make little overlapping patterns of damp circles on the bar napkin with the bottom of his glass. Suddenly Ralph laughed out loud. It was like a bark. Then he covered his mouth with a paw and coughed. Then he turned in his chair and began to rummage in Alice Ann's handbag again.

I have some of these Vantages, Judy said. —They're not very strong, but you're welcome to them. I'm trying to quit.

Never mind, Ralph said. —Thanks, anyway.

Feed pigs popcorn, Jim said. —That's another one of daddy's tips that saved my bacon.

When Alice Ann finally returned to the table, Ralph flashed her a broad smile.

We got the bill while you were otherwise engaged, Ralph said.

Terrific, Alice Ann said, and shrugged. She swirled her margarita.

You know, Ralph said, I thought my sirloin tasted like an old piece of boiled goat.

I adored my meal, Alice Ann said.

I sort of liked whatever it was I had, Judy said.

You had *pastitsio* with *kima*, hon, Alice Ann said.

Well, I adored my moussaka, Jim said, smirking at Ralph.

Mou-*suck*-a is more like it, Ralph said. —I hate this so-called restaurant like I've never hated an establishment before.

Ignore him, troops, Alice Ann said. —He's just getting into one of his little snits. He didn't have the imagination to order ethnic, so he wants to pout.

Ralph picked the bill up off the tray and examined it again in the lantern light.

Nope, Ralph said, and put the bill back on the tray.

Nope, Ralph? Alice Ann said. —Fucking *nope*?

Nope, sirree, Ralph said, and chuckled. —Nope, I'm not going to pay it.

Very funny, dear, Alice Ann said. —I just forgot to laugh.

I mean it, Ralph said. —I'm not going to shell out.

Well, er, who is, then? Jim was real curious to know. —I don't see old John Cheever anywhere.

I don't know, Ralph said. —Not me, that's for sure. That's not my bill. I don't see my name anywhere on that particular bill.

Hey, old dog, Jim said, this was supposed to be your treat. Alice Ann said so!

I don't care. I'm not going to shell out. I hate this restaurant. This restaurant stinks. This restaurant smells like Zorba's armpits.

Don't pay any attention to him, troops, Alice Ann said, and lit a cigarette. —Our anniversary boy has just gotten plastered per usual and peevish.

My sirloin tasted like goat, Ralph said. —I've got my standards. It's not my bill of fare.

Don't worry, gang, Alice Ann said. —I'm the keeper of the plastic in this so-called family.

Not tonight you're not, Ralph said.

Come again, sweetie-pie, Alice Ann said.

Look and learn, Ralph said.

Alice Ann stubbed her cigarette out slowly. She slid her bill-fold from her handbag and opened it to her card folder.

Very clever, Ralphie, Alice Ann said. —I just don't believe you sometimes. And this time you've achieved a new low-rent level. All right, Ralph, is it a scene you want? May I help you with a scene, is that it?

Hey, you two, Jim said.

Why don't we all just chip in? Judy suggested, and opened her own purse.

I think Ralph has his little heart set on a public scene, Alice Ann said. —I would hate to disappoint the anniversary boy. After that amazing six-second mercy fuck, I feel I owe the boy some-thing. Ralph just lives for public scenes, see. They give him some-thing to write about, after all. After all, if all Ralph could depend upon for his writing was his imagination, where would he be?

I don't care, Ralph said. —Raise the roof. Go on, throw some chairs and tables around. See where that gets you tonight. No one knows *me* here. I, for one, have never been in this smelly establishment before. Unlike you and whoever your Mediter-ranean Romeo is. I can just see that Greek goat now. Coarse and dark, hairy-armed, mustachioed. Reeking of garlic and olives and anchovies. Breath like feta cheese.

I guess the cat's out of that bag, Alice Ann said. —So tell me, Ralph, how long have you been spying on us, on Zorba and me?

Zorba! Ralph bellowed. —Too much, I say!

Oh come on, you two, Jim said.

I only have seven dollars, Judy said.

Hey, listen, old dog, Jim said. —We don't carry credit cards and I don't have my checkbook with me, or I'd gladly pick up the tab myself.

I just bet, Ralph said, then grabbed Alice Ann by an arm and hissed, Zorba, Alice Ann? Zorba?

I would! Jim told Ralph. —Why not go ahead and grab it for now and I'll write you a check when we get home. Now how's them apples?

I'll write you a check myself when we get home, Judy said. —And, Ralph, you know I'll keep my word.

You people just don't get the picture, Ralph said. —I can't use the plastic, even if I wanted to. They'll run a check on it, I know they will. Then they'll call the plastic police. At the very least, and I kid you not, they'll bring that card back on a little tray all cut to pieces.

Oh, don't be so goddamn paranoid, Ralph, Alice Ann said. —They don't have any reason to check that card.

They have all the reason in the world. *You* have been here before. You and Zorba. Zorba the goat. God only knows how much paper you've hung in this pathetic place.

Ralph, Alice Ann said, why did you smoke that dope before we got here? You should never smoke dope and drink, too. You always get so goddamn paranoid.

They'll cut up the card, Ralph said. —It's true. I know it will happen to us again. I can just feel it in my bones.

This is all just downright silly, Judy said. —This is your-all's wedding anniversary, don't forget.

Tell me about it, Alice Ann said. —Let me count the moments.

Well, buddy, what do you suggest? Jim asked Ralph. —Who's going to wash the dishes?

Why don't we simply walk away? Ralph said. —You know, vanish into thin air. Like Alice Ann said we should have done that night with John Cheever. It's not like we haven't walked our share of checks, Alice Ann.

Happy anniversary, troops, Alice Ann said, and raised her empty champagne glass. —Well, Ralph, I'll have to admit that walking an anniversary dinner check seems somehow so appropriate for us.

I won't do any such thing, Judy said in a huff.

Jim picked up the bill from the little tray and gave it a gander.

So, okay, Ralph, Jim said, what's your plan?

Jim! Judy squeaked, don't you even think about any such thing.

❦ ❦

We're all in this boat together, Ralph said. —Just remember that.

Don't worry, Jim told his first wife, I won't tell Melvin on you.

Who? Ralph said.

Jim, please, Judy said.

He's a friend of Zorba's, Jim told Ralph.

It will be a failure of imagination not to walk this check, Ralph said. —To coin a phrase. Hey, it'll be simple. I'll order some more champagne, see. Mumm's, this time. Two bottles of Mumm's. As though we've decided to celebrate some more, after all. As though we've decided the evening is young. As though we've decided life is too short not to celebrate until the cows come home. Then after a few toasts you two just get up and depart. As though you're simply leaving before we, the anniversary couple, are. As though you told the babysitter you'd be home a little before the cows. Then mosey on out and get the car warmed up and simply wait for us to effect our own clean getaway. See, you two are not really even involved in this business at all. Just wait for us outside, ready to roll with a moment's notice. Just be ready to peel out. To leave rubber, if it comes to that. Then Alice Ann can act as though she's going to return to the, er, little girls' room for another marathon poop, and she can simply slip out the bar-side's door instead. Then I'll slip out. I'll be the last one to go. I've already thought of a foolproof plan. It'll all be a piece of cake. Alice Ann and I have done this dozens of times.

Did you kids know I was once in an Off Broadway play? Alice Ann said. —I was. How many times have I told you that? But I was. I could have had a different life.

A cakewalk, Ralph said. —No fooling.

I've never done anything like this in my entire life, Judy said.

Fallen Homecoming Queens are capable of anything, Jim said.

Don't you see, Ralph said, the beauty of my plan is that none of you guys really runs any risk at all. I'll be the last one to leave. I'll run all the personal risk.

Risk, Ralph? Alice Ann said. —What do you know about personal risk? I once thought I was knocked up by a famous black actor. I banged on his door. I told him to his face. But he denied any responsibility. He told me to go back to my husband. So here I sit. End of story.

A cakewalk, Ralph said.

So here I sit celebrating my seventeenth wedding anniversary, Alice Ann said. —Hey, I have a bright idea, troops. Let's go parking tonight. While Ralph and I still have the convertible, anyway. Before the court takes it away. We'll find a place up in the hills so we can look out over the lights. We'll keep the top down. We can let the boys feel us up, hon. We'll all dry-hump and finger-fuck like in the old days. We'll get seriously nude. We'll lie there in that hot dark with absolutely nothing but the radio on.

So we won't really be involved? Judy asked Ralph.

Right, Ralph said. —Heck, even if they stop me, so what? What's the worst that can happen? I'll act as though there was a little misunderstanding about who was supposed to pick up the tab. Then, as a last resort, I'll try to push my plastic. Then, by golly, I'll wash some dishes, if it comes to that, sweep some floors, blow the cooks. But you guys will be long gone.

Ralph, sweetie-pie, Alice Ann said, if you're going to stiff a bill, stiff a serious bill. Do it with a little real flair, dearest. Why don't we set up the whole house? Tell the waitress the anniversary saps want to order the house's best champagne for everybody in the place. Including the cooks. So then everybody can get in on the celebration of our seventeenth wedding anniversary. Then we'll stiff that bill. Now, that would be a bill worth stiffing. You could even write one of your sad, ordinary, little stories about stiffing a bill like that. Use your imagination for once, Ralph.

You always want to go too far, Alice Ann, Ralph said. —You have never understood limits. There have to be some limits in life.

Oh come on, Ralph, Alice Ann said. —Please show a little imagination for once, please. You know, Ralph, that's always been your problem, Ralph. You must know that by now. You just don't have enough imagination for the big time, Ralph.

I have just as much imagination as the next fellow, Ralph said. —You just want to make a big scene, that's all. You're dying to cause a scene. So you can take the credit. Alice Ann loves to star in big scenes, folks. And the more sordid the scene, the better.

I'm simply doing what you want me to do, Ralph, Alice Ann said. —Deep in your heart, you want me to cause a scene. That's always been my main function in this so-called marriage. So you won't have to get up tomorrow and use your imagination, you cocksucker.

Hey, you two, come on, Jim said.

Two bottles should do the trick nicely, Ralph said. Ralph picked up the lantern and waved it in the air to get the attention of the waitress, who was several tables away. —You guys go ahead and order up some of their best bubbly. Meanwhile, I need another drink. A stiff one. In the worst way. Who else needs another drink? Why don't I just slip off to the bar and get us all another round, while we're waiting for that waitress to re-enter our lives.

Celestial Navigation

Through clicking windshield wipers Jim stared at stars and tried to recall those constellations he had memorized as a boy. Ralph's hands were high on the steering wheel, and now and then he twisted the wheel this way or that, as though turning into imaginary curves on the California shopping center's parking lot. Every now and then Ralph revved up the engine. But he made no move to put the ragtop into gear. The clicking wipers drew Jim's eyes to the windshield's curved glass, where he saw Ralph's and his faces reflected like death masks. Jim suddenly wondered who the real witness to these events in their lives was, Ralph or him, and whose memory they would fill meaningfully. For the very first time in their friendship Jim had this sudden fear of being lost, or submerged, as it were, in Ralph's memory or imagination or, worst of all, his future fame. Then Ralph reached forward and turned off the windshield wipers. Before Jim could break the focus of his concentration from their creepy reflections on the curved glass of the windshield, Ralph said, Let me get this straight, our wives are under arrest?

Not exactly, Jim said. —But there are threats. Our wives are sitting in the manager's office even as we speak. Alice Ann is raising hell. My blushing bride is seething. You might say our wives are being sort of held hostage.

How far has Alice Ann gone? Ralph said. He revved up the engine again, and then he began twisting the radio dial, until he settled upon a cool jazz station, where Chet Baker was singing "Let's Get Lost." —Has she struck anybody yet? She punched out a cop once. Down in Santa Barbara. What happened, anyway? Don't leave anything out.

Right now Alice Ann is in her mid-to-late snarling stage, I'd say. No blood has been drawn yet. She almost tossed her drink in the manager's face, but I caught her. The manager, who is this big, fat, oily fellow, by the way, saw you duck out, that's what happened.

Well, maybe I was simply stepping out for a breath of fresh air. Did anybody stop to consider that? Maybe give me the benefit of the doubt?

The manager watched you get in the ragtop.

I was careful, Ralph said. —I covered my tracks. How did that manager spot me, anyway? Did somebody finger me? Did you finger me?

I would have, you asshole, in a heartbeat, Jim told Ralph. —If I had had the chance. I knew you were up to something no good. The manager just had his eye on you, that's all.

From the start? You mean all night?

Who knows. Probably. They probably have profiles of people like you. Like they have of terrorist types at airports.

You think so?

I would if I owned a restaurant, Jim said. He took a joint from his shirt pocket and fired it up.

Can I have a little hit on that dooby? Ralph said.

Do you really think you deserve one, Ralph?

Please.

Just don't Bogart it as usual, Ralph, Jim said, and reluctantly passed that asshole the joint.

How did you escape? Ralph said, and then took one of his typical bug-eyed pulls on the joint.

I didn't escape, Ralph. I told them this was all just a sorry mix-up. I told the manager you had misplaced your wallet somewhere, and you simply went out to search in the vehicle. I'm supposed to be helping you find it.

And he believed you?

Probably not. But, hey, they have our wives. Actually, everything was relatively all right until Alice Ann got pissed. The manager just informed us that you'd been observed leaving the premises. Then Alice Ann went a little nuts.

See, I told you she was going nuts. Didn't I tell you that? She just has to do that, though, go really nuts, every once in a while. But that's another story. I can't talk about that.

My bride is properly mortified, of course. But that's not necessarily a bad thing. Basically, all Alice Ann really wants is to get her hands on you. Which I'm all for. I vote for that. I don't think those people even care about that big bill right now. I think they would almost be satisfied with getting Alice Ann off their hands.

Maybe that manager should call the police, after all, Ralph said. —That might be the best thing to do, you know, in the long run.

They made threats early on, but that was before Alice Ann really got hot and turned on them.

I can't go back in that wretched place. That would be not unlike walking into an ambush. What man in his right mind would deliberately do something like that, knowingly walk into a trap? Let me ask you that.

Well, you have to do something, old Ralph. You can't just sit here.

Okay, then. Well then, let's not panic. Let's consider everything. We'll just look carefully at our options.

Why don't you put the top down? Jim suggested. He dialed in a country-western station on the radio.

What?

The ragtop. Put it down, man. It's stuffy in here and smoky. Put it down, Ralph, while we consider *our* options.

All right, Ralph said. —That sounds like a good idea.

Ralph pressed the ragtop button and the top cranked slowly back. Jim rested his head back on the seat and looked up at the stars. It was a balmy night, with a whiff of eucalyptus in the warm breeze. The sound of traffic from the Bay Shore Freeway was a low, almost comforting rumble. On the radio the old Silver Fox, Charlie Rich, was singing "Behind Closed Doors."

Look up there, Jim said, and pointed to the sky with the joint. —There's the Big Dipper. Over there is Taurus. See those stars? Taurus the bull. There's Cancer. Were you ever interested in the stars when you were a kid, old Ralph?

No, Ralph said, wiggling his fingers at Jim for the joint. —Not much, anyway, I guess. They were just always up there, you know, blinking. I don't remember much about my childhood.

I wanted to be an astronomer when I grew up. I memorized the night sky.

Really? Ralph said. —That's nice. Can I have another hit of that dooby before it's history?

Those stars along the western horizon, they're known as the Great Chinese Dragon constellation. I know my constellations by heart. I know the night sky like the back of my own hand. Over there, see? That cascade of stars that looks like, well, a leak. Like they're dripping down the sky. That's called the Moon Maid's Menstruation. Right up there is the Great Celestial Salamander.

How stoned are you already? Ralph said. —Would it really kill you to share some of that dooby?

And right up there is the Giant Chimera.

You sound as flaky as Alice Ann sometimes, Ralph said. He pressed the ragtop's button and the top began noisily cranking back up.

Shit, wait a minute, Jim said. He took another joint from his shirt pocket and handed the thing to Ralph. —Here, asshole. Now keep the top down, dickhead.

Wonder what our wives are doing right now? Ralph said.

Cooling their heels while we search for your wallet, I guess, Jim said. —Ralph, would you explain to me why you were running the windshield wipers when I first came out.

I was just checking everything out. To see if everything was in working order. Sort of like a countdown, I guess. Like a pilot before takeoff.

So you really were thinking about doing it? Jim said. —Taking off. And leaving your best buddy in the dust.

It wasn't you I was leaving. But I was leaving, all right. I came within a heartbeat. And I might have done it. If you hadn't come charging out the door yelling your head off.

I've kicked guy's asses for less than what you tried to pull tonight, Ralph, Jim said. —And the night's young, buddy. Pass the dope, dicknose.

I'm not responsible for what I'm doing these days, Ralph said.

Are you pleading insanity? Diminished capacity?

Well, I'll tell you this, I'd get off in a court of law.

Where were you thinking about going, anyway? When you were thinking about dumping your best buddy.

Anywhere. Somewhere. I don't know. Well, I do know. Missoula, Montana, that's where. That's where the woman I really love lives. I really was thinking about doing it, too.

Does that woman love you?

You bet she does. I can prove it, too. I've got it in black and white.

It's not too late, you know.

What do you mean?

Let's go. Let's do it. You've got your paw on the pedal. Put the pedal to the metal. Let's run away from home.

You mean take off? Ralph said. Ralph looked over at Jim and started to laugh. —You know, Ralph said, they call Missoula the garden city of the Northwest.

We'll make a clean getaway. We'll be cowboys in Montana. If I didn't turn out to be an astronomer, the next thing I wanted to become when I was a kid was a cowboy.

Just take off, Ralph said, chuckling. —Put the pedal to the metal. Ranch by day and sing songs around the campfire by night.

Break wild horses for our pay.

Write Western stories full of vast distances under amazing sunsets.

And full of compound nouns and proper names, Jim said. —I've done it before, old Ralph. Run away from home. And I'm ready teddy to do it again. We're not waiting on me, buddy. Think of the story it would make. We'll be the talk of the town.

You want to take off? Just like that. You mean it?

You bet, Jim said. —I've been on leave this whole term and not written a fucken decent sentence. I need a change of scene. I need a change of life. Besides, my blushing bride is fucking some clown.

What? Ralph said. —What? You're kidding.

Nope. She's fucking some guy from work. Some sport who wears a white belt and white shoes with tassels. Too much, I say.

I don't believe you. Judy is? How do you know? Did you catch her red-handed? I don't believe it. Judy's not the type.

She told me. Judy's like that. She just thought I should know. Judy's all right. She just wants a normal, happy life.

She told you? That's crazy. You mean she just up and confessed? Why in the world would somebody do something like that?

Judy's not like us, Jim said. —She's basically a decent person. It's just something somebody like Judy would do. She feels guilty about fucking this guy, which I know is something difficult for somebody like you—or me, for that matter—to comprehend.

Gosh. Judy always put me in mind of, you know, Mary Tyler Moore. Holy moly. Did she tell you any, well, juicy details?

I pumped her for details.

I'll be damned, Ralph said. —I'll be damned. Did she tell you if she has engaged in any, you know, oral sex?

Hey, Jim said. —Fuck you and the horse you rode in on!

Gosh, old Jim, I didn't mean anything. I'm sorry. I'm just amazed is all. I just didn't have any idea, that's all.

Anyway, buddy, I, for one, am going on the lam, which is a way of life I can understand. I am going to practice some withdrawal of my own, I guess you could say, some serious withdrawal from ordinary life as I have come to know and loathe it.

You really are going to go, aren't you?

Hi-yo, Silver, away. Aren't you going to go with me, buddy?

I can't, Ralph said. —Not just yet, I mean. Not right now, exactly.

Oh come on, old Ralph. We'll live off the land. We don't even need maps. We'll use celestial navigation to guide our herd north.

I just can't, Ralph said. —Not right now, anyway. I've got too many loose ends to tie up. I'll come up later, though. I will.

Okay, I get the picture, old Ralph, Jim said. —Well, running away from home is a real perilous passage. It takes a cowboy with balls like a bull to run away from home. Okay, then, this will be my Western movie and mine alone, I reckon, pardner.

I can't believe this, Ralph said. —You're really going to do it. Will you do me a favor, old Jim?

I don't know. Maybe. What?

Will you take something to somebody for me? Sort of deliver a package to somebody for me?

Maybe. If it's not too big. And not out of my way. And if there are no strings attached.

Ralph turned off the engine, then got out and hurried around to the ragtop's trunk. Jim slid out of his side and followed Ralph back.

There's somebody watching us from the bar door, Ralph said.

It's the oily manager, Jim told him.

Wonder what he's thinking about all this business? Ralph said. He opened the trunk. —Wonder what our wives are doing now?

Jesus, Ralph, Jim said, who knows what the oily fuck thinks. Who cares. As for our wives, they probably have dates with the cooks by now.

Ralph rummaged about beneath piles of papers and books until he found an old battered yellow suitcase. It was covered with faded tourist stickers. SEE SILVER SPRINGS was one.

Nice suitcase, Jim said.

It's Alice Ann's. She's had this awful thing since childhood. The lock on mine was broken. I couldn't very well set off into a new life using a suitcase with a rope tied around it.

Ralph fumbled with the locks on the old beat-up suitcase,

then flung it open. It looked as though it had been packed in maybe six seconds, by furious fistfuls. It was stuffed with wrinkled shirts and pants and wadded gray underwear, all tangled among assorted, mostly uncapped toiletries. It also contained several cans of Campbell's soup, a couple of rolls of toilet paper, and what looked like a plastic bag of sandwich fixings.

So you really were thinking about taking off? Jim said, genuinely surprised and, yes, impressed.

I told you so, Ralph said. —I told you so, didn't I? I wasn't fooling. I packed this baby right after Alice Ann nailed me at breakfast. I was ready to hit the open road in a heartbeat if she turned on me again.

Jim saw the manager waving from behind the glass door of the bar. He was motioning for Jim and Ralph. Jim gave him the finger.

Here, Ralph said. —He took a large folder from the suitcase. —This is it. These are the letters I was telling you about. Lindsay's letters. And some of mine, too, actually. She sent them back to me. But she was angry. She'll get over it. Take them to her for me. Please, old Jim. Alice Ann threatened to burn these babies in the back yard. And she'd do it, too. Forget any concern for, well, you know, the interests of posterity. Tell Lindsay for safekeeping. Will you do that, old Jim? And can I trust you? I mean, these are private letters, old Jim. Meant for our eyes, Lindsay's and mine, only. You understand.

You know you can trust me, old Ralph. With anything.

Tell Lindsay I'm sorry. Tell her I'm coming as soon as I can tie up all the loose ends of my old, wretched life down here.

I'll tell her, old Ralph. You can count on me, pardner.

Hey, you fellas! they heard somebody call out, and they looked up to see the manager standing outside shaking his fist.

Old Missoula, Montana, Jim said to Ralph. —The old garden city of the Northwest, Jim said.

You fellas! Hey! they heard, and watched the fat, oily manager waddling hurriedly across the parking lot toward them.

Well, here comes old Zorba, Jim said. —Zorba the goat.

What? Ralph said. —Who? Who did you say?

Oh, you know, Jim said. —Old Melvin's buddy.

Yes! Jim thought. Fucken yes. Missoula, Montana. Why not? The garden city of the Northwest. A place on earth where he somehow knew he could come to belong. A cowboy-and-Indian town on the verge of things. Maybe even the uncanny edge of romance.

People of the Wolf

I

When Lindsay was thirty she divorced her first husband, this jerk who fancied himself an emerging great American poet and dangerous outlaw-biker to boot, after three pitiful years of marriage. For a time after her divorce and before her remarriage, Lindsay had lived as though she welcomed grief and ruin. In moments of sustaining illusion, she told herself that she, the *Lindsay*, was living legendary. In moments of less illusion, Lindsay saw her life as lost. A dead-end job selling real estate was a far cry from that glimpsed golden ideal of her future she had had as a scholarship girl going East to Vassar College. Although men now told Lindsay she was beautiful, she could only see herself as she had been in high school, a fat girl with pimples who played tuba in the marching band, was editor of the yearbook, and was brilliant in Latin. She had to admit, however, that after she had supposedly blossomed into a beauty in college her life had been full of romantic events, if not love. But where had they led her?

Lindsay's father had walked her onto the train that early morning she had first departed for Vassar, put up her carry-on luggage, and at the last moment had hugged her goodbye, the first time Lindsay could remember him hugging her since childhood. Lindsay's father had then told her out of the blue that if she slept with a boy he would know it. That night, somewhere in the darkness, hours east of her father, Lindsay had worked up enough nerve to go out and smoke on the open platform between cars like an adult, the first time she had smoked like that, a real grownup puffing in public. The vague sweep of the Western landscape felt so distant and dark, and Lindsay imagined herself a mysterious, daring woman in a veiled hat smuggling her life east. Lindsay's cigarette smoke trailed that train moving away from her father, like a ghost too thin to haunt.

Lindsay's acned face had rubbed raw against the train seat as she stared at endless, oily horizons, or tried to sleep, and by the time her train pulled into Poughkeepsie days later, her face was a bloody mess. Lindsay's roommate in Davidson Hall was tall, thin, blond, and as beautiful as the pale girls whose pictures Lindsay stared at in *Vogue* magazine. Lindsay's beautiful roommate wore a pastel-print McMillan blouse, a wraparound skirt, loafers, and a clunky bracelet of gold charms depicting crowning achievements in her life. As she felt her beautiful roommate giving her the once-over, Lindsay had tried to smooth her straight, bright-red, corduroy skirt over her bulging hips.

As the months passed, Lindsay would sit for hours at her darkened window overlooking Davidson Hall's front door and watch the endless moonlight French kissing of girls and the boys who loved them with all their hearts.

Rolf was Lindsay's first true love. A dark, handsome, German boy, he was a Yale student Lindsay had hired her freshman year to tutor her in German. Soon she dreamed of doing anything Rolf asked of her. She dreamed of his hands on her breasts, her nipples rolled gently between a thumb and forefinger while being licked like her one and only high-school boyfriend used to do, that pimply, big-hipped boy who was the marching band's drum major and always stuttered when aroused. One spring Saturday afternoon when Rolf came to campus to tutor Lindsay, he caught sight of Lindsay's beautiful roommate and fell head over heels in love with that blond vision. The beautiful roommate took a fancy to Rolf; such a dark, intense, handsome boy, he amused her. One weekend the roommate announced to Lindsay she planned on shacking up with Rolf in an apartment he had borrowed near the Yale campus. She was curious to see if he was as full of fire as he appeared. The beautiful roommate modeled her new blue nylon nightgown for Lindsay. The beautiful roommate danced a slow bump and grind about the room while Lindsay stared through that soft, flowing film at erect nipples red as blood. A few weeks later the beautiful roommate swore Lindsay to secrecy, then announced that their old friend Rolfie boy was full of fire all right, for she was knocked up.

What was Rolf to do? A scholarship exchange student, he had little money, but Rolf did the honorable thing, just as Lindsay had expected him to do. He begged the beautiful roommate to marry him. They could quit school, find jobs of some sort, manage somehow to make a future for themselves and for their son. When the beautiful roommate told Rolf she might abort, he begged her to bear his baby for the sake of the future, if nothing else. The beautiful roommate quit taking Rolf's calls. She began leaving campus early on Fridays for weekends in New York with other boys. Rolf began coming to campus during the week, lurking about, following the beautiful roommate around between classes, begging, begging her. She threatened to tell authorities. Lindsay would sit in her darkened window and watch Rolf pace below, smoking. He was growing so thin. Even Lindsay was losing weight with worry. Why wasn't she the one knocked up? It should have been her knocked up. She would carry Rolf's child, his son, his baby boy, under her heart gladly. Even if Rolf didn't love her at first. Rolf would learn to love her.

Perhaps Lindsay could talk the beautiful roommate out of the abortion! Perhaps if she offered to take the baby herself! Even if Rolf would not want the baby that way, without the beautiful roommate in the bargain, Lindsay didn't care. She would adopt the little baby as her very own, give it some beautiful name. Lindsay hated Vassar. She would leave Vassar in a heartbeat, get a job, disappear somewhere nobody would dream to look, Hoboken, say, and hide out there until her boy was a fully grown man.

Lindsay sat at her darkened window and imagined a brand-new love story. It was full of rescue and escape, and it had a happy ending. She would somehow rescue her baby boy and escape with him into a lifetime full of love, beyond worry, free from regret and guilt. Lindsay imagined the features of her son's handsome face, its shape, his lean, perfect, maturing body, his tender feelings and thoughts for her, his love for her, the words he would come to speak to her full of gratitude. One night, as Lindsay gazed out her window, a beautiful, dreaming baby appeared before her. It floated in midair, luminous among the dark leaves of the trees. Lindsay realized that dreaming baby's life was her mission on earth.

2

The night the beautiful roommate told Rolf the whole thing had been a dumb hoax, that she had never really been knocked up at all, that it was simply a dumb, bad joke (even she had to admit that!) which had gone too far, Rolf beat his fists bloody against Davidson Hall's front door and ran off into the dark. Lindsay went searching for him. Hours later she found him in a Poughkeepsie bar drunk. While Rolf wept quietly, Lindsay downed three Brandy Alexanders and two Pink Squirrels to catch up. Lindsay got drunk as quickly as she could, and she mourned along with Rolf for the loss of their son. A hoax, Rolf cried, and looked up at Lindsay through his tears. A detestable lie! Why would she tell a story like that? Somebody that beautiful.

That night would be like no other for Lindsay, full of events so new she would alternately attempt to reimagine or forget them all the rest of her life. In a drunken delirium Lindsay and her beautiful German boy circled back to a campus transformed in moonlight, whose old stone, ivy-covered buildings loomed lovely to Lindsay for the very first time. They found themselves lost on some dark path in the heart of Shakespeare Gardens, a park on campus containing every plant mentioned anywhere in Shakespeare's poems or plays. Rolf stumbled off the path. He pulled Lindsay down beside him, into a secret chamber beneath an oak.

That night the air of Shakespeare Gardens was like spice, thick with things nearly forgotten, faint melodies, lights in the leaves, a flickering lantern of moonlight over Rolf's dark, handsome face. If Rolf fell asleep, Lindsay would cross his lids with love's oil, and he would wake charmed with her in his mind. She would pluck the wings of butterflies, and she would fan moonbeams into his dark eyes. Hiding in this palace wood, she would carry his changeling under her heart. She would. She would. She would run away with Rolf. Anywhere. Hoboken. Germany. Marry him in a heartbeat, take his name as her own. Would she be worthy?

Rolf unbuttoned Lindsay's blouse, lifted her bra. Rolf took Lindsay's left breast in his hand, kneaded it a bit, rolled her nipple between his thumb and fingers just the way she had hoped he would, but then he suddenly just squeezed her nipple as though it were a zit. Ouch, Lindsay said, jerking back and banging her head against the oak. I beg your pardon, Rolf said. He unzipped his pants and pulled out his penis, which, even through the gloom, Lindsay could see was limp as a worm.

Look what she did to me, Rolf said, wagging his limp member for emphasis. —This tragedy is all her work. Touch it, Rolf said, and wagged it again. —Please touch it. Help me. Please help me.

Sure, Rolf, Lindsay said, and took Rolf's limp penis in her hand. It sure didn't feel like any of the other three members she had held before.

That awful blond bitch, Rolf said. —I am a ruin now. Now I can father no children for the future. There is no future for me now.

Sure you can, Rolf, Lindsay said. —You'll see.

Nothing can ever make it work again, Rolf said, and sobbed once. —I can never be a father now thanks to that blond bitch and what she did to me.

Sure you can, Rolf, honey, darling, Lindsay said, and wagged Rolf's limp member for him. —Really, you will. You just don't feel like yourself right now, honey, darling.

Did I ever tell you about how I was wounded seriously during the war? Rolf said. —Well, I was. I was just a little boy, but no matter. In Düsseldorf. One hundred yards from the Rhine. I have this scar. If you wish, I will let you look at it sometime. I let the blond bitch see it, for all she cared. My own grandmother was killed in the war. Well, she died. An uncle was killed by a bomb. I know history firsthand. Please pull on it a little more, please. There. See what I told you. Nothing will ever make it work right again.

I'm sure it will work again, honey, Lindsay said. —Darling. Sweetheart, you just don't feel well right now. Who would! Put your faith in us, Rolf, darling. I am German, too. Did I tell you that? Before it was shortened to Wolfe, my grandmother's maiden name was Wolfesburgher, which means people of the wolf in German, Lindsay said.

That is nice, Rolf said. —See there, nothing doing.

Lindsay pulled Rolf's limp penis up and down as rapidly, albeit gently, as she possibly could. Then she tried wagging it gently side to side.

It is no use, Rolf said, and sighed deeply. —I am the only child. I don't have any brothers. My brothers are all dead. All killed in that war.

That's awful, Lindsay said, as she alternately rotated Rolf's limp appendage clockwise and then counterclockwise. —How many brothers did you lose, precious, baby?

Eight, Rolf said. —Do that next thing for me, please. Please for me.

What next thing, darling? Lindsay said.

The next base, Rolf said. —Please for me. Go to the next base, please.

What next base, Rolf? Lindsay said. —Sweetheart, darling?

More like this please, Rolf said, and he pressed the back of Lindsay's head, his fingers in her hair. Had she washed her hair that morning? The night before? Rolf slowly pressed Lindsay's face down toward the limp penis she was currently whipping about in a path that vaguely resembled a figure eight.

I don't know, Lindsay said. —I've never done that before.

Please more for me, Rolf said. —The blond bitch would never. Not once even. For all she cared.

She wouldn't? Lindsay said.

Please for me, Rolf said. —Oh, see! Look! There. Look, it is working almost again. Please. Yes. Oh, thank you. Thank you for the sake of my future, darling. Please. Thank you, yes. Please. Yes, honey. Please. Oh, please, darling.

Rolf's damp crotch smelled like wet leaves. Lindsay had thought of rain, how it smelled, and how it might sound in the oak tree's leaves above the secret chamber. From somewhere in Shakespeare Gardens a cat yowled, and for all the world it sounded to Lindsay like the painful cry of a baby. And then, in Lindsay's mind's eye, the bald little heads of babies pressed up out of the earth in slow motion like mushroom caps after a rain.

The Garden City
of the Northwest

I

Jim Stark had never set foot before in the garden city of the Northwest, but from the moment he stepped off the bus late one spring night he knew he was home again. Due to a dumb little fracas Jim had foolishly gotten into at a dive near the Spokane bus station during a long layover the evening before, he was wearing shades to hide black eyes, and the knuckles of both his hands were covered with goofy-looking Band-Aids. Who was that mysterious, dangerous-looking, but dashing stranger, anyway? the drunken, late-night, riffraff, bus-station denizens must have surely wondered. What does he want in this town?

Jim took a third-floor corner room at the Palace Hotel, which overlooked Higgins Avenue, the main drag, and collapsed fully clothed onto a creaky old bed for his first dreamless sleep in years. The first thing Jim did the next morning was pour a finger of Jack Daniel's into a cloudy glass, and with a hearty gulp swallow a half hit of windowpane acid. Jim didn't even brush his teeth. Jim could do this with impunity now that he was out on his own. He could let his teeth rot and fry his brain at will now, with nobody around to boss him. Jim pulled a chair up to the window and positioned his feet on the sill. He fired up a fat joint and puffed on it like a tycoon. Soon he felt that magical old-timey light. It washed over him like water.

Jim had spent that whole first day fried but cool and relatively calm at that window, and then lingered there into the evening and the night, never even pulling himself away for nourishment, as best he could later recall. Jim had studied the native life on Higgins, the dangerous, drunken cowboys cruising their gaudy pickups; the peaceful, drunken Native Americans leaning about the landscape below, reddish-yellow with liver failure, glowing on corners like streetlamps. When they coughed, burped, or even laughed, they blinked as leisurely as caution lights. Higgins Avenue was aglow with neon. Every building front in town seemed to be trimmed with neon. What churches were still standing had been trimmed with neon, too, and transformed into bars, whose thin, blinking neon names seemed to change often, not unusually several times in the course of a single night.

The garden city of the Northwest Jim staggered around in those first fried days was mostly an imagined town for him. He stared at his haunted reflection in the blue-tinted mirrors behind bars, seeing a face he didn't know anymore, with a continuous shock of recognition. Who was that ghostly dead ringer for himself in the smoky mirror, and what wrong turn had led that tragic-eyed, handsome stranger down the dubious path into this forlorn, loveless, lonesome, but essentially heroic, country-song sort of life?

Jim discovered that the garden city of the Northwest was landlocked, surrounded by ancient Indian nations, but there were lingering rumors of lost coastlines of forgotten enormous bodies of water. The drumbeats and constant howls from those surrounding bare hills were unlike any heard in any other town. Once in a while an animal thought extinct wandered into town from the dark hills. For a glass of Thunderbird any Indian in town would interpret the ancient petroglyphs painted on the older buildings by the river. For a hit off your pint, any old derelict cowpoke would interpret the television set perpetually playing in the Sears store window. For a round, anybody would trade memories with you, stories of lost love and distant, happy lifetimes, until they became the same as your own. After a time, nothing needed to be said, time saved for drinking. You could sit for days in contented silence, among strangers who remembered the color of your mother's eyes.

The garden city of the Northwest was a town of patrons with hypothetical pasts. On certain nights, as you stumbled bar to bar, your past might gradually change. In some bars the foreignness of who you no longer were lay in wait. Sometimes you came upon evidence of a past you did not know you had. This happened to Jim one night at Eddie's Club on South Higgins, an establishment which served also as the de facto city hall. Covering the walls of Eddie's Club back in those days were row upon row of photographs of the honored town drunks. Each spring, when the snowbanks surrounding town melted, gold stars were pasted in the lower-right corners of the photographs of the revered drunks found frozen. One night on a dim back wall Jim found his own dusty photograph pasted with a celebratory star. Befuddled, Jim had asked the bartender for the story. Seems one spring they had sadly identified some stiff as Jim, the bartender related. The bartender offered to remove the star with a special ceremony conjured for just this situation. Leave it, Jim had told him, for luck.

There was no spot in the garden city of the Northwest safe from the possibility of memory, romance, or violence. One night Jim found himself drinking in the Flame Lounge on Front Street, a sort of fancy bar favored by the white-shoe crowd Jim could not recall entering. The realization had just swept over Jim that he was not a rich and famous author in town incognito, who was up in the Big Sky country as a sort of advance talent scout for the movie being made from his last bestselling novel, as he had confided to about a dozen folks over the course of that night, nor had his photograph once been featured on the cover of *Life* magazine, as he had intimated to one black-eyed bar babe.

When the tall woman with long, thick, fierce hair swept into the Flame, Jim recognized her in a heartbeat, and he knew exactly what was in store. Lindsay sat down at the far end of the bar, to be surrounded in moments by half the dipshit high-rollers of romance in the joint. Her mane of reddish-blond hair was lighter than in old Ralph's snapshot, which hadn't done this woman justice at all. This woman was a dead ringer for Lauren Bacall, back when she whistled Bogie in. Those slightly out-of-focus eyes, otherworldly gray and far apart. That moist, full-lipped, wide, generous mouth. She had a laugh that rang the room, and this dazzling smile, with big, brilliant, white teeth that snapped the tails off sentences. She was wearing white short shorts and a tangerine halter top, and with his fedora pulled low over his shaded, outlaw-of-love eyes, Jim stared unabashedly at her golden shoulders and pretty, round arms and trim, tan midriff and long brown legs, and, yes, at her full breasts straining that skimpy halter top, her great tits, yes, and great ass, that, too, and her breathtaking loveliness made Jim ache with a jealous amazement that old, rotten Ralph had actually tasted that wide mouth, licked and sniffed that smooth, glowing skin. The image of Ralph rooting around sweet, secret places popped into Jim's mind and ran amok.

Then, egged on by her admirers, a grinning, drooling audience of assholes, this shamelessly flirty hussy of a Lindsay character went fishing for the ribbony blue eel in the huge tank behind the bar with a piece of string and bobby-pin hook, and Jim flung himself sullenly from that wretched establishment.

2

Back in his hot hotel room, Jim flopped down on the creaky bed, clicked on the table lamp, and reread this Lindsay character's letters to Ralph for maybe the tenth time, and Ralph's to her. Her letters were wonderfully written, Jim had to admit, smart and insightful and funny, and, yes, real sexy, dirty even, you'd have to call them, but full of falsehoods. Jim reread parts where this Lindsay character proclaimed her love, her endless, undying, blah blah blah love for Ralph, which, judging from her flirty, hussy behavior at the bar, was clearly a cruel joke on poor old Ralph, that fool for love. Clearly Jim was going to have to take matters into his own hands, for his idiot buddy's sake. Jim just couldn't stand by and watch old dumb Ralph wreck his life any more than he already had, could he? What were best buddies for?

And then Jim reread his favorite dirty parts of this Lindsay character's letters once more intently, parts where this Lindsay harlot spoke of sexual secrets she and Ralph shared. Petting his parrot, Jim found himself somewhat inadvertently committing these juicy parts to memory. Jim called information for her phone number and memorized it. He dialed her number then, this Lindsay whory character, and lay there simply listening to the ringing. Somehow Jim knew he was getting closer to the real beginning of his life, or rebirth, as it were, and he imagined it dangerous and dramatic, like his teenage dreams of becoming a diver for sunken treasure, or a gunrunner, or a pirate.

Early the next morning Jim rented a car and located the address written on the envelopes. Jim parked up the street from Lindsay's townhouse on South 6th Street and waited. When Lindsay came out and drove off in her car, he followed her. He saw where she parked near her office, which was a real estate company in a restored old Victorian house at the edge of town not far from the university. Jim drove around for a while, took a spin out Rattlesnake Creek as far as Danny O'Brien Gulch, to get some air, clear his head, then got something to eat at a drive-through.

Jim parked up the street from Lindsay's vehicle and waited while he puffed a joint and sipped from a pint bottle of bourbon in a brown paper bag. He slouched down into the seat and gazed into that great blue bowl of sky that domed over the beautiful Missoula Valley, within whose long lap the garden city of the Northwest nestled. When there weren't any sounds of traffic, Jim could hear the low rumble of the Clark Fork River, which flowed through the heart of town, and upon whose banks at about any time of day you could find fishermen fly casting, the white filament of their lines gathering sunlight into curves, bright arabesques flicking out toward the swift current. Jim fired another joint and looked up at the steep slope of Mount Sentinel, rising behind the brick buildings of the university, to that huge design of whitewashed stones arranged in a shape not unlike the letter *M*, high up on the bare brown hillside, which shone intensely in the brilliant sunlight, like a landing signal to alien craft or the ceremonial snake sign of an ancient, fallen race, the nearly forgotten ancestors of the Salish Indian nation, say. He had heard various tales about that mysterious totem, and even initiated a few refried ones of his own. Jim puffed leisurely and let his gaze drift north to Mount Jumbo, which got its name because townfolks thought it looked like a sleeping elephant. In the distance, the snow-covered, high granite peaks of the Rockies glistened bluish in the sunlight as they ranged north toward Canada. Jim could hear the whistle of a Northern Pacific freight as it headed east up Hellgate Canyon toward Milltown and beyond. When this Lindsay character finally came out at lunchtime, Jim pulled his fedora low over his shaded, steely eyes and sank down in the seat. When she drove off, Jim followed her again; then he followed her when she got off work.

Jim followed this Lindsay character for days like that, snapping photographs of her at every opportunity with a cheap Polaroid he had picked up at a drugstore, photographs (if you could call them that) of her getting in and out of her car, and other people's cars, men's sometimes, as she came and went from restaurants, bars, and, on a couple of occasions, with this one clown in particular, from a fancy edge-of-the-river motel only a few blocks from her office. Some photographs captured this Lindsay character coming and going with this same man, who was an older fellow, in his late forties, say, who walked with a slight limp, from her own townhouse at the crack of dawn. Jim was doing detective work for his best pal, Ralph. Jim would do anything for his dopey friend. Jim was going to get the goods on this Lindsay character, amass so much incriminating evidence that old fool-for-love Ralph could not help but come to realize that this Lindsay character did not truly love him, and that her wonderfully written, smart, amusing, insightful, sexy letters were loaded with lies.

Shot through the curved glare of windshield glass, shadowy and grainy, as though culled from ancient newsreel footage, the pictures Jim took of this Lindsay were poor mugshots at best. In this one shot she seemed to be looking directly at him, although through her huge, dark sunglasses he could not see her lovely, gray, otherworldly eyes, so who could be sure. Lindsay seemed, however, to be making a face in Jim's direction, sort of clowning for the camera, touching her nose with her wondrous tongue.

Sitting in his rented car late one night, while he waited for Lindsay to emerge from that fancy motel at the river's edge, what Jim had let himself imagine as he studied that particular mugshot in the viridescent light of the dashboard was that trollop and her old coot lover up in that motel room, in the shower, say, soaping each other up, committing unspeakable, sudsy sexual acts. Then, out of the blue, old Ralph climbed into the shower, too. Then, holding hands and naked, Judy and Melvin showed up and asked to borrow some soap. Whereupon Jim had whipped out old nasty Mister Monkey for some serious spanking.

Black Widow

1

Lindsay goes to the party Buffalo Bill and Kathy throw for Ken Kesey after his reading at the university. Her old drinking pal Jim Crumley is there, up from Texas to show off his new detective novel, which is set in Missoula and dedicated to Dick Hugo, the grand old detective of the American heart. Buffalo had speculated that Crumley and this Jim Stark guy, Ralph's friend up recently from California, would rooster around each other when they met, but apparently it had been best-buddy love at first sight, and Buffalo, Crumley, and this Jim Stark regale the kitchen hardcore drinking crowd with outrageous tall tales of miscreant misadventures, while Kesey slouches in a doorway bemused. This Jim Stark guy is big and bearded and, when babbling with the boys, seems loud and bullshitty, but then suddenly terribly shy and awkward when Kathy introduces him to Lindsay. He looks down at his boots and mumbles something to Lindsay about having some items to deliver to her from Ralph, and Lindsay nods knowingly, and Kathy, who overhears, widens her blank, unblinking, Orphan Annie eyes with curiosity. Lindsay can't figure this Jim Stark character out, but in an aside she predicts to Kathy a lot more trouble in this old town in the near future. He is Ralph's trusted friend, and Bill's buddy from Bill's time at Stanford, and Kathy says he has published a novel. Another writer! God! Just what Missoula needs. So this guy is just splitting with his wife, according to Kathy, which, by the looks of him, translates to Lindsay that the poor wife probably parked his butt at the curb. Why did people think Missoula was a town where they could land on their feet?

Then through the screen door Lindsay hears a motorcycle roaring up in the yard outside, and alas, it is her ex-husband, Milo, on his brand-new Harley. He spots Lindsay immediately and is upon her in a heartbeat for old times' sake. Regales the audience with horrible but apparently hilarious stories of their three pitiful years of marriage, stories which he clearly thinks are a sitcom riot and demonstrate clearly how hip and long-suffering he was with the bride from Belview. Lindsay is stoned, the first time in days, for she is taking her turning-a-new-leaf-in-life seriously (two-drink limit most nights, six-cigarette limit daily, $23.67 on new vitamins the previous week, a mile run two mornings earlier, and off the pill for good so she won't even be *tempted* to slip). Lindsay has to admit to herself that she is stoned-paranoid, she knows that. And she is utterly stricken and sick to her stomach at Milo's onslaughts, but she attempts to maintain a bullshitty brave smile. She tries time and again to shove off, but Milo seems to be following her around, doing his fucking number on her.

Then this Jim Stark character comes up out of nowhere and starts mumbling to Lindsay, trying to make small talk about the possibility of life on Mars or some equal weirdness. Then Milo is upon them, and for some reason begins telling about the time his former wife, poor dopey Lindsay, who was Gracie Allen and Lucy rolled into one in the dumbbell wife department, once ran their transformed UPS hippie-mobile over the hill at Snowshoe on their way to go skiing when she got her left and right mixed up. Well, that is somewhat true, but why—why?—drag Lindsay's stupidity up for the world at large to savor? Then Jim Stark asks Milo very quietly to move along, that he and Lindsay are having a private conversation about the possibility of life on Mars. And just who in the fuck are you? Milo barks, huffing up all offended-biker and six-foot-two tough guy, flexing his tattooed, muscly arms.

Whereupon Jim Stark slaps Milo's face. Dear God! He just slaps the shit out of Milo. With the back of his hand. It sounds like a gunshot. How could this guy have read Lindsay like that? Is her pain that transparent? Everything simply freezes. Milo stumbles backward, his bloody mouth an O of astonishment. He pulls out a handkerchief and clasps it to his mouth. He is absolutely trembling with rage. A couple of his biker buddies move in behind him and puff up ready for action. Buffalo and Crumley (who looks like a fierce, bearded refrigerator) move in behind Jim Stark, which is like having the Grand Tetons of tough guys covering your back. Shades of showdowns in the Old West. Milo's biker buddies sort of say, Oh, never mind, and fade back into the woodwork. Milo snarls and hisses and splutters with rage, and sort of dances about flapping his arms. Stark just stands there grinning. Then Milo suddenly swirls and stomps out of the house, banging the screen door behind him. Poor Milo. Lindsay can hear his Harley roar and rage in the gravel as he peels out.

Lindsay walks directly over to Jim Stark and asks him if she can buy him a drink somewhere besides here, and he mumbles *shore* in this heavy, hicky accent, which cracks Lindsay up.

2

The next thing Lindsay knows, they are out at the Trail's End at the edge of town and they are talking about everything under the sun. They talk of Ralph, of Jim Stark's wife, of Ralph, of Jim's new novel, of Ralph of Ralph of Ralph. Seems the truth of the matter is that Alice Ann had found Lindsay's letters, read them through, then tossed them into Ralph's lap for a little anniversary surprise. Ralph had gone into one of his weasel who-me routines, according to Jim. Jim says that Ralph has a student girlfriend in Berkeley and also writes another lady in Iowa City. Jim says that Alice Ann does not have cancer, as Ralph had told Lindsay by way of explaining why he couldn't desert Alice Ann right now. It is not like Jim is ratting on Ralph. Lindsay has to pull this information painfully from him. Jim clearly loves Ralph and is really very loyal. Jim tells Lindsay a main reason he and his wife split is that he wants children and a real home life, while his wife, who he says is actually a wonderful woman, is into her career. Jim is on leave from Stanford until the next winter's term and hopes to have his new novel completed by then, and also his marriage problems resolved one way or the other so he can get on with his life. Lindsay asks Jim why he slapped Milo, and he just smiles and shrugs and says, no. 1, Milo is clearly an asshole who was making Lindsay feel bad, and no. 2, he wanted to make an impression on Lindsay, and no. 3, to be honest, he wasn't really being brave, for even with all Milo's leathers and tattoos and his big Harley, Milo was still basically just a fruity poet type.

After a third round of drinks, Jim tells Lindsay he has something he wants to confess to her, and he hopes Lindsay will understand and forgive him. Jim says he has been staying pretty much to himself since he hit town, and he has been amazingly lonely and sad. Jim tells Lindsay that on one particular recent hard night, he had read one of her letters to Ralph. He had felt so desperately alone and unloved, he read and reread one of Lindsay's letters he had pulled out at random, and he let himself imagine it had been written to him, written by a good woman who loved him. Lindsay tells Jim she understands. Frankly, Lindsay says, she is touched, and she is.

Kathy suddenly appears out of nowhere, saying she needs a break from her party, although things are still going strong. She flops down in her bored, superior way and Jim buys her a drink. Kathy announces that Jim's wife called the house a while ago and left a message for him to call her when he got a chance. What is it your wife does, anyway? Kathy asks Jim, blowing her perfect smoke rings into the air and leveling her Orphan Annies on him. Jim tells Kathy that his wife's career, such as it is, is the main cause of their split, that his wife insists upon pursuing a career in porno flicks. He asks Kathy if she has ever seen *Passionate Ponies*? And if so, does she recall the beautiful brunette in love with the Shetland with balls like cantaloupes?

Then suddenly Bill appears out of the blue, roaring drunk. He is furious that Kathy has scooted out of the party. Who is she planning to meet, anyway, Billy is real curious to know. Are you just dying to see some stranger's dick tonight, Bill is curious to know. And then, at the top of his lungs, Bill begins requesting that everybody in the bar who has one to haul out their hogs, please, so once and for all Kathy can get her eyes full of dicks. That is not necessary, Billy, Kathy says to him, then points to a table of cute cowboys and tells Bill their peepees will do fine. Billy goes berserk. Somehow Jim gets him out the door, Billy yelling all the way something about Kathy deserving a death by drowning in come.

Kathy lights a cigarette, blows a few perfect smoke rings, levels those cold blanks on Lindsay, and proceeds to lay her low with gleeful venom. First off, Bill is terribly down on Lindsay, Kathy says. He wants "that woman," viz. Lindsay, out of their lives. Kathy confirms to Lindsay that Bill has maligned her all along with Ralph, which may be the true reason Ralph has balked at commitment. Bill has told Ralph that Lindsay is infamous in Missoula as the "Black Widow," whose main hobby was to lay all the visiting writers who hit town to give talks and readings, especially the famous ones. Which is why Kathy is personally surprised that Lindsay is out with Jim Stark, a one-book boy at this point, instead of hitting on the really big-time Ken Kesey. Lindsay refuses to rise to this bileful bait and simply looks away, smoking furiously.

A half hour later Jim returns alone, saying he left Bill downtown at the Top Hat, dancing cheek to cheek with some black-eyed Indian princess. Kathy decides to retrieve Billy and return to the party. She says she doesn't care who he fucks, she is simply sick and tired of him getting his ass kicked every other night, as she was the one stuck with bailing him out and/or wiping up the blood and come off the backseat. That fucker is going to be killed before he pays the house off, Kathy says, and she is gone.

3

Ralph calls in the deep a.m. collect and Lindsay takes it in the guest room. Ralph tells Lindsay things down there are crazier than ever, which is why he hasn't been in touch so much recently, for he doesn't want to dump his misery in Lindsay's lap. Alice Ann is doing and saying crazy things; she is acting crazier than a bedbug; her breast cancer has driven her over the edge. Ralph tells Lindsay he finally told Alice Ann (cancer notwithstanding) that he really loves Lindsay and wants to be with her. Before he had given them to his best friend Jim Stark to carry to Lindsay for safekeeping, he had showed Alice Ann the stack of Lindsay's long, wonderful letters, which were the only things that had kept him from going nuts himself down there sometimes, to convince Alice Ann of the seriousness of the situation, to force her out of denial. No way, José, Ralph answers Lindsay, no way has Alice Ann read any of those letters. He would never let that happen. They are too private and precious to him. Those letters, and his to her, too, they are meant for their eyes only, and for whatever interest posterity might have in them. He has, however, promised Alice Ann that he will stick by her during her time of trouble. Then Ralph talks of his love for Lindsay and of what their life will be like together, of the exotic ports of call they will visit, of the fun and fulfillment they will share. Ralph mentions his increasing fame and solvency. They will be together soon, Ralph swears to Lindsay, just as soon as he gets a few more ducks lined up in his row. Meanwhile, and he hates to ask, but can he borrow fifty bucks until that big loan he is counting on from his mom comes through?

Suddenly Lindsay confronts Ralph with everything Jim has told her. She asks Ralph to tell her the truth about the letters and his endless lies and his other ladies-in-waiting and, most of all, why would he tell Lindsay that Alice Ann had cancer?

Ralph, clearly caught off guard, splutters that to begin with, Alice Ann *has* had a touch of cancer, but might be cured any day now. In fact, if the utter truth be told, he has already more or less left Alice Ann recently. Ralph says that he is at a writer's retreat, or somewhere like that, where he is pulling body and soul back together. And as soon as he does, which might be any day now, he fully plans to come to Lindsay at long last, to join Lindsay, and they will begin to live their life together. And then Ralph rails on and on about "that asshole" Jim Stark. Ralph says that Jim Stark is a legendary liar. Ralph implores Lindsay not to believe a single word about anything coming from the lying motormouth of that hypocrite deceitful running dog Jim Stark. Ralph says that Jim Stark would stab his own mother in the back if it would do him any good. Ralph vehemently suggests that for Lindsay's own sake she take his advice and cross the street anytime she sees that Jim Stark character coming.

Too late for that, is what occurs to Lindsay. Whereupon she cuts the conversation with Ralph short and returns to bed, to find that Jim Stark character wide-awake, smoking dope in the dark.

White Men in the Tropics

1

Appropriately enough, Ralph first read Jack London's 1913 alcoholic memoir, *John Barleycorn*, when he himself was drying out at a place called Duffy's, which was a clinic and sort of rest camp for recovering alcoholics three hours north of San Francisco and, by chance, hardly a stone's throw from London's famous Valley of the Moon. The major characters in London's book were London himself, a laborer, sailor, writer, a man of intellectual and physical vigor, impetuous, full of dreams and doubts and frustrations; his beautiful wife, Charmian, who lived with London in the Valley of the Moon; and John Barleycorn, alcoholism personified. Although London first got drunk at the age of five, again at seven, and drank steadily throughout his life, he proclaims at book's end that although he will continue to drink occasionally, he has the Long Sickness under control. It will never afflict him again.

Ralph was at Duffy's three days before he even tried to call Alice Ann (who had no idea where he was, for his student girlfriend had driven him to that sorry place, after a weeklong binge), enough time for him to get over the worst of the willies.

Alice Ann had not been at home then or any other time he had called since. Maybe Alice Ann just wasn't answering the phone. That was possible. Twice when Ralph called he had gotten a busy signal; then when he called right back, nobody answered. Ralph, after all these years, was on to all of Alice Ann's tricks. She was pissed, sure. All that *other woman* business. And Ralph had been hitting the old sauce a little too hard lately. Nobody had to tell him that. So sure, things had gotten a little out of hand of late. But Ralph had been under a lot of pressure, and he was just another weary human, after all. All Ralph really needed was a little peace and quiet, and some time alone to get body and soul back together.

Ralph just happened upon that copy of Jack London's *John Barleycorn* in Duffy's reading room one serendipitous morning. He read it through cover to cover that same day. Ralph realized that there was an important import for him, a terrible meaning, in the pages of that book, and he wanted to take it to heart, before it was too late for him, just as it finally got to be too late for Jack London, for all Jack London's physical vigor and strength and worldly success. According to Jack London, his own drinking had gotten out of hand those two years he had sailed the *Snark* throughout the tropics, for white men in the tropics undergo radical changes of nature. They become savage, merciless. And they drink as they never drank before, for drinking is one of the many forms of degeneration that set in when white men are exposed to too much white light.

This Duffy's was a high-toned joint, Ralph planned on assuring Alice Ann, if he ever got that woman on the phone. At Duffy's you were treated like a white man, Ralph would assure Alice Ann. Unlike some of these kinds of joints he had tried out in the past. At Duffy's they called you a patient, and a uniformed nurse was on hand. They let you taper off at Duffy's. The first day you got a stiff belt every waking hour, every third hour the second day. They called these "hummers." Finally, though, nothing. Finally, you were cast adrift hummerless, but a fellow probably would not go into convulsions on a program like this, Ralph would assure Alice Ann. Convulsions were Ralph's greatest fear in life. He would lie awake at night, sweating, gritting his teeth, waiting for the worst. The least tingle, the slightest twitch in his shoulder, say, or neck, made him go rigid with regret. What Ralph feared above all else was the same death as his dad had suffered, his dad, whom Ralph had loved dearly, a drunken man who drowned in his own vomit.

Nights really were the worst times there at Duffy's for Ralph. The shakes and sweats really were a scream. The willies primitive, uncanny. Doors slammed on purpose. Rats ran in the walls at night there at Duffy's, although the staff swore there were no rats around for miles. There was no television in your room. No late-night movies to blur your life with as you changed channels as fast as you humanly could. Worst of all, there was no phone in your room. No late-night long distance in your life. You couldn't even dial a goddamn prayer to keep you company. If there had been a phone in his room, Ralph knew he would live on it, dialing Alice Ann at all hours, letting that phone ring off the wall, half hoping almost anybody, no matter who, even a stranger, another man even, would answer. Some nights there at Duffy's the air conditioner, a noisy, leaky contraption at best, would go on the blink. You boiled in your own juices like a lobster in a pot. You could rattle your little claws against the walls all night for all the good it got you. You'd throw open a window. Moths would collect on the screen, their eyes swelling from their small, powdery faces, black, beady things, locking onto your every move.

Ralph spent most of that day he had read Jack London's *John Barleycorn* book sitting out in intense sunlight beside a drained swimming pool. He sat there in a hot aluminum deck chair as though doing penance. His shirt and pants stuck to his skin. His feet sweat in his socks and shoes. Not unlike Jack London, Ralph was one weary human, all right, and he knew it. He slowly rubbed a wrist over his sweating forehead and then studied and sniffed at the moisture. He took off his sunglasses and gazed about hopefully for something, anything, to look at that might brighten his spirits, that might lift his dark mood. On the tennis court next to the drained pool two middle-aged men listlessly lobbed an orange ball back and forth. Both were bareback and had sort of bewildered looks on their faces, as though they had both woken up that morning astonished to find themselves where and who they were. Their jiggling flesh looked feverishly yellow to Ralph. They were attorneys-at-law, Ralph believed. Big-time attorneys-at-law. Any number of professional and business bigwigs were at Duffy's, including that fellow who claimed he was the president of a bank and wept at meetings. A Stanford professor had the cabin next to Ralph's. You never saw that fellow, though, just heard his sad, noisome traffic all night. Strange fellows, all right, the lot of them. Drunks every one of them, true, but not one real derelict on the premises, a fact which provided Ralph with some small measure of comfort.

Then this strange fellow sat down beside Ralph at poolside. Ralph wasn't on the lookout for any company. Ralph had his own problems. The fellow had a helmet of white hair and a meaty red face. He was short and fat, and he wheezed when he talked. The fellow bummed a cigarette from Ralph as soon as he flopped down, and then, while he chain-smoked Ralph's cigarettes as relentlessly as Ralph, he started right up. I don't belong in this godforsaken dump, the fellow told Ralph. He had his drinking problem in a headlock, he went on, and he didn't have any idea why he was buried away here in this Duffy's place. He couldn't really recall how he got there, true. He remembered getting off a plane and tossing a couple at the airport bar, then bang, the next thing he knows he's buried here at Duffy's. He felt like a man who had been kidnapped, held against his will. Held for ransom. It was his wife, the fellow said. She was somehow behind all this. She wanted to bury him alive.

I'm not a drunk, the fellow told Ralph. To call a man a drunk is a serious charge. That kind of talk could hurt a good man's prospects. He was an important man who traveled to the four corners of the world on big business, he told Ralph. It was nothing for him to hop a jet to European capitals or, say, the Middle East, to meet somebody important on big business. He knew important people everywhere. Real earthshakers. He had bent elbows with the great and the near-great. Just who do you know, anyway? the fellow had suddenly asked Ralph out of the blue.

Who do you know big in London, Paris, Berlin, for that matter? Who do you know in Egypt? Ralph admitted he didn't know a soul in Egypt.

2

That hot day by the drained pool, after the strange fellow had shoved off, the sad pock sounds of the tennis ball made Ralph uneasy. He could feel his heart racing, and there was a twitch in his neck. He thought something was about to go wrong and he wanted to head it off. He wanted to escape it. Just close his eyes and pray it would pass by, maybe happen instead to one of those big-time attorneys. Or to them both. What did he care? Why not them instead of him? How old was Jack London, anyway, when he kicked the bucket? A chill passed over Ralph and he shuddered.

Ralph pushed himself up from the deck chair and shambled over to the edge of the drained pool. Shading his eyes like a salute, Ralph peered intently at the dry bottom. On a scorcher like today a fellow could sure use a little dip, Ralph thought. There was no serious drought this year. The hills weren't even baked brown yet. Here at Duffy's they let you flush your toilet to your little heart's content. So where was the swimming pool's water, then? That was one big mystery here at Duffy's. You had to imagine the worst. You had to imagine some poor devil, some so-called patient, found one morning floating facedown.

I *am* a patient, Ralph thought. He was a drunk now and then, too, but there at Duffy's Ralph was a patient with a little drinking problem, that's all. There was even an airline pilot at Duffy's as a patient. A fellow who flew those big babies, those 747s, all over the world. Now, that was something. That made you stop and consider. So Jack London claimed he could do the work of five men even when he was drunk. So Jack London could navigate a vessel through the reefs and shoals and passages and unlighted coasts of the coral seas. Dose and doctor, pull teeth, pull some poor Polynesian sailor back from death's door. One thousand words a day. Heave up anchor from forty fathoms. One thousand words a day rain or shine, even when he was drunk, was what Jack London claimed. But when it came to dosing and doctoring himself, when it came to pulling himself back from death's door, Jack London had come up short. In the saving-of-his-own-life department, Jack London had turned out to be nothing but chopped liver.

Ralph flicked his half-smoked Camel into the drained pool. When Ralph was a boy, he could hold his breath underwater longer than anybody he ever knew. He would swim underwater, close to the bottom, for hours, it seemed. He would hold his breath and dead-man-float for so long people would panic. Ralph could remember his dad shouting and shouting to him once from a lakeshore. He remembered his dad, half drunk from an afternoon of beer drinking in the sun, splashing frantically toward deep water to save his son.

3

Brew a liquor from molasses and sugarcane and put pots of it out in the jungle where the wild monkeys can find it. They get so drunk they can't jump. Catch those drunk monkeys and dress them up in red suits, then anchor them with small chains to posts in the garden. Their antics out there frighten all the other wild monkeys away. That is how the farmers of Paraguay make scarecrows.

That night the air conditioner went on the blink, and in moments Ralph felt like a monkey in a red suit chained in some foreign garden. Ralph paced his room, smoking like a stove. Sleep was a goddamn bad joke. Ralph felt nervous, irritable, less moral by the minute. Thank God, Ralph had a little something stashed in his cabin for snakebite. The quart of Four Roses was hidden in the toilet tank.

The thing about Duffy's was, if a fellow backslid on the premises, got caught taking a nip, just one, that fellow was cast out on his own, cast out from Duffy's forever. Ralph turned off the light and pulled a chair to the open window. He pinched aside the curtains and peered into the dreadful night. He could hear crickets and the traffic from a distant highway. Fireflies blinked from the hot dark like the cigarette embers of a posse.

Ralph splashed a finger of whiskey into a water glass and drank it down in a manful gulp. He poured another finger, then placed the bottle on the floor between his feet. Ralph wondered if there was a steady stream of traffic at his home in Menlo Park. Men coming and going. Truck drivers, bikers, sailors, marauders, hairy arms thick with tattoos holding his slender blond wife, monstrous acts of love. Ralph heard a door slam and his heart thumped. He clutched his chest. Somehow Duffy knew. The jig was up.

The toilet tank had been dumb. That's the first place an old ex-drunk like Duffy would look. Ralph sniffed at the water glass, then hurried to the bathroom. He held the glass under water hot enough to scorch his hand. He sniffed the glass again, dried it, put his toothbrush in it, and placed it carefully on the sink. Back at the window Ralph held his breath, listening and staring into the night for the least sign. Ralph picked up the bottle, tiptoed to the door, pressed his ear to it.

The deck furniture around the pool had been put up for the night, so Ralph sat cross-legged on the warm concrete. He took a pull of Four Roses, then placed the bottle before him. What he wouldn't give for a smoke. He wiped a hand over his sweating forehead, dabbed at his stinging eyes with his shirttail. What he wouldn't give for a little dip, some cool relief. If that goddamn pool had a quart of water in it, Ralph would take the plunge, clothes and all, what did he care, the heat was that intense. Ralph imagined himself swimming laps, up and back, on his way to nowhere, for hours, all night, until at last his old heart just caved in.

Ralph saw the glowing cigarette ember before he heard the footfalls in the road's gravel. He flattened onto his stomach on the warm concrete. The person approaching was humming softly, humming a tune of some kind, like a little ditty, it sounded to Ralph. Sailors hum ditties, Ralph thought suddenly. Seamen. Duffy had been a merchant seaman in his youth. Ralph's first thought was to sail the bottle of Four Roses out into the darkness behind him, letting it take its chances, hoping it would land softly on grass without a sound. But it wouldn't. Not in a million years. That bottle would smash on the only rock in that dark field, an explosion that would wake the dead. Clutching the bottle before him, Ralph crawled to the pool's edge. He stared down into that black abyss. The humming seaman approached. Ralph swung a leg over the pool's edge; his foot found the ladder. The humming seaman approached. Grasping the bottle neck with one hand, Ralph descended, vanishing without a trace.

Ralph crouched with his back pressed into a corner of the drained swimming pool that desperate night at Duffy's. Ralph watched the mysterious seaman who stood almost directly above him at the pool's edge smoking, a black silhouette against the dark sky. Coastal storm clouds covered the stars, and Ralph could hear the wind stir in the trees along the gravel road. Ralph felt a drop of rain. He felt another. The mysterious seaman looked up at the sky and held his hand out palm up. The seaman flicked his cigarette into the pool, where it splattered in sparks near Ralph's feet. Ralph gasped and slapped at an ember on his sock. Ralph shut his eyes. He held his breath and pressed even more painfully into the concrete corner. Moments passed. Minutes? Who could tell? Ralph opened his eyes and peered once again at the seaman's dark silhouette. Ralph took a long, burning drink from his bottle of Four Roses and clasped a hand over his mouth when he about gagged. The seaman turned slightly, seeming to peer back toward the road and cabins, then he turned toward the pool. Then the seaman took a drink. He did! Honest to God! He took a god-damn belt from a small bottle, or maybe flask, whatever, but he put it to his lips and threw his head back and drank like there was no tomorrow. Ralph could hear the gulps. So Ralph took a drink, too, in astonishment. Then the seaman fired up another ciga-rette, and in the lighter's flare Ralph saw his face. It wasn't Duffy at all. It was the fat, big-time businessman who knew important people as far away as Egypt.

Ralph buried his face in his hands. Tears squirted from between his fingers. He was breathless, choking with silent laugh-ter. Then Ralph felt the rain again, its drizzle warm on his head.

Jesus! Ralph gasped, and crawled crablike frantically from beneath the big-time businessman's golden shower. Ralph gasped and gagged and whipped his handkerchief out. Ralph spluttered and muttered and wiped his hair and neck desperately with the handkerchief and then tossed the damp, horrible thing away into the darkness. Up above, the fat businessman stopped pissing into the pool and stood there stiff as a statue. Then he seemed to lean out over the edge of the pool and peer into the blackness below where Ralph hovered and held his breath. Then the big-time businessman clicked on a lighter and waved it over the dark, drained pool. In the flickering light the fat businessman's mouth was agape with astonishment, and his eyes were bugged out like boils. Sounding not unlike the chains of a ghost, when he inadvertently tipped it over, Ralph's bottle of Four Roses rolled rattling down the concrete incline toward the deep end. By the time the ghost of the haunted swimming pool had stumbled to the ladder and awkwardly ascended, the big-time businessman was a blur beneath the dark trees as he flew like a fat bat out of hell down the gravel road through the drizzle, running with all his heart in the general direction, it had occurred to Ralph, of Egypt.

4

Ralph's hands shook as he slipped the quarter into the pay phone on the porch wall of the main building. Insects swarmed crazily about the bright porch light. They flicked in blind and confused from the darkness. Bright points in intricate elliptical motions, they were helpless. On hands and knees Ralph had searched in vain around the bottom of the drained pool for the lost bottle of Four Roses. Unless he could figure a way to rat out the big-time businessman, lay the blame on him, Ralph's number was up here at Duffy's. All Duffy had to do was check that bottle for fingerprints. Out beyond the frail light from the porch, the darkness under the trees was immense, inpenetrable.

Earlier on the night he died, Ralph's dad had been working the swing shift at the sawmill. He got home at midnight hungry for his big meal of the day: pot roast, homemade rolls, mashed potatoes, gravy, green beans with bacon, garden salad with Thousand Island dressing, fried apples, cherry pie à la mode, a fifth of Four Roses. Nothing out of the ordinary. Ralph's mom watched Jack Paar while his dad ate his supper and drank. She took a notion to stay up and watch the Late Show that night after she had bickered with Ralph's dad about the usual old stuff, and he had staggered off to bed with his bottle bitching and fuming as usual. Just another day in America. It was a hot August night and Ralph's mom was worked up from the argument and restless, and the Late Show was *The Moon Is Blue*, one of her old favorites, starring William Holden, in her opinion the most handsome star who ever came down the pike, a star who, in fact, she always fancied Ralph's dad looked like before the bottle had taken its toll. Ralph's mom often stayed up late like that, watching TV or writing a letter to her sister back in Little Rock. Ralph's mom had dozed off on the sofa and did not wake up until dawn to face another day in America. She put out a bowl, spoon, and box of Frosted Flakes for Ralph's breakfast, then headed off to bed herself, whereupon she had discovered Ralph's dad drowned in vomit.

Ralph let the phone ring twenty times, then decided to go for thirty. The hot night was thick, heavy, so sluggish a fellow could hardly suck air. Ralph wished with all his heart it would just pour down rain. He'd stick his head out in it. He'd wash that fat businessman's godawful urine out of his hair. He was sure he could still smell it, that godawful piss. God, that was awful. God, he hoped that fat businessman had dropped dead of a heart attack somewhere down the road. Ralph hoped those black clouds to the west were thunderclouds thick with lightning. Let the sky cloud up and Alice Ann gets edgy. A clap of thunder and she was hiding in a closet, trembling from memories of those terrible Midwestern storms of her childhood, when lightning seemed to seek appointed people out. How often had Ralph sat in a hot, closed closet holding that chosen woman? Dozens upon dozens of times, hundreds of times, that's how many. Ralph couldn't begin to count the times. Over the years.

When the rings reached thirty, Ralph decided to go for forty, give Alice Ann the benefit of the doubt. All right, Ralph thought when the rings reached forty, fifty was the limit. There had to be a limit. Ralph's trembling hands were bloodless in the bright porch light. Corpse hands, Ralph thought, and shuddered. Ralph froze when he saw a face in the porch-door window. It was his own reflection. His heart beat wildly.

At fifty rings Ralph hung up the phone. It was all over now, he thought. That chapter in his life was over and done. End of story. Well, at least he wouldn't have to accompany Alice Ann to that horrid bankruptcy proceeding now. Ralph was shaking by then almost uncontrollably. He looked out into the darkness beyond the porch and imagined the worst. Motion in those dark trees, the murmur of voices, low drums like heartbeats, returning alone and unarmed to his cabin, a white man in the tropics.

Ralph decided then to call long distance to Lindsay. Lindsay would answer the phone pronto, two, maybe three rings, and she would accept the charges. No question. Ralph would explain things. Standing under the porch's white light, Ralph trembled with the urge to travel. All he had to do was get body and soul back together, bail out of this Duffy's dump, tie up a few loose ends, then relocate with Lindsay in Missoula, Montana, the garden city of the Northwest, where life would be sweet for him, where he would write one thousand words a day, rain or shine. Finally Lindsay answered the phone and accepted charges, albeit, it seemed to Ralph, hesitantly. Whereupon out of nowhere Lindsay brought up stuff, blindsided Ralph with it, low-down stuff that that asshole Jim Stark had led her to believe, and Ralph had no real answers, or alibis, that he could make Lindsay believe, before she abruptly said good night and hung up.

The next time Ralph let the phone ring fifty-one times (one hundred and six was his record) before Alice Ann finally answered, whereupon Ralph gasped to her, Honey, honey, whatever you do, don't pay the ransom. I've escaped.

One-Whore Town

Lindsay took the two leftover pieces of cold pizza from the greasy box and put them on separate plates. She loaded up with items from the fridge and carried them over to the kitchen table. She sliced a tomato thinly and spread the slices over the pieces of pizza. She sliced an onion thinly, then some mushrooms, took a handful of black olives, then scattered them all over the pizza. Lindsay popped an olive into her mouth and suddenly laughed. She returned to the fridge for other items. On Jim's piece of pizza Lindsay layered sliced sweet pickles. She added a layer of sliced beets. She covered this piece of pizza with chocolate fudge sauce. She covered both pieces of pizza with slices of American cheese and placed them in her microwave.

Back up in the bathroom Lindsay placed the plates on a stool beside the tub. Several scented candles lit the room, and from her bedroom stereo floated a Mozart violin concerto. Lindsay removed her robe and tossed it onto the floor. Her flesh was golden and shadowy in the candle flame. Jim lay back in the big old-fashioned tub that sat up off the floor on lion paws, his arms resting on its rim, his old fedora tilted over his eyes as though he had died and gone to heaven.

You can't be asleep, you turkey, Lindsay said. —That's not fair. You made me go get the pizza. I almost fell down the goddamn stairs. God, I'm stoned. That damn dope of yours.

I ain't asleep, Jim said. —I just passed away and went to heaven. I am the late Jim Stark now. Please donate my organs, such as they are, to medical science. Donate my liver to the Budweiser Research Institute, for serious study.

Goody, goody, Lindsay said, as she slid into the steaming water. —The late Jim Stark ran more hot water before he passed.

The late Jim Stark likes to keep things steamy.

You want me to donate this little organ, too? Lindsay said, and wagged waves in the steaming water with Jim's dick.

Shore, why not? When I was a kid I'd stretch my nightly bath out until I'd used up all the hot water in the house, if adults would let me get away with it. The air would get to feel like the hot breath of some real big animal. Like the hot breath of an old bear in a close cave, say.

Why would you do that? Use up all the hot water in the house? Here, mister, you better eat your pizza, Lindsay said, and she held up a piece for Jim to bite. —Here you go, this is good for you. Let Mommy feed you, baby.

I can safely say, Jim said, as he chewed the bite of pizza Lindsay had maneuvered into his mouth, that this is unlike any pizza pie I, for one, have ever eaten before in my lifetime.

This is Mommy's mystery pizza pie, Lindsay said, and held the piece up for Jim to bite into again.

Somehow this don't exactly taste like that there perfectly predictable pizza we ate for supper, Jim mumbled as he chewed extravagantly.

Don't you just adore it? I used all my culinary skills preparing this special pizza for my own boy.

You don't say? All your culinary skills?

You don't adore it, I can tell. My culinary spirit is crushed. I distinctly recall you saying you would eat anything of mine. Even raw, I remember you saying. Were you being insincere with me, Jim?

To the best of my recollection, I didn't mention no mystery pizza.

But it is so good for you. It's covered with such healthful items. You'll be able to see better in the dark. And always land on your feet. And your boners will be the talk of the town.

Maybe I will have me another bite or two, Jim said, and gnawed off another hunk.

Eat your head off, honey.

Now, what's this here healthful thing? Jim said, and held up a greasy item between his thumb and forefinger.

That is either a very healthful beet or an enormous booger.

Well, Jim said, and popped the thing into his mouth, it shore hits the spot.

Would adults spank you if you used up all the hot water in the house? I'll bet when adults spanked you you wouldn't even cry, you're such a tough guy. I always cried. I wept for days sometimes. Even if I did something bad and didn't get caught, I'd cry and cry. I'd cry just imagining the spanking I should have gotten. I always believed what adults told me about God seeing everything, every little-bitty sin. So to get into heaven I was certain I would have to endure days, weeks, months of saved-up spankings from God because I had been such an evil girl. Anything that drew my attention to the sky, a soaring bird, beautiful clouds, a starry night, the moon, anything, would inevitably lead me to thoughts of heaven and the waiting hand of my spanker Lord.

Adults pounded the shit out of me, all right, Jim told Lindsay. —But not about the hot water. They would be too embarrassed at those times. Adults would just bang on the door and yell, You're using up all the hot water in the house, you little piece of shit.

Why would adults be embarrassed?

It was an adult's duty each night to come in after I had my bath and check out my deformed condition. This meant for an adult, usually my old drunk daddy, to finger and poke about between my slippery little legs and have me turn my head to one side and cough my head off. My slippery little pecker would bounce against the back of his or her adult hand. Sometimes I'd even inadvertently tinkle on his or her adult hand. Or my little weeny would start to magically bonerize. Now, that would really make an adult blush red as a beet.

Adults are so bizarre.

You can say that again.

Adults are so bizarre. Why do you wear your hat in the bathtub?

It's my lucky hat.

Why do you have to be lucky in the bathtub?

I like to be lucky everywhere. Fire up that last joint, why don't you. Did you and Ralph ever take a bath together?

That is an adult question. That's not playing fair.

Let me shave you.

Do I need one? Lindsay said, and rubbed her chin.

Let me.

I just shaved yesterday, Lindsay said, and rubbed her legs.

Under your arms, Jim said, and picked up the Lady Schick safety razor from the soap dish. Lindsay smiled sweetly and raised her right arm, and Jim soaped her. He ran the razor gently over the slick skin under her arm. He soaped and shaved under her other arm. Lindsay lifted each of her long, sleek legs in turn, resting her heels on Jim's shoulders, and he soaped and slowly shaved them while she hummed softly. Then Jim took the bar of sweet soap and rubbed it over her breasts.

Good God, Lindsay said, do my tits need a shave, too?

No, not quite yet, Jim said as he caressed Lindsay's breasts with his soapy hands. —Maybe tomorrow. I just like how they feel and look all soapy and slick in the candlelight. So, *did* you and Ralph ever take a bath together? I'm just curious, mildly curious, that's all. I don't care what you've done, you know, in the sex department, with other men. I can forgive you for anything you've done with other men.

You can *forgive* me for anything I've done with other men? Lindsay said, and tossed her head, laughing. —Well, lucky me.

I didn't mean it the way it sounded. But did you, you know, take a bath with Ralph?

Not that I can immediately recall.

Have you done it with many other men?

It? You'll have to be more specific, hon. Done what exactly?

You know, taken baths. Or showers. Those things.

A few, I suppose. I am a very clean-cut girl. I believe in a vigorous program of personal hygiene.

Plus you like to wash things before you eat them, right? Like a raccoon does.

I didn't say that, you did. But raccoons are pretty smart animals, you know, Lindsay said.

The phone began to ring from the bedroom. Lindsay didn't make a move to get it. It rang and rang.

Ain't you gonna get that?

Nope.

Why not? It might be somebody or something important.

I don't care. I'm happy right where I am.

Are you afraid of who it might be? What if it's old Ralph?

I don't want to speak with Ralph right now. The only man I'm afraid of is that crazy Larry I told you about. That nut. That nut made my life miserable. I tried to break off with him, but he wouldn't leave me alone. Even after I started dating Milo he would follow me. Once he followed me to Milo's. There was a terrible scene. He slapped poor Milo around in his own living room. I called the police. Larry ran out screaming it was not over yet. I've always been afraid crazy Larry is going to slip back into town and cause big trouble. That nut carried knives. He was always sharpening those knives. Larry was a very dangerous man. I'm sorry to babble. Just before you and I got together, I thought I spotted somebody following me around, and I thought maybe it was him. But I was just being paranoid, probably.

Slapping old Milo around is no big deal in the tough-guy department. I've known nuts like that Larry. You aren't being paranoid. You can't be too careful with nutcases like that. Did you recognize him as the nut who was following you around?

I couldn't tell who was following me. He was a stranger to me. I never got a good look, really. Maybe he wasn't anybody at all. Probably I simply imagined him.

You can't be too careful. That older guy I pulled those armed robberies with, that guy I told you about, Morris Hacket, he said that he planned on looking me up again someday, if he ever got out of the can, in order to reward me for ratting him out. I keep my eyes open. I look over my shoulder. You don't have to worry about that nut following you when I'm around, whoever he was. I can take care of that Larry creep for you. I can be a dangerous man, too.

Lindsay took Jim's hat off his head and placed it on her own.

Hey, I need that old hat.

I want to be lucky for a change.

That's more than my lucky hat. That's my magic fictioneer hat. I like to wear that hat when I write. I need it. Sort of like old Frosty the Fictioneer.

Are you writing right now?

You can never tell. Maybe. Well, so how many men would you say you've hopped in some hot water with? Offhand?

Does a sauna count?

Shore. If you were, you know, naked as the day you were born.

God. Offhand? Well, okay, let's see, Lindsay said, and began to count off on her fingers. —Honey, can it be off-foot, too?

Off what?

Foot. I've run out of fingers, Lindsay said. She lifted a foot from the water and began to count on her toes.

Just forget it, Jim told her. He took his fedora from Lindsay's head and replaced it on his own, where it belonged.

Oh, don't get pouty, Lindsay said. She patted Jim on the cheek. —Baby, she said, come on, baby.

I ain't gettin' pouty. I'm just kidding around. Besides, Missoula is just a small one-horse town.

What in the world does that mean? Missoula is the second-largest city in the state, as a matter of fact.

It is?

Yes, but that doesn't mean much outside Montana, I suppose. The population of Missoula probably isn't much more than, oh, thirty thousand.

Thirty thousand? Thirty fucken thousand?

Yup. What's the point?

There's no point really. The Buffalo told me you'd fucked about half the men in town. But I was under the impression that Missoula was just a one-horse town.

Did he say one-horse or one-whore? You jerks. He's such an asshole.

I'm just kidding around.

How wonderful to hear that my love life is such a hot topic of conversation among you bozo boys. Don't you boys think with anything besides your boners?

I'm kidding around, I told you.

Jim, it's you I love, Lindsay said. She took the fedora back off his head and replaced it on her own. —See. Now all I need is a black beard, about a hundred pounds, a hairy chest, and a peepee, and we'd be like the same person, we are so close. And it has happened so quickly. That's how I feel about us. I trust in us. I trust in you, hon. I've never really talked with another man about having, you know, rug-rats, as you call them. Really, I've never felt this way with another man.

I reckon we had best get hitched, then, Jim said.

Is that a proposal, Mr. Stark?

It ain't no proposition.

Wouldn't that effectively make you a bigamist? Isn't that against the law, even in California?

You know what I mean. As soon as I get divorced, let's go on and just do it.

Well, why not? I've always aspired to be some sort of hillbilly bride, barefoot and pregnant, Lindsay said, and laughed. —Are you really a dangerous man, Jim Stark? Lindsay said.

I can be.

Are you a fringy?

I can be.

How can you be a fringy and teach at a place like Stanford?

Stanford has fellowships just for fringies. I can just be a little dangerous now and then, that's all. I had to learn to fight when I was a kid. It was totally against my basically sweet, cuddly-teddy-bear nature, of course, but I had to learn. Because of those scars from the operations, the other kids liked to make fun of me. You know how kids are, cruel little fucks. Kids would point at me in gym showers and make fun of me and my scars, so I learned how to kick their asses for it.

I love my scar, Lindsay said. —My scar made me beautiful. Not that I've ever really felt beautiful a moment in my life. People just told me I was beautiful. I was a fat girl all my life. A fat fringy. Then I had to have an emergency appendectomy, and in what seemed like overnight I lost twenty-five pounds. I was deathly ill, but that was okeydokey by me. Well, afterward it was okeydokey. Suddenly I was this new thin girl. It was like having a baby in that respect, losing all that blubber. That is one dumb analogy. But anyway, suddenly everybody told me I was beautiful and love was just mine for the asking. Would you like to touch my scar for luck?

Anything for luck, Jim said.

Here you go, Lindsay said, and took Jim's hand. She traced his forefinger along the small blue scar on her lower right side. —Not much of a price to pay for becoming beautiful overnight, huh? Now it's my turn, Lindsay said.

Say what?

I could use some luck, too. You aren't afraid I'll laugh and make fun of your scars, are you? I'd never do that. I don't want to get my ass kicked, that's for sure.

It's nothing like that, Jim told her.

Lindsay smiled and softly jabbed a finger into Jim's stomach, whose muscles he attempted to tighten without grunting.

You can't really see my scars anymore, Jim told Lindsay. —I'm too fucken hairy.

I can feel them, Lindsay said. Lindsay slid her hand down onto Jim's lower abdomen, the back of her hand pressing against the back of his boner as her fingers felt through his hair for his scars.

I think I feel them, Lindsay said. —I really hope this will bring us luck. I want a houseful of kids someday.

We can do that, Jim said. —With just a little help from medical science, like I told you. How many kids? Jim said.

I've heard they're cheaper by the dozen, Lindsay said.

That's what I've heard, too. But I'd settle for a single son. I'd teach him stuff. I'd teach him the sort of stuff a son needs to live by.

You mean manly stuff? All-American-boy stuff? How to hunt and fish and play football?

No. I mean really important stuff. How to hot-wire a car. The ancient art of sucker punching. How to case a joint. How to be cool. You know, important stuff.

I see, Lindsay said, and laughed. —Really important all-American-Criminal-Boy stuff, Lindsay said, and cupped her hand under Jim's dick, gently rubbing her fingers over what passed as his scrotum. —Now exactly what were those meany adults hoping to find down here? Your tonsils?

My balls. Finally they just threw in the towel.

And you were at the Mayo Clinic three times?

Four. I was at the world-famous Mayo Clinic four times. For all the good it got me.

Turn your head to one side and cough, please, Mr. Stark.

Cough cough cough.

Again, please.

Cough cough cough.

Have you been eating your beets, young man?

I recken. I clean up my plate, Doc, ma'am.

You are an extremely good boy. Now you continue to eat all your beets and anything else your Mommy waves in front of your face and you will grow up with a great, big, amazing boner. That will be fifty dollars, please. Pay the nurse on your way out, please.

Fifty bucks was worth this.

I can tell, young man, Lindsay said, and squeezed Jim's hard dick. She moved her hand under the water between his legs and kept going. She slowly slid her middle finger up his ass.

Holy moly, Jim said. —Correct me if I'm wrong, but I believe you just stuck your finger up my, you know, behind.

Hurt, baby?

Nope. Well, yes, but I plan to be a very brave boy. Holy moly. What a neat maneuver, Nurse Nancy. Do you take all the boys' temperatures this way?

Only if they have been good. God, I've found it, honey!

Found what?

Whatever it was those meany adults were always looking for. I've found it. I've struck gold, hon.

You mean you really feel something? Really? Jesus. What do you feel? Is it like a, you know, lump or something?

I'm not certain, hon. But I think it feels like . . . Yes, that's what it feels like.

Like a lump or something? Jesus. Really?

No, not exactly like a lump, exactly. It's more like . . . like . . .

Jesus, Lindsay, more like what? Like what?

Pizza poop!

Sacred Cows

1

The pool was in the center of the motel courtyard amid a garden of palms and flowering plants. It was kidney-shaped, with a small cabana, tiled like the pool red and white at its larger end. At the pool's smaller end stood a small marble statue, a pink Cupid with a thin stream of water arching from its pursed lips into the pool. Blue and green spotlights were arranged in the palms with their beams playing on the pool. Here and there in the thick flowering bushes under the palms stood brightly painted plaster-of-Paris peacocks.

That first and only night they were there, Ralph sat, fully clothed, at a poolside table holding a glass of whiskey and ice. On the table was one of those motel-room buckets filled with mostly melted ice, a half-fifth of Four Roses (his daddy's favorite brand), and a small red transistor radio which Ralph had tuned to a Dodgers' game (his daddy's team). Alice Ann floated on her back in the center of the large end of the pool. She seemed to be staring up through the thick palm fronds into the darkening sky, and Ralph reflected on her thought. Several blocks west the sun was setting over the Pacific, and the darkening sky above the palms was the deepest purple. Ralph could smell the ocean, and in a warm, easterly breeze he felt from the Santa Ynez Mountains he thought he could smell blooming pittosporum, maybe jasmine. At a time like this, what *would* be on Alice Ann's mind? Ralph had to imagine the worst. Ralph had to be on his guard at every moment.

They were alone at the pool now. Earlier a couple of boys had spent a noisy half hour shooting forefingers at one another and grabbing shot guts as they took turns tumbling face first into the pool to float like little dead men. They had given Ralph a migraine, but now he missed the little shits. The pool's calm water looked like rosé wine to Ralph. In the aquarium-quality light Alice Ann's tanned flesh shone greenish, vegetal. In that light the pieces of her dark red bikini could have been blood leaking from wounds. Ralph shuddered. This scene became fixed before Ralph as though it was a moment carved from a bad dream.

It was a lovely evening, though, and Ralph had sat beside a pool in Santa Barbara, California, on the eve of his second bankruptcy hearing in seven years, and told himself again and again that things could be worse, for he and Alice Ann had been smarter about a bad situation this time around the bend. For one thing, they had *homesteaded* their house, which was simply legalese meaning they had filed the right papers so they wouldn't find themselves and their children out on the street. I am an American *homesteader*, Ralph kept repeating to himself. They had initiated the bankruptcy proceedings in Santa Barbara, three hundred miles south of their actual home in Menlo Park, a smart move to avoid local embarrassment and creditors. By hook and by crook, it looked as though Alice Ann would be able to hold on to her darling red Cadillac convertible, signing its title over to her sister for safekeeping. The convertible was parked in its appointed place in front of the motel. They had driven down that day in the thing. The drive had been leisurely. They had stopped at a seaside park just south of Big Sur for a picnic Alice Ann had packed of her famous fried chicken, some German potato salad, assorted cheese, and a good jug of Chablis. At one point Ralph had said to Alice Ann, Alice Ann, this is all just a crazy dream we'll wake up from.

Right then at poolside what worried Ralph the most was Alice Ann's calmness of late. There had been no recent snarls, no shouting, screaming, laying of blame, not one drop of recently shed blood. Ralph took a long drink. He watched his wife floating peacefully in Cupid spit in a pool shaped like a giant human organ. From the surrounding darkness under the palms fantails of terrible eyes fastened on Ralph's every move. Alice Ann was saving it up. Ralph was nobody's fool. It was not fair. Any moment plaster birds of prey would pounce shrieking across the crazy light for Ralph. Ralph exhaled, closed his eyes, and rubbed them until they hurt.

We have our health, Alice Ann suddenly said.

Ralph jerked and opened his eyes.

Our what? Ralph said.

Health, Alice Ann said. —Our health.

Health? Ralph said.

Alice Ann kicked and backstroked toward the pool's smaller end. Slivers of blue and green light twitched across the water's surface like a dance of severed nerves. Ralph drank down his whiskey. He put fresh ice in his glass and covered it once more with whiskey. He leaned toward the radio as though he hoped to catch the game's score.

We have our health at least, Alice Ann said.

Alice Ann draped her arms over the poolside near her glass. She rested her long chin on the backs of her hands and looked up at Ralph's face. Her eyes looked like black pools. Ralph could see the backs of her long legs floating out behind her in the pale red water. Behind her knees had been a favorite place for Ralph.

And our children have their health, Alice Ann said. —That's the main thing. My sister always says that when you have your health you have everything

Health, Ralph said. —What are you talking about, Alice Ann? What in God's name does your sister know about health? That

123

woman has been having the same pitiful heart attack for as long as I've known her. And what about her brain tumors, Alice Ann? A dozen of those babies over the years? Fifteen maybe? Don't ask me how many.

You're the one with all the little symptoms, Ralph, Alice Ann said. —All those little fainty vapors. The seven warning signs like clockwork.

A minute ago you said I had my health, Ralph said. —Which is it?

It's your diet, Ralph, Alice Ann said. —You have a rotten diet. Your stomach is a graveyard, Ralph. It is a cemetery for the dead flesh of fellow creatures.

I know the state of my health, all right, Ralph said. —I have no illusions. I know I'm a shell of the man I once was. I'm not even the man I was six months ago, and I know it. Or yesterday, for that matter. I don't kid myself. But it doesn't have a thing to do with eating meat, I'll tell you that.

Oh, come on, honey, Alice Ann said, perk up. You are in the prime of your life.

That is probably the cruelest thing you could say to me right now, Ralph said. He drank down his whiskey and poured another. He lit a cigarette and watched its smoke rise in the eerie pool lights.

This time tomorrow it will all be over, Alice Ann said. She pulled herself out of the water and sat at poolside, her back to Ralph. She hugged her legs to her chest and rested her chin on her knees. Her long hair was darkened with water and hung down her slender back in a rope. Ralph followed the soft slope of spine down her brown back to the deep dimples above her hips. Those dimples had been a favorite place. Ralph had licked champagne from those sweet pools.

Why don't you come over and sit beside me, Alice Ann said.

I'm listening to a game, Ralph said. —I'm smoking.

Let me have a puff, Alice Ann said, and wiggled a hand behind her.

You're all wet, Ralph said. —I'll light you one of your own.

No. Forget it. Later maybe. Are you getting hungry yet?

I don't know, Ralph said. —I hadn't thought about it, I guess. I guess my graveyard is still pretty full of that fellow creature you fried up.

Ralph, Alice Ann said, how many times do I have to explain to you that chicken is not red meat. Chicken is fowl, and fowl, like fish, is better for your blood than red meat.

You mean, in the great scheme of things, chickens are less our fellow creatures than our bovine brothers?

Red meat, Ralph, is simply not good for your blood, that's all, Alice Ann said. —I simply wanted to fix you something nice you liked, Ralph. That's all. I knew you wouldn't be satisfied with a nice salad. All I needed today was to have you carrying on about bean sprouts, choking and gagging around the way you do. I wanted us to have a pleasant picnic together, like old times. I didn't want us to drive down here today grim as death.

It was great fried chicken, Ralph said. —I mean it. It was a nice picnic, too. I don't remember a cross word, do you? I don't, anyway.

Remember the time we went skinny-dipping in that motel pool? Alice Ann said, and laughed. —Drunk as sailors. At three o'clock in the a.m. Those were the good old days, when we just flipped off the world.

That was all your idea, Ralph said. —You put me up to it.

Well, whose idea was it to make love in the water? Remember? We were all naked and slippery. You kept diving after me underwater. Muff dives, you called them. It's dark and dangerous work, you kept saying, but somebody has to do it.

We woke up the manager, that's something I remember. We were lucky he didn't call the cops.

Ralph, tell me how it's going to be after tomorrow, Alice Ann said. She finished her drink and handed Ralph her glass. —Light me a cigarette now, too, pretty please.

What it's going to be like? Ralph said. —What is that, Alice Ann, one of your trick questions?

It will be another fresh start, that's what, Alice Ann said. —That's the way we can look at this ordeal. What frightens me the most is that someday we'll run out of fresh starts. Let's really

125

do things differently this time around, Ralph. Let's pretend we really are new, different people.

What about the past, Alice Ann? Ralph said. —We just can't forget our sordid past, with all its trials and tribulations.

What's important is what we do now, from here on out. We'll live in the present and future. We'll set goals. Common goals.

What kind of goals? Ralph said. —I'll admit it, Alice Ann, talk like that gets me edgy. You talk about goals, and things like preachers and fund-raising and football pop into my mind. It's crazy, I know, but there it is.

I mean little things, Alice Ann said. —Just doing little things in our life differently. At first. To get started on a new road. Things like watching our health more. Getting some exercise. Really. Things like that. We could start taking walks. Long, brisk strolls after dinner together. Maybe start hiking in the woods on weekends. Who knows. Maybe later really getting back to nature. Backpacking into the high country eventually.

You must be going crazy, Alice Ann, Ralph said.

We could both quit smoking, Alice Ann said. —Now, that's something we really could do. We'll set a date and then just do it together, cold turkey. We'll encourage each other, Ralph. Give each other moral support. We'll be the two Mouseketeers of moral support, Ralph.

What about those two criminal children at home? Ralph said.

We'll cut back on the booze, too, Alice Ann said. —Think of the money we could save. We'll open a savings account. We'll take the kids on family vacations.

Sure, Ralph said, maybe take those criminal children backpacking into the high country with us.

I mean all of this, Ralph, Alice Ann said. —I do. We'll take family vacations. We'll go to places like, I don't know, the Grand Canyon maybe. Carlsbad Caverns, wherever they are. Places like that. Disneyland. We'll take the kids to Disneyland.

Alice Ann, honey, the boy is fifteen years old, Ralph said. —And he's a hood. Your daughter is sixteen, Alice Ann, and she's a hood-ette. The only way we could get those kids to go to Disneyland is high as kites on acid.

I want to take my children to Disneyland, Alice Ann said. —I've never even been to Disneyland myself. I've lived in this state all these years and not once has anybody ever taken me to Disneyland, Ralph. I want to take our kids to Disneyland, Ralph, and I want us to get a bumper sticker to prove it. We have to make a commitment to each other right now, Ralph, a vow. To take our children to Disneyland as soon as we get back on our feet.

Don't tell me you're drunk already, Ralph said. —Alice Ann, it's not even seven yet.

Before it's too late for us, Ralph. And we lose them for good. Are you willing to make this vow with me, Ralph? Here and now. I mean it, Ralph. Right this minute. If you still love me at all, you will. If you don't love me anymore at all, then you just don't. But if you love me, you'll make this vow.

Yes, Jesus Christ, yes, Ralph said. —Right. Wow. Disneyland. You got it. It's done. The check's in the mail. Disneyland is in the mail.

Take me seriously, Ralph, Alice Ann said.

I am, Ralph said. —I do.

2

Alice Ann stood up then at poolside and dove into the water. She swam underwater slowly to the pool's shallow end, where she surfaced in the spray from the Cupid fountain. She stood up and turned slowly, letting the spray fall over her body. She tilted her head back and let the spray splash over her face. She opened her mouth and let it fill with spray. Ralph followed the arc of water from the Cupid's pursed mouth to his wife's mouth. Alice Ann cupped her hands beneath her breasts. Water ran in thin streams from the corners of her mouth. Ralph turned off the radio. He heard sudden laughter from somewhere behind him and he jerked around in his chair.

What's the matter? Alice Ann said.

Nothing, Ralph said.

Ralph stood up and peered about. He could feel his heart racing. He sat down.

Is somebody coming? Alice Ann said.

I don't know. I heard something. I don't see anybody. Haven't you had enough of that water? You'll look like a prune.

Alice Ann breaststroked back to poolside near Ralph. Between the slight separation in her front teeth Alice Ann spit a long, thin arc of water toward Ralph.

Hey there, Ralph said, and scooted his chair back. —You got my shoes all wet.

Oh, bullshit, Ralph, Alice Ann said. —Come on in. The water's ripe and right.

I have a headache coming on. A migraine, Ralph said. Ralph turned the radio on and bent toward it.

I still say it's your diet, sweetie, believe me, Alice Ann said. She jangled her glass at Ralph and he bent to reach for it. He filled it with ice and whiskey and handed it back to her. Alice Ann took a long drink, then crunched an ice cube between her teeth.

I wish you'd go on that karma-cleaning diet I learned about at the Zen Garage, Alice Ann said. —You'd be a new man in no time.

I don't want to be a new man, Ralph said. —I just want to be the old me. The way I used to be. Back then.

Back when, honey?

I don't know. Back when I was about two or three, I guess. Back before all of this, anyway, Ralph said, and slowly waved his glass about him.

I think the worst is over, sweetie, Alice Ann said. —We've suffered, sure. But we're going to start getting some good out of this incarnation, Ralph. Both of us. I know it. And we're going to be made stronger for all our suffering in the long run. If not in this life, then in the next. We have to work off our karmic debts, that's all.

Alice Ann, would you just answer me something? Ralph said. —And don't fly off the handle, okay, please. This is just a simple, honest question. What's with you and those zen-birds, anyway? Where do they get off, Alice Ann? Just answer me that.

You never fail to amaze me, Ralph.

I just don't understand those birds, Ralph said. —I'll admit it. All right, so it's me being plain old ignorant. Maybe that's it. I don't know. But I honestly think they're all a bunch of nuts.

You are ignorant, Ralph, Alice Ann said. —You're right about that, anyway.

All right. All right. I've admitted it. I've said it out loud. So set me straight. Explain things to me. I'm willing to learn. Really. Okay, explain India to me, for instance. You take India. Over in India people are starving, right? Everybody knows that. It's a known fact. Starving people over in India. So, okay, explain cows over in India to me, Alice Ann.

Cows, Ralph?

Cows, you bet, Ralph said. —See, you don't have an easy answer for that one, do you? You could fill Texas twice over with all the cows they have roaming around over there in India. Cows roaming the streets. Cows all over the sidewalks. Cow poop everywhere. Cow pee. It's just awful. And you know why, Alice Ann? You want me to explain those cows to you?

I've tried everything to get you to expand your horizons, Ralph. There is a spiritual dimension to this world. You simply won't let yourself open up to new possibilities. You live in a closed system, Ralph.

Those people over there in India are starving, as we've established, but do you think they'd have the good sense to barbecue up some grade-A beef? Not on your life. Because they believe one of those bovines might be their dead daddy returned to life on the hoof. Amazing. My dad has been dead for years. I bet I've put away ten thousand hamburgers since my dad passed, and I'll tell you something, Alice Ann. I'm not one bit worried. You'll never in a million years convince me I ever took a bite out of Dad.

The final thing about you, Ralph, is you don't want to probe new possibilities. You don't have the imagination for it. And your stories suffer for it, too.

Leave my stories out of this, Ralph said. —My stories don't have a thing to do with this business.

Your stories are out of it, Ralph, Alice Ann said. —And this is the reason why. You don't have the . . . No, you won't let your imagination probe deeply enough. You won't let your imagination seek the deeper mysteries in this world of veils. That's why your stories are about colorless people going about the business of their mundane, colorless lives. There is no spiritual dimension to your stories, Ralph. And more's the pity.

That's crazy, Alice Ann, Ralph said. —Just utter nonsense.

It's true. It is. Malignancies, Ralph. Malignancies make up your stories. And bad karma. And that is one reason I pity you.

You pity me? Ralph said. —Now there's a laugh. What about those Zen looneybirds over there in India who walk around with nails in their dicks? Don't deny it, Alice Ann! It's a true fact. That's just what some of your Zen pals do, Alice Ann. They pound nails through their dicks, then roam around the countryside carrying these begging bowls. You'd never catch me giving a guy with a nail in his dick anything. I see a guy with a nail in his dick and I'm gone in the opposite direction. You call that spiritual? Are those the kinds of nuts you think I should write about? That's what is pathetic. You'll never convince me in a million years that pounding a nail through your dick is any way to worship God.

Well, Ralph, I'll bet it keeps them out of trouble, anyway, don't you agree? Alice Ann said.

There! Ralph said. —There it is! I knew it. I knew all day you were just waiting to drag up dirt. That nice picnic didn't fool me a minute, Alice Ann. All that fried chicken, done to a turn. That tasty potato salad. I knew all along you were just waiting to catch me off guard and nail me good.

That's not true, Ralph. I mean it.

That's a likely story. We weren't going to bring up old business, I thought. We agreed, I thought. That business was dead and buried, I thought.

You're right, Ralph, Alice Ann said. —Would you believe me if I told you I was sorry?

What? Ralph said. —What?

Would you believe me if I told you I was sorry?

I don't understand this, Ralph said.

Would you believe me if I told you I have never been unfaithful to you?

What? Ralph said. —What is this, one of your trick questions?

No, Alice Ann said. She drained her drink and placed the glass at poolside. She pushed off backward and floated to the center of the pool, where she treaded water.

You've got me all worked up now, Ralph said. He turned up the radio and poured more whiskey into his glass.

So what's the score? Alice Ann said. She breaststroked back to poolside.

I don't have the first idea.

Freshen my drink, too, Alice Ann said. She handed her glass to Ralph, and when he returned it, she drank deeply. —I may as well tell you something, Ralph.

Tell me something? Ralph said. —What? Tell me what?

You're not going to be very happy about this, Ralph.

Jesus, don't tell me, then. No, yes, tell me. Go ahead. Jesus, Alice Ann.

You'd find out sooner or later, anyway, Ralph. In fact, you may already know about it. God knows. But in case not, you may as well hear it from my lips.

Oh Christ, Alice Ann! You have me all worked up now. Just tell me and get it over with. Just do it!

Ralph, I wrote your girlfriend a letter.

What was that? Ralph said. He turned off the radio.

You heard me, Ralph.

Jesus Christ, Alice Ann! Jesus, what possessed you? That old business is dead and buried.

It is now, Alice Ann said. She took another long drink.

What in the world did you say? Alice Ann, I don't understand. What did you write her, Alice Ann?

Nothing but the truth, Alice Ann said, and smiled sweetly. —The truth about us, Ralph.

Alice Ann swam backward across the pool, then returned breaststroking. Ralph turned the radio back on, loud.

When she reached poolside, Alice Ann said, Why don't you go get into your swimsuit, sweetie? You need the exercise.

I didn't bring any swimsuit. I don't even own a swimsuit.

Well, we always have our birthday suits, sweetie, Alice Ann said. She undid her halter top and tossed it toward Ralph.

Are you going crazy, Alice Ann! Ralph said, and jumped up. He waved his hands at her. —Stop this, Alice Ann! Stop this!

Alice Ann bent beneath the water and tugged off her bikini bottoms. She swung them around over her head and threw them toward the nearest peacock among the flowering bushes. Ralph ran to them. He ran holding the bikini bottoms before him to the pool's edge. —Here, Alice Ann! Here! Ralph gasped, and shook them violently before her face. —Do you want to go to jail?

We're an old married couple, Ralph. We've seen each other naked a million times over the long years, Alice Ann said. She pushed off backward again from the poolside and floated to the center. Her nipples looked black in the vegetal light. Ralph watched the smooth muscles of her stomach and thighs flex. At some point in the last few weeks Alice Ann had, with no explanation, begun shaving her pubic hair.

There's somebody coming, Ralph said. He glanced about behind him. —Really, Alice Ann. It's probably the manager, Alice Ann. Jesus Christ, Alice Ann, this has got to stop somewhere. This is crazy, Alice Ann. Crazy.

Alice Ann arched backward into a dive and disappeared beneath the water. Ralph threw the bikini bottoms into the water after her. He kicked the halter top in, too. He turned away and then turned back and kicked her glass into the pool. Ralph stumbled to his chair and sat down heavily. He pressed his fingertips against his temples and shut his eyes. Somehow he would call Lindsay and try to tell her his side of things again. Give the lie to Alice Ann's letter, and to those horrible half-truths that asshole Jim Stark had told her. Tonight. Somehow.

Ralph stood up suddenly and hurried to the edge of the pool. He stared down into the pale red water. He knelt down at the poolside. Ralph braced himself as best he could, and he bent as far out over the water as he dared.

Alice Ann had been sound asleep when loud voices from the hallway stirred her. After a moment she remembered where she was, but she lay still with her eyes shut. She felt small and safe in this enormous bed, which continued to vibrate from the fistful of quarters they had stuffed into the slot on its headboard earlier in the evening for hours of healthful, fingertip toning touch.

Alice Ann and Ralph had paid an arm and a leg for this suite, and why not? What did it matter, she had asked Ralph. Even bankrupts deserve a bone. She had borrowed the money from a friend at the community college where she taught English and drama, so the debt was hers and hers alone. For the price of this suite a complimentary Continental breakfast was included, so tomorrow morning Alice Ann planned to put that one o'clock courtroom business out of her mind and pig out, while Ralph would suck one of his screwdrivers.

Alice Ann stretched and felt around for Ralph. The sheets on his side of the bed were still damp with champagne. Alice Ann had given Ralph a champagne-and-tongue bath, had licked champagne from his belly button. Alice Ann opened one of her eyes and peeked about. Across the darkened bedroom the huge color television screen was a silent red, white, and blue rippling American flag. The bathroom was dark. Alice Ann got out of bed and put on her robe. She heard her name called from the hallway.

Unhand my husband! Alice Ann screamed at the burly uniformed guard who had Ralph in a headlock in the hallway. Ralph, naked as the day he was born, was squirming and wiggling in the big man's clutches and trying to call out for her, but his voice was mostly muffled in a coat sleeve. —Alice Ann, help! Ralph gasped.

Remove your fucking hands from my husband this instant! Alice Ann screamed at the guard.

Listen, lady, the guard grunted, as he wrestled around with Ralph, falling against a wall.

That gentleman is my husband, Alice Ann said. —Now get your fucking hands off of him, please.

Jesus, lady, the guard grunted.

He's got me in a hold! Ralph croaked. —He jumped me by surprise, Alice Ann. Alice Ann, help me!

Lady, this man is naked in public, the guard gasped. He tightened his grip on Ralph's head.

Give him one, Alice Ann, Ralph whimpered. —Kick him!

My husband is ill, Alice Ann said, her voice calm now. —He walks in his sleep. He needs assistance, not this physical abuse. He is under a doctor's care. My husband needs medical attention.

Lady, what we have here is a real drunk man, the guard said. —A drunk, naked man.

A woman opened the door of the room across the hall from Ralph and Alice Ann's room. She stood there motionless, watching this scene, one hand on the doorknob, the other at her throat.

Would you call down to the desk for me, please? the guard asked the woman. —Get the manager. Get anybody down there.

Another door opened down the hall and a gray-haired man stuck his head out.

Are you people getting your eyes full? Alice Ann said. —A sick man is being assaulted before your very eyes and you people just gawk. This poor man needs somebody's help!

Call the desk, somebody, the guard said. —Have them send somebody up here quick. Please!

This man is an important American author! Alice Ann said. —How can something like this happen in America? Where is this, Germany? Are we in the Soviet Union?

Somebody just call the desk, please! the guard said.

Don't you people dare look upon my husband's nakedness! Alice Ann screamed. —Shut your fucking doors! All of you fucking rubberneckers! You shut your doors now! Alice Ann screamed, and stepped toward the woman. The woman backed into her room and slammed the door. Alice Ann glared at the man up the hall. He shut his door.

Call the desk, someone! the guard called out. —These are crazy people!

That does it, asshole, Alice Ann said. —Who do you think you are? Who are you, anyway? That man is an important American author.

Kick him! Ralph croaked. —Do it, Alice Ann!

Come on, lady, the guard said.

The guard ducked away just in time from Alice Ann's round-house right, but it caught him behind his right ear and knocked his cap flipping to the floor. Ralph broke the guard's hold and lunged for the door. Ralph slammed the door behind him. The guard bent to pick up his cap, and Alice Ann aimed a kick at his face which he barely blocked with an elbow. The guard ran several yards down the hallway before turning and shaking a finger at Alice Ann.

Lady, you are under arrest! the guard yelled.

I will sue you for every nickel you have, Alice Ann said. —We have friends in high places. Senator Ted Kennedy is a personal friend. And I mean really *personal*!

The woman from across the hall cracked her door again.

Lady, I just don't want no more trouble, the guard said, and he hurried down the hallway toward the stairwell exit.

God bless you, Alice Ann said to the woman hovering behind the door. —God only knows what that brute would have done to me if you hadn't been my witness.

The woman closed her door. Alice Ann knocked on the door to Ralph's and her room.

Open up, Ralph.

When there was no answer, Alice Ann pounded on the door.

Let me in, Ralph.

Who is it? Ralph mumbled from behind the door.

Who do you think it is, goddamn it! Open this goddamn door, Ralph!

Is there anybody with you?

Open the goddamn door, Ralph, or I'll kick it in!

This is the worst thing that has happened to me in my life up to now, Ralph said. He shut the door behind Alice Ann and locked it. He was dressed.

This is just too much for one man to handle, Ralph said. He stumbled over and sat on the bed. He put his face in his hands. —I was innocent, Alice Ann. I was just hunting for the bathroom. It was an honest mistake, Alice Ann. I just opened the wrong door. Which is the story of my life, I guess. This is the straw that broke this old camel's back.

Get your things together, sweetie, Alice Ann said. She began packing her overnight case on the dresser with her makeup.

Being nude out there in that hallway was my worst dream come true, Ralph said. He lay back on the bed. He pulled the covers up over his head.

Come on, sweetie, Alice Ann said. —Where did you put your shaving kit?

Let them come and get me, Ralph said. He rolled into a ball under the covers. —Let them just take me away.

This is like old times, Alice Ann said, and laughed. She put her robe and nightgown into the suitcase. She dressed quickly in her jeans and blouse. She quickly began packing Ralph's things into her suitcase. —Do I have everything of yours here, Ralph?

I guess, Ralph said. —Except my underwear. I forgot to put it back on when I got dressed. That's how rattled I was.

Where is it? I don't see it anywhere.

In my pocket, Ralph said. —I packed it in my pocket. Did you get that asshole with a good one?

Not really, Alice Ann said. —Come on, honey, get out from under those covers. You should have seen it all. He ran down the hall, then turned and announced that I was under arrest.

You mean you're under arrest? Ralph said, and peeked from beneath the covers.

Can't you tell, Alice Ann said, and laughed. She held the opened champagne bottle up before the television's light and shook it. She split its final inches between two plastic cups and carried them to the bed.

Am I under arrest, too? Ralph said.

Here, baby, Alice Ann said, and sat down on the bed by Ralph. —Look what Momma has for us.

Ralph pulled the covers from over his head and sat up. Alice Ann handed him a cup.

I guess we're just outlaws, Alice Ann said, and laughed. —No matter how rich and famous we get we'll just always be outlaws. Let's have a toast, Ralph.

To what? Ralph said. —My God, to what?

To whatever, Alice Ann said. —To our fresh start. I don't know, Ralph. You make the toast, sweetie.

All right, Ralph said. —I will. To Disneyland, Ralph said.

To Disneyland? Alice Ann said. —To Disneyland, Ralph?

You bet, Ralph said. —To our trip to Disneyland when we get on our feet. I want to be the sort of man who takes his wife to Disneyland if that's where she wants to go.

What about the kids? Alice Ann said.

What about the kids? Ralph said. —We'll get those little gangsters stoned out of their minds and drag them along. They'll love Disneyland. They'll think Disneyland is a trip, especially if they're on acid. We'll cover every inch of that Caddy convertible with stickers.

Ralph, what I said about your stories, you know I didn't mean it, Alice Ann said. —I think you're a genius, Ralph, you know that. I love your stories. I've always been your champion. Your stories are *spiritual*, Ralph.

Really? Ralph said. —Do you really think so, Alice Ann?

Your stories are the most spiritual stories being written in our time, Ralph, Alice Ann said. —And you are spiritual. You are a very spiritual man, Ralph. More than even you know.

Honest to God, Alice Ann?

You are, Ralph. Trust me on that, sweetie.

Sometimes I worry I'm just turning into an old worthless drunk, Ralph said. —Who'll be down on his luck for life.

We just need to get on our feet, Alice Ann said.

There was a loud knock at the door.

They're here, Ralph whispered.

To Disneyland, Alice Ann said, and raised her cup. —Come on, sweetie, to fucking Disneyland.

Right on, Ralph said. —You bet. Why not? To Disneyland.

Alice Ann and Ralph touched cups, whereupon they drank the champagne down.

Hey, Ralph said, furrowing his brow. —This stuff has already gone flat.

There was another loud knock on the door.

Well, sweetie, Alice Ann said, and grinned, we can always call room service.

Brand-New Life

1

Jim had returned to teach at Stanford in the fall, after a summer of amazingly emotional ups and downs with Lindsay, but he was desperately in love with her, and he had not minded the dark, cheap room he had rented at a midtown Palo Alto residential hotel, with its single-channel, blurry black-and-white, fifteen-inch television set and the scumbag bathroom up the hall he had to share with three outpatients from the V.A. hospital. Jim had not minded eating the cheap chop suey at the Seven Seas Café, or shuffling endlessly along in line with senile senior citizens at mystery meat-loaf cafeterias. Jim even let old coots ahead of him in line. Jim happily let a blue-hair have that last stuffed pork chop he coveted. Jim had not minded lying in that narrow bed in the dark listening to the lonesome sound of late-night downtown traffic, the sad sounds of distant sirens, faint midnight music from the bars down the street, a woman's sudden, drunken laughter from the sidewalk below, relentless coughing from the rooms around him, rats running in the walls. Jim had not minded the sad air of defeat at the end of the faded hallway, or the ancient air of loneliness and despair that settled like shadows into the corners of his crummy room. Jim breathed in a green cloud of desperate decay, and he did not give a shit. Happy as a clam, Jim lay there in the hot dark of his crummy room, sipping a warm bottle of beer, the television on soundlessly, his one window open. Down the street a country-western bar had its door propped open in the heat and Jim could hear a Merle Haggard tune about an outlaw moving town to town on the run. *Down every road there's always one more city,* old Merle sang. Jim grinned in the hot dark, a legendary outlaw of love who had found his one more city, whose running days were over.

Because Jim was in love, he was only bemused by undergraduate girls' winks and blinks. Night after night he killed time at the Oasis Bar on El Camino, carving heart-enclosed *Jim Loves Lindsay*'s in the thick wooden tables with his switchblade knife. Jim was in love with the astonishing idea that Lindsay, with those beautiful, wide eyes, that generous, smiling mouth, full, sensuous lips, loved a big bizarre bozo who affected a fedora. All that previous summer, Lindsay had kept a calendar of passion, had pasted silver stars marking each day's acts of lust. Jim would lie alone in bed in his dingy room like a monk astronomer whole nights sometimes poring over that celestial chart. He marveled at that calendar pasted thick with summer love's constellations of silver. Jim reimagined the memory of each star, its spinning planets and their moons.

Jim reimagined everything about last summer. Those silly, sentimental ice-cream-cone walks by the evening river. Making garbage bags full of buttered popcorn and watching old movies until dawn, then sipping coffee on the back porch in the cool birdsong sunrise. That trip up to Browning for the rodeo and Indian Days, the drunken cowboys' and Indians' sweaty eyes watching Lindsay sweep along. Fishing way up the Bitterroot that time, the sun hot on his bare back, the water icy on his waders, Lindsay lying on a quilt up in the long grass topless, that first bite. Jim had glanced up at Lindsay. She was up on her elbows, face tilted to the sun, eyes closed, her breasts getting brown. A picnic of two small, sweet trout fried fresh on the spot,

Chablis chilled ice cold in the river, oily, sun-baked sex on the bank. How they swept into the bars those cool Montana nights, brown and babbling a mile a minute, people looking up, that sudden silence, their envious eyes widening, their nostrils flaring in the sexual scent of Jim and Lindsay's wake. How they slow-danced to boogie music out at the cabin, at the Am-Vets, even at the Trail's End, where serious, high-betting, good-old-boy pool players paused to watch. How they wrote letters to each other daily, and talked on the phone for hours now that they were apart.

Finally Jim had landed a second-floor railroad flat in San Francisco's North Beach by sheer luck, by taking over another Stanford's faculty member's lease when he and his wife split up and fled for their lives. It was a fantasy flat, with working fireplaces, high beamed ceilings, old hardwood wainscoting, a stained-glass window at the end of the long central hallway, sliding wood doors, an ancient marble mantel in a huge front room that had a corner half-turret with windows of curved glass through which he gazed at the frozen flight of lights in fog. In that one sweeping view he could see Coit Tower on a nearby hilltop, and above the trees of Washington Square down the hill the illuminated spires of Saint Peter-Paul's Cathedral rising like huge sleek, elegant bones, and down descending avenues of fog toward the Bay, where far below at Fisherman's Wharf he could see a great red neon fish flashing before some restaurant. Beyond that was Alcatraz Island glowing through the fog like an enormous ship anchored in the dark bay.

Jim had moved his few boxes of belongings up from the low-rent residential hotel in Palo Alto into the flat, and he had spent all his spare time cleaning and polishing, polishing the broad windows until they cast the prismatic colors of light across the shining parquet floors; and at night, pooped from polishing, Jim would make a fire in the front room's fireplace and stretch out on his sleeping bag before it, listening to plaintive, trumpety Mexican music on his portable radio and sipping jug red wine while he imagined that firelight flickering on Lindsay's perfect, pretty titties.

2

Finally Jim got around to calling old Ralph. Let's get together for a drink and shoot the shit, Jim suggested. They both arrived at the appointed bar late and half loaded. They took one look at each other and began to laugh and punch each other in the shoulders. You are the real Running Dog, Ralph said. You always call me the Running Dog, but you're the real Running Dog around here. Well, Jim had to agree. Jim felt so magnanimous he was nearly wiggling with it. Jim fed Ralph a bag of what he knew in his heart was baloney about the nature of Lindsay's old love for Ralph, that Ralph was a great, no, maybe *the* great love of Lindsay's life, but that Ralph had let that love slip through his fingers. Jim told Ralph that if Ralph had been the one to go up to Missoula the previous May, Ralph would be the lucky dog strolling down that aisle in the chapel of love next spring and not Jim. What Jim really thought was that he and Lindsay were a celestial pair, a match made in heaven, destined legendary lovers, and that Ralph and Lindsay's puny little affair, if that's what you even wanted to call that little fling, was only a minor instrument of fate to get Lindsay and Jim together. Jim was only bemused instead of bored stiff and pissed as Ralph bragged on and on about new stories written and soon to be accepted by major magazines. Jim did truly love that old Running Dog, his old buddy who was doing his damnedest to hide his broken heart and who Jim did not really mean to do dirt, this old Ralphie boy.

Ralph asked Jim to read at his Thursday-afternoon class at Berkeley, and said they'd use the fifty-bucks honorarium Ralph could probably scare up for a nice dinner and drinks. By the time Ralph's class met on the selected afternoon, he and Jim had already drunk up the fifty bucks, and Ralph introduced Jim first as a distinguished panel and then, after several students pointed out the obvious, Ralph reintroduced Jim as Norman Mailer.

That night Ralph and Jim had found themselves somehow deep up in the Sacramento Delta, lost among the levees, in a beer joint with a bunch of pretty college coeds Ralph kept claiming he had never given A grades. Those honeys never got A grades from me, Ralph kept claiming. Except for the tall, black-haired beauty with the tattoo of a rose on her right shoulder, whose first-person stories always concerned the funny albeit sometimes fatalistic exploits of the female biker gang she apparently led. They were in some godforsaken, crossroads roadhouse named Dutch's, which had a low ceiling of polished antlers and walls covered with wild fur and the stuffed faces of animals, and after they had both fallen in and out of love with the tall, beautiful, tattooed biker chick several times, but had finally decided to give her up before she came between them, Jim put his arm around old Ralph's shoulder and he said, I'm sorry, old dog. You're like a brother to me, old Ralphie, and I did you dirt. But goddamn it, Ralph, I love the girl. No, not the beautiful, fucken tattooed chick, you can have her, I already told you. Lindsay. I love her. Lindsay. I love you, too, old dog. But I love the girl, Ralph. I do. We didn't mean for it to happen. It just did. Ralph, I feel terrible. I never wanted to cause you of all people in the world pain and suffering and any feelings of humiliation and inadequacy. I'd cut off my right arm, old Ralph, before I'd deliberately cause you, my best old pal, the pain and suffering that come with feeling like a loser, especially in the love department. But I love her, old Ralph. No, goddamn it, not the tattooed chick. Lindsay! Lindsay! Ralph, do you forgive me?

Sure, old Jim, Ralph said, and hugged Jim's shoulder back. —I forgive you. It's water over the dam.

Do you really forgive me? Jim asked. —Do you mean it?

I do. I swear I do, old Jim, Ralph said, shaking his woolly head in vigorous affirmation.

Ralph and Jim embraced at the bar. When Jim began to weep, so did Ralph. Men looked away from them, and the college girls, including the tall, beautiful, tattooed biker chick, began to dance with the incredulous locals.

I have a new girlfriend, anyway, Ralph said after a time.

Say what? Jim said.

I'm a fool for love, Ralph said. —I never learn my lesson.

You have a new girlfriend?

She's a babe.

Her? Jim asked, and nodded toward the tall, beautiful, tattooed biker chick, who was boogying wildly at that point with a bearded, one-legged, relentlessly hopping local man.

No, Ralph said. —No way. I told you you could have her.

Who, then? Do I know her? What's her name?

You've got to be kidding, Ralph said, and laughed, his big shoulders shaking, covering his mouth with his paw, the way he used to do.

Ralph and Jim had 4:00 a.m. scrambled eggs at a Nut Tree restaurant God-knows-where on Route 80, where they walked the check and Ralph stole a cherry-wood pepper grinder as an upcoming anniversary present for Alice Ann, to commemorate their eighteen years of marital bliss.

3

Lindsay and Jim were married on a beautiful spring afternoon, and she wore a long-sleeved, floor-length, light green dress, its material covered with small blue and yellow flowers, which she had made with her own hands. She wore a wide-brimmed white sail of a sunhat and carried a single white rose. Jim wore a new plaid sport coat he had bought the day before. It looked like something he could fashionably wear to sell used cars.

The party that night after the ceremony was a great success, and the police were called only twice. When Jim came to the next afternoon himself, he found his breathtakingly beautiful bride in bed beside him still wearing her lovely, albeit somewhat wrinkled, wedding dress, not to speak of her somewhat crushed white sail of a hat, whereas Jim was buck naked except for his brand-new snakeskin cowboy boots, Lindsay's wedding gift.

Only for Crumley's grumbling and threats two days later did the rented moving van get loaded with all of Lindsay's worldly goods for the move south to San Francisco to begin a new life with this new husband. The various Trail's End bar drunks

Buffalo had dragged along to help had moved like moonwalkers, and often their memories clearly failed them as they returned to the house with items from the truck. Lindsay visibly trembled as her beloved, inherited treasures were lucked into place on the truck and bound. When the Buffalo almost stumbled off the truck's loading plank with a box of her grandmother's priceless china, Lindsay gasped and then flung herself to the second-floor bathroom, where she locked herself in, lit up, and paced in rage and despair. The day had been packed with the portent of bad omens. As soon as she spotted her kitty-carrying case the morning of this moving day, little Sappho had hidden out wild-eyed and shivering in a closet. Finally Lindsay quit pacing the bathroom and simply flopped down on the commode lid, where she sat grinding her teeth and chain-smoking. Presently Jim began tapping on the door and begging Lindsay to trust in their future together.

Later on that day of their departure, when Jim pulled Lindsay's Oldsmobile Cutlass into a drive-through car wash in Lolo to remove the crude comments Buffalo and the boys had soaped onto the car, the crazy caravan of Trail's End drunks and grown men with the nicknames of boys had circled them honking and hooting and hanging mooning asses out side windows. Now and again some drunk fool would discharge his gun in the air. Lindsay had looked over at Jim with her smoky, country-song gray eyes, and shook her head slowly, and said quietly and simply, Good God, and I am just on my so-called honeymoon. Lindsay reached over and put her hand on Jim's big arm. Honey, Lindsay said, and Jim looked at her, honey, all I want is a normal life. A simple, normal life is all I ask of you.

Yessum, Jim had said, and grinned. —The normal life is in the mail.

4

A huge full moon hung above the Bay, and nearby the planet Venus shone that night far more brilliantly than any star, as Jim and Lindsay sped into Berkeley out of the east, Jim singing Shine on, shine on harvest moon, for me and my gal, above the radio blasting honky-tonk, the highway lights lushly coral, taillights bobbing in the tinted windshield like the blossoms of tiny electric red roses.

Lindsay rolled down her window, stuck out her head, let her long hair blow. She closed her eyes, opened her mouth, and ate air fresh from the Orient. Lindsay clapped her hands. I've never been so flipping excited, she exclaimed to Jim. I've never been so happy. God, Stark, I think I could eat you alive, Lindsay said, and then kissed and nibbled at Jim's neck.

Just remember, Jim said, you are what you eat.

When suddenly in the smooth flowing darkness beyond the road in the mudflats by the bay, the horrible shapes of creatures rose in Lindsay's vision from the black waters. Holy moly, Stark, Lindsay said, and pointed excitedly. —What in the world?

Them, baby, Jim said, are driftwood sculptures. People come out and build them at low tide. Driftwood dinosaurs, a sphinx of driftwood, tigers, trolls, demons, driftwood creatures in the form of spheres, an animal imagined by Poe, a minotaur, Swedenborg's devils, the elephant that foretold the birth of Buddha, driftwood metaphysical beings, nymphs, you name it.

Whatever you say, Stark, Lindsay said, rolling up her window and lighting a cigarette. She looked into the rearview mirror. She wanted to keep the past behind her but still visible, the way she liked to watch horror movies on television, from the next room while she was ironing.

Following a wide sweep of highway onto a massive bright boat of a bridge that seemed to float over a flood of low fog, Jim delivered Lindsay into the startling lights of a brand-new life.

Killer Is Cool

1

The fresh start that Ralph and Alice Ann made that same March when Jim and Lindsay were married was perhaps their best ever. They had been through the flames, Alice Ann declared, and now they were rising from the ashes of the past. They had gotten that bad bankruptcy business behind them, and Ralph's first book, that collection of stories which would eventually make him famous, was just coming out, and the early reviews—*Kirkus, Library Journal, Publishers Weekly*—were wonderful. All those years of dashed hopes, final straws, that life of low points, leaving towns under the cover of darkness, abandoning breakdowns on the highway and sneaking away burdened by defeat, bankruptcies like clockwork, were all somehow vindicated and made almost heroic by the stories in Ralph's book.

Ralph and Alice Ann had decided to use every dime of Ralph's remaining advance money to make their old *homestead* as glossy as a magazine layout. Alice Ann searched Sears for new bedroom rugs and drapes and kitchen curtains; they had to have new kitchen curtains, curtains like Alice Ann's mother once had, pale green with tiny pink apples on them, a few posters maybe, or prints, both, whatever, as long as they were bright, splashed with color, maybe in a Mexican motif (Alice Ann loved Mexico, and someday she and Ralph just had to get south of the border), as long as everything new in this fresh start was an aria of color and brightness and light, and plants, loads of new plants, exploding ferns, green jades, flowering plants, everywhere green, growing plants, galore with life, and lamps, two big new lamps for their showcase of a living room.

After getting estimates, Ralph and Alice Ann settled on a cheap Chicano crew to landscape their yard, which turned out to mean a week of overtime chopping jungle from the junked appliances beside the garage and peeling the back yard's layers of rotting oranges in a fog of flies.

Late one afternoon Ralph jumped his hoodlum son by surprise, got him in a pretty good hold, and tried to reason with him about the goddamn dinosaur of a Dodge which had been rusting on cinder blocks in the driveway for two years while the son tinkered on it with stolen parts. Although this discussion had ended in the back yard on the ground with the son holding Ralph in a headlock for nearly a half hour before Alice Ann returned home from work and squirted them with the hose, the goddamn Dodge was hauled, along with all the junked appliances.

After his hippie daughter had pulled one of her days-long disappearing acts, Ralph had stalked the house with a pillowcase one Saturday morning bagging the dozen or so stray cats whose karma, according to his daughter, had led them to his daughter's door. One by one Ralph tossed those filthy felines into the trunk of his car. Ralph would teach those cats karma all right, and his daughter, and Alice Ann, too, if she butted in. Ralph was going to put his foot down around this karma carnival, and he was going to shake those spraying, hissing, clawing cats out of his life like a bad habit. There could be no real fresh start with those creatures skulking around ready to pounce on it like a rat, and Ralph getting no respect.

Ralph fixed himself an eye-opener and sat at the kitchen table smoking. He was letting Alice Ann sleep in. She needed it after these last few days. Goddamn that hippie daughter. Making her mother sick with worry. Casting a pall over this fresh start. Ralph could hear those cats yowling from the car's trunk in the driveway. Maybe he should just pull the car into the garage, leave the motor running, close the garage door for a time. Wipe that slate clean before Alice Ann got up. No, he had to have Alice Ann's backing in this business. She had backed him at last about hauling the boy's heap. That was a first. Alice Ann had to realize that it was them against those kids. They had to stand up to those criminal kids shoulder to shoulder or be buried alive.

God, it's almost eleven, Alice Ann said when she walked into the kitchen. She poured a cup of coffee and sat down at the kitchen table and lit a cigarette from Ralph's pack. She exhaled through her nose and ran her fingers back through her long, tousled hair. She was wearing a short blue nightie, and Ralph could see that she had not shaved under her arms for days. —Why didn't you wake me up, sweetie? Is there any sign of her yet?

Not to my knowledge there's not.

Did you check her bedroom?

I checked her bedroom.

She could have slipped in and gotten some things and gone again. How would we know? I tried to listen for her. But I just couldn't keep my eyes open. The last time I looked at the clock it was nearly three.

She hasn't been here, Ralph said.

How do you know? How do you know that?

Elementary, my dear Watson, Ralph said, and jiggled his glass at Alice Ann. —We forgot to hide the vodka last night. We left it out like dopes and I left my cigarettes out here on the table, too, and everything was still here when I got up. She hasn't been near the place. For that matter, the lout isn't around either. As far as I can tell, he didn't stagger home last night either.

He didn't? He didn't ask to stay over anywhere, did he?

Of course not, Alice Ann. He's probably out casing some house to break and enter. And she's probably high in some hot tub engaging in unspeakable acts of sex.

Don't, Ralph, please. What's that noise?

What noise? I don't hear any noise.

I don't know. Some noise. Like babies crying or something. There it is. God, that's weird.

There are no babies around here, Alice Ann, that's for sure. Maybe some asshole neighbor is mowing his lawn. Maybe it's a siren in the distance. Probably the police chasing our children.

Ralph, we have to go look for our daughter again. I'll go get dressed.

That's crazy, Alice Ann. Just tell me where we start. Tell me that. You've called everybody who has known that girl since childhood. That's humiliation enough. I don't understand why you're so worked up, Alice Ann. She's pulled this disappearing act before.

She's our daughter, Ralph. Our only daughter, Ralph. I keep seeing her beside some road.

Right. Hitchhiking to Hollywood. Alice Ann, honey, this is old business. She wants that old car, Alice Ann. That's the long and short of this business. We just got rid of the boy's rattletrap, honey. You backed me on that business. We vowed no more eyesores rusting away in the driveway, Alice Ann. It has to be you and me and our fresh start or we're goners.

Our children have to be a part of our fresh start, Ralph. Sweetie, our whole family has to share in this new beginning.

The way I see it is that old business is going to ruin our fresh start. That's the way I look at it. I'm sorry, but there it is.

Ralph, are you calling our babies old business?

I'm calling a spade a spade. I'd like to enlist our old business in the Marines is what I'd like to do. Do you want an eye-opener, by the way? I'm going to freshen my screwdriver. Here I am getting all hot and bothered. I'm getting all worked up, and we said those days were behind us.

Is there any tomato juice? I'd like a Bloody Mary if there's any tomato juice.

Ralph opened the refrigerator and said, There's tomato juice here. But it's in a can somebody opened and just stuck back in here, who knows when. That could poison a person. When you open a can you should put any leftover contents in something plastic. Nothing would give those kids more pleasure than to poison me.

Settle down, Ralph. It's no big deal. Besides, you've never put anything in anything plastic in your life.

This tomato juice could be poison, I'm telling you, Ralph said, and shook the can and sniffed it. —Have you ever watched while that boy chugs right out of a carton of milk? He chugalugs half a goddamn carton of milk at a time and doesn't give a second thought to contaminating what's left for the rest of us with his awful germs.

You do the same thing, Ralph. Make me a Bloody Mary. Tomato juice is too acidic to go bad that fast.

I don't either.

Ralph, I've seen you do it a thousand times. I keep hearing that awful sound, Ralph, what in the world is it? Maybe something has crawled up under the house. Maybe you ought to get the flashlight and take a look, sweetie.

First thing in the morning, Ralph said, and turned on the radio. —Do you want a touch of Tabasco? Worcestershire sauce? The works, or what?

The works, Alice Ann said. —Why not? Some celery salt, too, Ralph. Ralph, that noise is making my skin crawl.

I've been the busy beaver all morning, Ralph said, and turned up the radio. —I started a new story. I think it's sure-fire.

Ralph, look at these goose bumps on my arms. Somebody is walking over my grave, Ralph.

When the doorbell rang, Ralph dropped the can of tomato juice into the sink.

Jesus Christ, Ralph said. —Who could that be? Don't answer it, Alice Ann.

Don't be crazy, Ralph, Alice Ann said, and got up from the table.

Me? Me crazy, Alice Ann? Don't answer it. Whatever it is, we don't need it.

Why are you so weird today? Alice Ann said, and left the room.

Ralph looked down into the sink at the spilled tomato juice as red as blood. Ralph turned on the hot water full blast and sat down at the kitchen table. He lit a cigarette and polished off his drink. He could hear Alice Ann speaking with somebody at the door. Steam rose from the sink. Ralph saw he had forgotten to close the refrigerator door. He saw an uncovered plate of something gone green. Ralph could hear an actual siren somewhere in the distance and the insane cries of those cats.

2

Where's my Bloody Mary? Alice Ann said when she returned to the kitchen and sat down. —I'm going to need it.

Jesus, Ralph said. —I knew you shouldn't have answered that door.

You had better make yourself a stiff one, too, Ralph. You're going to need it, too.

I told you not to answer that door, Alice Ann. Didn't I tell you?

Ralph stood up from the table and went to the sink. He turned off the hot water and then turned on the cold and rinsed his glass. He took a tray of ice from the refrigerator and that plate of green fur. Using a fork Ralph scraped the green fur into the garbage disposal.

Sweetie, just remember that no matter what the future holds we'll face it together. I'll stand by you, Ralph, through thick or thin. For better or worse, Ralph, that's us.

My goose is cooked, isn't it, Alice Ann? Just go ahead and tell me the worst.

Why in the world are you so paranoid today, Ralph? Alice Ann said, and laughed. —Why are you so paranoid, puppy? Have you been up to something I don't know about? We have a few checks bouncing around, but so what? What else is new? So what are you so paranoid about today, Ralph?

I am not paranoid, Ralph said. —Well, if I am, it's your fault. You're making me paranoid. You're the one. Who was at the door? Who was it, anyway? You're the one who's acting like it was the sheriff or something. You came back in here acting like there are armed men at the door with a warrant for my arrest.

Did it ever occur to you that it might be news about our missing daughter? Bad news maybe.

Well, yes. Sure it did. Is it? Bad news, I mean.

No, it isn't, Ralph. In fact, it wasn't bad news at all for a change. It was just a delivery I had to sign for, that's all.

Delivery? What delivery? A delivery of what? You know, Alice Ann, we can't carry this fresh-start business too far. We've been throwing money around like water. There has to be a limit, Alice Ann.

I don't know what it was a delivery of, Alice Ann said. —I, for one, am too worried about the old business of our missing daughter to pay much attention to anything else right now. It was a big box. Maybe it's the new twenty-five-inch color television set I bought on credit.

Ralph sat down at the table and put his face in his hands.

You big paranoid puppy, Alice Ann said, and laughed. —Get back up and fix my Bloody Mary, you big baby. And turn that radio down.

What's going on here, Alice Ann? Tell me, please.

Ralph, sweetie, it's your books. I'm just jerking you off, you big fuckhead. It's your fucking books, Alice Ann said, laughing, and jumped up from the table. She ran to the hallway and returned lugging a big box. —Your ten free copies from your publisher, puppy. Our books are here!

Oh golly, Alice Ann! It's the books! Look, it's the books! Here, let me have those babies, Alice Ann. Let me at that box! Get me some scissors. Or a knife. Alice Ann, get me an ax!

3

Ralph and Alice Ann had toasted the beautiful books stacked on the table between them. They toasted themselves. The white dust jacket with its dramatic black lettering was striking, they agreed, and toasted it. They toasted themselves. The jacket copy was brilliant, they agreed, and in his dust-jacket picture Ralph looked ten years younger, they agreed, and Ralph made them fresh drinks in the two new, long-stem Waterford-crystal glasses that Alice Ann had paid an arm and a leg for.

Read Lenny Michaels's blurb again! Ralph said, and then he read it out loud again himself: "Ralph Crawford's stories are extraordinary in their language, their music, and their huge terrifying vision of ordinary human life in this country."

It's true, Ralph, Alice Ann said. —Just because you and Lenny are friends doesn't mean he's not being sincere.

How would you, Ralph said, and held a foot-high, cherrywood pepper grinder up to Alice Ann's mouth like a microphone, you, a typical human-being-type person on the street, describe Ralph Crawford's vision?

Oh my God, Alice Ann said, and batted her eyes, am I on television or what? Is this live?

You are being broadcast live at this very moment, Susy Citizen. Please answer the question, please. Ordinary human life everywhere is waiting for your answer about Ralph Crawford's vision. Keep in mind you are speaking for ordinary human life everywhere.

I hope I can rise to this occasion, Alice Ann said. —Well, since you asked me, I think Ralph Crawford's vision is huge and terrifying. Just like on occasion his boner. Here, listen to this one, she said, and read from the back of the book: "Ralph Crawford's vision is somber and resolute, and the cumulative effect is powerful."

Somber as a toothache, Ralph said. —And why not? After all I've been through. Well, I'll tell you what I'm resolute about right now. I'm resolute about sucking another Screwdriver, that's what. Can I stir you up another huge, terrifying Bloody Mary, my dear?

Only if it's extraordinary in its vodka, so that its cumulative effect is powerful.

You name it, you got it. That Bloody Mary is in the mail, Ralph said, and stood up. Then Ralph sat back down. He lit a cigarette. Ralph placed his hand on the stack of books. —Alice Ann, do you know what these are? These are my babies. Our babies, hon. And they don't talk back or jump me by surprise or pull dis-appearing acts. They'll take care of me in my old age, these babies will. These babies are our tickets into the future, Alice Ann.

God, Ralph, Alice Ann said. —I don't know what I want to do the most right now. Fuck you or fight you.

Well, what's wrong with a little of both? Ralph said, and wiggled his eyebrows.

Alice Ann opened a book and read from it silently.

I remember the exact moment you finished this story, Ralph.

Which story?

The one about me selling the convertible just before we went bankrupt the first time.

These stories aren't really about us, Alice Ann.

I remember you were writing in bed, and God, it was almost dawn. I had to get up and go to work, and you had kept me awake all night wiggling around, but I didn't say anything, Ralph. You were smoking like a stove and jiggling your feet like you do and muttering under your breath. But I didn't say any-thing.

I don't remember that.

Then you started shouting, Hot dog, hot dog, hot dog! Then you shook my shoulder like I was asleep or something and insisted I sit up and read it on the spot. Then you insisted on a fuck. No, it was a blowjob you wanted. Then you insisted on three eggs over easy, pancakes, your little link sausages, your glass of orange juice with a splash of vodka, your strong black coffee with three sugars, some leftover coffee cake heated up, and then another blowjob there at the kitchen table.

I don't remember any of that, Ralph said, and laughed. —Really? Where were we? What were we doing then?

We were living in Sacramento, Ralph. In that horrible trailer park. I was working as a secretary in that insurance office. You were just collecting unemployment. Something like seventy bucks a week. You weren't even looking for work, but that was okay. You were writing so well. That was what was important to me. That was all that mattered to me.

Well, Ralph said, and patted a book, it has paid off, Alice Ann.

I remember every single draft of every single story in this book, Alice Ann said. She thumbed slowly through the pages of a book. —I know these stories by heart. And I know the stories behind the stories by heart, too.

Well, I'll admit I'm no elephant in the memory department, Ralph said. —I don't have memory one. But thank God for that, I say.

You never needed a memory, Ralph. You've always had my memory to rely on.

I use my imagination, Ralph said. —I've always counted on my imagination.

Remember this one? Alice Ann said as she scanned the table of contents. —When I was waitressing in that diner up in Humbolt, and you'd come in and hang around. And you'd get upset, but turned on, too, when those men would ogle me.

Whatever you say, Ralph said, and lit a cigarette.

Okay, sweetie, who do we call first? Alice Ann said, and closed the book. She scanned the blurbs on the back again. —Who do we call up and read what Cynthia Ozick has to say to? "There is something rock hard and unafraid about Ralph Crawford's fiction," says Cynthia, God love her. Call somebody, Ralph. Who do we call first?

I'd like to call old Jim, I guess, Ralph said.

I don't know. I don't know yet, Ralph.

Somebody has to break the ice. Sooner or later.

I know. I miss Jim, too. Let me get a little drunk first. Do you understand?

Sure. Sure I do. Maybe later. You know, though, we have to sooner or later. Maybe today is the day. But a little later. Let's get a little drunk first. You're dead right about that. Let's get a few drinks under our belts first. Hey, let's call the Buffalo. These blurbs will break Buffalo's heart. God, he'll stay drunk for a month, Ralph said, and laughed. —"Rock hard and unafraid." Jesus. Buffalo will shit a brick.

But you are, Ralph, Alice Ann said and took one of Ralph's hands, you are a very brave artist. And you are a brave man, too.

Even in the worst of times I've thought that. You are a survivor, Ralph. And so am I.

But rock hard and unafraid, Ralph said, and laughed.

You're just a little paranoid today, that's all, Ralph. Don't ever sell yourself short, sweetie, Alice Ann said, and she polished off the bottle of vodka evenly into the crystal glasses. —Here, make a final toast, sweetie. Then I'll throw some clothes on and run up to the pop shop and get us a magnum of serious champagne.

You make the toast, Ralph said. —You do it.

Okay. To you, honey. To Ralph Crawford, a great American author.

No, to you, Ralph said. —To Alice Ann Crawford. Without whom I couldn't have accomplished all that I have. Without whom I would have been chopped liver a long time ago.

To us, sweetie. And our book.

Okay, Ralph said.

To being rock hard and unafraid, Alice Ann said, and raised her glass. —To us and our book and to our fresh start and our future.

Here, here, Ralph said.

They touched glasses and drank the warm vodka down. And then Alice Ann laughed, and she sailed the crystal glass against the wall above the sink.

Jesus Christ! Ralph yelled, and dropped to his knees on the floor. —Alice Ann!

For luck, Alice Ann said, laughing. —We'll show the future what's what.

Alice Ann, Ralph said, and got up and walked over to the sink. He picked up a shard of crystal. —These glasses cost an arm and a leg, Alice Ann. Who do you think we are? The Rockefellers or something?

Oh come on, Ralph. For luck. Let's fly into the future with a flair. We'll be the Scott and Zelda of our day. Fitzgerald would toss his glass against a wall for luck in a heartbeat.

Well, maybe he would. But I won't. Not when they cost an arm and a leg, I won't, Ralph said, and sat down at the table.

Ralph gripped his glass with both hands in case Alice Ann got any more ideas. Ralph looked up past Alice Ann to the doorway, where his daughter stood leaning against its frame.

That was pretty far-out, Mom, Ralph's daughter said. —Why's the radio blaring like that?

God! Alice Ann said, and whipped around. —Where have you been? Do you even care about what you have put me through?

This is Paco, Ralph's daughter said, and nodded to a tall Chicano boy who stepped into the doorway behind her. The sleeves of his black T-shirt were rolled high on his muscular, tattooed arms. He wore motorcycle boots and a thick chain for a belt, and his hair exploded off his head like a mushroom of fur. —Paco is my new old man, Ralph's daughter said, and leaned back into him.

What's happening, man? Paco said, and shot a finger of greeting at Ralph, who flinched. Paco put his thick arms around the slender waist of Ralph's daughter and spread the fingers of one hand over her bare stomach.

Uh, Paco, Ralph mumbled, and pressed his empty glass against his lips. Ralph stared at a huge dog, which for all the world looked to him like the worst wolf of his worst nightmare, which appeared in the doorway beside Paco and began to growl.

This is Paco's dog Killer, Ralph's daughter said. —Don't sweat it. Killer is cool.

Honey, where have you been? Alice Ann said. —Why did you do this to me?

Me and Paco have just been, you know, around. Hey, Dad, it would be so cool if you threw your glass against the wall and busted it like Mom did. Wouldn't it, Paco?

I could dig it, Paco said, and nibbled at Ralph's daughter's neck.

Isn't this party a little early in the day? Ralph's daughter said. —Even for you guys.

Copies of my book came in the mail, Ralph said, and gestured vaguely at the stack of books on the table. —Your mom and I were just doing a little, you know, celebrating, that's all. Having a little toast or two.

You have no idea, do you? Alice Ann said to her daughter. —You just don't care about what you put me through, do you?

Look, what would be real cool is for somebody to explain why my cats are locked up in the car trunk, huh, Dad? They're going nuts out there!

What? Alice Ann said.

Could you clue me in as to why my cats are locked up in the trunk, huh, Dad?

Ralph? Alice Ann said, and looked at Ralph.

The vet, Ralph said. —I was going to take them to, you know, get their shots.

Sure, Dad! I'm totally pissed off about this, Dad, man! Ralph's daughter said. Killer began to growl again. —I think this is a real fucking bummer, Dad, man!

Ralph? Alice Ann said.

Ralph tossed the crystal glass over his shoulder and braced himself.

The Shadow in the Open Door
of the Future

1

Ralph balanced six of the ten beautiful books on the dining-room table, edge on edge, into a three, two, one pyramid. He arranged the remaining four copies in a semicircle before the glorious pyramid. He walked back and forth by the table smoking and looking at the pyramid from every angle. Now and then, at different distances, Ralph would stop abruptly and stare at the display of books as though seeing them in a bookstore window for the first time in his life.

Ralph took up a book and once again read the jacket copy and blurbs on the back. Rock hard and unafraid, Ralph read and chuckled. He stared at his picture on the inside cover. He peered into his photographed eyes. What had he done the moment before that picture was snapped? The moment after? What had he been thinking the moment the picture was taken? Ralph closed his right eye, as though taking aim, and looked deeply into those photographed eyes. He opened his right eye and shut his left and looked again. Ralph blinked his eyes rapidly.

Ralph walked into the kitchen to fix a little pick-me-up. At the kitchen door he glanced back over his shoulder down the dark hallway to the gleaming pyramid of beautiful books. As he ran warm water over an ice tray, Ralph gazed out the kitchen window. A cigarette dangled from his lips, and he squinted his eyes in its rising smoke. Paco's partially disassembled Harley was in the driveway. That had been part of the settlement with his daughter. Ralph's daughter was to give up six of the dozen cats, any immediate idea of getting a heap of her own, and make a promise not to get that skull-and-crossbones tattooed above her right breast, in return for Paco getting to work on his Harley in the driveway and sleep over. Ralph shut his right eye and gazed at the Harley. There were parts and tools scattered about it, and pools of oil shone like greasy little lakes of rainbows on the pavement. Ralph opened his right eye and shut his left. He blinked his eyes rapidly. Ralph shut both his eyes and let the warm water run over the backs of his hands.

Ralph sat at the dining-room table smoking and sipping his drink, and he thumbed through one of the beautiful books. He stopped at a random page and found a favorite passage. Ralph imagined himself as his old buddy Jim reading it. He imagined himself as Lindsay reading it, then Buffalo, then each of the sharks in his old Iowa writing workshop in turn reading it and weeping, then any writer of his generation reading it and weeping. Ralph imagined that high-school English teacher who had flunked him reading it, that sales manager who had fired him, that poet who had refused to lend him emergency money, the judges and creditors and asshole attorneys-at-law from his bankruptcies who had witnessed his humiliations. Ralph imagined Jackie O., Ann-Margret, Hanoi Jane, Susan Sontag reading it. He imagined that beautiful barmaid down at O'Rourke's reading it and getting hot to trot. He imagined John Cheever reading it. John Gardner. Mailer. Roth. Hemingway, if he were alive. Faulkner, Fitzgerald, if they weren't dead as doornails. Kafka. Chekhov. Chekhov, yes, yes. If they hadn't long ago gone to their rewards in that great library in the sky. Bill fucking Shakespeare. Move over, Bill! Ralph imagined his dad reading it, if he, too, weren't dead as a doornail.

Ralph fixed another drink and began to push the vacuum

cleaner around dutifully. He made his way leisurely through the house, room to room, passing up only the kids' hovels. Ralph hummed and turned over in his mind the list of people he intended to give the ten copies to. He had submitted a list to his publisher of about everybody he had known in his life who was remotely literate, supposedly for review copies, but the list for the ten copies on hand was different. This list was of folks he wanted to hand a book to personally and watch their faces. Tops on his list were Jim and Jim's blushing bride, which was like bagging two birds with one book.

Ralph began turning over in his mind what he would inscribe in the book he intended to give Lindsay and Jim that very afternoon. He would sign the book in front of them, with a flourish, as though whatever he made up to inscribe had come to him in a brilliant flash, today when the four of them were supposed to get together for the first time, to break the old ice. They were to tie up at a roadhouse in the hills west of Palo Alto. If things went smoothly, Ralph and Alice Ann planned to invite Lindsay and Jim back to their place to celebrate the book with several bottles of chilled Mumm's and the costly cuisine Alice Ann had slaved over the previous night. Ralph planned to give Jim's blushing bride a grand tour of the refurbished homestead, pointing out the new drapes and rugs, the posters, prints, the flowering plants, the lamps, and, most of all, that pyramid of glossy, glorious white tickets to sail into the future, his own personal *booking* for posterity.

2

In the living room Ralph used the nozzle attachment to get at the mounds of cat hairs between the couch cushions. He thought he heard the phone ring, and stopped and listened, and then switched off the vacuum. Ralph lit a cigarette and headed for the kitchen to freshen his drink. When he turned into the hallway, Ralph saw a man standing in the open back doorway. The man was a shadow against the bright light, and through the sheen on the screen door Ralph could not see his features.

Ralph could see a dark sedan parked in the driveway behind the man. Ralph stood there at the far end of the hallway, which was partially in shadow. Ralph held his breath and took a step backward.

Hello there, the man called out. —I rang the doorbell, but I didn't hear any response. I thought perhaps it was not functioning properly.

Yes, Ralph said. —Uh, yes?

The man stepped back and looked from a notebook he carried to the address numbers above the door.

This is 1422, is it not? You have a number missing. Your second 2 is missing. But this is 1422, am I correct?

The 2 fell off, Ralph said. —During a storm. I've asked my teenage son a dozen times to nail that number back on. Kids. What is it you want?

So, good, 1422 then, the man said, and closed his notebook.

Yes, Ralph said. —Yes, but nobody is home. I mean, my wife is not at home at this time. My wife is the one who handles these matters.

What matters?

Matters, Ralph said, and waved a hand vaguely. —Whatever.

Actually, I am interested in speaking with a Mr. Ralph Crawford of 1422 Wightman Street.

Who? Ralph said.

Is that you, Mr. Crawford?

What is it you said you wanted? I'm afraid we really don't need anything today. Maybe if you would like to speak with my wife later.

You are Mr. Crawford, then?

Perhaps you could leave a, you know, card.

I think I recognize you now, Mr. Crawford.

What is that?

Yes, indeedy. I heard you read from your work once, Mr. Crawford. At Foothill College. Just last June, as a matter of fact. My mother accompanied me that evening. It was a splendid reading, Mr. Crawford.

Oh, Ralph said. —Oh. Well. Yes. Yes.

Ralph hurried down the hallway to open the screen door.

Why, it is you, Mr. Crawford, the man said, and smiled. —I couldn't be certain with that screen door between us. But now I see that it is you in the flesh. Just imagine. Here I am face-to-face with you, Mr. Crawford. An American author to whom I owe so much. It was your voice that gave you away. Yes, your speaking voice is so very like your reading voice, Mr. Crawford. That is not always the case, you know. And more's the pity, if you ask me.

Well, yes, Ralph said. —Yes. How are you today? I didn't hear you drive up. I was . . . well, I was busy.

Were you composing, Mr. Crawford? I would hate to think I intruded while your creative juices were flowing.

I was just taking a breather. From, uh, yes, composing. I was running something. But I'm afraid my breather is just about over, however. I'll have to be getting back there shortly. To my composing, I mean.

I have attempted on occasion to evoke the muse myself, the man said. He wiped several strands of graying hair from his damp forehead with the tips of his fingers, a gesture Ralph found strangely graceful. He was a short, bulky man who wore a rumpled plaid sportcoat and a red knit tie. —Poetry mostly, the man said. —And that is where you come in, Mr. Crawford. Your work has been an inspiration to me. The way you write about such ordinary people simply going about the business of their ordinary lives. You make it seem so simple. As though simply anybody could do it. But of course they cannot, can they? I can't, for one. Yes, I have reconciled myself to my lack of expressive gifts. My real life will have to remain forever buried, I suppose. Unlike you, Mr. Crawford.

Yes. Yes, Ralph said, and chuckled. —Yes. Well, thank you very much for your kind words. Really, you are too kind.

Do you draw from your own life experiences when you write, Mr. Crawford? the man asked. —The characters in your stories, their desperation, their drinking, the unfaithfulness, the low moral standards, do you know many such people?

Not at all, Ralph said. —They're not people I know. A lot of the characters I write about, most of them really, I make up from scratch. And most of them, well, all of them probably, I wouldn't give the time of day in real life. Well, what can I say? I can't tell you how pleased I am you enjoy my work. You've made my day. Really. You've made me happy as a clam. Well. Well, well, I hate to cut this short, but I'm a very busy man, you understand. Just how can I help you?

I am very sorry, Mr. Crawford, but I have been remiss. I am Mr. Bell. Aubrey Bell, the man said, and took a wallet from his coat pocket. The man opened it to show Ralph a plastic-encased identification card with his picture on it.

That's you, all right, Ralph said, bending to study the picture.

Actually, it is not a very good likeness. My mother says that I have always taken a poor photograph. My weight fluctuates so dramatically, for one thing, Aubrey Bell said, and chuckled. —Mr. Crawford, to get down to cases, I am an investigator from the county prosecuting attorney's office. I need to ask you a few questions concerning a matter. Our office sent you three letters concerning this, but upon receiving no reply, well, here I am.

I've been away, Ralph said. —Out of town. For weeks. I was out of the country.

The letters were certified, Mr. Crawford.

It's a mystery to me, Ralph said. —Maybe my wife knows something about this. Maybe she signed for them and just forgot to tell me. I don't know. I don't know a thing about this.

I understand. Well, at least this little mix-up permitted us to meet in person, Mr. Crawford. Indeed, I asked for this assignment in hopes that you were *the* Ralph Crawford whose work I so admire. At any rate, I have to ask you a few questions about this matter. May I come in, please?

Questions? Ralph said. —What sort of questions? This really is a bad time for me, Mr. Ball.

Mr. *Bell.*

Mr. Bell.

Mr. Crawford, there is some confusion in our records. I am confident you can clear this little matter up quite easily. If I could please come in.

My wife will be home in a couple of hours, Ralph said. —She's the one in this family who takes care of these matters.

Mr. Crawford, according to our records, it appears that for a period of several months while you were being issued paychecks from the University of California at Berkeley, you were also collecting unemployment benefits.

What? That couldn't be! There must be some horrible mistake, Ralph said. —Some computer error. Something like that. A foul-up somewhere in the system. This whole matter is a mystery to me.

That is precisely the reason I am here, Mr. Crawford. To clear this little matter up as quickly as possible. If I may come in, we will get to the bottom of this mix-up in no time at all.

You know what, Ralph said, and scratched his head, it's not impossible I could have made some sort of silly mistake myself. That's not out of the realm of possibility. I'll admit it. I'm pretty ignorant when it comes to things like money matters. Financial affairs aren't my strongest suit. I've never had a head for, you know, numbers. My wife handles all the number business in our family. I'm always busy, uh, composing, as it were. My art takes all my attention. And as I said, I've been away for weeks. And things around this household, through no fault of my own, have gone to the dogs. My father has been ill also. That's why I was away for so long. I had to be on hand to handle matters. For my mother, you understand. Then Daddy died. My mother just fell apart. She hasn't been herself anyway for a long time. Her eyesight is failing, you know. Mom will be legally blind in a matter of weeks.

What painful news, Mr. Crawford! Aubrey Bell exclaimed, and threw up his hands. —What misfortune.

I don't know where I'm going to turn next, Ralph said.

I truly understand how confusing the world can become. Especially for an artist such as yourself, Mr. Crawford.

To me, Ralph said, my art is all. After my blind mother, of course.

There were benefactors for artists in bygone times, Aubrey Bell told Ralph. —Rilke lived in one castle after another, all of his adult life. Benefactors. Rilke seldom rode in motorcars. He preferred trains.

I've driven nothing but clunkers all my life, Ralph said. —Breakdowns on the highway are a routine part of my life.

Then look at Voltaire at Cirey with Madame du Châtelet, Aubrey Bell said. —His death mask. Such serenity, Aubrey Bell said, and raised his hands as though Ralph were about to disagree. —No, no, it isn't right, is it? Don't say it. But then, who knows. But one wonders if those great artists of bygone days, if they had lived in our own times without benefactors, would they have resorted to illegal means to secure funds in order to continue their work. Would Rilke, or Voltaire, for that matter, have risked going to jail, such as you may have, Mr. Crawford, for the sake of their art?

Sisters from a Past Life

1

On that day they were supposed to break the ice with Ralph and Alice Ann, Lindsay was nervous. Jim had never seen her so wired. He had packed a fancy picnic lunch, and they had driven two hours south down the coastal Great Highway to Pomponio Beach, where Jim figured they could hang out, wade in the surf maybe, maybe explore some of the cliffside caves, just relax before they drove on over the hills to tie up with Ralph and Alice Ann at the Alpine Inn. It was a chilly, drizzly day, though, and then when they were walking along the beach hunting for a spot to spread their blanket, it had started to really pour, so they made a run for a cave at the bottom of the cliffs.

Jim found some dry driftwood stored back in the cave and built a little fire at the mouth. He and Lindsay had cuddled up together and gazed out at the rain sweeping in off the ocean and the waves flopping in from China. They smoked some dope and passed a bottle of wine, and Lindsay began to calm down. Jim held her close to him, and rubbed her goose-bumpy, bare arms. Strands of her long hair kept blowing into his mouth, where he held them between his lips. They started to neck, kissing long and deep, and then the next thing Jim knew they were back deeper in the cave making love. When the rain let up, they walked on down the beach, where they came upon a really bad omen in Lindsay's book, the half-eaten body of a sea lion.

2

In the gravel parking lot of the Alpine Inn, a roadhouse on a thread of blacktop lined with peeling eucalyptus trees in the foothills west of Palo Alto, Lindsay and Jim sat sipping the last of the Chablis and listening to the Cutlass tick. The Alpine Inn looked like the stagecoach stop it had once been, a one-story, low-slung, wood-frame affair, its parking lot packed with fashionably funky BMWs, one maroon Mercedes, at least a dozen Harleys, several hippie vans, Volkswagen Bugs, countless tenspeed touring bikes chained in racks where once horses might have been hitched, and, beside their ticking Cutlass, Ralph and Alice Ann's ancient red Cadillac convertible.

Jim held the bottle up and gently shook it, then he offered it to Lindsay.

I've had enough, Lindsay said. —My tummy is jumpy enough already.

Down the old hatch, Jim said, and killed the bottle off. —Well, let's head on in and get it over with.

Let me smoke a cigarette, Lindsay said, and opened her purse.

Alice Ann is going to be nervous, too, you know, Jim told Lindsay, who was smoking and studying her split ends intently.

Somehow that is not particularly reassuring.

And poor old fucken Ralph is probably chewing his paws off. You know, if it gets down to it, I reckon you could probably take old Alice Ann. Watch out for her sneaky right cross, though.

Thanks for the fucking tip, asshole. Jim, do you love me?

A bushel and a peck.

I want to hear you say it.

I love you. Let me count the ways. Why don't we just go on in and get this show on the road?

Lindsay took hold of Jim's hand as they walked through the dim, low room packed with bikers playing clanging pinball machines. A big color television set blared a boxing match from above the bar. The air was thick with the smell of frying hamburgers and onions and old boards sour with a century of spilled beer. Just at the back screen door Lindsay suddenly chirped that she was sorry and she ducked into the women's restroom.

Lindsay sat down on the single commode's seat and held her face in her hands. She couldn't help but think about the last time she had been in this joint, that time with Ralph. When somebody tried the door, Lindsay about jumped out of her skin. She sniffed her underarms, which were swampy with sweat, and then unrolled fistfuls of toilet paper and tried to pat her underarms dry, whereupon she simply stuffed the wet wads of paper under her arms and held them there. She squinted at her reflection in the sliver of mirror above the cruddy sink, and then tried to smudge powder from her compact onto her sweating, flushed face. Lindsay thought she looked awful. Plus she was getting a pimple on her chin. Somebody knocked on the door. Wet bits of toilet paper stuck to Lindsay's armpits, and she tried to scrape her stinging flesh clean with her fingernails. Suddenly Lindsay realized that the crotch of her jeans felt wet. Jesus. Could it be her period? And that she was not pregnant, after all. Lindsay jerked her jeans down. Sweat, simply cascading sweat. Soaking with it. Then she still could be. After all. Lindsay unrolled more toilet paper and padded her panties. Somebody knocked at the door again. They knocked again. Lindsay lit a cigarette and opened the door just as Jim was about to knock again.

We're late, Jim said.

You asshole.

I don't like to make people wait on me.

My, my, aren't you the considerate dickhead.

Just fucken relax, will you.

They spotted Ralph and Alice Ann sitting far across the wide yard at a picnic table in the shade of a redwood near the creek bank in back. Lindsay saw immediately that it was the very same table she and Ralph had eaten at that evening in another lifetime. Lindsay and Ralph had sat at that same table in the shade and gorged on greasy burgers and then licked one another's fingers clean.

Jim and Lindsay wove their way across the yard among picnic tables packed with people. Barefoot children charged about in the dust, and along the creek bank barking dogs played chase. Rock-and-roll blared from speakers arranged in the trees. The bee-thick air smelled of sweat and suntan oil and fried onions. In the flushed, shifting light flies sparkled like fluttering specks of tinsel above oil-drum trash barrels. Mottled sunlight and shadow moved softly over Alice Ann's long, shining blond hair. Alice Ann looked up and saw Jim and Lindsay approaching. There was no expression on Alice Ann's long, lovely face.

Lindsay choked on a final huge inhale of her pinch of a cigarette. She began to cough violently. Patting her back, Jim led Lindsay across the yard of rubbernecking idiots to Ralph and Alice Ann's table and helped her sit. Tears streamed down Lindsay's face as she coughed like a consumptive.

Try this, hon, Alice Ann said, and offered a plastic cup.

Lindsay smiled a sappy thank you through her tears. When she gulped the warm, watery bourbon-and-Coke Lindsay knew she was a goner. Lindsay jumped up and staggered toward the creek bank. The redwood she braced herself against seemed to jerk away in a huff. Several children gathered about in time to observe Lindsay's lunch depart her system in a great green flood, which was in moments covered with a fist of flies. Joyous dogs bounded about barking. More curious, giggling children crowded about to point at the barfing lady and hoot. Lindsay felt an arm wrap around her shoulders and squeeze gently, and through her tears she saw that it was Alice Ann's.

3

Wonder what's happened to our wives, Ralph said. —We did have some wives here with us, didn't we?

They're probably inside making dates with bikers, Jim said.

Don't even say such a thing, Ralph said, and glanced toward the roadhouse. —Have you ever seen so many bikers in one place? I'll admit it, bikers give me the willies.

So, old Ralph, is Lindsay a sight for sore eyes?

Why, sure she is, old Jim. Sure. You know that. Lindsay is a wonderful lady. Wonderful. I hold her in the highest regard.

Lindsay was a little worried that things will be awkward. And I guess they did get off to a sort of barfy beginning. But I'm sure things will settle down and be cool. Has Alice Ann been cool about this little rendezvous, or can I look forward to her taking a swing at Lindsay at some point?

Sure, cool, Ralph said, so to speak. Sure, why not? Water over the old dam, and all that. You know. Where in the world do you think they are, old Jim?

Don't sweat it, Ralph. The wives are returning bikerless.

As they walked across the yard toward the table, Alice Ann had her arm around Lindsay's shoulders, and they sat down side by side on the bench, forcing Ralph to move around grumbling to Jim's side. Lindsay was pale and wearing her darkest shades. Jim got up and came around to stand behind Lindsay and rub her neck.

Are you going to pull through, kid? Jim said.

I'm in God's hands, Lindsay said, and then to Alice Ann said, Thank you again for the help. Really. I am simply mortified, of course.

You folks sure were gone a long time, Ralph said. —We were talking search party.

Speak for yourself, Jim said.

We're big girls, Alice Ann said. —We were getting acquainted. Now we are fast friends.

Get! Get! Jim growled as he kicked at several dogs sniffing about the table. —You too! Get the hell out of here! Jim barked at several bareback boys standing nearby staring at Lindsay. The kids scattered, and a big hippie with hair to his waist sitting at the next table requested that Jim be cool, brother. Whereupon Jim inquired about the depth of the hippie's desire to suck soup until his teeth grew back in. The hippie turned away.

The rhinestone redneck rears his hoary head, Lindsay said.

You exhibit very strange karma, Jim, Alice Ann said.

You got it, Jim said. —The strange-karma kid. Well, let us start this whole hello business over again. Alice Ann, kiddo, you look great as always. Wonderful, in fact. Ralph, you look like you're on a diet of dog shit. Alice Ann, please formally meet my blushing bride, the legendary but rather green-around-the-gills Lindsay. And, Lindsay, please formally meet the lovely Alice Ann Crawford, who deserves all our utmost respect and pity for that heavy burden she has assumed in this life, namely that pitiful old rugged cross called Ralph Crawford.

Oh, stuff it, Stark, Lindsay said, and took her compact out of her purse and looked into its mirror. —God, the damage done. I didn't repair very well, did I?

You look fine to me, babe, Jim said, and squeezed Lindsay's shoulders. —Look, I'm just dicking around. But it's all Ralph's fault as usual. He got me in a mood. He said you all were inside flirting with bikers.

I never! Ralph said.

You look beautiful, hon, Alice Ann said to Lindsay.

You look great, Ralph said to Lindsay. —You're a sight for sore eyes. Really.

It's good to see you, too, Ralph, Lindsay said.

Is Ralph a sight for sore eyes, too? Jim said.

As a matter of fact, he is, Lindsay said.

Everybody is in agreement, then, Jim said. —Everybody is a sight for sore eyes.

Why don't you guys go get us some Cokes or something, Alice Ann said. —Or maybe some cold beer. What would go good on your stomach, hon? Alice Ann asked Lindsay.

Hemlock, Lindsay said, and rolled her eyes.

Go on, you guys, get us come Cokes for mix, Alice Ann said, and shooed her hand at Jim and Ralph. —Get some french fries, too, Ralph.

I've got some Coke left in here, Ralph said, and jiggled his plastic cup.

Ralph, that's fifty percent cheap bourbon not fit for human

consumption, Alice Ann said. —And the rest is warm spit. Why don't you just go on and get us some Cokes and fries. I think Ralph is afraid for us to be alone together, Alice Ann said to Lindsay.

Oh, where do you get off? Ralph said.

And Jim is just afraid he'll miss something juicy, Lindsay said.

Hey, I'm just an innocent bystander around here, Jim said.

Oh really? Alice Ann said.

Come on, old Ralph, Jim said. —We're not appreciated around here. Let us just step and fetch it.

Why do we both have to go? Ralph said.

Give me a fucken hand, will you, Ralph? Jim said.

Go on, Ralph, Alice Ann said.

Ralph got up mumbling and followed Jim across the yard toward the roadhouse.

4

Alice Ann lit a cigarette. She handed it to Lindsay and lit another for herself. She blew long streams of smoke through her nose.

Thanks, Lindsay said.

I thought I was prepared for any way you turned out to be, Alice Ann said.

I take it you didn't exactly expect me to be so utterly collapsed, Lindsay said.

Well, no, Alice Ann said, and laughed. —I had you pictured as being très cool and oh so elegant.

Until I tossed my cookies into the creek?

Listen, hon, the très inelegant horror stories I could tell you.

Somehow I suspect we have had similar disastrous episodes in our life experiences, Lindsay said, and took off her sunglasses. She blinked her right eye rapidly. —Now I've lost a goddamn contact.

How did you have me visualized? Alice Ann said, and rolled the end of a long blond strand of hair around a finger. —Find it?

No, damn it, anyway. I hate when this happens.

Here, let me look, hon, Alice Ann said, and leaned toward Lindsay.

I can feel the damn thing, Lindsay said. Here. Here it is.

You found it? You have such beautiful eyes.

It was just stuck in a corner, Lindsay said. She tilted her head forward and popped the contact onto a finger. She put the contact into her mouth and moved it about with her tongue, whereupon she placed it back in her eye and blinked.

Do you ever get eye infections? Alice Ann said.

I know, Lindsay said, blinking her eye rapidly. —Jim tells me all the time how germ-infested the human mouth is supposed to be. But screw it. It's my eye and my big mouth and my germs. I've seen pictures of you. You're even more lovely than your pictures.

Did Ralph show them to you? The pictures.

In a way. What I mean to say . . . Well, they're the ones he carries in his wallet. Well, I guess I did show them to me. He was always so proud of how pretty you are. And he was always so proud of the kids. They're such good-looking kids. What I mean to say is that when I really looked and looked at them one time, Ralph was asleep. I was looking in his wallet for a, for a stamp. Oh, like hell I was. I was snooping, plain and simple. I wanted to look at your picture some more, and the kids' pictures.

That's the way I found your letters to Ralph. The old art of snooping.

Suddenly I feel mortified again.

Don't, hon. I don't want you to. That's not why I said that. Am I what you expected?

I didn't know what to expect, frankly. Ralph always spoke so warmly about you. And the kids. But I didn't know what to expect.

Ralph told you I had cancer, didn't he?

I think that was a horrible misunderstanding on my part. I always thought that under different circumstances you and I would probably be friends. I knew that I would like you. I was sure of that, anyway.

Thank you, hon, Alice Ann said, and patted Lindsay's hand. —I like you, too. You are a kind person. I could tell that much from your letters. Kindness is what I value above everything else in a person. Besides honesty.

I value kindness also. And honesty.

This is so corny, Alice Ann said, but I feel as though I have known you for a very long time.

Well, let's just be corny, then. Absolutely. This is so far from what I thought today might be like. Jim kept telling me not to worry, but he was also sort of setting me up.

Those assholes, Alice Ann said, and stubbed out her cigarette.

You have a point about that.

I never saw a picture of you, Alice Ann said. —I searched high and low, let me tell you. I turned over every one of Ralph's little secret rocks. We *are* going to be fast friends, I can tell. We're going to be more than fast friends.

I hope so, Lindsay said. —I would truly like that.

It is going to happen, Alice Ann said. —I can feel it. The vibrations between us are so positive. I'm never wrong about these things. I have a gift. A sixth sense. Call it what you will. And I know you and Jim will work out in the end.

God, I should hope so.

You will. Really. You will find happiness together. Happiness like Ralph and I have found together. Oh, we've had our rough spots, as you well know. But we have always come through the fire together. Adversity has just made our love grow stronger. We keep growing together. We have new realizations about each other daily. Ralph knows how much he needs me. He depends on me, Alice Ann said, and picked up the copy of Ralph's book beside her on the bench. She thumbed through the pages and then read from the dedication page: "This book is lovingly dedicated to my wife, Alice Ann."

That's lovely, Lindsay said. —And the book looks wonderful.

Ralph owes this book to me, Alice Ann said, looking up to watch Ralph and Jim coming toward them. —And he knows it.

5

The book doesn't look half bad, Jim said, and turned Ralph's white-jacketed book about in his hands. —Except for the photo.

What's wrong with the photo? Ralph said. —Alice Ann says it makes me look ten years younger.

Ten years younger than what? Jim said. —It's pitiful.

It is not, Lindsay said, and took the book from Jim's hands. —It's a beautiful book, Ralph. And you do look younger in your picture. You look distinguished, too. Younger and distinguished.

Really? Ralph said. —Do you really think so? You know, they did do a good job, didn't they? I think the photo is okay, too, no matter what Mr. Spoilsport says.

I still say it's a pitiful picture, Jim said.

Oh, Jim, Lindsay said. —It's a beautiful book, Ralph. This is so exciting. I'm genuinely excited for you guys.

Who took that pitiful picture, anyway, Ralph? Jim said. —You should get your money back.

Hey, old Jim, Ralph said, and pointed to the book in Lindsay's hands. —Read the blurbs. Read those babies and weep.

Read Cynthia Ozick's blurb, Alice Ann said. —It's the one about Ralph being rock hard and unafraid.

Say what? Jim said.

Rock hard and unafraid, Ralph said, and laughed. He covered his mouth with a huge hand and his big shoulders shook.

How well do you know Cynthia Ozick, anyway? Jim said.

I've never laid eyes on the woman, Ralph said.

We went to hear her read in Iowa City once, Alice Ann said.

I don't recall that, Ralph said. —Well, maybe we did. But that woman doesn't know me from Adam.

You rushed up to meet her after the reading, Alice Ann said. —Then later at the party you gave her some stories, Ralph.

Well, she never read them. She left them on the coffee table. That's where John Leggett found them the next morning. The party was at his house. And I wasn't the only one shoving stories in her face. Half the other sharks in my writing class were there waving stories in her face like little me-me-me flags. She just left them all on the goddamn coffee table. And there were stains all over mine, which happened by chance to be on top of the pile. People were using them for coasters or something. People put cigarettes out on them, like my stories, my babies, were ashtrays. Well, that's all in the past now. That's all behind me now. Rock hard and unafraid. That's my main motto from here on out.

Let's have a toast, Lindsay said.

Hear, hear, Ralph said. Ralph glanced about and then took a pint bottle of bourbon out of his windbreaker pocket. He glanced about again before pouring bourbon into his plastic cup.

So, who'll make it? Jim said.

Let me, Lindsay said. —Here's to Ralph Crawford, American author, and his future in literature. World literature. He is on his way now for sure. Fame and fortune loom on Ralph Crawford's horizon.

I'll drink wholeheartedly to the fortune part, Alice Ann said. —We've been poor people long enough.

Oh, for Pete's sake, Ralph said. —That poor business is ancient history. We're supposed to be celebrating around here. Let's toast the newlyweds. Let's toast happy endings. Let's toast all's well that ends well.

Jim watched Lindsay as she gazed out across the creek bed into the trees on the other side. Beyond the creek bed and trees was a sloping meadow where in the hazy late-afternoon light several horses grazed.

Hey, kids, why don't we go back to our house? Alice Ann said. —I could throw something together back there. Okay, to tell the truth, I busted my buns last night preparing all these fancy tidbits in case you guys came home with us.

Boy, that's the truth, Ralph said, and hooted. —I spent the day under threat of death if I so much as touched one of those tasty morsels. She even threatened the boy, that human garbage disposal, which was a first, I'll tell you.

Well, we're not waiting on me, Jim said.

We'll have to stop and get some booze, Alice Ann said. —Lindsay, you can ride with me, hon. We'll stop and pick up some vodka. Vodka is your poison, isn't it?

Oh, I've been known to drink a little vodka on occasion.

See, I told you. Vibrations. When I was a little girl I could foretell the future. I still can sometimes. I'll read your palm for you tonight, hon. Maybe we'll even break out the tarot cards and I'll tell you anything you want to know about your life and future.

We have champagne coming out of our ears at home, Ralph said. —We don't need to stop anywhere.

We don't have any vodka, Alice Ann said. —Lindsay and I will take the Caddy. We'll stop and get a nice bottle of vodka.

Why do we have to split up like this, anyway? Ralph said.

We're not spitting up, Ralph. Lindsay and I are simply going in our vehicle. You ride with Jim.

Why can't I ride with you two? Ralph said.

Thanks, dickhead, Jim said. —What am I, anyway, dogshit in the companion department?

You may find this difficult to comprehend, Ralph, Alice Ann said, and took Lindsay's hand in her own. —But Lindsay and I have become dear, dear friends in just this short time. Our vibrations are totally attuned. The only explanation is that we have met in other lifetimes. I mean it, Alice Ann said to Lindsay, and squeezed her hand. —You are the best friend I've made in ten years at least. God, I feel as though in some past lifetime we must have been sisters, Alice Ann said, and then she kissed the back of Lindsay's hand.

White Meat

1

Ralph Crawford's house could have been a ship afire for all the lights blazing from it when Jim Stark pulled into the driveway. And then Jim had to brake the Cutlass abruptly, tossing Ralph into the dashboard, when suddenly in the headlights loomed what could have been the world's largest wolf.

Jesus motherfucken Christ! Jim commented to Ralph. —Ralph, there's a giant wolf in your driveway.

That's Killer, Ralph said.

I'll say, Jim said.

If I were you I'd turn off my headlights, Ralph said. —Headlights seem to give Killer a headache.

You bet, Jim said, and turned off the headlights. —Ralph, who the fuck is Killer? Killer is growling, Ralph.

I've been advised that Killer is cool, Ralph said.

I, for one, am not getting out of this vehicle, Ralph.

Honk your horn.

Say what?

Lay on your horn. If he's not too busy, Paco will come out and take charge of Killer.

Paco?

Paco, Ralph said. —My daughter's significant other, so to speak. Paco has all these tattoos. If Paco is not too busy, you know, not engaged in some act of sexual perversion with my daughter, he might come out and call Killer off. Otherwise you better just make yourself comfortable. Honk your horn, old Jim.

You bet, Jim said, and honked the horn. —Ralph, will honking the horn give Killer a headache?

No, I don't think so. I've come to believe that a car horn must sound like some sort of kindred howl to Killer.

What makes you believe that, Ralph?

One night I sat out here in Alice Ann's Caddy honking the horn for well over an hour, Ralph said, and he lit a cigarette. He settled back in his seat. —Maybe it was two hours. Who can tell? I was honking and honking the horn and Killer began to howl. But it somehow struck me as a happy howl. He was sort of howling along with the horn, and it seemed somehow—what?—attuned, in a primal, joyous way. Finally Killer attempted to, well, you know, sort of mate with Alice Ann's Caddy.

Jesus, Jim said, and quit honking the horn.

You might as well honk it, Ralph said. —It's our only hope, so to speak. That's Paco's Harley over there in front of the garage. There are little lakes of oil all over the driveway. I slid in one the other day. I was carrying out the garbage. There I was one moment, just a regular fellow in America going about his everyday life carrying out his everyday garbage. The next moment I was flying through the air like some cartoon character. Then I was Dagwood Bumstead sitting on his butt in a pool of oil. Hair full of coffee grounds. An orange rind hanging off an ear. A lap full of shitty kitty litter. Surrounded by a snow of used tampons. I can't really pretend to understand anything about my life, such as it is.

You ought to put your foot down around here, Jim said. —Kick a little ass.

First thing in the morning, Ralph said. —What I should probably do is just stick my pitiful foot out the window right now and get it over with. Let Killer chew it off and bury it in the back yard.

You just don't know, old Jim. Things were turning around for us. The advance money for the book, money which is ancient history now. The book. Things were looking up for a week or two. Now there's a blizzard of bad checks flying back at us. We hired this Chicano crew to shape up the yard. To beautify it, in Alice Ann's parlance. The check we wrote them bounced and now they are requesting cash in hand in return for not coming back over here and plowing up the ground with my teeth. The electricity is going to be cut off. I'm in the process of plea-bargaining with the phone company. I'd get down on my knees and send up a prayer if I knew where to aim it.

Hey, old dog, Jim said, and tapped Ralph on his shoulder. — You just had a book of groovy stories published by a hardball house. Life could be worse.

Do you really think they're groovy, old Jim?

You bet. You know I do. And, who knows, what with all those swell blurbs from your famous friends, the book might not sink out of sight in a week like most collections of short stories.

Jim, I haven't told you the whole sad story, Ralph said. —All that rubber-check business, big deal. I've hung paper all my adult life. I've lived like a pathetic caveman without electricity in my life, too. Big deal. But the mess I'm in now is a different can of worms entirely.

What can of worms is different, Ralph?

This latest bad business. This is serious city. I'm going to jail, Jim, without passing Go. That's the long and short of it.

You mean there *is* some justice in this wretched world?

Yeah, you laugh. You think I'm fooling. Well, I'm not.

Why are you going to jail without passing Go, Ralph?

Hit the horn some more, Ralph said. It's a long and sordid story. It's a pitiful story.

All your stories are somewhat pitiful, Ralph.

The neighbors don't even speak to us anymore. They close their doors in our faces. They call the sheriff on us. And who can blame them, I ask you? Sometimes this whole driveway is packed with hoods on Harleys. Revving up their monstrous machines as they shoot up heroin in broad daylight. Paco and his pals drag-race up and down the street like crazy men. This is a residential street, for God's sake! This is a tree-lined residential white-bread street. Paco and his pals give each other points for running over the neighbors' pets. They take aim at the neighborhood kids. Not that I give a rat's ass for the scumbag kids in this neighborhood.

But why are you going to jail, Ralph? Jim said, and took a paper bag from beneath the front seat. He pulled a pint of Jack Daniel's out of the paper bag and opened it. He took a half tab of windowpane acid and downed it with a long drink and hit the horn.

Those little neighborhood scumbags turn over my garbage cans. My windows stay soaped with obscene comments. Every night in this horrible neighborhood is Halloween for my house. I don't suppose I could have a drop of that, could I?

Why are you going to jail, Ralph?

I don't belong in jail, Ralph said. —It's simply a big misunderstanding. So I made a little mistake. Why make a federal case out of a little mistake, that's my question. I really could use a little nip, old Jim.

Just don't guzzle it, okay, Ralph, Jim said, and passed the pint to Ralph. —Just cut to the chase, Ralph. Why are you going to jail without passing Go?

Okay. This fellow came to my door today. He caught me off guard. I hadn't heard him drive up. He was from the prosecuting attorney's office. That's how serious it is. So all right. So I mistakenly cashed a couple of unemployment checks after I started teaching that term at Berkeley. A very human kind of error in my book. A foolish mistake on my part. I'll be the first one to admit it. But you would have thought I'd robbed a bank or something.

How many unemployment checks did you mistakenly cash while you were teaching, Ralph?

Oh, I don't know exactly. I don't remember exactly. You know me, old Jim. I don't have any head for numbers.

About how many?

Eleven.

Goodbye, Ralph.

What? What?

Adios, amigo. I'll write you from time to time.

Really? Really do you think?

Cell-block city, old Ralph.

How do you know that? You don't really know that.

Look at it like this, Ralph. You'll have plenty of time to write. When you're not out on the chain gang anyway.

Now I know better than that. Chain gangs aren't allowed in an enlightened state like California in this day and time. Are they? Anyway, it's not like I'm some sort of hardened criminal like some people I know. I've never armed myself and gone out to commit criminal acts like some people I could mention.

You're going to be singing the cell-block city blues, old Ralph. That's simply the long and short of it.

I wasn't myself. I was muddled. I'll plead that, temporary muddleness. Something. Anything. Did I tell you my old mom is going blind? News like that would muddle a lot better man than me even.

Sure, Ralph.

She'll fake it, Ralph said. —I'll get her a white cane. She'll wear dark glasses and stumble into the courtroom. That old bat owes me that much. I think I'm going to just leave the country. Flee for my life, such as it is.

The law has long arms, Ralph, Jim said, and hit the horn. —Pass the bottle, Ralph.

I'll cross borders under cover of darkness. I'll vanish off the face of the earth. I'll live and write under an assumed name. Like that mysterious B. Travis fellow, or Tavern, whatever, who disappeared into the wilds of Mexico. I'll hide out in a little Mexican fishing village. I'll disguise myself, wear a wig, if it comes to that. I'll be the mysterious fellow writing at the corner table in the smoky cantina. Wearing a wig and writing under an assumed name. Alice Ann has always wanted to get south of the border.

Pass that bottle of Jack, goddamn it, Ralph, or whatever your name is, Jim said, and hit the horn.

Killer suddenly rose up on his great hind legs and put paws the size of pillows on the hood of the car. This was not a good thing in Jim's mind, especially since the acid had kicked in faster and more fireworky than he had expected. When the Cutlass seemed to tilt forward, Jim ducked around the steering wheel and banged his head as he tried to dive under the dashboard.

What is the wolf trying to do now, Ralph? Jim inquired, rubbing the rising knot on his forehead.

I think Killer is in love, Ralph said. —With your car. But don't worry too much. It will probably pass. Killer is sort of fickle for a wolf.

Jim peeked above the dashboard. He was almost in Ralph's lap. Killer's terrible yellow eyes flashed with a look of what? desperate yearning, lust? Killer bared teeth like dripping sabers. Killer raised his huge head and howled into the night. Frothing fiercely from his cavern of a mouth, Killer arched his enormous neck forward. With a blood-red tongue the approximate size of Jim's arm, Killer licked the windshield. Like filthy soapsuds, saliva blurred the glass, and without thinking Jim clicked on the windshield wipers. There was a great howl of pain and vast annoyance, then an astonishing silence. Jim pressed both hands on the horn and held them there. Ralph clasped his hands over his ears. Porch lights flashed on from houses up and down the street. The growl that followed was unlike any sound Jim had heard in his life. It seemed to grow from something huge rising from deep under the earth. The blaring horn was a small, feathered, fluttering, hopeless thing. When the car began to rock violently, Jim clutched Ralph around his neck. Ralph's eyes bulged as he struggled for breath.

An amazingly muscular young man walked out of the kitchen door. He stood there framed in the kitchen doorway's light, a glowing cigarette dangling from the center of his dark face. He was wearing only black bikini briefs. He flicked his cigarette and snapped his fingers. Killer belly-crawled across the driveway to him. The muscular young man opened the kitchen's screen door and he and Killer disappeared inside Ralph's house.

2

Ralph opened the refrigerator door and stuck his head in, while Jim, after shooing a big orange cat off a chair, sat down at the kitchen table. Two cats were curled up asleep on the tabletop. Other cats roamed about the kitchen counters sniffing and licking stacked dirty dishes. All the various cats around the room appeared to pulse, to grow larger, then noticeably smaller with each breath. They were pulsing pussies to Jim's eyes, and a rainbow of colors. A cat whose heart Jim could see visibly beating beneath its glowing green fur jumped up on the table and sniffed at a cup half full of cold coffee with cigarette butts floating in it like little dead albino fish. A purple cat drank from a dripping faucet, its pink little tongue darting in and out. When it had satisfied its thirst, the purple cat rubbed a paw over its face and then roamed along the counter until it came upon what appeared to be a small glass pyramid in which Jim was certain he could see an egg, a carrot, a piece of celery, and what could have been a blue-green sandwich.

What's that, Ralph? Jim said.

What's what?

The contraption on the counter over there that the purple cat is licking. The little glass pyramid thing, or whatever.

That's living proof, Ralph said. —This is the final straw, I'm here to tell you. I don't believe this. Alice Ann was up until the wee hours working on some of the world's most serious snacks. In case you guys actually came over. And for what I ask you?

Living proof of what, Ralph? Jim said.

I just really don't believe it, Ralph said. He took a large oval platter from the refrigerator and placed it on the table in front of Jim. On its wide white surface were four deviled eggs, three pieces of cream cheese–stuffed celery, maybe a half dozen tidbits of this and that. —That platter was jam-packed with fancy goodies, I'm telling you. And those were, too, Ralph said, pointing to two other empty platters on the kitchen counter that colorful cats were licking. Ralph stepped to the kitchen sink and scattered the colorful cats. He took an empty bowl from the sink and waved it in the air. —As late as three o'clock this very afternoon there was a tangy blue-cheese dip in this bowl.

We can always order in pizza, Jim said, and snatched a deviled egg from under a blue cat's nose. The blue cat looked at Jim and mewed fuck you.

And you know what was in that bowl? Ralph said, and pointed to a large, flat bowl on the kitchen floor by the door to the dining room.

Tell me, please, Jim said, and grabbed another egg in the nick of time. When Jim plopped the egg into his mouth, it possessed, like the previous egg, the texture of tiny feathers which fluttered faintly going down his throat.

Steak tartare! Ralph said, and sat down heavily at the kitchen table. He took a long drink of Jack Daniel's from the bottle Jim offered him. Ralph leaned forward and looked into the cup of cold coffee and floating tiny dead fish. —This is not my cup, I'll have you know. This place was neat as a pin as late as three o'clock this afternoon, which is when we walked out the door to meet you guys.

Ralph, you have to explain the little glass contraption to me, Jim said. —I need to understand, Ralph.

You mean you haven't heard about pyramid power yet? You spent too much time in Montana, old Jim. Pyramid power is all the rage these days. Among Alice Ann and her cosmic chums, anyway. It all has to do with these divine vibrations and cosmic energy coming in from the universe. Pyramids are sort of like television antennas you see. Pyramids attract and arrange all that cosmic energy raining in from the universe. If you tap in on pyramid power, you can have a better life. Just ask Alice Ann about it.

What's inside the little glass pyramid, Ralph?

You want to know what's inside that goofy, goddamn thing? You really want to know? Food for the gods, that's what.

Why, Ralph?

Living proof that pyramid power truly works. It can preserve things forever. Why do you think those old Egyptians put their dead pharaohs in pyramids? Pyramid power! That's why. To preserve those royal stiffs throughout the ages. Yeah, just ask Alice Ann and her fruitcake friends all about it. Here's what I, for one, think of pyramid power, Ralph said, and jumped up. He rushed over to the counter and picked up the glass pyramid. He smashed the egg in the sink and then ran water and turned on the garbage disposal.

Consider that a demonstration of my personal opinion about pyramid power and its living proof, Ralph said. He picked up the blue-green sandwich and waved it at Jim. —You hungry? Here, help yourself. This bologna sandwich has only been under here a month or two! Take a bite, Jim. Be my guest. You'll love it. It'll taste like goddamn King Tut.

I think I'd prefer some pizza, Ralph, Jim said. —With pepperoni. Jim held the nearly empty pint bottle up before his leaky eyes. —We need fresh supplies pronto, Ralph.

Where are those women? Ralph said. He started to throw the blue-green sandwich into the sink, but hesitated. He paused and then put it back on the pyramid's little platform. He took an egg from the refrigerator and gently placed it upon the platform and then repositioned the glass pyramid. —No sense in getting Alice Ann all riled up, Ralph said, and then he smacked his forehead and said, Mother of God!

Ralph rushed back to the refrigerator and threw open its door. He pulled out the vegetable bins in the bottom and jumped back and smacked his forehead again. —We had four bottles of Mumm's chilling. We had to drive almost all the way to San Jose to find a liquor store foolish enough to take a check of ours. Do you know what a bottle of Mumm's goes for these days? I'll tell you what it goes for. An arm and a leg is what. Will you look at what's left, Ralph said, and brandished a single bottle in the air. He slammed the bottle onto the kitchen table, making three pink cats leap for their lives. Ralph sat down at the table heavily and held his face in his hands.

I say we pop that sucker, Jim said as he polished off the pint.

Those wives are up to something, I'm telling you, Ralph said.
—They should have been here by now. I'm telling you, they're
out fucking bikers.

Bullshit, Ralph. Not Lindsay, anyway. Satisfied brides don't
go around fucking bikers.

Come on, Ralph said. —Let's go out to my office. I've got
some bourbon stashed there. I'll get us some ice to take.

Ralph threw empty ice tray after empty ice tray against the
kitchen wall, where they crashed and clattered like castanets.

Hey, Uncle Jim, Ralph's daughter said from the doorway. She
was wearing a black Grateful Dead T-shirt with a skull and crossbones on its front, and her unshaven legs were bare. —Hey,
what's all the fucking noise out here, anyhow?

Hey, kiddo, Jim said.

Why doesn't anybody but me ever fill up the goddamn ice
trays around this house? Ralph said, and threw one final empty
ice tray against the wall.

Don't lay that trip on me, Dad, man, Ralph's daughter said.

Did you and Paco graze all the goodies your mom made? And
I want the truth about this matter!

God, Dad, man! There wasn't nothing to eat in like the whole
fucking house, man. I guess you think it would have been cool
for me and my old man to like starve or some shit, huh? Did you
bring any toilet paper, Dad, huh?

I just got toilet paper the other night. I got a family pack of
toilet paper. Charmins.

Sure, Dad. Well, like there's not any shit paper in the house
now, Ralph's daughter said, and took a handful of paper napkins
from a drawer. —And you're looking at the last of the napkins in
the fucking house, too. My asshole is so sore I can hardly sit
down, man. Did Mom pick up my tampons, Dad?

What? How would I know a thing like that?

I'm getting pretty fucking bored with sanitary napkins, if you
know what I mean, Ralph's daughter said, and waved the napkins
at Ralph.

That sort of business is between you and your mother. Leave

me out of that sort of business. What I want to know is what happened to the three bottles of expensive Mumm's we had in the refrigerator. Was that your work, too? And Paco's? We were planning on having a celebration with guests here tonight before some criminal broke and entered this house and stole us blind.

So like where is Mom, anyhow? I need those tampons, man.

They're right behind us.

So that Lindsay chick is actually coming over? Wow! Far-fucking-out. Me and Mom read her letters. So how's married life, Uncle Jim?

Far-out, Jim said.

So where's the missing Mumm's? Ralph said. —Quit trying to change the subject. I'm going to get to the bottom of this matter. I'm going to put my foot down around here for a change.

Hey, Dad, man, me and Paco will pay you back okay, so how about being cool, all right! Paco's got some bread coming, dig? Anyhow, we were celebrating a little ourselves. I got my period, man.

Here, Ralph said. —Here, he said, and handed his daughter the bottle of Mumm's.

Hey, far-out, Dad, Ralph's daughter said, and took the bottle. —Sometimes, Dad, you aren't such a big asshole. Sometimes, man, you can be a really hip dude.

As Jim and Ralph started to leave the kitchen, Ralph stopped at the stove and above it removed an oddly out-of-place print of a green pepper, revealing a hole in the wall. Ralph fit his fist into the hole. —This is my work, Ralph said. —You know, I always dreamed of owning my own home someday. I dreamed it would be a house filled with laughter and joy and serenity and music, you know, classical music, and grace. That was once my dream, old Jim. I ask you, was that such an impossible dream?

3

Ralph turned off lights as he and Jim made their way back through the house. In the game room Ralph's sister-in-law Erin's twin blond boys were roller-skating on the flagstone floor. They skated about slowly, aimlessly, the metal wheels clacking over the flagstones. The boys' jaws were slack, their wet red mouths hung open, and their unblinking blue eyes looked as though they could have been painted on those faces, which were white as mushrooms. At the room's far end a television set blared unwatched. Somebody had dialed its light deep purple and it was tuned to one of Jim's favorite religious channels out of San Jose. A purple preacher dressed in a suit of sequins was praying at the top of his lungs for dollars to fight the devil, who, it seemed, was on the verge of winning city council seats for homosexuals. Ralph and Jim stood at the sliding glass doors that led out to the back yard, and they watched the skating blond boys. The twins skated slowly about each other, weaving, circling, sometimes one seeming to lead nowhere in particular, and then the other, like reflections freed and moving in and out of an invisible mirror. Clicking a switch on the wall beside the sliding glass doors, Ralph turned off the bright overhead lights of the game room. The blond twins skated on in their solitude and oblivion, around and around, slowly, enchanted in the purple light.

Those boys never give me a moment's trouble, Ralph told Jim as he clicked another switch and they stepped through the sliding glass doors into a back yard flooded with yellow light. When they reached Ralph's office, Ralph fumbled his keys out of his pocket.

They picked my locks again! Ralph said. —I've changed locks out here ten times at least. Nothing works. Nothing keeps the little criminals out.

Ralph hurried across the dark room. He turned on a desk light and picked up a coffeepot and shook it at his ear. Ralph chuckled and then drank from the coffeepot spout.

Fooled the little bastards this time, Ralph said, and handed the coffeepot to Jim. Ralph picked up two coffee cups from the desk and tossed their contents into a wastepaper basket, then ran his fingers around the cups' rims and handed one to Jim. —Wonder what our wives are doing, Ralph said. —We were fools to get those two together, much less leave them alone together.

They seemed to hit it off, Jim said, and took a drink. —Why are you so paranoid, Ralph?

It's Alice Ann's fault, Ralph said.

How so, Ralph?

It just is, that's all. She can't lay every single thing on my doorstep, Ralph said. Ralph cocked his ear as though he had heard something, and then he tiptoed across the room and stood up on the chair by the wall. He slid the framed photograph of Hemingway aside and peeked through the tiny hole.

Anybody home? Jim stage-whispered.

Nope. She's hardly ever home these days. More's the pity. Wonder what has become of our wives, old Jim?

How did you feel when you saw Lindsay today, Ralph? Jim said, and took a drink from the cup.

Me? What do you mean?

I'm just curious, Ralph. I don't mean anything really.

I already told you. She was a sight for sore eyes. I hold Lindsay in the highest regard.

I hold Alice Ann in the highest regard, too, Ralph.

Jim, we have to go look for our wives. We've got to find them before it's too late. I'll bet there's a happy gang of bikers somewhere right now.

I just don't understand you, Ralph. Your enduring paranoia and lack of trust. So Alice Ann may have made a few slips over the course of her life. Big deal. Considering your track record, you can't hold anything against her.

Slips? What do you mean slips?

Our wives are both wonderful women, Ralph. But human beings make slips, Ralph. To err is human, right, Ralph? After all, you weren't exactly being virtuous when you were involved with Lindsay, now were you, Ralph?

I want you to tell me what you mean by slips, Jim. Jim, you owe me the truth, as you know it. Go on. Tell me. Just do it. Come out with it, Jim. What do you know about Alice Ann and slips? You know things I don't know in the slips department, don't you, Jim? Okay, let me ask you this, do you have any solid evidence, Jim? All right, just tell me the worst. Don't hold anything back. Give me both barrels of the truth, Jim. No. No. Wait a minute. If it has to do with bikers or sailors or tattooed truck drivers, just keep the truth to yourself. If it's about sordid characters and blowjobs or any other monstrous acts of love, Jim, I don't want to know, after all. Jim, you don't know what I've had to deal with. Jim, Alice Ann has a tattoo on her behind. There it is. Out in the open at last. God knows when or where she got it. I hadn't taken a really good look at Alice Ann's behind in ages, when one night when I was about half sober she climbed out of the shower and was parading around nude, and by God I saw it. There it was! I thought it was a little bruise at first. But it wasn't anything of the kind. It was a parrot. A tiny green-and-gold parrot on my wife's behind. How does a man deal with that sort of revelation, I ask you? She said she just got it on a whim once when I wasn't around for a few days and she had no idea where I was, as though that were excuse enough for such outrageous behavior on her part. But even if that much is true, think about what it means. It means that at the very best she bared her behind so that some sordid tattooed stranger could get at it with a needle. Too much, I say!

Settle down, Ralph. Listen, I don't know anything about any slips. I've been busting your chops about the slips business.

But why, old Jim? You got me all worked up, Jim.

I know, Ralph. I don't know why I treat you mean sometimes. I love you like a brother. No. I know why I'm being mean to you tonight. You've seen the naked body of my wife, Ralph. I hate that about you, Ralph.

You can't lay the blame for that on my doorstep. What difference does it make, anyway? Besides, since we're on the subject of Lindsay, a subject you brought up, do you have any idea how I felt when I heard that you had gotten involved with her? Do you have any idea of how I felt to have the lie put to so many of my hopes and dreams?

You were and are a married man, Ralph, so to speak.

I don't want to think about these things, Ralph said, and sat down heavily. —All I know is this. I'm going to set my house in order once and for all. I'm going to try, anyway. We've got an appointment with some shyster the day after tomorrow. For all the good he's going to do me. I'm not walking into that shyster's office with any illusions, I'll tell you.

You probably won't go to jail, old Ralph. Not a first offender like you. If your mouthpiece is any good, that is. And if the prosecuting shyster isn't out to make an example of you. Anyway, what's the worst you could pull? Six months maybe. A year at the outside. Eighteen months. Probably easy time at some white-collar criminal country-club farm. Hoeing in the fields. Milking some cows. And if you're lucky enough not to spend any time in a county lockup you might not even get buggered.

What? Get what?

Buggered, Ralph. You know, butt-fucked.

Butt-fucked? Me? I don't believe that for a minute! They go for boys. I'm too old. I'm a man of forty or so. I'm nearly over forty. I thought they went in for boys. Young, tender boys. Tender chickens is what they call those boys. I'd hang myself if I ever got buggered. I swear I would. I'd hang myself in my cell. With my belt. With my shoestrings, if I could manage that.

They confiscate your belt and shoestrings, Ralph.

Then I'd choke myself with my own bare hands. What's holding our wives up? That's what I'd like to know.

You see, Ralph, rape is an act of power and aggression. It doesn't really have much to do with sexual attraction or gratification. Basically, Ralph, you'll just be another piece of white meat for the brothers to shame and humiliate and cornhole.

But why me? I've always been, you know, a liberal when it comes to, you know, civil rights. I, for one, just thought the world of Martin Luther King. I read most of *Malcolm X*.

But how are the brothers going to know that? Nope, Ralph, you'll just be another white-meat avenue in old payback city.

Did you ever get buggered when you claim you did that time?

I'll tell you what I did. As soon as I hit that lockup, I found out who was supposed to be the meanest motherfucker in the joint. I took the cat on. I'm not claiming I won, but I fought him good enough that nobody ever wanted a piece of my ass.

I've had two fights in my life. And both of them were before I was ten. I lost them both. And one of them was with a girl.

I'll teach you some moves and holds. So you won't be totally defenseless. But you'll probably have to get an old man.

An old man? What old man, Jim? I don't want an old man.

Some tough brother who'll protect you for sexual favors.

Sexual favors? Never! Exactly what kind of sexual favors?

It'll be either him or an endless line of brothers or Paco's tattooed cousins. You be good to him, be his sissy, sit down when you pee, spend some quality time on your knees, and he'll be like your motherfucker in shining armor.

Never! Ralph said. —Not in a million years!

Take my advice, Ralph. As soon as you hit that cellblock, be mentally prepared, and don't try to bullshit your boyfriend or think you can outsmart him. The first thing that big motherfucker will ask you is do you want to be the momma or the poppa. And you, Ralph, thinking you're making the best of a bad situation, and that you're somehow smarter than him because you've been to college, you'll probably say you'd rather be the poppa, right, Ralph. Well, forget outsmarting him. Your boyfriend will just give you a big grin and drop his drawers and say, Okay, Poppa, you just come on over here then and suck Momma's big dick.

I think I'll just go hang myself right now, Ralph said, and put his face in his hands. —While I still have my belt. I wish those women would get here.

Ancient Eggs

Contrary to Ralph's greatest fear, Alice Ann and Lindsay had not searched the seedy bars for bikers or tattooed truckers or sailors; instead, they had remained at that roadhouse in the hills above Palo Alto drinking and telling one another all, which did, however, confirm his second-greatest fear.

I want to go ahead and say this, Alice Ann had said at one point, taking a long drag on a freshly lit cigarette. —I never really blamed you for anything that happened between you and Ralph. I know Ralph lied to you about our situation, so how could you know the truth about Ralph and me. I finally couldn't even really blame Ralph for what happened between you two either, if the truth be told. Finally I came to realize that I had only myself to blame. Ralph, well, Ralph was simply being Ralph, for one thing, and he was also trying to deal with his own pain and sense of betrayal. I'll never forgive myself for the agony I caused Ralph. We were childhood sweethearts. We were both virgins when we made love for the first time. It felt fated. I got pregnant from that very first time. We both swore we would never make love with anybody else. We were each other's everything. And neither of us did make love with anybody else. For years and years, anyway. Until I went outside the marriage. I broke Ralph's heart. So he was just getting back at me through you. In some ways maybe I deserved it. Didn't you say Ralph showed you pictures of our kids?

Yes, Lindsay said. —He did. They're handsome kids.

You've never had children, have you?

Not yet. But Jim and I are trying.

They're both just great kids. Our daughter can't decide whether to follow me into the theater or study to be a veterinarian. She loves animals. Our house is a zoo, of course, but so what is my attitude. Our son aspires to be a police officer, or an attorney-at-law maybe. Did Ralph tell you I was an actress in New York at one point?

I think he did mention it.

Off Broadway, of course. But not Off Off Broadway. One play I starred in later made it to Broadway. Actually my part was the second lead, but my notices were amazing. But I had to drop out. I had to take a job to support the family so that Ralph could write full-time. I do community theater occasionally, and of course my current job is teaching drama at a very prestigious community college. Now and then out of the blue I'll get a call from New York. Or Hollywood even. Some old friend or admirer offering me a part. Now that the kids are almost grown I may consider an offer. If only Ralph could get on his feet.

Alice Ann took Lindsay's right hand and studied its palm. She then studied her own palm as though for the first time in her life. Alice Ann took a pack of small tarot cards from her purse and began arranging them on the picnic table.

They, she and Lindsay, had been more than even sisters in other lifetimes, Alice Ann declared, staring at a card of stars. In two lifetimes they had been twins. Twice they had died in fire together, and once in water. In ancient Egypt four thousand years ago, they had been royal sisters, their mother a queen of the Nile. Alice Ann had been Lindsay's mother in one life. And Lindsay had been Alice Ann's mother more than once. In a Roman life their souls had merged. Ralph had been Lindsay's son once. And her father. And Alice Ann's father and son. And once Ralph had been their sister. It never ended, this ageless soup of seeds and ancient eggs.

In this lifetime Alice Ann had dreamed about Lindsay since childhood, Alice Ann declared, and gripped Lindsay's hand across the table. She had waited for Lindsay to come to her. She had known Lindsay was coming into her life. She had dreamed of Lindsay's childhood face. After she had met and married Ralph, Alice Ann had begun to dream dreams of Ralph holding another woman in his arms. Ralph naked, and the woman naked, and they had made passionate love in the dreams, and at first Alice Ann had been inconsolable. Until she began to realize the woman in her dreams of betrayal was her sister, her mother, daughter, was herself, who had been lost to her in this lifetime. It was as though one of Ralph's missions on earth in this lifetime had been to seek out Lindsay for Alice Ann and make them whole.

As soon as I saw you today, Alice Ann said to Lindsay, I knew who you really were. I didn't see Jim at first. He was walking behind you. But as soon as I saw you walking toward our table, I recognized your face from a thousand dreams. We are exceptional beings, you and I. We will be safe in this lifetime together.

I hope that means we won't be burned at the stake again anytime soon, Lindsay said, and stubbed out her cigarette.

We have one another now. We will be safe now.

And we won't go down with any ships at sea again, will we?

We are both due long, good lifetimes. Our lifelines about wrap around our fucking hands, see.

Now there's a comfort.

Ralph told me that when you two made love he would come to a point he thought, or rather, he made himself imagine he was fucking us both.

Hon, Lindsay said, and drained her glass of beer, don't you think we should be going? The boys will be pissed. Jim is so anal about time.

I knew every time you two made love, Alice Ann said, and lit a fresh cigarette. —I could always tell. I would get these strange vibes. Every time Ralph comes, he pictures my face. He can't help it, he just does it automatically. Ralph can be a thousand miles away and having a wet dream, and if he comes, I can feel it. I can feel his eyes, even in his dreams, on my face. And it's as though I can feel his hot seed shoot up inside my body. Every time Ralph even masturbates, and believe me Ralph jerks off like a monkey, I know it. Ralph and I are thinking about having another child. Before it's too late for us.

I think that's simply wonderful, Alice Ann, Lindsay said. —I think I may be pregnant.

This may sound bananas, Alice Ann said, and laughed, throwing her head back and shaking out her long blond hair, but I ordered this kit, this wild kit. Ralph thinks it's bananas, of course. But Ralph thinks that just about every goddamn thing I do is nuts. He wants to keep me under lock and key. I'm always trying new things. I'm always trying to broaden my horizons. That is the only way one can grow as a human being. But not our Ralph. Ralph is terrified of change. Show Ralph something new and he turns tail. Ralph is gone like a shot. But anyway, I've ordered this sort of kit. It's for a, well, tent. Or more like a canopy. To put over our bed. You assemble it, you know, then install it, rig it up, whatever, over your bed. And the wild, wonderful thing is that it's in the shape of a pyramid. Isn't that wild? I don't think it's bananas at all. Ralph will shit a brick. And they are really quite lovely. They come in all these lovely colors, and the fabric part is pure silk from the Orient. They're really sort of what you could call designer pyramids. But the important part about all this is the pyramid shape. It creates a force field. This is a scientific fact. It has been proven by scientists more advanced in their thinking and fully documented. The pyramid shape is a mysterious and magical force. It can preserve things, for one thing. I mean, look at the goddamn mummies, for God's sake. It can revitalize things, too, which to me is the most important consideration. People who sleep under these pyramids make the most amazing claims. Bald men grow new hair suddenly. Wrinkles disappear overnight. And talk about pyramid passion! Couples who haven't had the urge in years start screwing like rabbits. Not that Ralph and I need any help in that department. But the most important thing is what it can do for fertility. They have accumulated scientific evidence to prove that sleeping under a pyramid can cause a woman to double, even triple, her chances of conception. And it can increase a man's sperm count by a billion or more. An extra billion of those little buggers! Can you imagine! Anybody can make babies. There was a report of a sixty-seven-year-old woman who became pregnant for the first time in her life. And believe me, she wasn't even trying. But I will be trying. I will be trying with all my heart and soul.

All Wet

1

Where had Ralph and Jim not searched high and low for their errant wives, driving bar to bar up and down El Camino Real, passing a fresh pint of Jack Daniel's, Jim chain-lighting joints. They toured the dives on Whiskey Gulch in Palo Alto's east end, a low-down area which according to Ralph Alice Ann had been known to haunt. The hot, humid air smelled like chicken frying; traffic from the nearby Bayshore Freeway sounded like heavy rain over a huge body of water. Country music, shrieking laughter, rebel yells poured out of the cowboy and biker bars' open doorways, where evil-eyed hombres lurked impassively as Ralph and Jim lumbered along bar to bar.

Okay, goddamn it, anyway, where are they? Ralph asked Alice Ann the moment he and Jim found the women sitting together on a couch in the living room of Ralph and Alice Ann's house looking through a photo album.

Where are whom, may I ask? Alice Ann said.

The riffraff, Ralph said. —The greaseball bikers.

The scumbag sailors, Jim said,

You just missed them, Alice Ann said, and she lit a cigarette.

I'll bet, Ralph said. —You've probably got a tower of turds or two hidden around here someplace.

I never could fool you, Ralph, could I? Alice Ann said.

Alice Ann has been giving me a tour, Ralph, Lindsay said. —I love your home.

Where were you, anyway? Ralph addressed Lindsay.

Oh, tarrying and talking, Lindsay said.

For hours? For hours? Ralph hissed. —Where have you two been? What have you two been up to? We have a right to know. We're your husbands, after all. Don't forget that.

You, Ralph, are the one around here who forgets important things, Alice Ann said.

I asked you where you two have been, Ralph said. —I demand an answer right now. And don't bother to lie. If you're thinking about telling lie one, just forget it. It won't wash around here.

I love your new lamps, Ralph, Lindsay said.

I don't think I like your tone of voice, Ralph, Alice Ann said.

My tone of voice? Ralph said. —Well, forgive me, please. Pretty please.

Ralph, we were simply chatting, Lindsay said. —We lost track of time. We had a lot to catch up on. About four thousand years' worth.

My so-called goddamn tone of voice? Ralph said. He picked up a champagne bottle from the coffee table and shook it. He tilted his head back and polished off what was left, whereupon he threw the empty bottle across the room against the brick fireplace. The bottle exploded and shattered glass showered the room. Lindsay screamed and jumped up from the couch. Ralph clutched Lindsay by an arm. —How could you? Ralph said to Lindsay through gritted teeth.

Hey, Jim said, and shoved Ralph. As Ralph turned toward him, Jim cocked his right.

Alice Ann is bleeding, Lindsay said. —A piece of bottle hit her.

From a spot at her hairline a thin stream of blood ran down the right side of Alice Ann's face. Alice Ann smiled and took a deep drag off her cigarette. The blood was forming and dripping off the point of her chin. Alice Ann flicked her cigarette ashes into a large ashtray on the coffee table.

Let me look at that, Jim said, and hurried over to Alice Ann. He pulled a handkerchief out of his back pocket and pressed it to Alice Ann's forehead.

What the fuck's going on out here? Ralph's daughter said.

She was standing in the hallway door with her hands on her hips. She was wearing a different black T-shirt with a Day-Glo devil on its front, and her unshaven legs were still bare.

This business out here is none of your affair, young lady, Ralph said to her.

Lindsay, Alice Ann said, this is my daughter in this lifetime. Honey, I'd like for you to meet Lindsay, your uncle Jim's new wife.

Hello, Lindsay said. —I understand you want to be a veterinarian.

So you're her, Ralph's daughter said. —So what's happening out here anyhow, fucking World War III or some shit? Mom, could you clue me in as to why the fuck your head is bleeding, Mom?

Or follow your mother into the theater, Lindsay said.

It's just a scratch, Jim said. —We'll just wash it up and put a Band-Aid on it.

This business is far from over, Ralph said. —I'm all worked up about this business. There has to be a limit.

I couldn't agree more, Alice Ann said. She stubbed her cigarette out in the ashtray on the coffee table and then picked the ashtray up over her head and threw it into the fireplace.

Holy moly! Jim said.

Alice Ann, honey! Lindsay said.

You think that's something, Ralph said, and picked up one of the new lamps, a heavy pottery affair shaped to resemble a Mexican peasant having a siesta, his sombrero pulled low over his droopy-mustachioed face.

You're fucking crazy, Dad, man! Ralph's daughter informed him.

Jesus, old Ralph, Jim said. —Cool it, man.

Ralph, Lindsay said. —Please.

I'm not the crazy one around here, Ralph said. —I don't know why you people can't get that straight.

Just go ahead and do it, Ralph, Alice Ann said. —We are all waiting with bated breath.

You think I won't, Ralph said.

Tick-tock, Alice Ann said.

I'm going to call the sheriff again, Ralph's daughter said. —I will, Dad. You know I will, man.

Why not? Ralph said. —Let's get everybody in on our own personal, private family dirt.

I will, Dad. I will!

Please, Ralph, Lindsay said. —Please don't, hon.

No, you won't either, young lady, Ralph said, and carefully put the lamp back down on the end table by the couch. Ralph walked over to the phone on a small table by the hall door. With a single jerk Ralph pulled the phone cord out of its wall socket.

Real cute, Dad. Ralph's daughter said.

That ends any unnecessary outgoing around here, Ralph said, and wiped his hands. —And any incoming, too, for that matter. Who needs them? That phone jumps when it rings. That phone rings only in alarm.

Ralph never finishes anything he starts, Alice Ann said. She stood up and unplugged the large matching lamp on the table at her end of the couch. Alice Ann heaved it up and swung it under-arm into the fireplace, where its smash sounded like a huge egg being cracked.

You're the cause of all this shit in the first place! Ralph's daughter screamed at Lindsay.

Lindsay flung herself from the room.

You had no call to say that, Jim said to Ralph's daughter.

Hey, man, I just call 'em like I see 'em was Ralph's daughter's reply to Jim.

2

When Jim reached Lindsay she had her huge purse on the car fender and she was searching through it frantically.

Looking for something important? Jim said, and leaned back against the car.

I intend to get the fuck out of this nuthouse, Lindsay said, and started to sob. Tears streamed down her face. —If I can ever find my fucking keys.

These guys? Jim said, and dangled the keys he took from his pocket.

Thank you, Lindsay said, and held out her hand for them. —Now let's go.

I'm not going anywhere just yet, Jim said, and closed the keys in his fist.

Would you please return my keys to me?

What's your hurry? Where do you want to go, anyway? Maybe you're exactly where you belong.

This is my car.

So?

Prick.

Cunt.

Lindsay lunged for the keys in Jim's hand, and they began to struggle, Lindsay grabbing at the keys and Jim dangling them out of her reach. Finally Lindsay fell back against a car door gasping for air.

You better quit smoking, kiddo, Jim said, and leaned back against the car also. —Ralph still loves you, you know? Is that a two-way street, Lindsay? Is that why you called him "hon"?

God, what a mistake this has all been, Lindsay said.

You said it first.

God knows I've tried to get this marriage off the ground.

You have lied to me from the first, Jim said.

I never did. You lied to me.

Not me. You must be confusing me with old rotten Ralph again.

You lied about loving me. Just give me my car keys, please.

Who do you think I love, then?

Your first wife, that's who. Why don't you just go back to her? Don't think I couldn't.

Well, do it, then. Let her finish raising you. At least you liked to fuck *her*. Just give me the keys to my car, Jim, so that I may leave this place.

You said I should consider this vehicle *our* car.

That was before.

Before what?

Before I decided to divorce you.

I hope you and Ralph have a long and happy life together.

They heard shouts from inside the house and then the sound of shattering glass. They heard something else glass being smashed, and then Ralph's daughter ran out the kitchen door.

I told them I would, was all Ralph's daughter said as she ran past Jim and Lindsay in the driveway.

Alice Ann said that she and Ralph are trying to have another child, Lindsay said.

Bullshit, Jim said. —Ralph would drown it in the toilet.

Is that what you would do?

What kind of question is that?

You have never loved me. You don't even like me much, do you? Lindsay said, and grabbed the keys from Jim's hand. Jim caught her wrist and squeezed, and Lindsay dropped the keys onto the gravel. When Jim bent down to scoop them up, Lindsay took a kick at his hand.

You bitch! Jim said, and grabbed Lindsay by the shoulders.

Is this where you strike me? Lindsay said, and lifted her chin.

I've never hit a woman in my life, Jim said, and let her go.

Well, why don't you simply think of me as merely your soon-to-be second ex-wife, if that makes it easier.

I'd never hit you. You know that.

You hit people. You hurt my wrist.

I didn't mean to.

You just don't know your own strength, is that it?

Sometimes I don't.

We have not made love in over three weeks.

I don't believe that. Anyway, you know how hard I've been working lately.

Over three weeks. It's the truth. You don't love me.

What about this morning? Jim said.

You mean our funny-fuck? Well, actually it was simply peachy-keen. But does that mean we won't make love unless there happens to be a cave nearby?

Cute, Lindsay.

Is our marriage bed too boring?

I didn't say that.

Oh, I see. So, when I get laid from now on, I'll just have to settle for getting some foreign substances like sand up my ass. That's really something to look forward to. A sex life with sand or fog up one's rear end. And one's tits turning blue.

I think I best mosey along on down the old trail now, Jim said, and opened the car door.

That is my car, Jim.

Think I'll mosey back up to Montana and try again, Jim said, and closed and locked the door.

Jim.

Thanks for the memories, ma'am, Jim said, and started the engine.

I bought that car with my own money.

Hey, I'm just borrowing it for a spell. Lighten up, ma'am.

Don't call me that.

I'll park it in front of your folks' house, ma'am, Jim said, and rolled up the window. —Happy trails to you, ma'am, Jim mouthed silently through the window.

I'm the one who is really from Montana, Lindsay said, and got down on her knees in the driveway. Lindsay rolled onto her back and scooted with some difficulty partway under the car. Jim turned the engine off and got out of the car. He knelt down beside where Lindsay's legs stuck out.

Okay, Jim said. —Game's over. Time out. Everybody's in free. Everybody's home free.

I am quite happy where I am, thank you.

I'm not going anywhere without you, kiddo.

I don't trust you any longer.

So how long do you plan to stay under there?

Who knows. Who cares.

You'll have to speak up. I can hardly hear you under there.

It doesn't matter.

What?

Nothing matters.

What about all the spiders and bugs under there? Creepy-crawlies getting in your hair.

I don't care.

The sheriff is on his way, Jim said, and took Lindsay's foot in his hand. He slipped the sandal off and examined the fine blue veins so near the surface of her skin. —You could find yourself under arrest in a matter of minutes.

For what, may I ask? Please let go of my foot.

I'm not hurting your foot. I like your foot. I love your foot. You have beautiful foots. There are plenty of laws against acting drunk and dopey in public and giving the nosy neighbors an eyeful.

It is not illegal to lie peacefully under one's own bought-and-paid-for automobile.

You could get arrested for being a bad public joke.

I would consider it protective custody.

Okeydokey, Jim said, and stood up.

No man has ever really loved me. My own father didn't really love me.

Say what?

In my whole life. Men just like to fuck me.

What was that? Jim said. —About getting fucked.

Never mind.

I couldn't hear what you said exactly. What did you say exactly about getting fucked?

I said to fucking forget it.

Okeydokey, Jim said. Jim strolled over and picked up a hose coiled at the edge of the driveway by the house. He turned the water on at the spigot.

Last chance to behave like a reasonable adult, Jim said.

I said for you to just fucking forget it.

Okeydokey, Jim said, and adjusted the hose's nozzle to fine spray.

3

Ralph was sitting at the kitchen table examining what appeared to be a blue-green sandwich in his hands and Alice Ann was sweeping glass shards into a dustpan when Jim came in the kitchen door.

There you are, Alice Ann said. —What do you like on your pizza?

You like anchovies, don't you? Ralph said.

Sure, I like anchovies, Jim said.

What does your wife like on her pizza? Alice Ann said. She emptied the dustpan full of broken glass into a garbage pail under the sink. The little pyramid's bent, glassless frame sat in the middle of the kitchen table.

Jesus, but I'm hungry as an old goat, Ralph said. He turned the blue-green sandwich about in his hands, studying it intently. —Let's get at least one of those pizzas with the works.

How are you guys? Jim said. He pointed at the Band-Aid on Alice Ann's forehead.

Ralphie Nightingale nursed Momma back to health, Alice Ann said, and smiled, and she touched the Band-Aid with her fingertips.

I could have been a brain surgeon, Ralph said, chuckling, his big, round shoulders shaking.

He even gave the little hurt a little kiss-kiss, Alice Ann said. —A healing lick, lick. Ralph's got saliva like a dog's.

You betcha, Ralph said, and sniffed the sandwich.

So everything's cool? Jim said.

You betcha, Ralph said. —Water over the dam. Let's get moving on this pizza-pie business. What does Lindsay like?

Where's your wife? Alice Ann said. She sat down at the kitchen table and began looking through a small wicker basket of envelopes and clippings. —I've got a coupon somewhere in this mess for two dollars off a king-size pizza. Where's your wife?

She's pouting, Jim said. —She's all wet, so to speak.

I've never been so hungry in my life, Ralph said. He licked at the blue-green sandwich in his hand.

How are you going to phone for pizza without a phone? Jim said.

We have phones coming out our ears around this house, Ralph said. —In the bedroom. In our daughter's room. In the boy's room. We've got more phones than you can shake a stick at around here. Our daughter could have used a phone here to call the sheriff. Our drama-queen daughter just likes to run out into the night for effect. Beating on a neighbor's door in the middle of the night to use the phone is just a lot more dramatic and satisfying and humiliating for her parents.

So what happens when the sheriff shows up? Jim said.

We'll offer him a piece of pizza like always, Ralph said. —Don't forget, Alice Ann, he likes mushrooms on his.

Now where did I put those damn coupons? Alice Ann said.

In the first place, Ralph said, I seriously doubt that any of the neighbors will open their doors to our daughter. In the second place, the sheriff didn't even bother to come out the last time, and the time before that, he was two hours getting here. You can't count on anybody these days.

Here they are, Alice Ann said. —But they're only for a dollar off each pizza.

Who cares, Ralph said. —Somebody get on the horn.

Oh, Alice Ann said, but if you get two king-size pizzas you get three dollars off.

Get two, Ralph said. —Get four, for God's sake! There's not a morsel of food in this entire house.

Eat your green sandwich, Jim said.

Sure, Ralph said, and waved the sandwich in the air. —King fucking Tut, remember?

What happened? Jim said, and picked up the pyramid's bent frame.

It had a little accident, Ralph said. He sniffed the blue-green sandwich again and then nibbled at its crust. —But maybe Alice

Ann has something with that pyramid-power business. Somebody better get some pizza here pronto, I'm telling you.

Why don't you go out and get Lindsay? Alice Ann said. —See what she wants on her pizza.

When Jim stepped though the kitchen door, he was hit square in the face by a blast of water. Jim stood where he was as Lindsay aimed the stream of water up and down him. She circled Jim slowly, hosing him head to foot. Finally Lindsay turned the hose off at its nozzle, and she began to coil it up.

What do you like on your pizza? Jim asked Lindsay.

The Last Straw

1

There's the girl, Alice Ann said when Lindsay came in the kitchen door, followed by Jim.

I hope you like anchovies, Ralph mumbled, talking with his mouth full.

I went ahead and ordered, Alice Ann said. —Ralph was driving me nuts.

I adore anchovies, Lindsay said.

Hey, Ralph said, and waved his half-eaten blue-green sandwich at Jim and Lindsay. —Hey, you guys are all wet.

A sudden cloudburst, Jim said. —We were caught without cover.

You guys are dripping wet, Ralph said. —You really are.

God, what happened? Alice Ann said. —You guys really are dripping wet. You'll catch your death like that. I'll get you some towels.

Oh, we just felt like singing in the rain, Lindsay said. —It seemed so romantic at the time.

What in the world did happen? Ralph said.

We decided to wash the car, Jim said.

I may take it on a long trip soon, Lindsay said.

Sort of like a getaway, Jim said. —A clean getaway.

Let me get you some dry clothes, Alice Ann said.

Oh, don't bother, Jim said. —I'll just drip-dry.

No, you guys need something dry to put on, Alice Ann said.

I wouldn't wear anything of Ralph's if you paid me, Jim said.

Let him drip, Lindsay said. —He's good at it.

I wouldn't want you in any clothes of mine, Ralph said, and pushed the final bite of blue-green sandwich into his mouth. —I'd have to turn around and burn the things.

Well, big boy, Alice Ann said to Jim, what about some of my things, then?

Got anything that will match my eyes? Jim said.

I've got just the cute little number for you, Alice Ann said.

I don't want anything, you know, too revealing, Jim said.

It's a little low-cut, but I think you'll find it suitable. Come on, hon, Alice Ann said, and tugged at Lindsay's hand. —Let's get you into something dry right now. You'll catch your death.

I thought I was safe in this lifetime, Lindsay said, from a death by water.

You are, Alice Ann said. —Trust me about that.

2

Did you actually eat King Tut? Jim said.

It was a desperate measure, I'll admit, Ralph said. —It was either eat King Tut or faint from hunger. You know, maybe Alice Ann has something with this pyramid-power business, after all.

I've seen everything now, Jim said. —Old Ralph actually ate King fucken Tut. Your basic pharaoh food.

I did. I admit it. But like I said, there may be something to this pyramid business, after all. I wish I had a little piece of that action. Get into some kind of pyramid franchise. No fooling, Jim. Hey, old Jim, speaking of pyramids, I've got a little pyramid of my own in the dining room. A little pyramid of my new books, by golly. Talk about pyramid power! Talk about prosperity!

Is it a franchise? Jim said.

By golly, it is sort of a franchise, Ralph said. —I'll show it to you when the girls get back. No, come on, let me show it to you now. You'll want to weep with envy in private.

Don't forget, Ralph, I've already published a book of my own. Big deal.

I know, I know, Ralph said. He took a bottle of vodka from a paper sack on the kitchen table and opened it. He filled two water glasses nearly full and handed one to Jim. —I sure wish we had some ice, Ralph said, and slurped a drink from the glass.

Jesus, Ralph, don't you at least have some kind of mix? Some juice of some kind? Didn't the girls get any mix?

Well, let me take a look, Ralph said, and opened the refrigerator. —Nope. There's none in the bag either. They forgot, I guess. As late as three o'clock this afternoon there was a gallon of fresh orange juice in here. Oh, hey, here's a taste of prune juice. It's kind of old. My mom had it here a few months ago when she was trying to move in on us.

Old? Well, that shouldn't bother you one bit, Ralph. A prune-juice chaser for King Tut. Okay, give me a hit.

Okay, here you go. Okay, now follow me. Just walk this way, please.

Okay, Jim said, and imitated Ralph's shambling walk down the hallway behind him.

All right, Ralph said, and stopped at the door of the dark dining room. —Now you've got to get the picture. You're walking down the street of a city. Up in San Francisco, say. Or in L.A. Or New York. Some great city. And you come upon this bookstore. A huge bookstore. It's unlike any other bookstore you've seen in your lifetime. With great shining windows. Windows that gleam in the sunlight. And great pyramids of brand-new books are being displayed behind the gleaming windows of the great bookstore.

Okay, Ralph, I get the picture.

I mean, Ralph said, all the world's bestsellers are on display. And not only that, but *collected* works are on display. There's a whole window of Hemingway's books. Every book Billy Faulkner wrote in his lifetime has been reissued and is on display in this great bookstore's windows. All the writers you've read and admired. All the books you've loved in your lifetime. They are all in print with shiny new covers and they are stacked in pyramids in these gleaming display windows for all the world to see. And right there among them is your own book. Get the picture, old Jim?

I said I get the picture, Ralph. —You've got us looking in display windows at the books of the immortals.

Right, Ralph said. —Well, right there, in a window all your own, I mean, all *my* own in this case, among the immortals, as it were, there it is. My own book! Are you ready?

Ready Teddy, Ralph.

Da ta da, da ta da da da! Ralph chirped, and clicked on the dining-room lights.

Copies of Ralph's book were scattered all about the floor of the room. Most looked as though they had been half eaten. Two books left on the dining-room table looked as though they had been merely bitten. Ralph clutched his throat and ran to the table. He slowly picked up a bitten book as though it were a small, wounded pet. He ran his fingertips over the tracks of great teeth marks on the book's shining, glossy white surface.

This is just awful, old Ralph, Jim said.

Ralph held the bitten book against his chest, as though giving it comfort. As he left the room, Ralph turned out the lights. Jim followed Ralph down the hallway to the kitchen. In the kitchen Ralph sat down at the table. Jim leaned in the doorway. Ralph turned the bitten book slowly about in his big hands. He opened it and looked at his photograph on the inside cover. He blinked his left eye shut and studied his picture; then he looked at his picture with his right eye closed. Ralph read the dust-jacket copy, his lips moving, and then he read the blurbs. Ralph put the book down on the table gently, with both hands, and he patted it gently. Ralph lit a cigarette and waved smoke away from his face, coughing. His eyes were wet.

What a bummer, old Ralph, Jim said. Jim walked over and sat down at the table across from Ralph.

I feel so bad right now, old Jim, Ralph said. —It's crazy, I know, but I feel about as sad as I did when I buried my dad.

It's a bummer, all right, old Ralph, Jim said. —Man, you gotta put your foot down around here. I'd shoot that dog for starters.

My dad would have been so proud of me, Ralph said. —If he hadn't drunk himself to death.

Bummer city, Jim said. —You want me to shoot that dog for you?

There's not a day goes by I don't miss my dad, Ralph said, and stood up slowly. He walked over to the kitchen sink, then turned around and walked back to the table.

I couldn't really shoot any dog, Jim said. —You want me to whip Paco for you, though?

Ralph picked up his book and returned with it to the sink. He put the book down gently on the counter within easy reach. Ralph turned on the cold water and let it run. He fetched several of the empty ice trays from the refrigerator and one by one filled them with water and returned them to the freezer. Ralph looked at his reflection in the window above the sink and let the cold water run over the backs of his hands. He drank some water from his cupped hands and then he splashed his face and rubbed it. Ralph covered his face with his wet hands, and then his big shoulders began to heave with sobs.

Jim walked over to Ralph and patted his back.

What a bummer, old Ralph, Jim said, and patted Ralph's heaving back. —Paco's ass is grass and I'm the fucken mower.

What's wrong? Alice Ann said as she and Lindsay entered the kitchen.

Ralph? Lindsay said. —Jim?

Looks like that fucken Killer went and ate Ralph's new books, Jim said. He had to bite the side of his tongue to keep from laughing.

Oh, baby, Alice Ann said, and rubbed Ralph's heaving shoulders. —Honeybunch, baby.

Bummer city, Jim said, and in spite of himself snickered, which he coughed to hide. Jim felt Lindsay's hand on his back. He looked at her and saw that her eyes were teary. She smiled faintly, and Jim reached up to touch her cheek.

What a day, Ralph said, and put his hands back under the running water. He splashed his face. —Whew boy, Ralph said.

Everything is going to be all right, baby, Alice Ann said, and she hugged Ralph from behind. —And this is the last straw. That dog is out of this house as of now.

Do you mean that? Ralph said. —Really and truly?

Really and truly, hon, Alice Ann said, and she ran her fingers through the back of Ralph's woolly hair.

What if Paco leaves, then? Ralph said.

Tough titty, Alice Ann said.

What if our daughter threatens to leave with him? Ralph said. —What if she does leave?

I'll tie her up in her room if I have to, Alice Ann said. —Everything is going to be all right, Ralph. I promise.

Whew, what a day, Ralph said, and rubbed his forehead with his fingers.

Maybe we should be heading home, Lindsay said to Jim. Jim had his arm around her shoulders, and he pulled her gently against him and kissed her forehead.

No, now you guys can't leave yet, Alice Ann said. —The evening is still young, you guys. And we have these two giant pizzas with the works on the way.

I sure wish that pizza would get here soon, Ralph said. —I sure wish I didn't have to go to jail.

You won't have to go to jail, Alice Ann said.

Jail, Ralph? Lindsay said.

Buggery city, Jim said, and hung his head.

You promise I won't have to go to jail? Ralph said. —Really and truly, Alice Ann?

I promise, Alice Ann said. —Really and truly.

I sure wish that pizza would get here soon, Ralph said.

It will be here in less than eleven minutes, Alice Ann said, looking at the clock on the wall above the stove.

Really? Ralph said.

I promise, Alice Ann said.

In less than eleven minutes? Ralph said. —How could you know something like that, Alice Ann? And, for God's sake, don't give me any of that you can predict the future business, please, please, Alice Ann. Not tonight.

They have a strict policy, Alice Ann said. —If they deliver the pizza later than one half hour from when you place your order, they have to refund five dollars.

On each pizza? Ralph said, and looked over at the clock.

Right, Alice Ann said. —On each pizza.

No fooling? Ralph said, watching the inexorable movement of the second hand on the clock above the stove.

No Shelter

1

In late June Lindsay and Jim throw a birthday party for S. Clay Wilson, a good friend of Jim's who is an infamous underground cartoonist. Clay is a big hairy hulk of a guy originally from the Midwest and quite insane. Clay provides a half-dozen cases of Anchor Steam beer, and his girlfriend, Mary Mississippi, an artist, a painter of some local note, makes a crazy birthday cake shaped not unlike an enormous chocolate cock. Lindsay considers this her own coming-out party, and she is determined to get acquainted like crazy, focus on people whom Jim seems to like the most. Lindsay is determined to be fun and interesting and just generally irresistible. She labors floor to ceiling on the flat, until everything absolutely shines and sparkles. Lindsay produces a table groaning with food that looks catered. Classical music wafts through the rooms, for a time anyway, before Clay takes over the machine with his throbbing dork Delta Blues. Lindsay wears her black dress and her grandmother's pearls, discovering herself way overdressed, but so what!

The place is packed by nine o'clock, when suddenly Clay, who has been holding forth at the kitchen table, begins yelling, "What the fuck! What the fuck! Where the fuck am I?" Another guy at the kitchen table slumps over and begins to drool uncontrollably. A girl falls out of her chair laughing hysterically. Then somebody starts yelling that nobody should smoke any more of the grass going around the room. Bad grass here, somebody else shouts. And, dear God, is it ever! PCP perhaps. People are freaking out right and left.

Lindsay considers trying to close the party down, but everybody is simply too stoned by that point to safely depart, too paranoid to do much more than stand around and weep or laugh insanely. Finally this big hairy ape of a biker, all tattoos and chains, identifies himself to Lindsay as the asshole who is passing around the bad dope, announcing that he considers himself a catalytic agent for sudden startling change, who comes to parties and spreads the crazy grass and waits for the tone and tenor of things to become very interesting. When Lindsay tells him to get the fuck out of her house he simply laughs and tickles her under the chin like a child. Lindsay has no idea where Jim is at that point, not to mention Ralph and Alice Ann. Lindsay decides to slip into their bedroom and simply hide out for a while. No such luck. She turns on the light to discover some couple screwing on the bed. Lindsay mutters something like "Excuse me." She turns off the light and shuts the door to her own bedroom.

Lindsay decides it is definitely time to locate Jim. The crowd is dense and more people keep pouring in. Lindsay wrestles her way through the flat. She finally finds Jim sitting out on the back steps with little Sappho on his lap. He is angry with Lindsay and darkly broody. He tells Lindsay she has been an outrageous flirt all evening and has humiliated him. He tells her that he had seen her touching, no, pawing, Ralph while she was talking with him, clearly giving Ralph and everybody else the wrong idea. At least he hopes it is the wrong idea. Whereupon Lindsay blurts out about the biker asshole passing the bad dope around the party and how said asshole had laughed at her when she told him to leave and tickled her under the chin.

Jim jumps up and hands Lindsay the kitty and tears inside. Lindsay follows, holding her kitty close. Jim scans the room from

the kitchen door. Where is the motherfucker? Jim growls to
Lindsay when she comes up behind him, and she points said asshole out across the room, who really is a pretty big guy, bigger
than Jim. Who knew who would win. Lindsay doesn't care. Jim
plows a path across the crowded kitchen. When he arrives at the
asshole, Jim grabs him up by his throat and slams him up against
the wall. Jim gets very much into the asshole's face, whose eyes
are bulging like boils. Jim says something to him Lindsay can't
hear. Whatever it is works, and when Jim lets the asshole loose, he
practically runs down the hallway.

Jim wades back across the room to Lindsay, and he takes her
in his arms and holds her for a while amid the chaos, and then he
kisses her on the forehead gently. Then Jim turns back to the
party, and the party is still going strong at 8 a.m., when Lindsay
rolls a naked chick off their bed and crawls under the covers.

2

Lindsay and Jim and Ralph and Alice Ann fall by (oh so reluctantly on Ralph's part) Jim's Hawaiian gangster biker-buddy
Shorty Ramos's house on Valley Street (across the street from
Jim's old doper hippie commune) for some of Shorty's wife
Edna's famous *pétales* (Edna makes her famous *pétales* from three
kinds of meat, man, Shorty always declares, some pork, man, some
beef, and some meat from roof rabbits, you know, man, those
furry little fuckers that crawl around on roofs at night going
meow). (And you really expect me to eat that stuff? Ralph whines.
Are you crazy?) So after pigging out on Edna's *pétales* (except for
Ralph, who orders in an extra-large pepperoni pizza, of which,
after Shorty's five sons get their cuts, Ralph ends up with a single
slice and falls into a profound pout), everybody goes out to
Shorty's Noe Valley hillside back yard to sit in the cool evening
air and watch the lights of downtown buildings begin to blink on
through fog that rolls in like low, slow waves over the hills. There
is a crescent moon and higher in the clear, blackening sky above
the enveloping fog more stars than Lindsay has seen since she
moved down from Montana. Lindsay sits on the back steps and

wraps her arms around her knees. She thinks of the star-filled skies of her girlhood, sitting on the porch of that cabin high in the mountains, looking up through the sharp, clear air into the night. Lindsay starts to shiver, and she slides her bare arms inside her T-shirt.

Jim and Shorty stagger on out to the small level area at the top of the yard and begin their karate dances. Shorty is the star of countless stories Jim has told Lindsay, a seriously "badass" dude with greased-back black ducks and the goatee of a devil. Shorty was a founder of the Sons of Hawaii badass biker gang, bikers so bad that even the Hell's Angels hire them to break bones and put people into the waters of the Bay, according to Jim. Shorty is, well, short, but built like a fire hydrant, and crude jailhouse tattoos cover muscular arms that bulge beneath a Hawaiian shirt bright with blue parrots crying from pink palms, and he and Jim circle each other, spin, kick high in the air, flail their arms, boys skinned to their animal. Alice Ann sweeps out onto the plain to join them. Ralph sits down on the steps behind Lindsay (Shorty frightens Ralph to death). Lindsay can feel Ralph's knees touching her back.

The layer of light over the downtown buildings is rosy and an impossible purple. The night air smells like exotic spices. Lindsay watches her husband kick at demons in the dark, and questions come to her as clear and mysterious as lines from poems. How dependent is she upon desire? Can she discard the plots of her old dreams? Can she imagine moving into yet another runaway life? Can she patch up her life in secret? What are the causes for love? Is surviving saying yes to everything? Is ruin an impossible habit to break? What was the nature of this longing that could find no shelter? What does dear old rotten Ralph hope to gain by rubbing his bony knees up and down her back as she watches her new husband dance madly in the dark?

Alice Ann laughs and swirls about the dark yard, her beautiful white face an image of smoke, her thin, pale arms lifted above her head, long blond hair thrown back, as though in a spell, an apparition weaving in and about the shadowy swim of Shorty's and Jim's shapes. Jim's trick, Lindsay has come to understand, is to catch people up, making up the rules as he goes along. Lindsay feels Ralph's bony knees press and rub almost painfully into her back as she watches Jim carry on and on, the sort of guy who might set his own hair on fire so that one would notice him in the dark.

When Shorty pulls out his ceremonial Jap hari-kari dagger and begins to flash it about, Jim entertains a bright idea. It is high time he and Shorty became blood brothers. They would cut their thumbs and clasp their bleeding wounds together. They would mingle their blood, let their stories and memories mingle, let themselves fold into one great mutual myth. Shorty thinks it's a groovy idea, freaking far-out, man! Ralph mumbles something to the effect that he is utterly appalled by such an idea. The idea! Ralph mumbles disdainfully. Jim takes the dagger and carefully nicks Shorty's thumb, which Shorty holds aloft, and hoots into the night. Shorty excitedly takes the dagger, and while Jim stoically gazes toward the lights of the city, Shorty nearly severs Jim's thumb. For a few moments Jim simply stares at the gushing blood. Shorty is flabbergasted at his work, his jaw drops in shock. Ralph clasps his hands over his mouth and gags. Alice Ann strolls leisurely over to Jim and touches his face. Jim looks up at Lindsay with an expression of sappy surprise bordering bewilderment on his face, and he grins bravely for a moment or two, before his eyes roll back in his head and he keels over in the grass.

At Mission Emergency the Chicano doc informs Jim that he is one lucky dude to get off with merely nine stitches, man, and no apparent serious damage done, for all the good that news does Lindsay, who cannot stop shaking for hours.

Out of the Blue

Ralph studied his face in the restroom mirror and dabbed tenderly at his nose with a damp paper towel. The bleeding had stopped, but there were still traces of blood around the edges of his nostrils, and it looked to Ralph as though his nose had about doubled in size and was rapidly turning purple. Before his very eyes, Ralph's nose was rapidly beginning to resemble an eggplant. It occurred to Ralph that the stricken look on that sorry face with an eggplant for a nose staring back at him from the mirror might have been a visage carved from his worst dream of public humiliation. His whole face looked purple now, in that godawful fluorescent light, as though some purple veil of sick, sad flesh had been lowered over the features of his real face. Ralph shut his left eye and looked intently at that stranger with the purple face and purple clown nose. Then Ralph shut his right eye and took a long look at that purple face full of grief and pain and astonishment, for all the insight that provided him.

A man came into the restroom and, glancing at Ralph, walked over to the urinal against the far wall. Ralph coughed behind his hand and turned on the hot water again. He made a big production of punching liquid soap into his hands from a container above the sink, and then thrust his hands in the hot water and soaped them vigorously. Ralph cleared his throat several times, and he studied the man's back in the mirror. He was a handsome, white-haired man, tall and distinguished-looking in an expensive suit, as though he might be a big-time business executive, or a doctor, or an attorney, or even a judge maybe. Ralph wondered if the distinguished gentleman had been a witness to the recent humiliating events in the restaurant's bar.

When the restroom door banged open and Alice Ann charged in, the distinguished gentleman did a double take (as did Ralph), then jerked around away from her. The distinguished gentleman took a quick look down at his dick, did a little dance in place, bent slightly, and zipped up.

That miserable sonofabitch, Alice Ann said to the distinguished gentleman, and pointed at Ralph, and I have business to conclude. This is a private matter. So do you mind? she said, nodding toward the door.

Not at all, the distinguished gentleman said as he backed around Alice Ann toward the door.

Thank you, Alice Ann said. —Would you care to wash your hands first?

Not in the least, the distinguished gentleman said, holding his hands out palms up as though for Alice Ann to examine, and then the distinguished gentleman disappeared through the door.

For God's sake, Alice Ann, Ralph muttered. He smacked the button on the hot-air hand-drying machine beside the sink. When it didn't come on, he smacked it several more times. —I hate these contraptions. These contraptions never work right. Never, Ralph said. He held his dripping hands helplessly beneath the quiet machine and watched Alice Ann out of the corner of his eye.

I have just one final question to ask you, Ralph, Alice Ann said. —When exactly did you decide to ruin my evening?

I don't know what you're talking about, Alice Ann. This is all just crazy and I refuse to be a part of it.

Did you set out, Ralph, to ruin my evening? Did you actually plan on it? When did it come to you, Ralph, the plan you devised to ruin my anniversary evening?

Alice Ann, you're way off base. Can't you see how way off base you are?

When we were getting dressed up to go out, Ralph, did you know it even then? Or was it earlier? What time today did you know it, Ralph? Just answer this one last question for me. This is the last thing I will ever ask of you, Ralph.

We have to get out of here, Alice Ann. You can't be in here like this. They already threatened to call the police when you belted me at the bar. We're going to get arrested yet, Alice Ann.

Did you know it as early as this morning, Ralph? Please tell me, please.

No way, Ralph said. He shook his dripping hands in the air before him and then blew on them with great puffs.

No what, Ralph? Alice Ann said, and took a step toward him.

No to everything. You're not going to catch me up with one of your trick questions.

Here we have come through the flames, Ralph. We are on the verge of a new life. We are on the threshold of the future. Things have finally begun to go our way. And then you had to break my heart one last time.

Go our way? Our way? Ralph said, and flapped his hands like crazy little wings in the air. —Are you really bonkers, Alice Ann? Our house is a hotbed of dopehead hoodlums. Things are a shambles in our house. Holes knocked in the walls. Dozen of godawful cats pooping everywhere in sight. Pooping right on the kitchen sink. One of them had a giant bowel movement on my typewriter the other day. It's true! The electricity is about to be shut off again. I'm on the verge of going to jail. Where God only knows what sort of sordid events lie in wait for me. And most of all, you went back on your word to get rid of Paco and Killer. And now you can talk about how things are going our way? Crazy, I say.

This has always been your biggest problem, Ralph, Alice Ann said. She glanced in the mirror behind Ralph and touched her hair. —You have never been somebody who could look on the bright side of things.

Bright side of things? My God, Alice Ann! One minute we're sitting here in a tony bar having a nice after-dinner drink, and the next minute I'm flat on my back.

You broke my heart. You called me by another woman's name.

I never did.

You did, Ralph. You broke my heart.

Your ears are playing tricks on you, Alice Ann.

My ears are just fine. It's my heart that is broken.

You were hearing things, Alice Ann. Maybe one of your ancient Egyptian mummy buddies was trying to get through to you, and you just thought you heard me.

You called me *Lindsay*, Ralph. That's the bottom line.

You just misunderstood me, that's all.

I know perfectly well what I heard.

I might have been saying something about calling Jim and, you know, Lindsay. I might have been saying something about the fact we haven't seen them, Jim and Lindsay, lately.

You called me by another woman's name, plain and simple.

I didn't either. I didn't. And even if I had made some slight slip of the tongue, that doesn't give you the right to clip me out of the blue.

You have ruined everything once again, Ralph.

You didn't have to come unglued. You're the one who has ruined everything. You've ruined this tony place for us, for one thing. Now it's just another fine establishment where we are no longer welcome as customers, no matter what the color of our money. Which, come to think of it, is probably not such a bad thing, considering the prices here. Which were outrageous, didn't you think?

Is Lindsay who you really want to be with tonight, Ralph? Is that the reason you called me by her name?

You'll never pin that on me, Alice Ann. Not in a million years. You were just hunting for an excuse to clip me one. And I'll tell you this, if I had been looking, you would never have landed that punch. Not in a million years, Alice Ann. You just got lucky, that's all. You had to go and suckerpunch me. Fine anniversary present that was, a suckerpunch out of the blue.

It wasn't a suckerpunch, Ralph, Alice Ann said. —I gave you ample warning.

No, you didn't, either. Just wait until tomorrow when you sober up, see how you'll feel about these humiliating public events tomorrow. You'll be sick with shame and regret tomorrow, and it will be too late. Mark my words! Ralph said. Ralph suddenly punched the hot-air machine solidly with his fist.

—Oh oh oh ouch! Ralph cried and hopped up and down. He held his hand up before his face and blew on his knuckles. —Now you've really gone and done it, Alice Ann. This is your fault, too. You got me all worked up. I'd never have hit that infernal contraption if you hadn't got me in a state. Now I have a broken hand on top of everything else. None of this would have happened, Alice Ann, if you hadn't come unglued in the first place. I lay every bit of this pain and misery and my broken hand right on your doorstep.

Goodbye forever, Ralph, Alice Ann said.

What? Ralph said and blew on his knuckles. —What are you talking about now, Alice Ann?

Goodbye forever, my darling, Alice Ann said, and turned toward the door.

Turkeys in the Rain

1

TGIF, Lindsay thinks as she begins that day throwing up into the toilet for a solid half hour, which as usual Jim either does not notice or refuses to acknowledge. Then Shorty calls up with an apparently interesting itinerary for a full, fun-filled day of criminal activity to share with his blood brother Jim, which means all day Lindsay will have the pleasure of half-expecting a call from authorities to come down to juvie so that her delinquent husband can be released into her custody.

As usual Jim walks Lindsay down the hill on Union Street to see her off, passing a paper cup of coffee back and forth. They stop on the corner of Bush to let an almost empty trolley car clang through the intersection, then they step carefully over the slick, humming rails. On the far corner the green-and-white-striped awning of Fugorios Resturant flaps in the breeze, and the cool air is full of the slightly scorched but freshly clean smell of baking bread. Down the corridors of streets sloping toward the Bay, they can see the vague outline of a large ship making its way slowly through the fog off Alcatraz Island. Lindsay and Jim sit on a bench in Washington Square Park with two old Italian ladies wearing long black coats, who are chattering loudly and eating small pieces of bread they take turns tearing from a long, slender loaf in a white paper sack. When Lindsay shivers, Jim puts his arm around her shoulders and draws her to him.

Are you okay, kiddo? Jim says.

Nope, Lindsay says, then says, Actually, yes. It's just chilly this morning. And I'm tired. The day hasn't even started and I'm tired to my bones. But that's being whiny and boring, I know.

It ain't whiny and boring, Jim says.

Lindsay lights a cigarette and they sit there on the bench passing the cup of coffee and silently watching the gulls circle and glide and land to stagger like drunken sailors across the damp grass. On the far side of the little park, before a statue of Benjamin Franklin, thirty or so old Chinese men and women go through their slow, graceful tai chi exercises. They look like apparitions in the thick fog, as they do their soundless dance. A big man with a long gray-black beard wearing a raggedy pea coat sits down on the next bench. Now and then he takes a pull from a bottle in a brown paper bag. He seems to be glaring at them, but Jim doesn't appear to notice, which is probably a good thing. When Lindsay sees her bus, the 30 Stockton, rumbling up Columbus Street in the slow but surprisingly quiet traffic, Lindsay puts out her cigarette and begins rummaging in her purse for change.

Well, fuck a duck, Lindsay says. —I'm off to another day in America.

It'll be a dandy day in America, Jim says. He hugs Lindsay to him and gives her a quick kiss on the lips.

A dandy day in America is in the mail, right? Lindsay says.

You bet.

And you love me, right?

You bet, Jim says, and they get up and walk toward the bus stop.

Don't get into trouble with Shorty today, okay?

I'm just giving him a hand. He's got a line on a load of frozen turkeys that fell off a truck somewhere, or something crazy like that. I'm just going to drive down to San Jose and help him cop a few. I'll meet you at Powell's for drinks.

Frozen turkeys? You bet.

You bet, Jim says, and hugs and kisses Lindsay again like an affectionate brother. Jim finishes off the coffee and crumples the cup and tosses it into a trash container. Just as they pass the bearded man on the next bench, he shakes his bottle at Jim and growls, What the fuck do you know about love, anyway?

Jim stops and Lindsay can feel the muscle of his arm tense through his leather jacket. Her heart skips a beat.

But Jim simply grins and says, Not nearly enough.

And they walk on.

2

Lindsay goes to bed alone. Lindsay goes to bed alone.

Sometimes Jim does come to bed, but only to fall instantly asleep. Or sometimes he will tuck Lindsay in, even rub her back, when she has been a good girl and not bugged him about anything, especially his booze and dope and dealing. Then back up the long hallway to the kitchen, where he turns to the TV, or his music, country-song-sad and shit-kicky, but most of all to his trusty manuscript, his book and its beauty, night after night given over to its celebration, celebration and then more booze and dope, waxing sacramental until early morning, when the wine, the real blood in his veins, usually wins out.

They do still have some high times together, Lindsay and Jim, but more and more often only out at the bars with other revelers, who see them as this fun-filled rather outrageous couple, or when they have troops back to the flat, which is often, perhaps too often, for high old times around the kitchen table, Jim's tableaux, where he holds forth, telling story after story; the tales getting taller with each telling, and more funny, truly, turning the disastrous daily events of their lives into high comedy, everybody in stitches; and Lindsay does have fun and she feels love for Jim and even pride, and for extended moments sees their life together in another light.

But this night Lindsay waits awake in the darkness, per usual, slow-dancing in her mind to an oldie-but-goodie station on the radio. Jim doesn't come to bed, per usual. Finally Lindsay masturbates, angry and deliberately imagining other men, imagining Ralph, that's who.

3

On that early August night of particularly wanton nakedness Jim borrows Shorty's Harley so that he and Lindsay can make a grand entrance at the opening of Mary Mississippi's "Handsome Suicidal Sailors" show at a gallery south of Market Street. It is evident immediately to Lindsay that Jim does not really know dick about the handling of a Harley, and Lindsay buries her face into the back of his leather jacket as they roar around turns on shining, rain-slick streets. The short red-leather skirt Jim had begged that Lindsay wear is hiked high on her spread legs and cold spray stings her bare thighs. Adjusting his fedora once as they bounce over old trolley tracks, Jim almost drops the huge machine and Lindsay's heart jumps into her throat. At least, Lindsay begs at the top of her lungs into Jim's back, take off those fucking shades so you can see the fucking road! But to no avail. The gallery is in a converted warehouse and Jim shudders the Harley up to the open double doors and then idles it on inside the huge, hot, barn-size room as the startled, staring crowd at first spreads away like a sea of hip people parting, but then folds back in about them gawking and impressed just as Jim has hoped.

The striptease starts back at Mary Mississippi's loft after her show, when for no particular reason Jim tosses a boot in Mary's direction and she tosses it back along with one of her own little red cowgirl numbers. Mary's show has been a great success, and she sold several of her huge paintings depicting handsome sailors naked save for their caps, heavily tattooed and amazingly hung, leaping off brightly illuminated ships that look like floating ocean cities into the high seas at night.

The big drink, Jim says, as he takes off his other boot. —That's why I dig your paintings, Mary. I understand them things. I almost took the big drink myself one time, Jim says, and he tosses the boot at Mary Mississippi's boyfriend, the aforementioned S. Clay Wilson.

Now why ever did you want to take the big drink, darlin'? Mary Mississippi asks Jim, in her relentlessly Southern-belle, blinky, breathless mode. Mary is sitting on a white rattan couch beneath the skylight beside S. Clay, who is busy cleaning his fingernails with a switchblade knife. The high, whitewashed brick walls of the big loft are illuminated by spotlights directed onto paintings selected from some of Mary's earlier series: a couple from her "Falling Window Washers" series, three from her "Hotel Chinese Insomniacs" series, a few from her "Sacrificial Virgins and Assorted Burning Saints" series.

As Jim relates how he once almost committed suicide by jumping off a bridge because he had lost the true love of his high-school honey, Lindsay walks around the huge room looking at the illuminated paintings and touching the odd collections of items Mary has piled high on shelves and tabletops everywhere: including a whole shelf covered with the severed heads of dolls and tiny torn-off dolly limbs, little dolly arms and legs, which Lindsay runs her fingers over gently. They make her feel sad. When she picks up a tiny, plastic head, its blue eyes blink open and Lindsay quickly puts it down.

Mary Mississippi leans forward, her elbows on her knees, a look of sappy rapt attention on her pretty face as she listens to Jim hold forth about that time he balanced himself on the railing in the center of that bridge and listened to the dark water rush below, cold rain coming in gusts across his face. Lindsay flutters her fingers over enormous feathers that are arranged like exotic flowers in antique glass vases lined along a wall which is covered with a collection of feathered masks. No, one would have to describe Mary Mississippi's face as more than simply pretty, Lindsay decides. It is an odd face but beautiful in its way, with a slightly upturned nose, faint freckles, a bud of a mouth, short coppery-blond hair rich with flickering highlights. Mary always wears long, dangling, silver-and-turquoise earrings which she designs and makes herself and often sells for a bundle. Lindsay has not been able to wear earrings since that night years earlier when she had undressed hurriedly drunk and ripped an earring caught on a pullover sweater through her left lobe. Lindsay had not realized this until the next morning, when she awoke sick as a dog, dizzy, still half-drunk. Lindsay had awoken to discover the head of a man whose name she could not for the life of her recall beside her own on a blood-soaked pillow.

But Jim had got himself an acute case of the old whirly-birds and had fallen backward onto the bridge instead of forward into the cold, dark big drink, and he had passed out cold there in the cold rain, a real fortunate pilgrim that night. Which explains why Jim responded so strongly to Mary Mississippi's depictions of naked, well-endowed sailors leaping overboard to practice their dead-man floats, for he could understand why men could do such a thing. Jim tells Mary Mississippi that he wishes she had a hot tub handy, or some such body of water wherein he could demonstrate his own dead man's float.

Well, darlin', all I got is a big ol' hot and steamy shower. Mary Mississippi winks and blinks from the deep old South.

I have known suicidal sadness in my lifetime, too, S. Clay pipes up. —My old ma croaked when she gave birth to my baby brother, who is this crazily carnivorous Cyclops child.

Your momma isn't deceased! Mary Mississippi exclaims. —You are such a sick puppy for uttering such a thing.

My baby brother shits through his ears, S. Clay says.

We could pretend we are singing in the rain, Jim says. —In your hot and steamy shower.

I just adore singing in the rain, Mary Mississippi says.

I hate to bring this up in mixed company, my little candy lamb, S. Clay says to Mary Mississippi, my little main squeeze for the moment, my own little hot, many-holed honey, but, toots, it is just about time to give your old pork pirate his 3:13 a.m. blowjob.

S. Clay, darlin', Mary Mississippi says, why don't you just retire to a far corner all by your lonesome and play nice with your old baloney bayonet.

We can look up and open our mouths and pretend we are all singing in the rain in your hot and steamy shower, Jim says, and unbuckles his belt.

I, for one, S. Clay says, am juiced to the tits.

Turkeys have been known to drown in the rain, Lindsay says. —But that is because they are stupid creatures, not suicidal.

Say what? Jim says.

Turkeys, Lindsay says. —They are too stupid to come in out of the rain. And sometimes they drown in it.

Turkeys? Jim says. —No shit?

Turkeys, Lindsay says. —Rain starts dropping on a stupid turkey's head and it gawks up at heaven in utter amazement. Then sometimes they forget to shut their stupid mouths, and gulp gulp gulp, they are goners. Mary, maybe you should paint a stupid-turkeys-drowning-in-the-rain series.

Right now, hon, Mary Mississippi says, I am busy as a little bee painting a botched caesarian section series.

Mary Mississippi does the cutest bump and grind as she matches Jim's silly striptease piece for piece. S. Clay gets in the act, stomping about the room in his motorcycle boots to the beat of the Stones blaring "Satisfaction." So then Lindsay, feeling as though she is being caught up in some sacrificial fiction, peels off the tight-fitting, sequined, truck drivers' dream black blouse Jim had begged her to wear. She swirls it about her head a couple of times and then somewhat surreptitiously folds it neatly on a table.

Mary Mississippi's naked body is as beautiful as Lindsay has feared, perky little tits, strawberry nipples, two perfect handfuls of hips, a haze of pubic hair the same soft reddish hue as the tiny tufts under her tanned, toned arms. Lindsay feels not unlike a heifer lumbering about to that rock-and-roll beat Mary swings her tight pretty little ass in perfect time to. As the four of them bop about the room becoming naked, Lindsay tells herself the trick is to adapt to the moment, to utterly love the present as an exciting place full of possibility where you have never been before, that she should push out of her mind those pressing pre-monitions of dark turns, escapes too narrow, that she should resolve to a bottom line of behavior that will include quitting smoking the first thing tomorrow and losing ten pounds in a week.

Hey, take a look at clownbody, S. Clay calls out, and Lindsay's heart stops. —Get down, jellybutt, S. Clay hoots, but he is pointing at Jim as Jim spins the perfectly naked Mary Mississippi under his arm. Jim is still wearing his jockey shorts and he has his fedora pulled low over his eyes and at some point he has pulled his boots back on.

Hey, jellybutt, S. Clay calls to Jim, you fetid son of a homely whore, why don't you stick your thumb up your jellybutt and bark for us? Hey, get a load of Lindsay! Lindsay's got a pair of tits that won't fucking quit! Come here to Daddy, you big-boobed babe, you, S. Clay calls out to Lindsay, who vows to herself on the spot to befriend and defend S. Clay Wilson from this day forward to all those multitudes of people who claim he is probably the world's greatest walking talking asshole.

I dig your haunting perfume, is what Lindsay overhears Jim say to Mary Mississippi once when he swings her near.

Bald Boy

1

Ralph Crawford's house could have been a ship afire as usual, for all the lights blazing from it as he pulled into the driveway. After Ralph had suddenly felt compelled to heave his outrageously expensive dinner into the toilet, he had searched the restaurant high and low for Alice Ann, who had clearly bolted, but without the car. Who knew where she had run off to or how. Who cared. Maybe she had gotten a ride home somehow.

Ralph kicked his way though the cats lurking in the kitchen. He snapped off light after light as he made his way back through the house to the bedroom, where in his most secret inner sanctum he had a little something stashed for snakebite. At the closed bedroom door Ralph stopped abruptly, frozen to the spot, his hand on the knob. He placed his ear against the door. There was no mistake about it. Ralph could hear low voices, whispery voices, coming from behind that closed door, and low laughter, too, coming from his and Alice Ann's bedroom. Ralph backed away slowly, quietly, down the hallway.

In the living room Ralph sat down heavily on the couch. He reached up and turned off the lamp, and then sat there in the dark. His hands shook as he lit a cigarette. Ralph sat there in the dark and tried every trick he knew to quiet his runaway heart. He thought about those whispery voices and the low laughter back in the bedroom and his mind buckled, filled with a swarm of unthinkable images. Ralph shook his head violently, tried to create other possibilities, other conclusions. But Ralph knew the worst. Had he called Alice Ann *Lindsay*? Had he been that dumb? But he thought about her all the time, Lindsay, every waking moment. So maybe he had been that dumb, called Alice Ann *Lindsay* and brought this terrible turn of events down on his own dumb head. He knew what Alice Ann was capable of, like bringing some tattooed low-rent biker home to fuck in their bed. His mind roared with that terrible knowing.

Was this rock bottom, then? Had he and Alice Ann finally sunk to it? Had all their yesterdays together, all those yesterdays with their incomprehensible yet relentless logic, added up to this sorry state of affairs? Ralph reached up and turned the lamp back on. He blinked in the sudden light and his eyes teared. Ralph let the tears come. He sat there, his purple face and nose in his hands, and shook with sobs. He could feel his purple nose running into his hands, and he could taste his own snot and tears. He gently pressed one painful purple nostril and then the other, exhaling violently, blowing gobs of snot onto the new carpet at his feet, then he ground them in with the soles of his shoes. Ralph picked up a copy of his book on the coffee table and studied his picture on the back. He turned the book over in his hands, examining the bite marks. He opened the book to the dedication page and ripped it out. He crumpled the page in his fist and tossed it into the fireplace. Ralph threw his book into the fireplace.

Ralph got up stiffly and walked over to the fireplace, where he picked up a cast-iron poker. He tested its heft. He smacked it lightly into the palm of his good hand. Back in the hallway outside the bedroom, Ralph put his ear against the door. The sound of voices rose suddenly, followed by laughter, and Ralph thought that he had never heard anything so frightening in his life. His heart was jumping as if he had been running up a hill. His legs were ropes of water. He remembered how as a boy, when his dad took him hunting, how he would consciously will himself cold and unrelenting, heartless, every nerve alert, ready to pull the trigger on anything that moved, or not, ready to kill anything, or not. Ralph lifted the cast-iron poker above his head and turned the doorknob slowly.

2

The radio had been a Christmas gift from somebody sometime somewhere. Ralph had never liked the thing. It had never worked worth a damn from day one. That radio was no friend of Ralph's. It had brought no comfort into his life. Its sound rose and fell randomly, its tuner roamed all over the face of the dial like it had a mind of its own, stations cross-fading crazily with other stations amid screams of static; its alarm went off when it felt like it. The news that radio had brought into Ralph's life was news he didn't need, news of airplanes dropping from the sky, families burned up in unexplained fires, mass murderers on the prowl, news that seeped into his sleeping brain as he turned in the current of his already dark dreams and left him at daybreak full of an abiding dread. Sudden loud laughter from that radio gave him a start; then a voice rose and faded away, and Ralph was left with an inexplicable but profound sense of loss, as though he had just heard his dead dad's voice again for the last time. Ralph felt on the verge of sobs again. Ralph smashed the radio with the cast-iron poker, swinging it like a ball bat. Ralph was the sultan of swat, the Babe Ruth of serious radio bashing, as he sent blinking, spluttering parts of that radio over the fence.

Next Ralph attacked that pyramid contraption Alice Ann had for some unfathomable reason erected above their bed. He bent the thin hollow metal tubing of its frame and then bashed the whole shebang onto the floor and stomped it flat. Ralph beat the abandoned, unmade bed until he was breathless, dizzy, and coughing. He flopped down on the edge of the ruined bed, then sat there panting. Ralph felt as though a huge, cold hand was squeezing his heart. He lit a cigarette with his shaking hands. He lay back on the tangled, yellowing sheets and pillows that smelled of their scents, his, Alice Ann's. Maybe if he simply closed his eyes and let himself drift off, he might get lucky and not wake up in this world. Had it been a mistake when Ralph, once upon a time, married the darling, clear-eyed girl he loved. Had it been wrong for Alice Ann to marry the hopeful, ambitious boy she loved? Had his and Alice Ann's days been numbered from the beginning? How long could he and Alice Ann go on telling themselves they could still turn out to be the people they had started out believing they would become? The thought occurred to Ralph that we are all identified finally by what we do to other people, and that betrayal is simply another word for loss. He put those thoughts out of his mind in a heartbeat. Ralph felt as though somebody had rearranged his organs and his heart was thumping from somewhere down in his stomach. Suddenly Ralph had the notion that he was a man without a true human interior, that his soul had no inner landscape upon which to move.

Ralph got up and hurried to the closet. As Ralph pushed his way back through the hangers, he was amazed how just the scent of Alice Ann's clothes gave him a little chubby. He got down on his knees at the entrance to the narrow tunnel he had constructed between the piled boxes of old Christmas decorations, ruined toys, torn teddy bears, tattered, outgrown baby clothes Alice Ann steadfastly refused to discard on the faint chance they might be needed again in this family. On his hands and knees Ralph crawled deeper and deeper into the starved closeness of the closet's darkness, as though he were descending into the midnight recesses of some Kentucky cave. Ralph felt his eyes grow large and lustrous. He imagined he could hear the sound of dripping water and smell a damp, earthy odor not unlike mushrooms growing rampant and huge in the dark, an aroma that put him strangely in mind of sex, whereupon he entertained another little chubby. But Ralph pressed forward, and after a time the darkness began to feel accommodating and safe and even sweet, and the memory of the outer world of light began to fade away like some dim dream from childhood, and Ralph imagined that he was slipping through some strange ring into another realm. At last Ralph arrived at that tiny, hushed clearing at the closet's deepest part. He could not see a thing in the pitch black, but sight was not necessary now. Ralph opened that old battered trunk handed down to him from his dad and ran his hands over the hidden treasures.

As always Ralph sniffed at that old shirt of his dad's, rubbed it over his face, imagining that he could still inhale that faintly sour, smoky smell he had loved. He touched the old tackle box that held those elaborate lures his dad had spent the happiest hours of his life fashioning, sitting at the kitchen table night after night, sipping whiskey or beer, tying flies and talking of secret hot spots for fishing that only he and his boy knew about. Ralph picked up the pearl-handled pocketknife with the bottle opener and closed his fist about that precious item. Ralph pictured his dad's hands whittling with that old knife, carving, cleaning nails, popping open beers, gutting fish in the grass of riverbanks, those big hands silvery with scales, fingers stained with the dark blood.

Ralph's dad used to take him fishing all the time, even in winter. His dad fished for whitefish mostly, using a belly reel, and pencil-length sinkers and red, yellow, or brown flies baited with maggots, which his dad used to keep alive and warm under his lower lip. This was the only thing about his dad that ever made Ralph's skin crawl. Ralph had quit letting his dad kiss him good night because of the thought of those godawful maggots, which his dad had misunderstood. His dad had thought it was somehow cute, that Ralph was trying to act too grown-up to kiss his old dad good night.

Ralph had always imagined he would teach his own son to fish, that he would show his boy all the secret hot spots to fish his dad had shown him back home up in Oregon, teach his boy all the tricks about fishing his own dad had taught him with patience and exactness and love. Ralph had taken his own boy fishing just once. Back before things had grown so bad between them, back when the boy was about four, Ralph figured. All the boy had wanted to do was throw rocks into the river. The boy had had his little heart set on bashing some fish. Now Ralph wouldn't be able to find any of those old fishing hot spots back home if his life depended on it.

What Ralph wished the most was that he had never stopped kissing his dad good night. What Ralph wished was that he had turned out to be more like his dad, for all his dad's faults. Even though his dad had died a drunk. Ralph was going to quit drinking himself. He meant it this time. Just as soon as he and his dad polished off the last of that bottle of ancient Scotch Ralph had paid an arm and a leg for and kept stashed in the secret inner sanctum. And what Ralph and his dad could use right now was a little bracer. Whenever he and his dad were hoisting a few together there deep in the inner sanctum and talking rainbows, Ralph would take one drink for himself and one for his dad. Tonight Ralph planned for them to kill that half-full bottle of ancient Scotch and then that would be it for Ralph. His drinking days would be behind him. Ralph rummaged through the old trunk. He ran his hands along the sides and across the bottom and into the corners. Ralph emptied that old trunk in a New York minute, tossing his dad's treasures over his shoulders into the darkness. But there was no bottle of ancient Scotch to be found. That hooch was history.

So it had finally come to pass. The little devils had finally found and violated Ralph's last secret place. Ralph closed his eyes and simply sat there listening to his own breath. He had nowhere left now. He could never escape the surface of his life. Ralph felt around on the dark floor for his dad's treasures, and one by one placed them back in the old trunk. He came upon the precious pearl-handled pocketknife with a bottle opener. Ralph opened it and rubbed its dull old blade over his wrists. Ralph ran the blade slowly up and down his pant leg, as though cleaning it, imagining his own hands silvery with scales, his own fingers smoky with blood.

3

Ralph had come to truly believe in the existence of evil, and he believed that evil lurked about the edges of our world waiting for the least opening to squeeze through, like a rat. Not long before these events, Ralph had let Alice Ann drag him to a movie called *The Omen*, in which Gregory Peck and Lee Remick played a handsome, highly successful couple who had, because of either pure bad blind luck or an evil contrivance of fate, ended up raising a child they had thought was their own flesh and blood but who was in reality the Son of Satan loosed into this world to fulfill his biblical destiny as the Antichrist. After much bloody mayhem and murder, the movie drew to its climax with a wounded Gregory Peck dragging the screaming, struggling boy toward a church altar in the dead of night in order to ritually stab him to death and thus save the world from dark dominion. Ralph had sat in the dark theater finishing up the last of his buttered popcorn and watching this desperate act unfold with a profound sense of appreciation.

Ralph went to his daughter's bedroom, for she was his chief suspect, especially now that Paco had more or less moved back in, with the understanding he would confine his criminal activities to Ralph's daughter's bedroom, such as selling drugs to the scumbag neighborhood children out of the bedroom window instead of the kitchen. As always, a low, persistent growl was emanating from behind the door of Ralph's daughter's bedroom. Ralph was no fool, and although they denied it, Ralph knew his old pal Killer was back lurking about the premises. And he had evidence of it. Just the other day Ralph had found a turd the size of his arm in the back yard. When he thought he could see his own breath in the chilled air before his daughter's bedroom door, Ralph realized that he was the one going crazy, not Alice Ann. And his daughter's door felt cold to the touch. Just the other day, upon catching Ralph holding a cat's head under the faucet at the kitchen sink, and not buying his excuse that he was simply giving kitty a drink, Ralph's daughter had expressed her displeasure by spinning her head around on her neck a few times and growling with guttural animal sounds unlike any Ralph had ever heard this side of a horror movie. Ralph decided to forgo discussing the purloined liquor with his daughter and her beau for the time being, and he tiptoed backward away from her door. Ralph would clean out that nest of vipers first thing in the morning, in the bright light of a brand-new day, when Alice Ann was home.

Ralph was astonished that his son's bedroom door, which was pulsating with the insane vibrations of rock-and-roll, was unlocked. As Ralph turned the doorknob, which felt hot to the touch, it occurred to him that he had not entered his son's room in years. The first thing Ralph noticed, once his eyes adjusted to a flashing strobe which froze the room in bursts of painful light, was that the walls were now painted black, which did wonders to frame the Day-Glo posters advertising those killer, cannibal bands Ralph's son revered so, who played that pure Charlie Manson music loaded with catchy lyrics extolling the kicks kids could cop cutting the throats of their parents. In the confusion of the flashing light and throbbing music, Ralph didn't spot his son at first. Then he saw him lying over on the floor beside the bed, a form motionless except for the nervous, twitching illusion created by the light. What Ralph realized immediately was that his son was as naked as the day he was born.

Ralph tiptoed across the room to his naked son. He reflected upon the fact that he had not seen his son naked since he was a little boy. The first thing Ralph registered, with a strange twinge of pride, and then with a wave of resentment, was that his boy was hung like a horse. And then Ralph recalled bathing his son as a little boy, and how even back then Ralph had been amazed that the tot had a tool that looked like a third leg. What Ralph realized in the next moment in amazement was that his son was wearing a rubber.

Ralph glanced about the room, fearful some beautiful, naked teenage girl would suddenly sit up and scream at the lurking, leering, dirty old man for being where he did not belong, there in his own son's room in his own house. Ralph looked on the far side of the bed and then tiptoed to look in the closet. Then Ralph noticed the used rubbers scattered all over the floor, a dozen or more, a snow of shed skins and opened condom packets. Ralph picked up one of the torn-open condom packs from the floor and studied it in the flashing light. It was his brand, all right. And the girly magazines all around the floor Ralph recognized immediately as being from his own private stash, which he kept under lock and key in a file cabinet in his office. Oddly enough, each of the magazines was turned to pictures of some of Ralph's own favorite babes. Ralph looked back at his naked son and shook his head in confusion. Why would anybody, even somebody as weird and weak-minded as his son, waste a perfectly good, not to mention expensive, rubber just to jack off, that's what Ralph wanted to know. There was no explaining it. It was a notion beyond all comprehension.

When Ralph's eyes fell upon the neck of the bottle sticking out from under the bed, he was not surprised. He bent and picked it up. Ralph knew that the bottle of ancient Scotch was a dead soldier even before he lifted it to his lips. There was evil in the world, there was. Pure, palpable evil that pushed at the world and made it turn, and it had leaked into the world through the lust of Ralph and Alice Ann's own loins. This evil naked bad omen at Ralph's feet was their fault alone. They had brought forth this abomination with their abandoned fucking, and now the whole world would have to pay the price. Ralph studied his son's reptilian face, glistening with sweat, his jaw working, his little lizard lips twitching even in his coma in time to the blaring beat. Ralph looked around the black walls of the room at the posters which glared at him in the throbbing light like leering, evil icons, mocking him and all he stood for, mocking the truly moral man he knew was buried somewhere deep inside him. Ralph rushed around the room slashing one poster after another with his dad's precious pearl-handled pocketknife, which until that very moment Ralph had forgotten he was carrying open and ready for business.

In that scary movie, *The Omen*, what had finally convinced Gregory Peck that the boy he had thought of as his own son was really the Son of Satan was the birthmark the boy carried, triple sixes, 666, on his scalp, which Gregory Peck had uncovered when earlier he had cut the sleeping boy's hair in order to find out the truth once and for all.

Consciously willing himself cold and unrelenting, every nerve alert, ready to do anything necessary in order to find out the truth once and for all, Ralph knelt down beside the naked boy. The boy's hair was as beautifully blond and long as Alice Ann's, but Ralph could not believe how slimy it felt running through his fingers, as he lifted it section by greasy section and sawed away as close as he could to the boy's scalp, which was slow going with the dull blade of Ralph's dad's precious pearl-handled pocket-knife. Ralph was dripping with sweat, exhausted, and his hand actually ached by the time he had cut away enough handfuls of the boy's hair to fully examine his scalp for the telltale birthmark and finally convince himself that the evil boy was truly his own son and responsibility and nothing he could blame on the devil.

Ralph held his drunk, passed-out, naked, and nearly bald boy's head in his lap, and he reflected upon how much they were alike, after all. Holding his nearly bald boy in the strobing light like that, Ralph couldn't be sure where one of them started and the other ended. Ralph had always thought that his son had the sort of personality you could store meat in, but maybe he had been wrong from the start. Maybe it wasn't too late to take his nearly bald boy fishing again, teach him those tricks the boy in turn could pass down the generations, and perhaps Ralph could, if he searched his memory long and hard enough, recall some of those secret hot spots his own dad had shown him beside the lost rivers of his childhood.

Ralph kissed his boy on the mouth, kissed him good night on those dear, lizardlike lips. Ralph began to weep then without sound, something else he had learned to do from his dad, how to cry your heart out without making the least sound. Ralph began to rock his naked, nearly bald boy in his arms. What *could* Ralph teach his son so that he wouldn't go down some of those same old wrong roads? What sort of advice could Ralph give his poor, weak-minded son that he wished his own dad had given him that might spare the boy some of the heartbreak and misery and moves under the cover of darkness from town to town? Ralph put his lips against his son's somewhat elfin ear, and in order to be heard above the blaring madman music in the remote chance that anything could actually penetrate his son's alcoholic coma, Ralph shouted lovingly, *May you not be like your dad! May you not be like your dad! May you never be like your dad!*

Crying at Will

Lindsay flushes the toilet twenty times at least. Until there can surely be no trace of the blood that had gushed from her body. Lindsay curls there on the floor and hugs her knees to her bare breasts. She is still bleeding. She clutches a fistful of toilet paper into her crotch. Lindsay's eyes seem to float away from her, to float up slowly, and then they stop somewhere near the ceiling, and they look back down with disgust at the abandoned body of some naked, bleeding girl curled up into a ball on the cold floor.

Then Lindsay hears her name being called: *Lindsay. Lindsay.* Her called name comes floating in under the door. *Lindsay.* Softly. *Lindsay*, are you okay? Are you all right in there, kiddo?

Lindsay reaches up and unlocks the door.

Are you okay? Jim says. Jim holds Lindsay and says, What's wrong? Are you all right?

I'll never be all right again, Lindsay says.

What? Jim says.

You don't understand.

Huh? Jim says.

My heart is broken, Lindsay says.

What? What did you say?

My stupid period just started. Or something started.

Your period? Jim says, and strokes Lindsay's hair.

I haven't had a real period in weeks, months. Did you know that, Jim?

Your period?

Oh, I spotted some. But I really thought I might be pregnant. I really did. Did you know that, Jim?

Pregnant?

If I had been pregnant, Jim, what would it have been for you?

For me?

Would it have been wonderful or awful?

It would have been all right, Jim says, and rubs the back of Lindsay's neck.

Well, it doesn't matter now. You needn't worry now.

Maybe we should get you to a, you know, hospital or something. You know?

I don't need to see any fucking doctor or go to any fucking hospital. I don't need any fucking doctor to tell me I'm not going to be a mother. I don't deserve to be a mother.

Sure you do, honey, Jim says.

I feel awful.

Maybe we should call somebody or something.

I'll be all right, okay? I just feel awful right now. And I smell awful.

I don't smell anything.

Don't patronize me, Jim! Just don't fucking do it! I know how awful I smell. I want to get in the tub, Jim. Help me up.

Come on, Jim says, and helps Lindsay to her feet. With his arm around her shoulders Jim leads Lindsay from the hallway toilet around the corner into the bathroom. Lindsay begins to shiver violently. Jim grabs a large towel around her and helps her balance on the edge of the huge old tub. Jim puts the plug in the tub and turns on the hot water.

I want a bubble bath, Lindsay says.

Jim picks up a box beside the tub and sprinkles the steaming water with blue bubble-bath beads.

I want the candles lit, Lindsay says.

Sure, Jim says. He gets up and lights the dozen or so scented candles Lindsay keeps arranged on top of her grandmother's old oak towel cabinet. He turns off the overhead light and then kneels and swirls the blue, sweet-smelling beads around in the hot water with his hand.

Don't burn your hand, honey, Lindsay says.

Jim turns off the hot water and begins running a thin stream of cold, swirling it into the hot, testing the water constantly. A small blue bubble breaks from the surface of the foamy water and floats up into the air before Lindsay's face. She watches it rise in the candle flame like a tiny golden balloon and then disappear.

Here, Jim says, and slips the towel from around Lindsay's shoulders.

I'm just crazy. Everything is crazy.

Jim helps Lindsay ease down into the steaming fragrant blue bubbles.

Does it feel okay? Jim says.

It feels okay.

I'll wash your back if you want, Jim says.

I'm still just a fringy, Lindsay says. —I'll always be some sort of fringe-element character who doesn't fit in. I've never fit in anywhere in my life. Not in high school. Not in college. Not even in my own family. I'll never be a real wife and mother.

You're my wife, Jim says. —The last time I checked.

I don't feel like it, Jim. God, I just want to have a normal life. I don't care anymore if I'm not even really happy. Just so I'm not desperately unhappy. I'll settle for that. I just want to be at peace with myself. I'm just tired of feeling that the only place I want to be is far away from myself. Jim, do you love somebody else?

Say what? Jim says.

Are you in love with another woman, Jim?

What other woman?

I just want for you to tell me if you are. I won't cause any trouble for you. I promise I won't. I'll simply go away quietly. You'd tell me the truth, wouldn't you? You wouldn't lie to me about something like that, would you?

No, Jim says. —Is the water okay? Is it too hot?

The water is perfect, hon. Jim, hon, get in the tub with me. Would you?

Oh, I don't know. Let me wash your back. Would you like me to wash your hair?

Are you afraid of something? Are you afraid some of my smelly blood might get on you?

No. Nothing like that.

Please.

Okay, Jim says. He slips off his clothes and eases into the hot water at the end opposite Lindsay.

Jesus motherfucken Christ holy shit, this water's hot! Jim says. —I mean, it's really hot.

Lindsay cups sudsy water and lets it fall over Jim's chest.

Ouch ouch fucken ouch! Jim says through clenched teeth.

I love bubble baths, Lindsay says, and lies back in the blue bubbles, her breasts like little islands on the surface of the water. — Jim, honey, are you still getting those nosebleeds?

No. I mean, hardly ever.

What does that mean?

It means hardly ever.

That really frightens me, hon. That morning I woke up and found blood all over your pillow scared me to death. Will you agree to see a doctor if I do? Would you let me make you, us, an appointment tomorrow?

I can't tomorrow.

I mean simply make the appointment tomorrow.

Okay.

Do you mean it? And none of this the-doctor's-appointment-is-in-the-mail business.

Sure. Okay.

It's the dope, Jim, that's what's making your nose bleed. And you, we, should really slow down in the booze department, too.

I know, Jim says. —I've already started. I've cut way back.

I just don't want to be worried sick all the time, Lindsay says, and she slowly rolls some of Jim's chest hair around a finger.

—Worried about your nosebleeds. About the booze and dope. Worried about your and Shorty's dope deals, which I know are dangerous.

They're not so dangerous.

Worried about you getting caught and going to jail.

At least you'll know where Ralph and I are.

Right, Lindsay says, and laughs. —But most of all I'm worried about your health.

I'm okay.

I'm tired of being worried and sad all the time.

Please don't start crying, honey.

Like this? Lindsay says, and gets up on her knees in the tub and leans forward over Jim, her long hair falling like a curtain about his face. —I can cry at will, Lindsay says, and lets her tears fall on Jim's face.

Are you crying at will right now?

Sure, Lindsay says, and lets the tears drop.

Cool, Jim says, and touches Lindsay's wet cheeks with his fingertips. He brushes the tears away.

I learned that when I was on the stage in college, Lindsay says, and eases back in the water. —I can cry on cue.

I know, Jim says. He rubs strands of Lindsay's hair in his fingers.

Do you love me?

I do.

I hate feeling old and ugly.

You're not old and ugly.

I always feel as though I'm smelly or something. I don't even care if we fuck, necessarily. I just need to feel a man's arms around me.

Any man's?

The man who loves me. All I ever felt like I was good for with that asshole of a first husband was washing his socks and sucking his cock. But at least the sonofabitch would roll over every couple of weeks and want to stick it in my mouth. I felt desired that much at least. You're the one who makes me feel old and ugly and smelly, Jim. And you're the one who promised to love and cherish me until death us do part.

Let's talk about this later.

But you always put me off. You never want to talk.

I talk.

Why do you make me feel so fucking awful?

Thanks, Jim says. —Put all your problems at my doorstep.

Now you sound like fucking Ralph.

That's probably the worst thing you ever said to me, Jim says. —Look, I'm trying to write a book. It's taking about everything I got.

That's not good enough. Jim, honey, we need to talk. Even when it's painful. Tonight is the first time we've even come close to talking about anything since I don't remember when.

I know, Jim says.

We have to stay in love, Jim. We have to try, anyway. Staying in love is the most difficult thing to do on the face of the earth. But we can do it. We simply can't keep drifting apart.

I know, Jim says.

Two people are capable of loving one another all their lives, I know it. I have to believe this. If I don't believe anything else in the world, I have to believe this. Your book is no reason for us to drift apart.

I'll do better.

Do you really still love me?

I love you.

God, I hope so, you big bozo. I love you. I do.

I'm glad.

Well, I'm glad you're glad, Lindsay says, and laughs. She strokes Jim's nipples through the hair on his chest with her thumbs. Jim touches the sides of Lindsay's breasts with his fingertips. He cups her breasts and squeezes gently.

The Kindness of Strangers

Ralph had to look high and low, rummage around in countless drawers, before he found a functioning pair of scissors, which he then arranged in his son's left hand (the boy was a lefty, another suspicious sign in the devil department). In the boy's right hand Ralph arranged several fistfuls of greasy hair and, as an afterthought, a ripped section from one of the evil posters. Ralph locked the boy's bedroom door behind him, and he fled the scene of that crime against nature with hopefully no solid clues pointing in his direction.

In the kitchen Ralph lifted the print of the green pepper above the stove and reached into the hole behind it. He wiggled his fingers around until he found the little bottle. It was only a half-pint of bourbon, but an unopened cherry, and in a pinch what else could a man hope for. Ralph unscrewed the top and took a long hit and, after swatting a cat off the chair, sat down at the kitchen table. He reached up and clicked off the overhead light and then sat there in the dark chain-smoking and sipping from the little half-pint, one sip for himself and one for his dad, as he watched the driveway. He reflected upon that naked, nearly bald boy in that bedroom of black walls. At this point, Ralph reflected, it was all out of his hands.

A car Ralph did not recognize pulled into the driveway and stopped. It was a big, black, expensive-looking affair, and who-ever was driving left the engine and high beams on. Ralph ducked back away from the window and stubbed out his cigarette. The backseat's door was flung open and Alice Ann tumbled out onto the gravel on her knees. Ralph killed off the pint in a single gulp. Alice Ann was laughing hysterically. The driver's-side door of the car swung open and Ralph saw a pant leg.

Ralph blinked his eyes in the bright overhead light when Alice Ann clicked it on with the switch by the door, and spots spun in his vision. When he was able to focus, Ralph peeked out from behind the refrigerator. Alice Ann was being supported on either side and guided along by a couple, an older couple, who were complete strangers to Ralph. They were a tall, handsome couple, and the woman had beautifully coiffed white hair. The man looked like that junior-high-school principal who had expelled Ralph for smoking in the boys' room. The woman made encour-aging cooing sounds at Alice Ann, and kept saying, "There, dear; there, dear; there, dear." At this point Alice Ann was weeping uncontrollably. Suddenly Alice Ann began to laugh again. Both the man and woman had stricken looks on their otherwise pleas-ant, kindly faces.

Over there, Alice Ann said after a particularly wrenching combination sob and hoot, and she pointed at Ralph, who ducked back behind the refrigerator and held his breath. —Over there is Mr. Crawford, the man who happens to be my husband of all these wasted lifetimes. We are the Crawfords, my husband and I. Come out from behind the refrigerator, Mr. Crawford, you miserable sonofabitch, and meet the Myerses, the kindest human beings on the face of the fucking earth, who just saved my life.

Hello, Ralph said, and stepped out from behind the refrigera-tor. —I was looking for something. I dropped something back there. Hello, hello, Ralph said, and offered his hand to Mr. Myers, who shook it once.

She—your wife, I mean, Mr. Myers said to Ralph, in a whisper Ralph supposed he meant to somehow fly over Alice Ann's head, she was walking on the side of the road.

Your wife was stumbling, Mrs. Myers stage-whispered, her lips pursed and her wide eyes suggesting her utter astonishment. —She was stumbling on the roadside. We had to stop, Mr. Myers and myself. We had to help her some way.

This is the third house she has asked us to stop at, Mr. Myers said, his kindly eyes crinkled with confusion and concern. —We really didn't know quite what to do.

We had to help her, though, if we could, Mrs. Myers affirmed, nodding her white head vigorously.

She is not deaf and dumb, Alice Ann said. —*She* is not a dead person or a child or somebody simpleminded.

My wife has been under the weather lately, Ralph said. —And she's been taking medications. Prescribed medication, of course. She had a glass of wine with dinner. Two tops. Nothing like this has ever happened to us before.

These kind people, the Myerses, were kind enough to drive me home after you dumped me on our eighteenth wedding anniversary. Mr. and Mrs. Myers, I will never be able to adequately thank you enough for your kindness. Mrs. Myers, I would bet my life that Mr. Myers has never been an inconsiderate cocksucker to you, has he? Unlike Mr. Crawford. By the bye, Mr. and Mrs. Myers, would you care to have a little drink? A nightcap?

I looked everywhere for you, Alice Ann, Ralph said. —I thought you had left me. I did, I did, Ralph said to the Myerses.

We really have to be going, Mr. Myers said, looking at his watch. He took his wife by her elbows and edged her toward the door. —Mr. Crawford, Mr. Myers stage-whispered, perhaps she, Mrs. Crawford, should see somebody, somebody, you know, professional.

Please, Mr. and Mrs. Myers, I implore you, Alice Ann said. —Permit my husband, Mr. Crawford, to fix you a little drink. Pull up a couple of chairs and let's get better acquainted. My husband's first name is Ralph. Call Mr. Crawford Ralph from here on out, please. My first name is Lindsay. Call me Lindsay like my husband, Mr. Crawford, does, I implore you. Mr. Crawford, will you please fix us all a nice little drink and we will explain to the Myerses how things went astray tonight. So they will understand and hopefully not think too badly of us and hopefully will give us a second chance, as I have given Mr. Crawford. Mr. Crawford has had more chances than you can shake a stick at. Mr. Crawford, Ralph to you, went outside the marriage, you understand. A woman's charm, as we all know, is fifty percent illusion, but when a thing is important, I tell the truth, and this is the *truth*. I, for one, have never cheated on Mr. Crawford as long as I have lived. Is it that I am not young and desirable enough any longer, Mr. Crawford? Is that why you were fucking my sister royally? Look at dear Mrs. Myers here. Mrs. Myers is no longer young and desirable, but does that mean Mr. Myers would fuck her sister royally? I think not. I have always believed that whatever good you possess is good enough to merit your salvation. Something has happened to Mr. Crawford and myself while we weren't looking. But what was it? Mr. Crawford, why don't you see if our children are awake. I'd love for the Myerses to meet our children. They're wonderful kids. They want to be lawyers and doctors.

Not tonight, Alice Ann, Ralph said. —Some other time.

We have to leave, really, Mr. Myers said. —Really we do. We are sorry, you understand. We truly are.

Our kids will be heartsick if they don't get to meet you folks, Alice Ann said. —Ralph, goddamn it, fix the fucking drinks.

Really, not for us, Mr. Myers said. —Perhaps another time. We really have to be going. People are waiting for us. We are expected somewhere.

At three or four o'clock in the fucking morning? Alice Ann said. —Don't make me laugh. Our children are not at home, is that it, Ralph? Ralph, tell me where our children are at three or four fucking o'clock in the morning.

Mr. Crawford . . . Mr. Myers said.

Ralph to you, Alice Ann said.

Somebody professional, Mr. Crawford, Mr. Myers said. —Somebody recommended. A good doctor.

Did you know, Mr. and Mrs. Myers, that my husband, Mr. Crawford, is a famous author?

Please, Alice Ann, Ralph said. —Please.

Don't be so modest, Mr. Crawford, Alice Ann said. —Haven't you folks heard of Ralph Crawford, the famous author?

Well, to tell you the truth, Mr. Myers said, I'm not very conversant with contemporary authors. A fact I am rather ashamed to admit, since I'm a professor of literature at San Jose State. My area of concern is the Victorian period. I am something of an Arnoldian, I must confess.

He is very prominent in his field, Mrs. Myers said.

I will make it a point to look up your work, however, Mr. Crawford, Mr. Myers said, and withdrew a small notebook from his coat pocket. —Perhaps you could give me some of the titles of your books.

No, that's all right, Ralph said. —Really. Just forget about it. I'd much rather that you forget everything about tonight, if you can.

My husband, Mr. Crawford, won't forget anything about this night, Alice Ann said. —My husband is probably making this into a story right now. Tell him the stories of your lives, Mr. and Mrs. Myers. Go on, I dare you.

Well, it has been nice to meet you folks, Ralph said to the Myerses, who stood there frozen in an attitude of departure. —Even under these trying circumstances.

Mrs. Myers, Alice Ann said, and raised a hand toward Mrs. Myers, I simply cannot tell you how much you remind me of my mother. She was beautiful and kind, as you are. I got my hair from her, and my voice. My mother would have looked exactly like you, Mrs. Myers, if her brain had not exploded, Alice Ann said, and picked up the empty half-pint bottle from the table. She shook it and looked at it in the light.

I'm afraid that little baby is history, Ralph said. —To tell the sad truth, I don't think there's a drop of anything in the whole house for a nightcap. I don't suppose you have a little drop of something with you, do you, Mr. Myers?

When Mr. and Mrs. Myers turned hurriedly for the door, Mr. Myers stumbled over a scrambling cat. Alice Ann jumped up from the table and rushed after them.

Let's stay in touch, Alice Ann called from the doorway to the departing Myerses.

Sea of Love

1

The Beach Chalet was a two-story Byzantine dream of a bar. Once a fabled watering hole for the wealthy, it was now an aging, once-grand Beaux Arts building on the curb of the Great Highway, with the Pacific Ocean as a view and inspiration for serious boozing. A vast cathedral of a gin joint, it was flooded with a smoky lyric light that left you with an illusion of flying buttresses and a floating cloudy dome of a ceiling dim and distant and rich with mysterious portents as meaningful for some as a Sistine Chapel, beneath which its generally lowlife but dedicated disciples could get truly religious about their drinking—graybeard biker types and their sagging bleached-blond babes; old salts nodding with nostalgia as they nursed the last, sad beers of their lives; fading, tattooed trollops tottering around the room, as they slow-danced in lonely self-hugs and awaited the second coming of desire. They all took turns plugging silver into an enormous Mexican folk altar of a jukebox packed with those sentimental, plaintive country tunes in which self-pity just comes natural, in which at the end of long suffering you get to be just who you have always suspected you are, the real star of the song.

Jim gazed across the room, that smoky shadowland of sudden love and its attendant loss, to where Mary Mississippi was shooting pool with a tall, one-armed biker whose pure white hair hung in a ponytail nearly to his butt. Mary had taken off her motorcycle jacket, and each time she bent forward to shoot a ball her small, firm breasts pressed against the cotton of her sleeveless cut-off black T-shirt. Her hair was still damp from the rainy day outside, and its red ringlets were pasted around her shining penny of a face. As Mary took each studied shot, Jim looked with lust at the supple ripple of sleek muscle beneath the tanned, toned flesh of Mary's arms. Her wide sea-green eyes had that show-me-something-I-haven't-seen-before look in them, and when she raised a fist in the air after a very good shot, Jim could see a haze of red hair under her arm. Within that slant of autumnal ocean light in which she moved languidly around the table, Mary's hair and flesh shed the soft glow of a sunset. The aging biker, who had your basic battered, been-around face and, Jim had to acknowledge, a true elegance of motion as he deftly handled the pool cue one-handed, was clearly entranced by Mary, and Jim knew the name of that song.

Jim saw Mary touch the old biker fart on his shoulder when he made a poor shot, and she fluttered her fingers there as they spoke for a few moments, their heads inclined intimately. Mary poked the old biker in the ribs with a forefinger as she nodded her head against his chest and laughed at something wonderfully funny he said. After another game of pool, they strolled over to the jukebox together, Mary and the old biker fuck, and Mary stood with the side of her hip pressed against the old biker's leg, while they took turns punching selections. When they began to slow-dance, the old biker bent forward so that his face was against Mary's upturned face. They barely moved as they danced in place in front of the jukebox, and Mary's eyes were closed. The old biker's one huge hand, his left, rested at the upper swell of Mary's hips. Mary had one of her hands up under the old biker's white ponytail on his neck and the other she had hooked over the back of his belt by a thumb. When the song ended Mary stood on tiptoe to whisper something into the old biker's ear, and then she stepped back away from him and smiled wide-eyed and blinky up into his old, craggy, take-no-prisoners face. The old biker wagged his head in what appeared to Jim's trained eye utter disbelief, and then after saying something to Mary, he hurried off toward the entrance to the men's room. Mary looked over her shoulder at Jim with that sexy, shadowy smile he knew so well, and then she turned and walked toward him, looking down at her feet as she came, her hands clasped behind her back, biting her full lower lip, like a naughty little girl who had some big explaining to do.

Mary Mississippi nuzzled her face into Jim's neck and ran her tongue along the side of his beard to his ear, whose lobe she sucked between her lips. She hooked the fingers of her right hand behind Jim's belt buckle and pressed the palm of her hand against the amazing bulge of the boner strangling in his jeans.

Well, my gracious, Mary said, laughing, you old hot dog, you.

What's a boy to do?

So, how've you been amusing yourself while I was off shooting pool with that old guy?

And slow-dancing.

Yup.

Oh, not much. You know. The usual. I've just been sitting here brooding about the fact that the bottom line of life is the indestructibility of hope.

I'll say. Been lonesome for me.

You bet. So how have you been amusing yourself besides rubbing up against that old fart?

That's about the long and short of it, darlin', Mary said, and cocked her head cutely. —Here's the problem, sugar, I haven't been a real bad little girl much this past week hardly at all. I hardly have any juicy stories for you at all. Oh, let's see. I fucked Spain on Tuesday, but I wasn't much in the mood and we didn't do anything real dirty. I fucked Clay last night. I ran into him down on 24th at the Celtic Tavern and one thing led to another and I really hadn't fucked Clay in a month of Sundays and he was peeved. Oh, and we did do a little trick that might tickle your fancy. You ever heard of a snowjob? I hadn't, which is pretty hard to believe. What Clay did was put a line of coke on his boner, which I did just before I gave him head. That's what Clay called a snowjob. That just about cracked me up! I could hardly suck him off I was giggling so bad. Anyway, that's about all she wrote in the old suckin' and fuckin' department this week. So what will that add up to, anyhow? About five or six little spanks is all, I bet. My little bottom will hardly get rosy with five or six little spanks. Sugar, will that snowjob get me a few extra little spanks when we get back over to my place?

A couple, I reckon, Jim said, and patted Mary's ass.

Shootfire, boy, is that all?

Let me guess, Jim said, and cupped Mary's hips in his hands. —You got your heart set on doing that old fart?

What's a girl to do? Mary said, and pressed her pelvis against Jim's leg. —I mean, I have never made it with a one-armed man before. Hey, and he tells me he's got a dick that needs a dashboard! I won't do it if you tell me not to, sugar.

Do what you want to do.

Okeydokey. I just plan on giving him some head, so it won't take too long, I betcha. Do you want to watch?

Not today.

Okeydokey, babe. When I lick my lips and come up smilin', I'll be thinking of you down in my heart, and only you. And I'll commit every single little juicy thing to memory, and when we get back over to my place, I'll drive you plum nuts with the dirty details, sugar. It'll be my little goodbye gift to you, okay? Mary said, smiling up at Jim like a choirgirl. —Jim, you may have my heart in your back pocket, baby, but I have your number good.

When the old fart of a biker returned from the restroom, Mary was waiting for him by the front door. As he opened the door for her, Mary slipped a hand into one of the old biker's back pockets. Mary gave Jim a last look over her shoulder and a big smile, and Jim tipped his fedora toward her just as the heavy door swung shut behind the happy couple.

2

As soon as Jim saw the old biker stagger back in the door maybe twenty minutes later, looking palsied and dazed, Jim polished off his shot of tequila and headed out. At which moment, as that farcical cosmic gravy called fate would have it, he ran right into S. Clay Wilson coming in the door. Clay was leading his usual entourage of sleazy, shanghaied strumpets, thundering dummies, and cave-life cretins, all of whom, Clay informed Jim grandly, had spent a typical morning touring the low-rent bars to hunt and gather and collect offerings of any sort for the Higher Echelon Fallen Angels Beer Blast, Barbecue and Swimming Party Fund, of which Clay was the master of last rites.

Gah'damn, sumbitch, it's my old pal Jimmy, Clay had yelled at the short, muscular woman with a mustache, whose name was Femme Fatale and who was Clay's main squeeze for the morning. It's fucken farcical cosmic gravy, Clay yelled into Femme's ear, for he had been thinking about his old pal Jim ever since that morning when he took this monster dump and that giant two-toned turd laying there grinning up at him had looked just like his old pal Jimmy.

Jim begged off, had to almost wrestle Clay to get loose, saying some shit was hitting the fan elsewhere, one of his and Shorty's deals gone sour, a situation he had to attend to pronto, but he'd call Clay tonight and they'd tie up. Clay hovered at the door, however, and watched as Jim made his way across the rain-slick Great Highway to the parking area, where Clay spotted that chopped-top, lowered, midnight-blue '52 Hudson classic, a car Clay recognized even before Jim reached it and hopped in. Whereupon the Hudson peeled out, leaving rubber even on the wet pavement, and Clay knew the name of that song. Whereupon Clay did what seemed sensible and rewarding. He joined his scumbag entourage at the bar and began downing double shots of Sausa Commemorative tequila with warm Dutch beers back.

For a few forlorn minutes, S. Clay considered the possibility of swearing off women and the pain they caused as routinely as taking a shit. Returning perhaps to that fag bar in the Castro he and his thundering thug buddies had terrorized earlier in the morning, the Mildred Pierce Annex, where he had harassed a covey of cute cabin boys off a Swedish liner anchored in the bay until all the sweet things swore they would never disembark in

America again. Perhaps Clay could make things up to them, those cute cabin boys, convince them to take him in, care for him, be gentle and understanding and patient with him as he learned their secret ways. Then Clay felt Femme Fatale, who could read him like a book, cozy up beside him. Whereupon, cooing the soft sounds of sympathy, she took things in hand, rubbing his horn of honey beneath the bar. As he tried to focus his wet, crossed eyes upon the thick, muscular form of this angel of masturbation, who was also one of a hell of a professional wrestler, Clay suddenly perceived the wondrous light emanating from her lonely but lovely inner self. What Clay had come to understand was the wisdom of loving a selfless, ugly woman, who was also perfectly capable of kicking some ass.

3

Mary Mississippi and Jim drove across town from the Great Highway to Mary's loft south of Market Street at the edge of the Mission. Jim placed his hands on Mary's softly swaying hips as in the drizzly air they climbed the rickety outside stairs to her loft, which took up the entire top floor of an old three-story brewery building. As Mary fiddled with the lock of the big sliding iron door, Jim took in deep breaths of air rich with the smell of freshly baked bread from the bakery down the alley, and he gazed out over seeming acres of wet warehouse rooftops that stretched all the way to the waters of the Bay, where he spotted the dim outline of a ship making its way to the docks in Oakland.

Mary undressed slowly as she walked across the big room toward the brass bed along the far wall. Her skin glowed pink in the pearly light that streamed though the huge skylight. Mary lay back on the wide bed and opened her arms and legs toward Jim, smiling that cute, crooked smile, the red hair around her labia outlining an impossibly pink core. She bit her lower lip as she watched Jim walk across the room toward her, tossing his own clothes as he came.

As it turned out, Mary's old biker had had a dick that could put to good use not only a dashboard but fender skirts and the grille of a Cadillac car. Hence Mary truly got what she craved from Jim as she related all the low-down, blow-by-blow details of the various dirty deeds she had done to that old coot with a great cock and Jim spanked her bare ass black and blue for her. What Jim reflected upon as he whacked away at Mary's cutely dimpled behind was that the one thing they had always really shared was the craving of that fruit called pain. In a nutshell, they were both fools for pain, Jim and Mary. They were pure pain simple.

Jim flopped back on the bed breathless, sweaty, his arms a ton of bricks. Mary crawled up onto him. She licked the damp hair on his chest and sucked on his left nipple. She buried her face in his chest hair and inhaled deeply. —Boy, you have got to be the best-smellin' man I have ever personally had the extreme pleasure of smellin'. Sugar, what I can't figure out is if you're this boy who may really love me like he claims he does or if you're just some sort of intrepid nooky hound who fooled me good. Sugar, the time has come for you to shit or get off the pot. Are you gonna move back to New York with me or what?

I told you I'd be back in a few weeks.

I'm not talkin' about some little bitty visit, boy. You know just what I'm talkin' about.

I know what you're talking about.

How the fuck did I ever get on the lonely side of love, any-how? I know all about the crazy road I'm on. I've been down it before. I figured I'd learned a long time ago not to try to hold on to something I never had in the first place. But I guess you never learn when it comes to nasty old love. I don't know how I got to be a goner over you. You are so extreme is what I think it is. I've never met a man as hard and as soft at the same time as you. You're just so weird and extreme, and also, I love how you smell. So what have I been to you, then, sweetie, some kind of six-week stand? You still love her, don't ya?

You know I care for you. She loves somebody else.

Fuckin' *care* for me! You asshole! You're just one of those kinds of old boys who like to fuck fantasy. I knew that about you right off. Well, I didn't do half the low-down, dick-suckin' shit I told you. I just told you a whole bunch of that shit for the pure sake of your boner. So who does she love, anyhow?

Oh, really? You made stuff up?

That's the long and short of it, you asshole. So who is he?

Just somebody, that's who. What wasn't true?

Oh, a whole lot of it wasn't true.

What about the stuff with Clay, for instance? The snowjob. That time he had you tickle his asshole with his own toothbrush.

Well, yeah, that stuff was true, I guess. Hey, you're trying to turn the tables. I'm the one with the big questions around here. You're stalling on me, aren't you, boy?

I just can't move back to New York with you right now.

I know the score. I just want you to know there were real, true feelings involved here on my part, anyhow. All this wasn't just some big fat joke to me. I meant things and I'm real sad right now 'cause I know you'll never leave her. Not for me, anyhow. I'm real disappointed in how things turned out, and most of all I'm real disappointed in you, Jim. I've really liked being in love with you. Being in love makes me feel like a million bucks. I believe in love. True love, too. I'm a sucker for it. There's a whole sea of love, and I'm just a little boat on it. I was, anyhow. Now I'm gonna have to stop being in love, and I could just cry my eyes out on account of it. I'm a real unhappy girl right now, Jim, thanks to you. Jim, just don't go making a joke out of my true feelings. Don't play this for laughs in some old story. Please don't do it. Give me that much anyhow, all right? Show me that much consideration, will you, huh? Well, let's go ahead and fuck anyhow. I'll fuck your brains out of your ears and you just remember what you'll be missing, boy. I just hope she breaks your fucking heart. You got it coming, boy, big time.

The Lights of Buenos Aires

1

Ralph knew it was time to get out on his own. He could no longer endure the endless accusations and pain and potential violence, nor one more night of Alice Ann's efforts to raise the dead from this and a hundred earlier lifetimes of turmoil. Ralph had had enough of Alice Ann sitting at what had once been their dining-room table with her space-cadet friends, talking in tongues, the room ablaze from skull-shaped candles and musky incense smelling morbidly like overripe roses and worms.

More than this even were the criminal kids, who were finally totally out of hand. His daughter had gotten that tattoo of a skull and crossbones above her right breast, after all. Paco was back to weighing drugs on the kitchen table, and Killer roamed the house freely. Ever since that night when the boy had in a drunken delirium apparently cut off great strands of his own long blond hair, he had taken to shaving his head, except for a Mohawk strip down the center, much in the mode of his latest hero and role model, that crazy character Robert De Niro had played in *Taxi Driver*, full of hatred, sexual hang-ups, and an affection for violence and revenge, after whom Ralph's son had decided to pattern his life. Most of all, though, Ralph had to demonstrate to Lindsay that he was now a free agent.

He needed to be alone for a few days is what Ralph wrote in the note he left Alice Ann. He needed to get body and soul back together. He'd be in touch, Ralph wrote in the note. Ralph took a room in a cheap East Palo Alto hotel which had two narrow windows overlooking the Bayshore Freeway. As he sat on his bed at night, smoking and watching the endless traffic of people with places to go, Ralph could sometimes glimpse an airplane descending from the dark western sky toward the San Francisco airport. It would sink softly in the night as though through liquid, its lights blinking in languid sequence, and Ralph would fill with both an unspecified remorse for the past and longing for the future.

Ralph had to use a pay phone in the hallway for calls. Time after time he tried to get a call in to Lindsay, but Jim always answered, and Ralph hung up. Ralph called his old home a dozen times a day at least, let the phone ring off the wall, simply to see who would finally answer, and when somebody did, he would hang up. What Ralph liked best about his little room was the small refrigerator which stood next to the bed. When he woke up in the middle of the night confused and dying of thirst, all he had to do was reach out, even with his eyes closed, blindly, and open the door, and there was that cold bottle of vodka.

One afternoon Ralph parked his car down the street from the house and sat there smoking and sipping vodka for over an hour, looking for the least sign of life. When he was reasonably sure nobody was home, Ralph entered the house and poked around. He examined the dirty dishes piled precariously on the sink and reflected upon what their stains revealed about the eating habits of a household to which he no longer belonged. Ralph felt like some sort of archaeologist sifting through the debris of a vanished people. He checked out the little pyramid of butts in the ashtray on the kitchen table for evidence, such as unfamiliar brands. He checked out the contents of the refrigerator to see what they would reveal about the life of these lost people. He drank directly from a half-gallon bottle of milk and then poured the rest down the drain. He poured a bottle of orange juice down the drain. He ate several bitefuls of leftover Chinese food from cartons, and then threw the remainder in the garbage disposal. He dumped half a dozen eggs down the garbage disposal. He crammed lunchmeat and cheese, half a loaf of bread, and a jar of Alice Ann's favorite pickles down the garbage disposal and turned it on and lingered there listening to that satisfying grind.

The bedroom was as straightened up as Ralph had ever seen it, the bed made, no piles of dirty clothes. Ralph noticed that Alice Ann had bought new sheets and pillowcases. In a sudden fit he tore the bed apart, left the bedcovers in a pile on the floor. Ralph checked the medicine cabinet in his and Alice Ann's bathroom for evidence. Ralph dumped all the toothpaste and toilet paper he could find in the house into a pillowcase, and on top of that piled all the canned goods he could carry, and forsook that place.

One night when the house was closed up and dark, Ralph spotted a strange car parked at the end of the driveway, a battered old Mercedes. When Ralph skulked over to check it out, he saw that it had a flat tire. That could only mean that Alice Ann and somebody, God only knew who, were off together somewhere in her own rattletrap. Even he, Ralph Crawford, was handy enough to change a flat, for God's sake, Ralph reflected with disdain. He listened with great pleasure to the hiss of freed air as he deflated the Mercedes' other three tires. He bent its antenna into a question mark. He stood there in the dark driveway breathless and looked up and down the street. A dog barked in the distance and he could hear the faint hum of traffic from the freeway. Ralph leaned against the car and smoked another cigarette. He flicked the butt out into the driveway, its glowing ember like the tracer of a bullet spinning through the dark. Ralph looked up and down the street once more and then unzipped his pants. He began urinating on the driver's-side door handle, then raised his aim and sent his golden arc streaming through the open window.

And then one morning Ralph found a FOR SALE sign in the front yard. When he tried the front door he found it was locked, something of a first. Ralph tried his key, and every other key on his key chain, to no avail. He circled the house, pounding on the locked doors and windows, and calling out for Alice Ann, to no avail. Ralph's next-door neighbor, that nosy old goat, came out onto his porch and stood there with his hands on his hips glaring at Ralph. Ralph ignored him, lit a cigarette, and flopped down heavily on his front stoop. After a time the neighbor went back into his house shaking his head, and Ralph pulled out the pint he had in his coat pocket and took a pull. What came to Ralph's mind was that John Cheever story where this poor fellow gets unstuck in time, where somehow in the course of strange events one day the poor fellow in the story arrives in the future only to find that he has no place in it. The poor fellow arrives at his house after a day of terrible misadventures only to find it locked against him, and apparently long empty, and his lovely wife and children apparently long gone. It was as though that poor fellow's future had vanished without a trace.

Ralph jumped up and ran over to the FOR SALE sign. He pushed it back and forth, jerked on it, put his arms under it, and heaved with all his might. When he could not uproot the wretched thing, Ralph stepped back and kicked it. He kicked it until the board broke, and then he stomped on that wretched sign and kicked it in the teeth while he had it down. When his nosy neighbor came back out onto his porch, that perfect asshole who would as soon call the sheriff on Ralph as look at him, Ralph pulled his pint out for all the world to see. He waved the bottle toward the nosy neighbor, then took a long pull. Ralph smacked his lips mightily, then stuck out his tongue at that nosy neighbor.

There came a day when Ralph had about three bucks and some change to his name. While Ralph shaved that morning, he mulled over his options. Who had he not already borrowed from? His mom wouldn't even answer her door. When he heard the drone of a low-flying plane overhead, Ralph stopped shaving and simply stood there looking at his wretched kisser in that cracked mirror. What he wouldn't give to be on some flight out. Clean-shaven and wearing his freshest shirt, one which had but a single coffee stain on its front, Ralph braced himself to face a new day. He dribbled the last drops from his last pint into a few cold swallows of yesterday's coffee. He carried the cup and his change out into the hallway to the phone on the wall.

Jim answered almost before the phone rang, and Ralph began rattling along a mile a minute, afraid to let Jim get a word in edgewise. My back is up against the wall down here, old Jim. Down to my last dime, the rattletrap is on its last legs, two weeks behind in the rent for this fleabag room, my mom needs an operation or she'll be legally blind in weeks, and what if she croaks, what then, I ask you? I can't bury the old bat. Who knows where Alice Ann has run off to. Or with whom. The wolf is at the door, old Jim, not to mention the sheriff. I'd run away from home if I had one, old Jim, Ralph rattled on and on in that public place, that hallway pay phone, with old men eyeballing him as they passed in the narrow hallway, a couple of the old farts even stopping to listen in on Ralph's lament, and one old coot came up behind Ralph to wait for the phone, jabbering loudly to himself, drooling, rolling his milky eyes, waving his cane wildly.

Old Jim, what I need down here is a helping hand, Ralph rattled, trying to keep his back turned to the insane old shit, whose spittle Ralph could feel spraying the back of his neck, saliva infected with old age and hopelessness. —A helping hand, old Jim, until my ship comes in. Jim, I am currently up a creek of shit with no paddle. What? Say what, old Jim? You've been trying to run me down? For what? A party? For me? A birthday party for me? You've got to be kidding. I didn't even remember I had a birthday coming up, old Jim. I am welcome in your home with open arms? You are rolling out the red carpet? You've missed me of late? You forgive me my transgressions? Old Jim, don't take this the wrong way, but what's the catch here? Who do I have to kill? Do I have to perform unnatural acts while on my knees? Well, I'll do it! Whatever it is, I'll do it. You name it, old Jim, and I'm your man. What, old Jim? Your ship? Your ship has come in? You sold your what? You sold your new novel? You sold your new novel for how much? Dear God, old Jim! Dear God in heaven! Yes, I'm on my way, yes, I'm leaving in two shakes. Say what, old Jim? Come up and stay with you guys for as long as I want? A roof over my old woolly head for the rest of my natural life if it comes to that? Grow old with you guys if it comes to that? Holy moly, old Jim, I'm out the door down here. Which may be a little tricky, as I owe back rent and the manager is a sly, evil old coot and pretty frisky for a paraplegic, but I'm on my way, old Jim. Old Jim, how much was your advance again? Dear God, old Jim! I'm really happy for you, old sport. I'm happy for you and happy for Lindsay. You guys deserve it, by golly. Okay, here I come. I'll be knocking on your door before you know it, old buddy, Ralph said, and hung up. Ralph barely managed to dodge the cane-wielding, crazy old coot who pushed past him to grab the phone and, without inserting a single coin or pretending to dial, commenced a conversation with J. Edgar Hoover.

Ralph sat on the edge of his bed and fired up one of his last three cigarettes. Jim had sold that silly teenage hoodlum novel to Harcourt Brace Jovanovich for how much did he say? That was a lie of, course. Jim had sold his novel, no doubt. He couldn't get away with a lie like that. Something like that would be too easy to check out, as Ralph was certain any number of Bay Area authors were doing right then. Wonder how much that old pirate did get, though. Ralph threw whatever of his clothes he could find fungus-free into that old yellow suitcase of Alice Ann's, along with four rolls of toilet paper and three tubes of toothpaste left over from his home visits. He was happy for old Jim, he was. Ralph picked up a pillowcase and looked around the room. There wasn't a thing worth taking in that sorry dump. Ralph put the pillowcase in the suitcase and closed it. And he was happy for Lindsay. He was. Ralph wrapped the rope around the suitcase twice and tied it tightly. He was happy for them both. Ralph heard the sound of another plane landing or departing, and he imagined himself on it, at the end or beginning of some flight pattern of the future. Ralph cracked his door and peered into the dark, narrow hallway. The old coot was still raving to J. Edgar Hoover about the Commie in room 34. Clutching his suitcase under his arm, Ralph scurried down the hallway toward the burnt-out EXIT sign above the door to the back fire escape.

2

Many years later, Ralph Crawford and his second wife, a woman whom Ralph considered to be the person who had finally saved his life, would have to catch an early-morning flight from Buenos Aires back to the States, after a combination vacation and reading series Ralph had presented as a part of a cultural exchange program under the auspices of the State Department. As Ralph and his second wife passed through the early-morning airport, they noted how still and deserted it was, and his second wife, who was a celebrated poet herself, commented that for all its bright lights and shining floors, the deserted airport had the aura of a place of mourning.

As the plane taxied down the runway in a light snow, Ralph, whom flying gave the willies, wished to himself that his second wife had not used that bummer word "mourning." As the plane lifted off to return Ralph and his second wife to their rich, full, famous lives in America, Ralph turned in his seat for one last look at the lovely lights of Buenos Aires, where they had enjoyed such a fulfilling time together. Ralph then settled back in his seat and closed his eyes, hoping to grab a nap on this first leg of the long trip back. Ralph began to drift off, letting his mind wander, as he listened to the easy drone of the plane. But then Ralph's mind started jumping around wildly and landed in the past. Suddenly Ralph shot up in his seat and looked about the cabin in utter panic.

Living for the Record

1

Sure, Jim had billed the party as being in honor of Ralph's birthday, but Ralph got the real picture fast enough. Jim was using Ralph's good name and highly successful book of stories as bait. Jim had invited about every author of note in the Bay Area to the party supposedly for Ralph, and Jim was sucking up to them all shamelessly. Jim was turning this gathering of just about anybody who was anybody in the Bay Area literary scene, supposedly on hand to celebrate Ralph's birthday, into a sort of coming-out party for his own new book and himself.

At one point Ralph overheard Herb Gold, who was escorting two cute albeit it very young chicks, tell Jack Hicks that Jim had confided to him that Jim's book advance had been in the six-figures range, which was double the amount Jim had lied to Ralph about in the first place. Ralph watched Jim as he held forth over where he had strategically positioned himself beside the dining-room table, which was groaning under succulent mounds of food that looked catered, where many of the Bay Area's noted authors were grazing like cattle.

Jim had his arm around Lindsay, who looked absolutely ravishing in this flowing, flowery-print affair, silky green and off her creamy shoulders, which glistened in the candlelight. Jim had not let Lindsay out of his sight for a moment all evening, the poor woman. In fact, Jim had made sure Ralph and Lindsay were hardly ever alone together in all the past week Ralph had stayed there. Sure Lindsay looked lovely that night, but Ralph could see beneath that. To Ralph's eagle eye Lindsay looked stricken, miserable, breathless in Jim's bear hug of attention, even though she was trying bravely to hide it with all that laughter and feigned gaiety.

Ralph wandered out to the kitchen, where he found some of the Stanford crowd, including Dick Scowcroft, a funny, courtly man who had been his and Jim's dear old Stanford teacher. The wall phone, which was difficult to hear above the din, was ringing. Finally, Dick Scowcroft turned around and lifted the receiver and waved it at Ralph, saying, I bet it's for you, Ralph. Ralph said, Oh no. It couldn't be. Dick put the receiver to his ear and said, Hello. What? Oh my gracious, Dick said, and then he handed the phone to Ralph again, saying, Oh yes, I'm quite certain it's for you, Ralph. Ralph took the receiver and put it to his ear. Hello, Ralph said. The voice on the other end, a voice Ralph vaguely recognized, said, As I was saying, you faithless, fetid flotsam of a betraying asshole. Ralph said, You've got the wrong party, I believe. But the angry voice bellowed on. Just wanted you to know, you cocksucker, I know all about the hot-to-trot affair you're having with that bitch boner-breath Mary Mississippi. And what I mean to do is revenge-fuck you, pal. Revenge fucks are the absolute best fucks in village life. And I got some payback blowjobs coming, too, motherfucker. Lindsay is a class-act lady and she don't deserve your vile shit. And when I rat out your worthless act, I'll bet she'll agree with my revenge-fuck theory. Adios, pigshit, the voice said, and hung up. Goodbye, Ralph said, and hung up the receiver.

At last Ralph saw Lindsay without Jim. She was making her way amid the crowd up the hallway toward the kitchen carrying a tray full of empty beer cans. Ralph stepped into her path. Hi there, Ralph said. Lindsay said, Well, hello, birthday boy. Having a good time? Ralph said, I've got to tell you something. Can it wait?

Lindsay said. No, it can't, Ralph said. Lindsay and Ralph were nearly shouting to be heard over the noise. Well, Lindsay said, cupping her hand around her mouth to Ralph's ear, shoot. Cupping his own hand around Lindsay's ear, Ralph said, Look, I love old Jim. But the fact of the matter is, I love you more. I hate to do this, rat old Jim out, that is, but I just heard something you ought to know. Lindsay said, What are you talking about? Ralph said, I'm talking about the fact, which I heard on good authority, as it were, that Jim is carrying on with some woman. Apparently it's the talk of the town. Lindsay said, Is the woman's name Mary? Why yes, Ralph said. Ralph, would you do me a favor and do some picking up? Lindsay said, and held up the tray of empty beer cans she was carrying. If I don't stay ahead of the mess, I'll be in deep shit tomorrow. Do you mind? No, Ralph said, I don't mind. Thanks, hon, Lindsay said, and wove her way on down the hallway.

As the noted Bay Area authors sang "Happy Birthday," Jim carried out Ralph's cake, German chocolate with chocolate icing, Ralph's favorite, which Jim had baked with his own bare hands, as he announced to the world at large several times. To the noted Bay Area authors' glee, Ralph huffed and puffed himself blue in the face attempting to blow the candles out. The noted Bay Area authors were greatly amused when it finally dawned on Ralph that they were trick candles, impossible to blow out. Ha ha, Ralph thought, as he hacked and coughed in an attempt to catch his breath and hopefully not faint, which he really felt he might do. Then when the general laughter had died down, Jim, wiping tears of amusement from his eyes, announced that he wanted to make a little toast in old Ralphie boy's honor.

He wanted to take this opportunity, Jim said, to thank old Running Dog Ralph Crawford for all the little words of encouragement Ralph had given him during those dark, discouraging days Jim was struggling to complete his new novel, soon to be published by Harcourt Brace Jovanovich. Stay the course, Ralph had suggested to Jim, when Jim was feeling defeated. Never say die, Ralph had recommended. All's well that ends well. The end justifies the means. It's not over until the fat lady sings. Yes, those kind clichés from old rotten Ralph had meant a lot to Jim in his hours of creative struggle, and in many ways Jim had old Ralph to thank for the big-bucks sale of his new novel soon to be published by Harcourt Brace Jovanovich.

Here, old dog, Jim said, and handed Ralph a knife, it's your cake, so you get to do the honors, boy. Led by Jim, the noted Bay Area authors hooted and laughed uproariously at Ralph's expense as soon as the knife hit that hard object buried in the heart of that cake Jim had baked with his own bare hands. Where you're going, old Ralphie, Jim said as he drew the file from the cake and cleaned it off to present with a great ceremonial flourish to Ralph, you'll want to employ this little item as soon as possible to break out, hopefully before your sexual orientation gets totally turned around. Ha ha, Ralph thought. So the whole room of noted Bay Area authors knew the status of Ralph's legal problems. Wonder who spread that sorry news around. Ha ha. Although, Jim informed the room full of smirking noted Bay Area authors, there was probably no way our birthday boy here could make good his escape in time to avoid at least one serious (how shall we put this in polite company?) tush-tapping. But what's a little buggery really in the great scheme of things? If Oscar Wilde could survive behind bars and even transform funny fornications into high art, then so could the birthday boy.

Ha ha.

Ladies and gentlemen, Jim said at this point, and pretended to play an invisible trumpet fanfare, then bowed and with great sweeping gestures said, I wish to present the birthday boy's beloved ball and chain, as Alice Ann walked slowly toward Ralph through the parting crowd of noted Bay Area authors. In spite of himself, when Alice Ann leaned up to kiss his cheek, Ralph flinched. Happy birthday, Ralph, Alice Ann said, and took Ralph by the hand, to the applause and cheers of the noted Bay Area authors.

Although she and Ralph had not had a civil word for each other in over a month, Alice Ann informed the noted Bay Area authors she was on hand this special evening to give Ralph his birthday blow job, a tradition in their long marriage she was loath to break, especially because it might be the last blow job he received, from a woman anyway, for quite some time. For, unfortunately, she had some bad tidings for the birthday boy. It was bad news that Alice Ann felt they, she and Ralph, should share with Ralph's many friends and fans, for he would be needing their support and understanding in the hard days to come. She, for one, planned to stand by her man, for better or worse, as she had promised to do those many years ago. Upon her arrival home from work earlier that very evening, Alice Ann had found a telegram from Ralph's attorney-of-record, who was representing Ralph in his current difficulties with the state of California, which, as everybody knew, was prosecuting Ralph for fraud and perjury and general bad citizenship, among many other misdemeanors and possible felonies. She had immediately contacted Ralph's attorney, who claimed that because people rarely answered the phone at her house he did not feel he was in any way at fault or remiss for informing Ralph at such an eleventh hour that he, Ralph, was due to appear in court to face the music tomorrow morning, and perhaps Ralph would be wise to bring along a toothbrush.

2

Ralph ran to his room and began throwing his clothes, which Lindsay had kindly laundered for him, into Alice Ann's old yellow getaway suitcase. Alice Ann strolled into the room and sat down on the edge of the bed. —I thought I had thrown that old suitcase out, she said, and lit a cigarette. She sat there smoking and watching Ralph scurry around the room, trying to recall all the places he had hidden items purloined from Jim: books, pens, pencils, typing paper, cans of Campbell's soup, tins of sardines, two more tubes of toothpaste for his collection.

If he pulled out right then, Ralph speculated aloud, and drove lickety-split and nonstop, he figured he could make Reno by midnight, which was safely across the California state line. And then it would be a clear straight shot south to old Mexico. Or maybe Canada would be the best bet. What he needed to know was which border would be the easiest to cross. Why had those fainthearted draft dodgers fled to Canada instead of old Mexico is what he wanted to know.

Ralph, Alice Ann said, and stubbed out her cigarette, only to light another. —You're not going anywhere. We are in this together, both our marriage and the criminal matter. We have had this date with the music from the beginning, Ralph, and we are going to simply face up to it finally.

Sure, Ralph said, that's easy for you to say. You're not the one who's going to get their brains buggered out.

You aren't going to jail, Ralph. I've sold the house. In all honesty I planned upon selling the house, which was bought with my inheritance, if you recall, out from under you and pocketing the proceeds to finance a new life for the kids and me. But I've changed my mind. Your worthless attorney-of-record informed me that if restitution is made to the state for the funds you stole by fraud and malice aforethought, and if you throw yourself upon the mercy of the court, you'll get off with a white-collar criminal slap on the wrist. Probation and maybe some community service.

What sort of community service? You mean things like road work?

What does it matter? The important thing here, Ralph, is that I'm coming to your rescue again. And, Ralph, I am going to ask you for only one thing in return.

What one thing?

You must give me my just due. Ralph, in any success you may have in the future, you must not forget what I've done for you. You must not forget the hopes and dreams we have shared. Over the long course, Ralph, everything but hope lets you go. Then even that, I suppose, finally loosens its grip. Ralph, why hasn't there ever been enough of anything in all the long years we've shared together? But we have had some sweetness and light in our lives, haven't we? Ralph? Haven't we?

I guess.

You once swore you would love only me forever, Ralph. You once gave me a ring and asked for me to come along with you in your life's journey. You told me I could trust you forever. Things to that effect. You once quoted me something, Ralph. You quoted somebody who said, The world is the world, and it writes no histories that end in love. Do you remember that?

Not really.

Well, anyway, happy birthday, you son-of-a-bitch. Let's just get this over with, Alice Ann said, and she walked over to Ralph and began to beat on his chest and shoulders with her clenched fists, which Ralph let her do, not even grabbing her wrists or flinching away, until her arms grew weary. And then Ralph had simply stood there, his arms hanging at his sides, as Alice Ann sunk onto her knees in front of him and unzipped his trousers.

3

Jim enlisted the aid of Max Carver, a mutual friend of his and Ralph's who was this big, burly, red-neck, rhinestone Commie from Texas, to help drag Ralph down the stairs early the next morning and then shove him into the backseat, where they lodged Ralph between them, so that Ralph could not leap from the moving vehicle or make a frantic grab for the wheel as Alice Ann drove, and they set out through the foggy morning south for San Jose and the Superior Court Building for Ralph to face the music.

Ralph alternately whined and mumbled incoherently. What, Ralph? Jim said. What? When he was a little kid, Ralph mumbled, a little, rambunctious boy true, but not evil, his mom had hooked him up into one of those barbaric kiddie-harness affairs, and she had fastened it to a clothesline out in the back yard, where she had left Ralph to spend most of his formative years, a little, lonely fat boy, trotting a trench beneath that clothesline, up and back, up and back, until he was exhausted sometimes with all that effort of running nowhere with all his heart. But by the time that trench was waist-high, Ralph had felt a fierce pride in it, that wonderful hole that held the perfect shape of his determined escape to nowhere but deeper. Well, Jim said, Momma tried.

Ashen, shaking, his trembling legs buckling at every other step, his heart beating visibly beneath his shirt, Ralph still found the strength to resist, and he had to be manhandled into the courthouse by his snickering buddies. Ralph's oily attorney-of-record took one look at Ralph and strongly recommended again that Ralph simply plead guilty and throw himself upon the mercy of the court. When it became apparent from his opening comments the avenger-asshole of an assistant district attorney had his flinty heart set upon making a white-collar-criminal example out of Ralph, Alice Ann insisted upon taking the stand in a last-ditch effort to save Ralph's bacon.

Your Honor, sir, Alice Ann said to the judge, a white-haired man who looked like God, let me say first of all that I am prepared to write the court a check on the spot to cover all fines and to make full restitution for the monies my husband in his drunken stupor falsely received from the state. Let me say also that my husband, Mr. Crawford, has two wonderful children at home, who need and love him very much, in spite of all the pain and hardship and general humiliation he has caused them over the years. Please don't let those wonderful children go through this incarnation with the onus of having a jailbird for a father, I beseech you. Let me say also, sir, that my husband intends to join AA tomorrow, and I will drive him personally to and from meetings. Your Honor, sir, I am not up here to praise my husband, for I am not that foolish, but simply to attempt to save his bacon. I have always believed, sir, that what good one possesses was enough to merit one's salvation. In spite of all the overwhelming evidence to the contrary, sir, there is some good in my husband, Mr. Crawford. Things I will have to relate to you, sir, are very painful for me. Mr. Crawford would probably prefer I bite my tongue. But no matter how painful, I cannot bite my tongue. To talk about the tragic events of Mr. Crawford's and my marriage is very painful, how from the beginning we have overexisted, how on too many sad occasions we have been so foolishly operatic in our behavior. Your Honor, I never lie to myself or to others in my heart, so, sir, let me assure you from my heart that the pathetic person you see sitting before you, Mr. Crawford, my husband, is not simply the man who, in order to save a few dollars on dog food, was capable of purloining his children's puppy, their beloved pet, and driving it to a distant neighborhood, where he tossed the poor thing out to fend for itself. Yes, he was capable of that, and did it, and he was also capable of using such a despicable act as a source of inspiration for a story, and I might add one of his very best stories. Sir, there will always be those rare individuals who must stare into the darkness of themselves in order to really see for us all. My husband, Mr. Crawford, is one of those damned yet blessed individuals who must both suffer and soar because of the gift of that burden. Because of that burden Mr. Crawford drinks like a fish, and lives about half the time in some parallel world of story. It is because of this that my husband has a diminished capacity to recognize and act upon notions of right and wrong in the real world. What happened to him . . . no, what has happened to us both, is that we reached that point where the fiction of our lives began to feed on itself. Sir, I would like to offer the fiction of our lives into evidence as exhibit A for the defense, Alice Ann said, and she held up a copy of Ralph's book of stories for all to see.

And, Your Honor, I would like to swear an oath on the lives revealed in this book, Alice Ann said, and placed her right hand upon Ralph's book, I would like to swear an oath that Mr. Crawford has been rehabilitated by this book and he is full of remorse for the horrific events of his life that he drew upon in order to write this book. He is sick at heart also about all that he has stolen from others for the sake of these stories. I, for instance, Your Honor, am a person who has been living for the record all her adult life. It is not easy, let me assure you, sir, always living for the record. Living for posterity is no picnic, sir. As you may discover after today yourself, Your Honor. For today, sir, you are living for the *record according to Ralph.* For my husband, even in his stunted state of mind, is playing with these proceedings somewhere deep in his twisted imagination just as he would play a hooked fish into his boat, reeling it into his own sick reality. My husband, Your Honor, will fry us all for dinner if we are not careful. Finally, sir, I would ask you to look closely into that man's sorry face. Is not his bitter grief, and his shame, yes, that too, are they not apparent and proof enough? Sir, please just look carefully at that pathetic shell of the man who was once Ralph Crawford. Mr. Crawford is clearly not a pretty picture. He needs your compassion and understanding, not punishment. Your Honor, with the court's kind permission, I would like to enter Mr. Crawford's wretched personal appearance into evidence for the defense.

Lucky Old Dog

1

Ralph sat in a chair pulled away from the kitchen table, chain-smoking, sipping a glass of what he swore was pure orange juice, glancing back and forth between the cartoons on the television set on the kitchen counter and Jim, who was at the stove churning hash browns about in his favorite heavy cast-iron skillet. Lindsay was moving about the kitchen attempting to make a dent in the previous night's damage, closing open drawers, dumping the dead soldiers and empty Chinese-food cartons and pizza boxes and overflowing ashtrays into a big plastic bag.

I don't see how anybody could drink vodka this early in the morning, Jim said over his shoulder.

Hey, Ralph said, I told you already, this is pure OJ. Call it a will of iron, but I, for one, never take a drink before 11 a.m.

You bet, Jim said.

I once met a fellow whose drink of choice was Listerine, Ralph said. He was coming down off Scotch. That poor devil still got drunk as a skunk, but he had the freshest breath.

Jim stepped over to the table and picked up the glass in front of Ralph and drank it down.

Hey, there! Ralph said. —No fair!

Jim took a nearly empty bottle of vodka from inside a kitchen cabinet. He waved it at Ralph, then drank it down straight and smacked his lips.

Hey, Ralph said, and looked back at the cartoon chases flickering across the television screen, what am I supposed to do when 11 a.m. rolls around?

There's a bottle of Listerine in the bathroom, Jim said, as he began breaking eggs into a blue bowl. —Fix yourself a fucken screw-gargle.

Alice Ann swept into the room. She was already dressed and made up for the day. She sat down at the kitchen table and lit a cigarette, which she pointed at Lindsay's Bloody Mary. —That looks like what the doctor ordered.

I'll stir you one up in a jiffy, Lindsay said, and took an unopened bottle of vodka from beneath the sink. —You look nice. I'm still dragging around in my ratty old robe.

You're the hostess with the mostest, Alice Ann said. —I've got to get down there and get the kids settled in with Ralph's mom. Then I have at least a half-dozen rental houses to look at and see about storage and movers.

Me too, please, Ralph said to Lindsay.

Before 11 a.m.? Jim said, then said to Alice Ann, How do you like your eggs?

Scrambled, but I have to run.

Oh, I'll make an exception this morning to be sociable, Ralph said. —Hey, old Jim, how's that grub coming, anyway? If I had a horse, I'd eat the nag whole. Alice Ann, do you happen to have any of those little LifeSavers handy? Those little fruity babies you always carry around in your purse.

Nope, I don't think I do.

But you always have some in your purse. I could really go for one of those little cherry LifeSavers right now. Or an orange one. I like those green ones, too.

Sorry, Alice Ann said, then said, I dreamed about you last night, Lindsay. I dream about you a lot, actually. I don't remember much about last night's dream, but you were beautiful in it. I dream exclusively in black and white. Your skin absolutely glows in black and white, Lindsay. Your skin is absolutely luminous in all my dreams, even if they're bad dreams, horrible dreams, even when they're my worst nightmares.

Well, hon, Lindsay said, for a girl who grew up with the nickname Pimple Plantation, that is not unwelcome news.

They'll make the film of my life in black and white, Alice Ann said, blowing a series of perfect smoke rings, while she observed Lindsay's movements about the kitchen. —Color is too much a record of the world. Black and white takes one beneath the surface to the real mystery of the world. Black and white signals that we are in another world. I want the movie of my life shot in a sort of fragmented black-and-white light. I want the shadows to jerk like fucking war footage. Faye Dunaway will play my beautiful tragic part. And she'll win an Academy Award. That movie will make people bawl like babies when they see what I've had to endure with Ralph. Lindsay, I just hope that in our next incarnations you get stuck with Ralph for a fucking change.

Hey, Ralph said, what did I do around here? How come you're picking on me so early in the morning, Alice Ann?

On the television a mouse made its hole, barely. A cartoon cat crazy with anger and frustration and desire banged its head against a wall.

You called me by another woman's name again last night, Ralph, Alice Ann said. —So what else is new? I'm nobody's fool, you fuck. I can read the handwriting on the wall. I've been living under the illusion that while Ralph's and my marriage has sustained serious damage over the years, it was still, oh, maneuverable. *Maneuverable*, as on *Star Trek*, when Spock radios Captain Kirk that while the *Enterprise* has sustained serious damage, it is still maneuverable. Well, folks, I have to run, Alice Ann said, and dunked her cigarette in her unfinished drink. —I'll be late as it is. I'll see you guys this evening if I don't die in a car wreck or something. Don't anybody do anything I wouldn't do, she said, and hurried from the room.

Hey, old Jim, can I have Alice Ann's eggs? Ralph said.

You may or may not get any grub, you old dog, Jim said over his shoulder from the stove. —I ain't decided yet. Plus I gotta meet Shorty and I'm running late, too.

I'll fix Ralph some eggs, Lindsay said.

Well, I, for one, don't have to take this ongoing abuse. I, for one, will be up on the deck minding my own business if anybody cares to bring me some breakfast sometime today, Ralph said, and snatched the bottle of vodka and headed out the back door.

Okeydokey, Jim said to Lindsay. —You fix Ralph's fucken eggs. I gotta roll.

And why are you in such a rotten mood, too? Lindsay said.

Never mind, Jim said.

And just what are you and Shorty up to today, anyway? Lindsay said, and sat down at the table.

We got a couple of little errands.

How long will these little errands take? Five or ten years in prison?

So just who do you love, anyway? Jim said. —Have you figured that one out?

So just who do you love? Lindsay said. —That's the real question around here.

The fuck it is, Jim said, and tossed his spatula onto the stove and strode from the room.

2

Lindsay walked up the back stairs carrying a plate of eggs and hash browns, and she noted the particulars of her immediate life with a feeling vaguely like penitence. In the shade of a soaring pine below in the next courtyard several Chinese women squatted while they sliced vegetables into a wide white bowl. When Lindsay smiled at them they looked away, and she was suddenly filled with an aching sadness. Wind chimes tinkled in a slight breeze that smelled of bread baking and fresh wash hung out on lines strung on the surrounding flat rooftops, and tears flooded Lindsay's eyes. As though seen through a lens, or in a fever, the colors of the vegetables in the white bowl far below, luminous in a shifting flush of light, the greens and reds of peppers, snowpeas, stringbeans, mushrooms white as pebbles, were pure enough to blind. Here I am in San Francisco and I am carrying Ralph's eggs up to him, Lindsay told herself, and looked at eggs so yellow they hurt her eyes. This was the intense, timeless light Lindsay had waited in for her childhood to end. As she had felt her body change cell by cell. Atom by atom.

Is that my plate? Ralph said. He was sitting in a chair beside the round glass-topped table on the far side of the deck. Ralph's expression was anxious, vaguely baffled. He looked so helpless somehow, sitting almost crouched, smoking intently, pinching a cigarette against his lips with those huge, hairy fingers Lindsay had sucked on.

Lindsay placed the plate she carried in front of Ralph, who finished his butt and pulled his chair up to the table.

Where's yours? Ralph said, as he shoveled eggs into his mouth.

I'm not hungry, Lindsay said, and sat down at the table.

Where's your husband?

He took off in a huff, not unlike your wife.

That man you're married to is a nut, Ralph said, chewing mightily. —Jim Stark is crazy. Just plain crazy. Jim and Alice Ann are like two peas in a pod, a padded pod. Whoever sold them their tickets from Mars ought to be arrested.

Ralph, don't start up, Lindsay said. A foghorn sounded from the Bay and the chimes from Saint Peter-Paul's Cathedral rang forth, and Lindsay gazed for a moment more lightheartedly over her glorious postcard of a view. Although she couldn't see Sausalito yet, the sun had burned most of the morning fog off, and already the white sails of boats flicked about in the dark green water. Rising above the trees of Washington Square Park down the hill, the cathedral's spires looked white as bones in the clear, washed light. But all of this was lost to Lindsay, now that Jim loved another woman.

What did Jim say about that Mary Mississippi business? Ralph said, as though reading Lindsay's mind. —You didn't tell him who tipped you off, did you?

I didn't tell him anything, Ralph. I haven't even mentioned it. I haven't found the right time. I don't know. Right now I try to put it out of my mind. For the time being, anyway.

Do you know something? This is about the first time in weeks we've even been alone. I'm amazed Jim actually left us alone. Sometimes, too, I've had the impression you were trying to avoid being alone with me.

Don't be paranoid, Ralph.

Well, you can't imagine how much I've missed talking with you. You're my best friend on earth, Lindsay. I mean that.

What about your best friend Jim?

You've been my best friend from the first day we met. I've never gotten over that.

Well, Ralph, no matter what else transpired between us, or didn't, I have always thought of you as a dear friend.

I am your dear friend. Your dear, dear, dear friend. And more. In my book, anyway. Much more. And I can talk with you like I've never been able to talk with anybody else in my life. I can open up with you like I've never been able to do with anybody.

What about your wife, Ralph? What about Alice Ann?

Not even with Alice Ann when it was still good between us. You can't imagine how good it is to talk with you again. You can't imagine how much I've missed it.

I've missed it, too, Ralph.

I've missed it more than anything. I mean it. That's the honest-to-God truth.

What really is the honest-to-God's truth, Ralph? What's the truth about your life?

My life is crazy, and getting crazier by the day. I've finally arrived at the end of my rope. Alice Ann and I are history.

I'll say. About eight or nine thousand years' worth, Lindsay said. —According to Alice Ann, you two have shared countless lifetimes together. And she has inspired your work. She has lived your stories with you. She gave birth to your two children, Ralph. Your family.

Right, Ralph said. —Remind me to write her a fat letter of thanks about that. If I wrote monster stories I could use those kids as inspiration. Maybe I could rent them to Stephen King.

You are talking about your children, Ralph.

God, but I wish we could have had kids together, Lindsay. I wish we had a son of our own.

Oh, Ralph, don't you think we already had our shot at happiness?

Did we? Do you only get one shot? You know, Lindsay, I can remember exactly what your kisses taste like.

My, my, what an amazing memory the boy has. What do you think Jim would do if he caught you kissing me?

Give me a knuckle sandwich, I guess, but it would be worth it. I love old Jim. I do. We go at each other a lot, I know it. But I do love him. It's just that you went and married him. And the last good kiss I ever got I got from you. Lindsay, we could still sail into the future like we used to talk about.

Which way is that?

I mean it. Finally everything in my household is just too crazy. Alice Ann is convinced she's some kind of medium. That spirits, you know, of dead people, can speak through her. Can you beat that? And then there's her old Egyptian spirit pal Horus, who she apparently got real tight with down in the lower delta during the Old Kingdom. So old Horus gives Alice Ann a ring from the beyond now and then to shoot the breeze. Talk about long-distance bills. And I'll probably get stuck with those charges, too. Like all the other outrageous charges Alice Ann levels at me day and night. Outrageous charges from other lifetimes. I can hardly get through one day at a time intact in this lifetime and I'm being held accountable for crimes I committed in other lifetimes. Did you know that in Roman times I once tossed Alice Ann, who was this Christian virgin martyr, to a lion. And once in ancient Egypt I supposedly had, you know, carnal knowledge of Alice Ann's royal sister down on the banks of the old Nile.

Well, did you, Ralph?

Probably, Ralph said. —But after six thousand years, so what, I say. Cut a fellow some slack. There has to be a statute of limitations, doesn't there? Let sleeping dogs lie is my motto. Especially six-thousand-year-old sleeping dogs. Well, I, for one, am out of all that ancient history now. Let somebody else look back on the long, sorry record, its scraps and tirades, the deadly silences and innuendos, the screams in the night, and let them figure out what it all adds up to. Goodbye, I'm saying. Goodbye to that history of heartbreak.

Really, Ralph? Goodbye? Goodbye to eight or nine thousand years of togetherness?

I'm kissing it all goodbye, Ralph said. —I'm laying it all to rest. I should have taken a hike out of that tragedy four or five centuries ago. And I'm going to turn over a new leaf in this lifetime while I still have time. For one thing, I'm going to stop drinking. Any day now, I mean it. And I'm going to become the sort of man a son could look up to. The sort of man a son, a son like our son, if we had had one, or ever have one, could be proud of. God, Lindsay, but it really is good to talk with you.

It's good to talk with you, too, Ralph.

Really. To talk my heart out. To be able to get things off my chest like this. I have always, no matter what the course of events, thought I could count on you as my best friend.

Thank you, Ralph. I feel as though I can count on you, too.

That settles it, then, Ralph said. He got up and stepped over beside Lindsay and rested a hand on her shoulder. —We can count on each other. Through thick or thin. Come hell or high water. For better or worse. Until death us do part, Ralph said, and put out his hand as though to shake.

Come hell or high water, Lindsay said, then took Ralph's outstretched hand and shook it, laughing.

God but I wish we had hours and hours to talk, like we used to. Talk the day and night away. Talk and make love until the sun comes up. Can you remember that?

Yes, Lindsay said.

Talking. Telling stories, gossiping, dragging all our friends through the mud, eating about a dozen scrambled eggs at three in the a.m., making love about every fifteen minutes.

You, my boy, are a cracked record, Lindsay said, and laughed. —But I'm happy you feel you can talk with me. I'm afraid I'm out of practice. The practice of opening up.

Opening up, Ralph said, and patted Lindsay's cheek. —That's something we can practice on together.

Oh, Ralph, Ralph, Lindsay said, and slowly stood up to hug him. —You can be such a dear old dog, she said, and kissed Ralph on the cheek.

Gosh, Ralph said. —Thanks a million. I'm a lucky old dog is what I am. Really. I needed that. What did I do right, anyhow? Tell me what I did right so I can do it again. I mean, that really hit the old spot, that kiss did. Well, it almost hit the old spot.

Almost, Ralph?

Well, you sort of missed my mouth.

Oh, not by a mile.

Hey, I'm not complaining, you understand. A kiss from you is a kiss from you, and I was a lucky old dog to get it. I'll take any kind of kiss from you I can get. Hey, hold the horses. Let me ask you something. Is the reason you missed my mouth on account of this little cold sore I have?

Cold sore? Lindsay said, and laughed. —I hadn't noticed any cold sore, Ralph.

Right here, Ralph said, and touched a red spot on the left corner of his mouth. —This little devil. I know it looks bad. You're just being kind, as usual. I didn't get enough milk or green veggies as a kid. That's how a doc explained why I'm always getting these godawful sores. It's just another carryover from what passed as my childhood. My childhood is always rearing its miserable, hoary head. Such as now. Deprived of an innocent kiss on the mouth from a dear, dear friend because Momma raised me mostly on lard and sugar sandwiches. Well, I don't blame you one little bit. I wouldn't want to kiss me on the mouth either. Even if I did know, which I do, that this little devil isn't in the least bit contagious. This little baby has about run its course.

Oh, Ralph, you nut, Lindsay said. She put her hands on Ralph's chest. —You make me laugh. I miss laughing.

I wish I knew some jokes. I can never remember jokes.

Neither can I. I always forget the punch lines.

Me too. Hey, here's one I remember. Have you heard the one about . . . Ralph said, and stopped when Lindsay reached up and kissed him on the mouth. When Ralph opened his mouth, so did Lindsay. They kissed for a full minute.

When did you say Jim would get back? Ralph said.

I didn't say. But my best guess is that it will be a while. Long enough, anyway.

Long enough?

Let's go downstairs, Ralph.

Downstairs? You mean, you think we should go downstairs?

I don't want to think about it, Ralph. I want us to just go downstairs while we can.

Well, yes. Yes. Let's do that. Go downstairs. And you're sure Jim won't be back anytime soon?

God, yes, Ralph. I'm sure about that, anyway, Lindsay said and took Ralph by the hand and led him across the deck to the stairs.

Lost Highways

1

The house was dark when Kathy returned from rounding the bars. She fixed herself a nightcap in the kitchen and then walked upstairs to what would have been the baby's room. She sat in the rocking chair she had bought when she was six months pregnant. In the slant of light from the street the little lambs on the wall-paper were luminous. All around the room bits of light reflected from the bead eyes of stuffed animals. Kathy rocked while she smoked a cigarette in the dark.

Kathy turned the light on in Bill's bedroom to see if per-chance he was already home passed out. As soon as she entered her own room she heard the faint sounds of muffled hiccups coming from inside her closet, and the clink of ice against glass. The sliding closet doors were cracked. Kathy undressed slowly. When her six-foot-plus body was naked she carried her phone over to her dresser, where she sat down facing the mirror and began brushing her long blond hair. After a time Kathy picked up the phone and, holding the button down, pretended to dial.

Hello, honey, Kathy said into the phone. —Yes, I'm home now. Just got in. I wanted to hear your voice again before I tucked in. What, honey? No, I have no idea where he is, and I don't give a goddamn. Out romancing some barroom rosy, I guess. No, hon, you don't even have to think about something like that. Don't even think it. Old Billy hasn't brought a boner home in years. What, baby? Me too, baby. It was. Really, baby. I've never before in my life like that. God, hon. I hope the walls were thick enough. I've never screamed out like that. What, baby? Nothing on, as a matter of fact. That's right. I'm stark. Bare ass, baby. Yes, I was going to step into the shower. I mean, God, you can smell sex all over me. What, hon? Oh yes, baby. Yes. I'll do it right now. My right nipple. Now my left, baby. I'm doing it. I'm pinching them. You're pinching them. You're sucking on them hard now. You're biting now, baby. Bite harder, baby, harder. What, baby? Honey, I only have one free hand. What, sweetie? Honey, my tongue's no way long enough to do that, unlike your own. What? Honey, I don't see anything around I could use for that. I'm at my dresser, precious. Wait a minute. I've got a bright idea. There are some enormous cucumbers downstairs in the fridge. Could you hang on a sec, sweetie? Oh, me too, baby. God, yes, yes. Yes, I love you, too, honey. I love your huge cock. I just live to have your big black cock in my mouth, Rufus.

You bitch! You bitch! Bill bellowed as he took down the closet door in a single lurch.

Why, Bill, you're home, Kathy said, and hung up the phone.

2

When Bill awoke early the next morning he discovered that he must have dozed off in his car in the driveway with the engine running. But there he was, sure enough, his forehead against the top of the steering wheel, a little lake of drool on the floor mat between his boots. He also discovered that he was in a great amount of discomfort, mostly in and about his head. When Bill looked in the rearview mirror he made even further unhappy discoveries. Both his eyes were black, for one thing, and his nose was bloody, for another. A great knot had risen on the back of his head, which he touched tenderly with his fingertips. It also appeared that many of his worldly possessions—his clothes, for instance, his favorite books, a couple of boxes of his own manuscripts, his fishing gear, several guns, his old high-school football helmet, the framed picture of his mom, all this and more were strewn about the car, in both the front seat and the back. Oh, that's right, Bill recalled, he had been in the process of leaving this place and its attendant woman forever. He had been in the process of running away from home. Well, okay, then, why not simply do that very thing?

But where was he going, and why exactly? Bill pondered as he rinsed his mouth and gargled with a swig from that half-full bottle of vodka he had happily discovered between his legs and swallowed. Well, he was going to go *there*. But where exactly was that? Looking for what? Call it desire and pursuit of that dim aura glowing over the horizon we call possibility, or excitement. Hadn't Henry James once said there are two mental states, excitement and lack of excitement, and that unfortunately excitement was more interesting than the lack of? Who was Bill to argue with Henry James? Or call that chasing away from home the pursuit of that whole we call love. Why shouldn't he, Bill, have some of it, too, *love*, like that evil betrayer, butt-kicking woman in that house he didn't care if he ever set eyes on again in his lifetime.

Bill headed out of Missoula, Montana, upstream along the Blackfoot River, the asphalt weaving and dipping and the morning light lime-colored through the leaves on the aspen. He put a tape of fine, thin, fragile music on the tape deck, a Vivaldi cello concerto, music as clean as the air across the mountain pastures, music that didn't encourage Bill to think. Later, he knew, there would be plenty of thinking. But all Bill needed at that point was the purity of that music and the motion of going, the very notion of it, that going, and somehow ending up as far away as he could get from that illusory sheltering semblance of coherency he had once called home. But with some restraint, sure, Bill thought as he passed a cluster of those little white crosses you see everywhere along the roads of Montana, marking those places where other travelers have died, many of them drunk, sure, and most of them searching, too, and unable to name what it was they were missing at home.

Bill was well aware that lonesome traveling could get tricky. It was a delicate passage, lonesome traveling. Aloneness could lead to loneliness, and self-pity, and paranoia, and things like that. Such a trip could break down into dark questing after dubious companionship. But the advantage of going it alone lay, of course, in spontaneity and freedom. You don't have to consult anything but your inclinations. You are in your old white Buick convertible and you are rolling, you are riding away and long gone. Shit fire, Bill thought, they don't need me, not today. Or tomorrow. Maybe never. I'm sick. This is sick leave. You know it's true, Bill told himself. You've been sick and now you are going to cure yourself elsewhere far away from that evil butt-kicking betrayer woman and old broken-down way of life.

It had always seemed like a good idea to Bill when driving up along the Blackfoot to stop at Trixie's Antler Inn just as the doors were being unlocked. One single quick drink for the road and some dirty banter with the pretty hippie chick tending bar. But wrong. After that first hesitation Bill found himself stopping at other establishments, all enjoyable, one after the other. The Stockman's in Arlee, the Buffalo Park in Ravalli. He moved on to the 44 Bar north of St. Ignatius, then made the Charo turn to Tiny's Blind Pig. Then the Wheel Inn on the near outskirts of Lincoln, the Bowman's Corner over south of Augusta, with the front of the Rockies rearing on the western skyline like hope and possibility personified.

Soon that fine blue bowl of heaven and Bill's exquisite freedom were forgotten, and he found himself lying to strangers and himself about his role in life. No more Vivaldi. By noon of the second day Bill was playing Hank Williams tapes and singing along, wondering if he could have made it in the country-music business. By then Bill knew he was a long and dangerous way from that ticking stillness he recalled as home, and he was somewhat disoriented. The bartenders had begun to study him like a potential serious problem. Bill had drifted into another mythology called lost highways, an emotional rat's nest of rootlessness, a country music worn-out drifter syncopation that could be a theatrical but finally real thin way of life.

Bill began to stop at historical markers, and then mull over the ironies of destiny as he drove on. This was maybe the third day and Bill was listening to bluegrass, in fact a tape from a Seldom Seen concert. Bill was experiencing no despair at that point. He thought of elk in the draws, buffalo on the plains, the complex precision of predator-prey relationships. Bill was becoming a philosopher. And he was willing to learn from his past mistakes. For instance, Bill reflected, as he touched his still-sore, swollen nose, never again would he fuck with a six-foot-plus humorless woman. Bill was finding himself interesting, and enjoying his own company mightily. There was no need to get drunk and kill somebody on the road, not to mention himself. At twilight Bill stopped in some little town and checked into one of the two motels along some river. He showered, shaved, changed shirts, and then ambled on over to that tavern across the road, where he intended to make some new best friends and share his pretty new vision of life.

Which was about the last clear memory Bill would have, strolling relatively sober through the sweet Montana twilight toward the sweet blinking blue lights of that tavern, humming his favorite Willie Nelson tune, "You Were Always on My Mind," his heart full of a sort of sweet and gentle melancholy and all the best intentions in the world, until he more or less came to, driving across the Bay Bridge into San Francisco at night God-only-knows how many days later, rock-and-roll blaring ungodly from the radio, his gas tank on real-near-dangerous empty, a very young and lovely woman with long, dark hair and a sleeping child on her lap sitting in the seat right beside him, her hand on his knee.

The Queen of California

1

I'm here to make you all stars, Bill said, wagging his huge, shaggy head, when Lindsay finally arrived at the bottom of the stairs to answer the door.

Good God, Billy! Lindsay said. —Where in the world did you come from?

Meet the love of my life, Bill said, and stood aside in the doorway to draw forward a young woman with long black hair and black eyes carrying a sleeping child. —This is Lulu, the woman I love more than life itself. Lulu, meet Lindsay, a woman I loved once, true, but you have nothing to fear from Lindsay, little darlin', for that was in another lifetime.

The name's Lucy, the young woman said.

Well, hello, Lucy, Lindsay said. —Hello. Welcome.

Yeah, Lucy said. —Right.

Well, Lindsay said. —Well well. Good God, Billy, come on in. And, Lucy, come in, please. What a lovely child. Is it a boy, Lucy?

Right, Lucy said.

What a pretty baby, Lindsay said, touching the back of the baby's head of thick, black hair. —How old is he?

About a year, Lucy said. —Give or take a few weeks.

What's his name? Lindsay said. —He is so cute.

I mostly just call him Kid, Lucy said.

I see, Lindsay said. —Well, why not?

That's our own boy, Bill said. —I plan to give the little fellow my own good name. Meet little Bill, Bill said, and tapped the sleeping baby on the head.

Hey, Lucy said, turning the baby away. —You watch it.

Well, folks, just come on up, Lindsay said. —Just make yourselves at home. The old gang's all here.

2

Holy moly! Jim said as Bill lumbered into the room.

Jim and Ralph and Alice Ann were seated about the round oak table in the turret, candlelight flickering over their faces and upon Lindsay's grandmother's china and ornate silverware, and gathering in rich points of flame within the curved glass of the broad, old, wavy windows, beyond which the lights of North Beach spread around and down the steep streets toward the dark waters of the Bay and the glow of Alcatraz Island.

Look! It's the old Buffalo! Ralph said, and jumped up.

Billy! Alice Ann said. —You old good-looking devil you.

Meet Lulu, folks, the woman I love more than my own life, Bill said, and reached back to take Lucy by an arm and direct her into the room. —And meet little Bill, my own boy. God but I love this woman. No more looking high and low for love for this old buckeroo. The life I'm living with this little woman is real grownup in nature. No more finding myself trapped at every turn by foolish enterprises I keep mistaking for purposes. This is the most realistic relationship I've had in years, folks. Little Lulu here is one wonderful gal, folks, a plum wonderful gal.

Well, Jim said, why don't you folks pull up some chairs and take a load off your feet. Lulu, you and old Bill just sit right down and pile up a plate.

The name is *Lucy*, Lucy said.

Lucy, hon, would you permit me to hold your little boy while you fix a plate? Lindsay said.

Be my guest, Lucy said, and handed the baby to Lindsay, then sat down. —So what about your buddy here? Lucy said, and nodded at Bill, who was busy spearing pieces of roasted baby lamb onto his plate. —Is he really making a big movie down here or what?

If I've said it once, I've said it a hundred times, Jim said, the old Buffalo has been floundering in the same freeze-frame for twenty years.

I mean, is your buddy here really making an Indian movie down here or some shit? Lucy said as she removed her jean jacket to reveal a clinging, low-cut, red halter top and creamy brown shoulders and arms and the ample upper swelling of beautiful breasts covered with tiny tattoos.

As I told my little darlin', Bill said between great bites of food, I am making a movie of the final interior. By interior I mean a dream of the center of America as a place that can most precisely be defined as a last chance to be yearned toward. Ralph, don't you hog that macaroni now.

That ain't fucken macaroni, you big dumb shit, Jim said. —That's *lasagna inbottite*, stuffed noodles, which is a traditional dish on the wop-wedding menu, for this is a second honeymooners' wedding feast to end wedding feasts, and Lindsay has been slaving over it for days.

I've never had a meal so divine, Alice Ann said.

Yummy, Ralph said.

Ghost Dancers will be the name of my movie, Bill said between bites and gulps of wine. —It will be about the final return of the ancient Indian spirits to the lost center of America.

Just where did you two kids meet? Alice Ann asked Lucy.

Nevada, Lucy said. —Where I been working. He said he was gonna drive me and my boy down here and put me in a movie. I got a cousin down here, too. I've been trying to get down here.

Yes, Bill said, I met my little darlin', as best as I can recall, over hard-way sixes at four o'clock on the luckiest morning of my life in one of those heartbroke Nevada gambling towns where she clearly didn't belong. I see my little darlin's role in my movie as a sort of Indian Madonna.

I'm a full-blood Paiute, Lucy said. —And fucking proud of it.

I see, Alice Ann said. —Lucy, I hope you don't mind me asking, but what is the meaning of those mysterious hieroglyphic-like tattoos etched on your lovely breasts?

To tell you the truth, I don't rightly know, Lucy said, looking down at her breasts and touching the tiny tattoos gently with her fingertips. —This one is a fish crying the blues 'cause he's out of water. Which is what my boyfriend says he felt like in jail. This here is a cross, a upside-down one, though, 'cause my boyfriend don't like Jesus. And these little ones that look like more tears are really 6's, my boyfriend's lucky number. My boyfriend gave me all these, and they kinda hurt, the way he done them with a knife and ink. He learned how when he was in Folsom. You ought to see the ones on him. Him and his jail buddies didn't have nothing better to do. I didn't want all these, but when my boyfriend is feeling bad, it's what he likes to do.

Isn't my little darlin' here something else? Bill said. —Didn't I tell you folks the whole truth about my little darlin'? Little darlin', all I ask of you is that in the end you don't go stomping my old heart flat.

Here, Ralph, Lindsay said as she returned from the kitchen with the ketchup and white bread Ralph had requested. The baby was asleep over her shoulder.

Ketchup and white bread, Jim said. —The idea! Ralph, you put that shit on Lindsay's lamb, I'll pound you with the bottle.

Ralph puts ketchup on everything he eats, Alice Ann said. —I've seen hard-boiled waiters weep watching Ralph empty a bottle of ketchup on filet mignon. I've seen Ralph pour ketchup on apple pie.

Ketchup was an acquired taste for me, Ralph said. —A defensive measure from when I was a kid and had to smother stuff that was looking back at me and blinking.

Is anybody ready for their salad? Lindsay said. —I have a nice chicory salad prepared, and there is *cassata alla Siciliana* for dessert.

By this point Bill had drawn Lucy onto his lap, where she perched clinging to his big belly while he entertained her with a lingering French kiss and caressed her tattooed breasts.

Billy, Lindsay said, could I interest you and Lucy in some salad? Billy?

Is Billy being bad? Bill said, coming up for air, both his and Lucy's lower faces wet and shining in the soft candlelight.

What about dessert? Lindsay said.

I could go for some dessert, Lucy said. —You got any ice cream? Chocolate?

Well, actually the dessert is more like cake, Lindsay said. When the baby stirred she began patting its back. —A sort of cream tart. But there is some chocolate in it. But a sort of bitter chocolate. I'm a chocolate nut, too.

Are we all having fun yet? Bill said. —That's the real question here. Is this the jumping-off place for fun, or what? Folks, I, for one, am experiencing no despair, Bill said, and he buried his face between Lucy's tattooed breasts, while Lucy smiled and looked about the table with unabashed eyes.

3

Presently the people around the table in the turret simply sat there in silence, their stunned faces glistening with sweat and their eyes glassy, breathing fast and shallow, as they watched the candles burn down and, over the murmur of Italian opera turned low on the stereo in the next room and the muted sounds of traffic on Union Street and the occasional clang of trolley bells down the hill, listened to the heavy industrial sounds of one another's digestive tracks.

I, myself, Jim said, holding aloft his long-stemmed glass, have just about enough warm spit left in here for a final toast.

What in the world is there left for us to toast? Lindsay said. She was still patting the baby on its little back.

There is always something left in this old world worthy of a toast, Jim said. —The foggy, romantic night beyond these windows of old, curved glass. The flicker of candle flame upon that sleeping child's face.

Your buddy there has shot his wad, Lucy said, pointing her thumb at Bill who was sound asleep and snoring, his great shaggy head bent forward with his chin on his chest, his breath ragged and his snores juicy.

Your buddy's got something stuck up his nose, Lucy said.

Good Lord, Jim said, bending forward for a better look. —Lulu's right as rain.

Will you look at that, Ralph said, leaning over the table. —What in the world is it?

I think, Jim said, that it is one of the most amazing boogers ever seen by human eyes.

It looks like a fucking worm, Lucy said. She took a compact and lipstick from her small red-sequined purse.

Why, it's a noodle, Ralph said. —The old Buffalo has one of those tasty stuffed noodles caught in his nose.

Dear God, Lindsay said, as she shifted the sleeping child from her right shoulder to her left. —How did Billy manage to do that?

Here, Alice Ann said to Lindsay, opening her arms. —Let me hold him for a while. May I? she asked Lucy.

Just don't drop him, Lucy said, as she applied black lipstick to her full lower lip.

Well, Jim said, he *was* grazing his last helping of *lasagna inbottite* pretty close to the plate. It boggles the imagination. Ralph, reach over there and jerk that noodle out of Bill's nose.

Who says that's my job? Ralph said. —I wouldn't touch something coming out of Bill's nose for all the tea in China.

Oh, I'll do it, Lindsay said, and stood up.

No way, José! Jim said, and jumped up. —Just don't you dare touch that thing! I'll do it. Why me? Why always me?

How far is the Mission District from here, anyhow? Lucy said.

About ten or fifteen minutes by car, Lindsay said; then said: Jim, you don't intend to stick that fork up poor Bill's nose, do you?

How much would a cab cost over there? Lucy said.

Five bucks. Six, Jim said, as he slowly speared the noodle and pulled it from Bill's nose. Jim placed the fork and noodle on Bill's plate. Bill's breathing immediately became more regular and relaxed. —I coulda been a brain surgeon, Jim said.

Poor old Billy, Lindsay said, and patted Bill's head. —He's down for the count.

Don't bet on it, Jim said. —He's just recharging his Buffalo batteries.

Bill snorted from the profound depths of his snooze, and burped and smacked his lips wetly. When he attempted to reposition himself more comfortably, he let out an enormous fart and almost tipped the chair over backward.

We'd better get Billy stretched out somewhere, Lindsay said.

Good luck with that, Jim said. —I, for one, am not about to risk life and limb trying to get about a ton of half-baked Buffalo bullshit to bed.

It's no sweat, Lucy said, and cupped her tiny hand in Bill's crotch. Bill did not open his eyes, but he immediately mumbled mightily and sat up straight in his chair. —So where do you want to park him? Lucy asked Lindsay.

I'll show you, Lindsay said.

Come on, big boy, Lucy said, and when she gave Bill's crotch a hard squeeze, he stood up like a soldier at attention, whereupon like a sleepwalker Bill followed the directional flow of Lucy's expert touches and tugs, as she walked beside him with her hand fluttering like a tiny bird about the front of his jeans and led him safely from the room.

I don't think, Alice Ann said, I've ever seen a seeing-eye whore before.

The moment Lucy left the room, the baby awoke and blinked its eyes. He looked up at Alice Ann and began to cry. His face remained oddly expressionless as he cried, but streams of fat tears rolled down his plump brown cheeks.

There, there, my precious baby, Alice Ann said, and began walking around the room patting the crying baby's back, which only seemed to add a slight hiccup to the unabated weeping.

Soon the baby was wailing. —Your momma hasn't left you, baby. Your momma is here. She is right here, little lamb, Alice Ann said.

Gosh, Jim said, doesn't that wailing have a strange, old-timey quality to it? Like an old-timey Indian chant, maybe. An ancient, ritualized keen of infinite loss and mourning for the passing of a whole people.

It sounds old, all right, Ralph said. —And it's getting older by the second.

When Lindsay re-entered the room, she hurried directly to Alice Ann's side. —What's wrong with the little baby-baby? Lindsay cooed, and tickled under the child's chin.

Well, Jim said, as nearly as we can figure out, some kind of infinite loss or other.

Does him miss his mommy? Lindsay cooed.

He doesn't miss his so-called mommy, Alice Ann said.

Alice Ann, hon, Lindsay said, would you like for me to take him?

Why should you take him?

I don't know. Maybe he would be more used to me.

I do have some experience with babies, you know, Alice Ann said. —I have had two babies of my own, you know, to care for night and day virtually alone.

Alice Ann sat back down at the table and placed the baby on her knees, where she bounced him playfully, to no avail. His sobs seemed to come from a place in him ever deeper.

That squawking kid is driving me batty, Ralph said. —Can't its own mother hear the thing squawking? Maybe somebody should go get the thing's mother.

He doesn't need his so-called mother, Alice Ann said. —I was a young mother once.

You'd think its own mother would come running, Ralph said.

Maybe he simply needs to be changed, Lindsay said.

I'm telling you-all, Jim said, what's bumming the kid out is that old infinite-loss syndrome.

Maybe Bill is holding that girl against her will, Ralph said. —We all know what he's capable of. Maybe somebody should go bang on their door. Or put that squawking kid outside it.

Did Lucy have any baby bottles with her? Lindsay said. —I didn't see any. Did anybody see a, oh, baby pouch or something? For, you know, diapers, bottles, a pacifier. Jim, honey, look around, will you?

I understand this baby's needs perfectly well, Alice Ann said. —God knows I've had experience. My own babies were such healthy, happy babies, she said, and she began to unbutton the front of her blouse.

Alice Ann! Ralph said.

Alice Ann, hon, Lindsay said.

Alice Ann, Ralph said, for the love of God.

Ralph always did act funny about this beautiful, perfectly natural act, Alice Ann said, as the child, who had stopped crying, dimpled the flesh of Alice Ann's breast with his grasping little fingers and took her nipple into his mouth.

I'm sure there are baby bottles around here somewhere, Lindsay said.

Have you no shame, Alice Ann? Ralph said. He unfolded a cloth table napkin and spread it over the head of the suckling child and Alice Ann's breast.

This is a beautiful act and a God-given woman's right and duty, Alice Ann said, and tossed the napkin back onto the table.

I, for one, Jim said, agree wholeheartedly with Alice Ann on this matter. Little Tonto there is clearly going to grow up to be a serious tit man.

Jim, Lindsay said, do you always have to egg things on?

Baring her bosoms for a crowd was always one of Alice Ann's favorite stunts, Ralph said. —On public transportation was always big with Alice Ann. When our brats were babies and one of them would make the slightest peep, Alice Ann would haul out one of the old faithfuls and pop it in the kid's mouth for every Tom, Dick, and Harry to gawk at the beautiful act.

I think the little fellow is dropping off again, Alice Ann said, smiling down at the baby, whose eyes were closing. —Ralph, I have wanted to put forth an idea all evening, but the time hasn't been right. Ralph, I want us to keep this beautiful child to raise as our very own.

This time, Ralph said, you've gone around the bend, Alice Ann.

We could give this beautiful child our name, Alice Ann said, and bent over to kiss the baby's forehead. —We could begin again, Ralph. Before it's too late.

You've gone over the edge, Ralph said.

Now now, Jim said, you don't have to always be automatically a wet blanket, Ralph.

Jim, Lindsay said, zip your lip.

Ralph, Alice Ann said, we could be reborn in this beautiful baby. He could redeem us, Ralph. Couldn't you, little Ralph; couldn't you, sweetheart?

How could you even suggest such a thing, Alice Ann? Ralph said.

Spoilsport, Jim said. —Killjoy.

Offer that Indian whore money, Ralph, Alice Ann said. —Any amount. The sky's the limit. We still have the house money.

How's Billy doing? Lindsay asked Lucy as she walked back into the room at that moment.

Fuck your buddy and the horse he rode in on, Lucy said, and then stopped dead in the middle of the room. —Hey, what's going on here, anyhow? Lady, just what the fuck do you think you're doing with my kid?

Snack time, Jim said.

Fuck you, pal, Lucy said.

Ditto, Lindsay said.

Lucy, hon, Alice Ann said, we, meaning Ralph and I, Mr. Crawford and I, would in all good faith, with your own best interests at heart, and the baby's best interests, and we mean this sincerely, we would like to make you an offer, a proposal, as it were, one that we hope you will find truly impossible to refuse, one that will help you make something out of your life, help you secure a good future, become somebody even. Lucy, we would like to adopt your beautiful baby and raise it as our own. Wouldn't we, Ralph?

Lady, Lucy said, you are one fucking fruitcake.

Wouldn't we, Ralph? Alice Ann said. —Simply name your price, Lucy. The sky is the limit here, Lucy, dear. And you would be welcome to come visit little Ralph sometimes. Just let us know a little in advance when you're coming. That's all we would ask. And we would make little Ralph well aware of his Native American heritage.

Lady, Lucy said as she strode to Alice Ann, you better get your fucking tit out of my kid's mouth right now if you know what's good for you.

Lucy, Alice Ann said, and attempted to hold the baby against her breast as Lucy reached for him, it would be in little Ralph's best interests. You could see that if you would just be honest with yourself. Think of all the advantages we could offer little Ralph.

Let go of my kid, Lucy said, and pulled the baby from Alice Ann's arms. Lucy held the baby to her as she grabbed her purse from the table and her jeans jacket from the back of the chair.

Alice Ann, Ralph said, please cover yourself up, please.

Just consider our offer, Alice Ann said. —Is that asking too much?

All you people are fucking nuts, Lucy said, and, hoisting the baby onto her shoulder, she hurried to the doorway. —And that includes your bullshit buddy. I've never seen a crazier bunch of white people in one place in my life. Except maybe for you, lady, Lucy said, and looked at Lindsay. —You're a nice lady, but I sure can't say much for the company you keep.

You don't have to leave, Lucy, Lindsay said.

Me and my kid are out of here, Lucy said, and turned away.

Goodbye, Lucy, Lindsay said.

They all listened to Lucy clomp down the stairs, and then they heard the glass-paneled door slam.

Ralph, Alice Ann said, go after her. Before it's too late.

Let her go, hon, Lindsay said.

Alice Ann, honey, Ralph said, cover yourself up, honey, please. Button your blouse, Alice Ann.

Bummer, Jim said. —This is going to break the poor old Buffalo's big prairie of a heart.

It's still not too late, Ralph, Alice Ann said. —If you hurry.

Indians can be so infuriatingly fickle, Jim said. —The way they giveth and taketh away.

Here, hon, Lindsay said, and moved to Alice Ann. Lindsay knelt before Alice Ann and buttoned up her blouse.

Somebody, Ralph said, and held up his empty glass in the dying flicker of the candle's flame, is going to have to break down and make a booze bolt soon.

Well, how about you, little Ralph, Jim said, for a change.

4

Moments later Bill lurched into the doorway and stood there swaying and glaring around the room. His wild, shaggy hair looked like a recently abandoned nest of a flock of terribly frightened prairie chickens. His shirttail was out, his cowboy belt buckle was undone, plus he was bootless.

Old Buffalo, Jim said, I got some real sad news for you, partner. Brace yourself, buddy, but your little darlin' has flown the coop.

I'll fucking say, Bill said, and lumbered on into the room. He waved his wallet in the air, then threw the thing down on the table. He picked it up again and held its bill compartment open to demonstrate that it was empty. He threw the wallet back onto the table and then hit the table with his fist, making Lindsay's grandmother's china and silver jump and rattle.

That little whore, Bill said, his big, bright face pulsating with incredulity, took me to the cleaners, I'm here to tell you. I had six or seven or maybe eight hundred bucks on me until real recently. I had just cashed my paycheck before I headed out of town. I didn't even stop long enough to pay off any bar bills in my haste to ride off into one more great foolishness. The little whore stole me blind is what I'm saying here!

I don't believe Lucy would do that, Lindsay said. —Could you have lost it? Maybe you spent more than you remember.

I always spend more money than I can remember, Bill said. —But I got gas the minute I hit town, and I had it then. I even counted it. Almost a thousand bucks in crisp tens and twenties, which I counted in the men's room twice while I enjoyed the first real dump I had stopped to take in three days. Well, Lulu was the woman I deserved, I guess. What I don't understand is why I always go to my doom with such relish.

Well, I, for one, Alice Ann said, fully believe that the little whore took Bill's funds. And I think Billy is being awfully big and brave about it. Which is true to his old, sweet, big, brave Buffalo nature. I personally would feel absolutely murderous.

The real sad thing is, Bill said, deep in my heart I only wanted to do what was best by Lulu and little Billy. I really wanted to star her in that film I've been preparing to make all my adult life. I wanted to make the little whore a star. I wanted to make that little whore the Queen of California. I gave that little whore my all, and all she left me with was a reason to drink.

Not around here, Ralph said, unless somebody breaks down and makes a booze bolt.

Billy, Alice Ann said, I think we should rush out and find that whore. Before it's too late and she gets away with what is ours.

You are dead-on right about that, Bill said, wagging his head. —Which way did the little whore go?

Out, Jim said.

I'll track her down if it's the last thing I do, Bill said. —I'll choke in her whore dust all the way to Texas, if it comes to that.

Billy, Alice Ann said, and jumped up from the table, let's head the little whore off at the pass.

Alice Ann, Ralph said, just what do you think you're doing now?

Coming, Billy? Alice Ann said, and rushed to the door.

There, folks, Bill said, and pointed at Alice Ann, there is the true Queen of California.

Shake a leg, Billy, Alice Ann said.

The queen's wish is my command, Bill said, and lumbered to the door. —I'd die for my queen, if it came to that.

Billy, Lindsay said, you can't go out on the streets looking like that. You'll get yourself arrested.

Not in San Francisco, Jim said.

Thanks, Lindsay, Bill said, and patted at his hair. He stuffed his shirt in his pants and buckled his cowboy belt.

Time's a-wasting, Sheriff Billy, Alice Ann said, and took Bill by the hand, you old posse, you.

Don't you do it, Alice Ann! Ralph said.

Hi ho, Silver, away, Bill said with a wild grin, and followed Alice Ann out the door, clomping down the stairs.

Billy forgot his boots, Lindsay said.

Happy trails, Jim called out just as the front door slammed.

Vast Club

1

After the posse had disappeared into North Beach that night, Ralph had paced and smoked and mumbled and grumbled. Lindsay had started doing dinner dishes back at the sink in the kitchen, while Jim entertained a half tab of acid and attempted to decide between catching either an old Bogart flick or a silver-tongued preacher program out of San Jose. Every now and then, smoking like a stove, Ralph would scurry mumbling and grumbling down the hallway to peer out the front windows for any sign of Alice Ann and Bill. Who knows what sort of trouble those two nuts are capable of getting themselves into, Ralph muttered vehemently time and again when he loped back into the kitchen. *Somebody* should have stopped those two from going out into the night like nuts, Ralph opined and opined, puffing furiously each time he loped back into the kitchen to pace and pout and fume, until Jim abruptly turned the silver-tongued preacher off and suggested they all undertake a combination booze bolt and search for the Lost Posse and the missing Queen of California.

That night San Francisco's North Beach was ancient Egyptian in nature to Jim as the acid kicked anciently in. For one thing, the unusually warm wind that blew in off the Bay smelled both vaguely vegetal and as oceanic as sperm, as though it had passed through blooming bushes of pittosporum and palms thick with parrot life and over the ancient backs of crocodiles. And that full yellow moon truly looked tropical and serene and suggestive of a world of mystery in Lower Egypt during the Old Kingdom, which Jim, not unlike Alice Ann, found himself recalling vividly.

Neither the Lost Posse nor the Queen of California was to be found in Powell's or the Washington Square Bar & Grill, nor were they to be found at Capp's Corner, where the bartender, Hal Tunnis, insisted on buying a round. Nor were they to be found at that little hideaway Basque joint on Broadway, where the mostly blue-haired but hip old bohemians were dancing to the bouncy albeit sad accordion music of a tiny, amazingly wrinkled, prune-faced French woman wearing a long blond wig, who was reputed to have been the most celebrated courtesan in Paris between the Big Wars, and who wept copiously as she played her accordion and sang the old songs of Edith Piaf. Honey, Lindsay said at one point, and took Jim by the hand, are you crying? Not me, Jim said, batting his eyes like a flirty homecoming queen.

Across a traffic-clogged Broadway, Chinatown was a great glowing caterpillar of neon and noise, hosed sidewalks smelling like burnt oil and eels and the fresh blood of chickens. Waiting for the light to change at Columbus and Broadway, Jim and Ralph and Lindsay entertained the corner strip joint barker's urgent entreaty to enjoy the infinite allure of totally nude coeds dancing within. Are they really coeds, do you think? Ralph asked Jim. Naked, you know, coeds? Yup, Jim said.

Jim gazed on down that Broadway boulevard of blinking neon fallen-angel signs while reflecting on the nature of forbidden desires. Ralph said, You think they might be in that place, the, er, Condor Club? Maybe we should take us a little look in the Condor Club, Ralph said, referring to the club across Columbus, above whose open doorway a giant red neon figure of Carol Dodo and her famous huge breasts blinked. Lindsay said, Ralph, you just want to gape at some big tits. No, Ralph said, you've got me wrong about that. Jim was wondering if it was ever possible to drop your membership in that vast club of the betrayed and the betrayers. Simply stop paying your dues and quit cold turkey. Or was that vast club of the betrayed and the betrayers like the Mafia, where, once you were initiated, only death could set you free. What Jim wanted to do was concentrate on somebody outside himself for the rest of his natural life, like his lovely wife. Jim took Lindsay by the hand and she looked at him a little surprised and she smiled at him warmly and his heart leapt.

They poked their heads into Vesuvio's, where the bartender, Danny Brannon, bought a round. Larry Ferlinghetti was playing chess at a back table. They dodged through traffic across Columbus into Adler Alley and Spec's. They ordered vodka martinis, and Jim studied his handsome, tragic face in the mirror behind the bar. In the mirror he watched Lindsay and Ralph lean toward one another to talk. Jim strolled back through the low, dark, smoky, packed room toward the heads. The walls were plastered with pictures, posters, old signs, dusty funky memorabilia, all that privileged junk which made Spec's the neighborhood museum.

In the narrow back hallway, Bobby Diamond was talking to two blond dancers from the club upstairs. All night the topless dancers from the strip club upstairs snuck down the inner staircase to Spec's between sets for quick smokes or belts or to pick up a few extra bucks giving blowjobs back in Spec's head. Both girls were tall and thin and pale as mushrooms. They leaned back against the wall smoking and talking with Bobby Diamond languidly, their bored, painted raccoony eyes dark and sad and their mouths red as blood. Their tits, which Jim could see through their filmy robes, were way too enormous for the frail stems of their bony bodies. Neither of the hard-faced, big-titted girls acknowleged Jim as he walked up. Bobby Diamond had an unlit cigarette dangling from his thin, scarred lips. Player was Bobby Diamond's nickname among his small-time hood and has-been pug pals. It meant *pimp* in street talk. Maybe 120 pounds dripping wet, Bobby Diamond was a hard-nosed little banty rooster of a boxer, who could bob and bang and punch all night with pure heart for fuel. But he could get caught cold and cut easily. Bobby Diamond had done some time. Between bouts for chump change Bobby Diamond worked as a bouncer in cheap bars and nude encounter parlors and spent every free afternoon in those fleabag hotel rooms he called home writing a novel about a down-and-out boxer heartbroken because he had blown his one big chance for love with a good woman. Suddenly the hard-faced, big-titted girls flipped their cigarette butts to the floor and ducked hurriedly through the beaded curtains to head back upstairs to the club, their high heels clacking crazily on the steps.

Bobby Diamond turned to look at Jim with angry, albeit sad, eyes. How did you blow it with that great woman? Bobby Diamond hissed at Jim, punching him in the chest with a finger. Yeah, and don't go acting fucken cool, you dumb jackoff, Bobby Diamond hissed. Jim said, Say what? Bobby Diamond said, I saw your old lady up at Café Trieste today, man, and this big dumb goofy-looking guy was hitting on her, man. They were holding hands and he was fucken mooning around. So how did you let that happen, man? You been fucken off, man? Lindsay'd never fuck off if you weren't fucken off first. I ain't rattin' her out, man, 'cause I figure you're the fuckoff here. Jim said, Yeah, I'm the fuckoff. Bobby Diamond said, Well, you want me to do that big dumb goofy guy for you, man. I'll do him gratis. Jim said, No, man, he's my job. I'm on top of this situation, man. I got my own plans for that puke. But I gotta wait for the right time. Thanks, anyway, man. Bobby Diamond said, Okay, man. But if you need me, man. Listen, man, what are you holding, man? Any good blow, man? Jim said, Me and Shorty got stuff coming in. I can cover you tomorrow, man. Bobby Diamond said, Okay, man. Now listen, don't act fucken cool and don't act fucken stupid, man, and get your situation taken care of, man, you dig? Jim said, Yeah, man, I dig. Can I buy you a belt, man? Naw, man, I'm back in training, Bobby Diamond said, and pointed to the unlit cigarette dangling from his lips. I've been hitting the heavy bag down at Newman's for a couple of weeks. I'm making a comeback, man. I'm getting a six-round prelim next month. But I could do with some blow. Blow is what you need for comebacks. Jim said, You got the blow, man.

Outside Spec's, the night air about Jim and Lindsay and

Ralph was palpable with purpose, like breath, like a gathering and release of air from the lungs of the ancient royalty of a lost race. Jim was certain at that moment he had the future by the short hairs as soon as he took care of business. The lights of North Beach shuddered with energy as Jim and Lindsay and Ralph turned back toward Broadway and Carol Doda's red blinking tits. They angled onto the narrow, alleylike Grant Street amid the hordes of hooker-witches, drug thugs, and refried freaks left over from a bygone subterranean time. They peeked into the Grant Street saloon, then meandered up the narrow street window-shopping the gaudy funk boutiques, the refugee hippie head shops, the secondhand shops of fancy old clothes, crazy costumes, hats from the thirties and forties, racks of feathered boas, the exotic Chinese herbal shops, and a hardware store with a collection of mystery tools from the Orient in its window.

They threw a left onto Green. Ralph didn't like the looks of Gino & Carlo's on Green, a dark narrow cave of a bar packed with its usual crowd of old wop gangster winos punching operatic arias on the jukebox and scar-faced Sicilian waiters from the Café Sport and working girls getting lit for the long night ahead of them, plus an assortment of Grant Street pimps, queens, and dopers. Gino & Carlo's was an establishment which gave Ralph the willies, and he, for one, wasn't ashamed to admit it; hence Jim entered that place alone, leaving Ralph and Lindsay outside on the sidewalk smoking. When Jim maneuvered his way into a spot beside him at the bar, Charlie McCabe looked at Jim over glasses perched halfway down his huge bulbous nose and grinned. A heavy, white-haired old fart of a character, Charlie McCabe wrote a column called "Himself" for the *San Francisco Examiner*, and the corner bar stool nearest the door at Gino & Carlo's was his office, where he had his own phone, and stacks of papers, magazines, and books abounded. Jim bought Charlie a black brew as thick as molasses and himself a double Jack over. As he and Charlie chatted, Jim gazed through the open doorway at Lindsay and Ralph talking and smoking outside. At one point Lindsay leaned toward Ralph to say something and he bobbed his head in acknowledgment, whereupon Lindsay reached up to pat him on the cheek.

Jim said to Charlie McCabe, Charlie, I got an item for your column, old sport. It's about an impending cold-blooded murder in the form of a serious ass kicking, which I predict will occur before the weekend is over and the perpetrator of said ass kicking will get off in a court of law on account of justifiable mother-fucken homicide. We are talking about body parts scattered throughout the neighborhood here.

2

As they walked up Russian Hill in the early morning, Ralph continued to mumble and grumble and gripe about Bill and Alice Ann probably being under arrest somewhere at that very moment and just who was supposed to come up with bail? Lindsay walked along in silence, as did Jim, who had been stuck carrying the booze-bolt bag. Lindsay had her arms folded over her breasts, as though she was chilly, or simply hugging herself. Now and then she took a long drag from the cigarette that dangled from her lips. The fog had rolled in, and the lights along the street had little yellowy halos glowing around them, and moisture crackled on the wires overhead.

When they reached the corner of Hyde, Lindsay nodded toward a revolving bubble of blue light atop a police car parked in front of their building on up the hill and said, I have a sinking feeling that Ralph may have a point.

They're probably waiting to pick Ralph up, Jim said.

This may not be funny, Lindsay said. —That's Bill they're talking with. God, what now?

Ralph ducked into a doorway.

Ralph, you chickenshit, Jim said.

Why should we be implicated, Ralph whisper-hissed. —In anything Bill has done?

Old Harry and Jake, Jim said as he and Lindsay walked up to the two uniformed officers who were standing on either side of Bill in the middle of the sidewalk in front of their building. The officers were out of the station on Green Street, right around the corner from the cop watering hole, Powell's, where Jim

joined them often. —My two favorite law dogs in the world.
What's up?

Do you know this character, Jim? Jake, a heavy-set, acne-
scarred Irish cop, said, shining a flashlight on Bill's face.

I've never seen this sorry sonofabitch in my life, Jim said.

He's ours, Lindsay said. —As much as I hate to admit it.

This is all just a real big mistake, Bill said, rolling his eyes and
wagging his head empathically.

Is this asshole under arrest? Jim said. —If not, he should be.
And so should that shady-looking character lurking in the shadows right down the hill. Yeah, him. Take both the sonsofbitches
and throw them under the jailhouse is my best advice.

Just a sad, sorry mistake, Bill said. —That's what this is.

He was trying to break into your building, Officer Harry, a
young, handsome cop, said. —He about scared your landlady to
death. Mrs. Chou called us about a big break-in. She's not real
happy right now, Jim.

I can tell, Jim said, and gave a little wave and shrug of his
shoulders to Mrs. Chou, whose tiny face, its eyes pinpoints of fear
and fury, he could see peeking from behind a curtain in her first-
floor flat. She ducked back out of sight.

And then there's that one, Officer Harry said, and pointed his
flashlight at Alice Ann, who was sitting in the entryway smoking.

There you are, Lindsay said, and walked over to her.

We were just trying to get in, Jim, Bill said. —That's the
absolute long and short of it. A sorry mistake.

You got a real choice friend here, Jim, officer Jake said, shining his flashlight back on Bill's stricken, sorry face.

Your pal here was trying to jimmy open Mrs. Chou's side window, Officer Harry said. —He's lucky she didn't plug him.

I was just trying to get in, Bill said. —We didn't have a key
and Alice Ann had to go potty pronto.

Jesus, Billy, Jim said, you big dumb fuck. I live on the second
fucken floor.

I forgot, Bill said. —I got confused. I'm not from around
here, Officers. Alice Ann had to go real bad, Jim. I was doing it
for her. I told her to just squat and do it in the entry, but you

know how women are bashful about some silly stuff. So, strictly speaking, this is all Alice Ann's fault.

Just do us a favor, Jim, Officer Jake said. —Get these people off the street. And keep them under lock and key.

Thanks, boys, Jim said. —Christ on a crutch, I'm sorry about all this bullshit. I owe you guys a couple.

Don't sweat it, Jim, Officer Jake said. The officers walked to the patrol car shaking their heads. They got in, turned the flashing light off, and pulled out from the curb.

Hey, Alice Ann, Jim said, and walked over to the entry.

Hey, your own self, Alice Ann said, and stubbed her cigarette out in a flower pot. —If I don't get upstairs in about ten seconds, I'm going to become very damp.

Lindsay pulled her key from her purse and hurried across the entryway.

Goodbye, Billy, Alice Ann said over her shoulder as she passed by Lindsay at the opened door.

Adios, Alice Ann, Bill said.

Ralph! Jim yelled down the street. —Get your worthless ass up here, buddy!

Hush, Lindsay said. —Quiet down.

Well, Jim said.

It was all a sad, sorry mistake, Lindsay, Bill said. —I swear it.

As soon as the patrol car had passed through the light down the hill at Union and Powell, Ralph stepped from the dark doorway and scrambled up the hill.

Hey there, old Ralphie, Bill said.

Hey there, old Buffalo, Ralph said.

Another close call, Bill said, and he and Ralph laughed and hugged each other around the neck.

Another disaster narrowly avoided, Ralph said, and he and Bill banged each other on the back and hooted with laughter.

You guys, Lindsay hissed, quiet down.

Okay okay, they mouthed in unison, clasping their hands over their respective mouths.

Lookie! Bill suddenly said, and whipped a fat wad of bills from his jeans' front pocket and waved it in the air. —My little darlin' didn't do it! My little darlin' was innocent the whole time. My little darlin' didn't rob me blind, after all.

I told you, Lindsay said.

Holy cow, Ralph said, where did you find it?

Down around my balls, that's where, Bill said. —Pardon my French, Lindsay. I guess I had stuffed it down in my jockey shorts at some point. For safekeeping, I guess. Because I didn't have the good sense to trust my little darlin', and that's why I went and lost her in the end. Let that be a lesson to you boys.

So, when did you find it? Jim said.

Oh, I didn't find it. Alice Ann found it.

Say what? Jim said.

What? Ralph said. —What?

I mean, Bill said, it fell out. When I got out of the car at some point. We were, or had been, you know, driving around hunting for Lulu.

Lucy, Lindsay said. —I knew Lucy was innocent.

Right, Bill said. —We were driving around looking high and low for my little darlin'. Then I pulled into a, oh, gas station. To get gas. And to take a, you know, leak. That's when Alice Ann found it.

When you were taking a leak? Jim said.

No, amigo, Bill said. —When it fell out. On the ground by the car. It had sort of worked its way down my pant leg, I guess. That's what. And it fell out and Alice Ann spotted it.

Old eagle-eye Alice Ann, Jim said.

Right, Bill said.

You better buckle your belt, Buffalo, Jim said. —You must have forgotten to buckle up after you took your leak. The old Buffalo, as everybody knows, always sits down like a sissy to pee. Right, Bill?

I sometimes do. I do. When I'm dog-tired or drunk, I do. Well, folks, it's been fun, but I gotta hit the road. Adios, amigos.

Bill, just where do you think you're going? Lindsay said. —It's almost two in the morning.

Home, Bill said. —Back to the Big Sky country, where I really belong. I just remembered I'm supposed to give a final bright and early Monday morning. I owe it to my students to be there. I've taken some sick leave lately.

Bill, Lindsay said, you need to get some sleep first.

No, ma'am, Bill said, it's time for me to leave now. My work is done here. Like Shane, it's time for me to ride off alone back into the mythological mountains, those mystical Tetons, never to be seen or heard from again. I showed my class *Shane* and they thought it sucked. They thought that it was dopey and sentimental. They didn't understand the holy and innocent hero who comes in from the wilderness to do civilization's dirty work, then rides away like a movie star, like Shane, like me, folks. They didn't understand the nature of that lonely outsider with rules and magical skills and a code of conduct. I tried to teach the little shits, but I didn't get anywhere. Heroes are an ancient problem. Especially old, worn-out heroes like Shane, like me. Oh well, like I always say, when the old way of doing things wears thin, you gotta find a new one. When the story we're in isn't working out right, we make up a new one to inhabit. I'm gonna give those little smartass sumbitches that final on Monday, then I'm gonna flunk them all. Anyway, like I said, my work is done here. Adios, amigos. Bye-bye, Bill said, and lumbered down the hill.

Billy, Lindsay called out, what about your boots?

Billy! Jim called out. —Come back, Billy! Ralph needs you, Billy! Alice Ann wants you, too!

Bill paused at the corner of Mason and stood there weaving under the streetlight for a few moments, while he gazed about for his vehicle and tried to recall the best road back to Montana, and then Bill lurched across Union Street and was gone.

3

Back upstairs Lindsay found that Alice Ann had disappeared into the spare bedroom. Lindsay went into the bathroom and locked the door. She sat on the edge of the tub and smoked a cigarette, flipping the ashes into the sink. When she had finished, she ran water over the butt, then dropped it into the wastebasket. She filled the sink with hot water and washed her face, then rinsed it with cold water. She studied her face in the mirror. She began to reapply makeup, but stopped.

Lindsay found Ralph standing at the stove in the kitchen stirring something in a pan. Jim's little black-and-white television set was playing soundlessly on the counter by the sink. Ralph didn't look at her when Lindsay walked into the room.

I'm making me a little soup, Ralph said. —If that's okay?

It's okay, Ralph, Lindsay said.

I'm sorry about all the problems Alice Ann has caused around here, Ralph said.

It's not Alice Ann's fault, Ralph.

Well, I know I'm a part of the problems. And I'm sorry.

We are all a part of the problems, Lindsay said. —We are all in the same boat of bullshit.

Well, Ralph said, poop floats.

Maybe so, Lindsay said. —But you can't keep pretending that a turd in the punch bowl of life is a chocolate ice cube. Dear God, where did that one come from? I sounded like bullshit Billy. Bill shows up for a single evening of craziness and his special brand of bullshit and I am utterly undone. Where's Jim?

I don't know where your husband is.

Maybe you should find your wife, Ralph. See if she's okay.

Right. Maybe tell her a bedtime story. Except my wife knows all my stories by heart. She made up most of my stories anyway herself. Just go ask her. Why don't you sit down for a minute? Let's smoke a cigarette. Where's the harm in us having a nice relaxing cigarette together? You want any soup?

Go check on your wife, Ralph, Lindsay said.

I want to talk some more, Ralph said. —We need to. Nothing is settled. We need to talk some more.

Everything *is* settled, Ralph, Lindsay said. —Oh, Ralph, Lindsay said, and mussed his hair. —Ralph, Ralph. I need to go check on my own husband.

Jim was lying bareback on his old sleeping bag before the front-room fire with little Sappho curled asleep on his broad hairy chest. Lindsay studied Jim's bearded face in the faint light of the dying fire. Who was he? Whom did he love? Lindsay sat down on the sleeping bag beside Jim. She put Sappho on the hardwood floor in a slant of streetlight, where Sappho had an immediate cute-attack, rolling about on her back, twisting her head, the star of her own little kitty movie. Lindsay laughed quietly and rubbed her cat's tummy.

Lindsay ran her fingers over the skin of Jim's muscled arms. She loved the feel of his skin, faintly moist, smooth. She loved his skin's smell and its taste. Milo's skin had been dry and had an acrid odor. More than anything, Lindsay wanted to be a real person at last. She wanted to be a real woman, a real wife, a real mother with breasts filled with real milk. How in God's name was her life going to turn out? Would she ever have a life with her husband full of common purpose, shared motives? Shared vulnerability, security, repetition? What scared Lindsay the most about Jim, besides the facts that he drank too much and did too many drugs and was essentially a criminal who could end up behind bars, was the manner in which he always seemed to be writing things up somewhere in his mind, always mining his life, their life, for material. What Lindsay feared the most was becoming a character, *the* wife, in somebody's collected stories, forced into fiction. Please God, no more fucking hopeful beginnings, crises, crash landings. Please God, no more three-act fucking melodramas.

Lindsay slowly unzipped Jim's jeans and spread his fly wide open. She gently tugged his shorts down and took his penis in her hand and studied it intently, rolling its foreskin gently with her thumb. Jim farted a little fart and smacked his lips in his sleep, and Lindsay laughed quietly. She squeezed his penis lightly and he farted again. Sappho lifted her little black face and looked at Lindsay and mewed softly. Lindsay scratched the top of her little cat's head, and Sappho licked her fingers and then yawned greatly.

Lindsay bent forward and licked the skin of Jim's shoulder then sniffed it. She rubbed her nose lightly around the ridges of an underarm. She parted the hair over a nipple, then flicked it lightly with the tip of her tongue. Then suddenly Lindsay thought of Ralph, his huge wonderful, gentle hands, the wonderful way *he* smelled. Lindsay shut her eyes and shook her head. When she opened her eyes, she traced a finger along those two long scars barely visible through thick hair that carved a V down Jim's lower abdomen, whose point was his limp penis, which she began to rub gently, until Jim mumbled in his sleep. It sounded as though he had mumbled a name. Lindsay bent over him, put her ear next to his mouth, as though listening for her husband's last words.

Jim mumbled again. *Natalie*, was that the name? Natalie, Lindsay whispered back into Jim's dream, while she gently pulled upon his stiffening penis. Natalie, Jim mumbled again, then mumbled another name. *Sally?* Sally, Lindsay whispered in Jim's ear. Whereupon Jim mumbled Susie. Then Jim mumbled Annie, Peggy, Jenny, Belinda, Bobby Ann, Bobbie Jean, Lolita, Mary Louise, Robin, Janet Sue, Jackie, June, Mae, Martha, Megan, Diane, Donna, Molly, Margaret, Annie, Lynn, Camille, Connie, Amy, Leslie, Debbie, Bev, Beth, Bossy . . .

You turkey, Lindsay said, and laughed. —You're not asleep, Stark. Bossy? Who the fuck was Bossy?

I loved Bossy, Jim mumbled, grinning, but with his eyes still shut. —When I was a boy back on the farm, Bossy and I would meet out in the old barn late at night. Mooooooo, Bossy would go when she came. Mooooooooooooooo.

You turkey, Lindsay said, and gave Jim's member a mighty squeeze. —Consider this one extremely choked chicken.

Yeow, holy cow! Jim cried, then gasped, Lindsay Lindsay Lindsay Lindsay Lindsay Lindsay Lindsay . . .

Whereupon Jim sat up and rubbed his eyes. For a time he simply sat there staring into the dying fire.

What are you thinking about, honey? Lindsay said.

Nothing much, Jim said. He stood and zipped up his jeans, then walked over to the table in the turret. He took a drink of wine from a long-stemmed glass, then picked up a roach resting in an ashtray and lit it. He clicked on his little portable radio, which was on the table, dialed to that station he liked out of San Jose that played Mexican music all night; border-town gunfight music, Jim always called it. Jim sat down and began cleaning his gun, which was on a newspaper spread out on the table. Jim looked up at Lindsay as she walked over to the table.

What are you doing, Jim? Lindsay said.

I'm cleaning my heater, Jim said. —My rod, my roscoe.

Why are you cleaning your roscoe, Jim?

You never know when you might need your roscoe, Jim said, and took a long drag on the joint, letting the smoke swirl dramatically up over his shadowy face.

You know I hate that thing.

Shorty and I are going target-shooting. Take a gander out at Alcatraz tonight. It looks like either a great ghost ship anchored in the dark bay or an island city of the dead. I can't make up my mind. Are you glad you married me instead of Ralph? Jim said.

Ralph was never serious about marrying me, Lindsay said.

That don't really answer my question, ma'am.

I hate when you call me ma'am. You know that. I love you, Jim. So, are you going back to New York?

I ain't studying on no New York. Where is everybody?

Here and there. I'm going to bed.

I'm right behind you.

Good night, honey.

I'm right behind you, I said.

Good night, Jim.

5

The canopy draped above the bed resembled a pyramid only vaguely. The thin hollow metal tubing of its frame had been bent and wobbled like delicate old bones when Lindsay sat down on the edge of the bed. The tent's tie-dyed fabric felt wet and slippery like silk and was as thinly translucent as a scarf.

When in the world and why did Alice Ann put this up, Lindsay wondered. Lindsay undressed and lay down naked on top of the covers, gazing upward at the canopy. In the soft glow from her vanity lamp across the room the filmy material above her shimmered like stained glass turned molten with her breath. A foghorn sounded its distant, forlorn low from the Bay, like the boohoo of some pathetic, drowning cow. The plaintive albeit menacing Mexican music drifted in from the front room, where Jim sat drinking his wine and smoking his dope and cleaning his roscoe. Good night, Jim. Sleep tight, Jim. The pang Lindsay felt she thought would burst her heart. Across this box of broken dreams was her grandmother's antique vanity and chiffonier and that ancient cradle wherein she and her mother and grandmother had been rocked to sleep. Lindsay felt her life tremble. Her memories felt like an undertow.

Sappho jumped up on the bed and came mewing toward her, then stopped to sniff between Lindsay's legs. Come on, honey, Lindsay said, and reached down to scratch her kitty's head. Don't be a dirty little kitty. Come on, Lindsay said, and lifted her kitty up beside her own face on the pillow. They breathed into each other's faces for a few moments, and then Sappho curled up on the pillow in the cusp of Lindsay's neck. Lindsay bit her lip until it hurt. She made her mouth water, then tasted and swallowed it like a bitter kiss. She touched her right nipple. Good night, Jim, Lindsay said to herself as her fingertips brushed her nipples. She felt the heat rise in her stomach. Good night, Ralph. Good night, Alice Ann. Sleep tight, Lindsay whispered as her fingertips traveled slowly down the starry sides of her night body.

He was a shadow in the doorway for a moment, then closed the door behind him and walked slowly across the room to bed.

Say Uncle

1

Lindsay awoke to loud voices. For a moment she lay there with her eyes shut, Jim's big arm resting across her bare stomach. He was sound asleep. Lindsay reached beneath the covers to reposition Sappho, who was nestled between her legs, and Sappho gave an annoyed nip to one of her fingers. She blinked open her eyes and looked at the glowing alarm clock on the table beside the bed: 3:23. The voices were coming from the kitchen. Lindsay slid from beneath Jim's arm and slipped into jeans and a sweater in the dark.

Alice Ann and Ralph were sitting at the kitchen table in the dim light of the little black-and-white television on the counter. When Lindsay clicked on the overhead light, they both turned to look at her. Alice Ann stood up and swirled around. She was wearing a long, lovely, full-flowing white dress, that billowed about her as she spun around. It had long sleeves and a brocade front with mother-of-pearl buttons.

Oh, hon, Lindsay said, that is absolutely gorgeous.

It's my second-honeymoon dress, Alice Ann said. —I paid an

arm and a leg for this thing, God knows. I got it especially for our second-honeymoon trip.

That's what we're having a little discussion about, Ralph said. —Just what constitutes an arm and a leg.

I was going to save it for later, Alice Ann said. —I think I've already told you, I made Ralph and me reservations at a really fancy hotel in Seattle, and I thought I'd make Ralph take me out dancing wearing this. In one of those fancy rooftop-restaurant nightclubs overlooking the romantic lights of the city. And if I can't get Ralph out on the dance floor, I'll dance the night away with strangers, if it comes to that.

I love Seattle, Lindsay said. —And your hair. Your hair looks terrific, hon.

How much did that dress cost? Ralph said. —Tell me.

You look ravishing, Lindsay said. —You look breathtaking, really. You look as lovely as a bride.

A blushing bride? Alice Ann said. —Does it make me look young and innocent? Ralph, does it?

You bet, Ralph said. —You look real pretty. You do. How much did it cost, really?

What's up? Jim said as he strolled into the kitchen. He was wearing jeans and a T-shirt and his cowboy boots. —Is it time for breakfast or something? What time is it, anyway?

Come on, Ralph, Alice Ann said. —Dance with me. Let's dance and think about it later. Let's dance with utter abandon. Let's be abandoned like in the old days, Ralph.

You know I have two left feet, Ralph said. —I'd stomp on your foot, and then you'd bop me one, and then where would we be. Lefts and rights. We better leave well enough alone, is my best thought on this matter.

Goddamn it, Ralph, Alice Ann said. —Get up off your fat ass and dance with your wife. If you love me, you'll get up and dance. If you don't love me, then you won't. End of story.

It's been a real long day, Lindsay said. —Maybe we should all just retire for the rest of the night, get some shut-eye.

Hey, Jim said, I've got a bright idea. I got you guys some stuff for your second-honeymoon trip, a sort of surprise package that I was going to give you to take along and open up later. But, hey, why wait?

Jim, honey, Lindsay said, I don't think it's such a good idea for tonight. Or this morning, I should say. Everybody is dead tired and a mite strung-out. It's been a long, stressful day.

It'll be fun, Jim said. —It'll be a riot. I'm wide awake now.

I've had about all the fun for one day I can handle, Lindsay said.

A surprise package you say? Ralph said.

It'll be a million laughs, Jim said and headed back toward the door. —I've got it stashed in the bedroom. Nobody move, Jim said, and hurried from the room. When he returned in a blink, he placed a paper bag whose top was tied with a pink bow in the center of the table.

They're just some gag gifts, Jim said. —They'll be a hoot.

I really think we ought to wait until morning, Lindsay said.

Oh, Lindsay, Jim said, don't be such a spoilsport, baby. So, here you go, folks, one honeymooners' deluxe package of delightful items to be utilized for debauchery and decadence and just plain old dirty sex. I took a bus all the way down to the sleazy Tenderloin to shop for these sinful little items. Well, go on, old Ralph. Open it up, boy.

This isn't one of your tricks, is it, old Jim? Ralph said. —Nothing is going to, you know, spring out at me and explode or something, is it? A trick like that could, you know, put a person's eye out.

Here, for God's sake, Jim said, and opened the package. —Here, Ralph, here's something I got just for you. Something you've always needed from what I hear, Jim said, and handed Ralph a small blue jar.

What's this? Ralph said, and held the jar up to read its label. —*Doctor Dick*, Ralph read, and laughed, his big shoulders shaking. —*Doctor Dick*, the ultimate prolong lotion.

Just rub some of that blue stuff on your dick, Ralph, and your problems are over, Jim said. —No more humiliation and heartbreak in the droopy-dick department, old Ralph. And here, Jim said, rummaging in the sack, some Kamasutra Nipple Nectar. Listen to this: "Let him taste the sweet, full fruit of your ripe breasts. As soon as this invisible drip of pure pleasure meets his lips, he will kiss, nibble, lick, and suck you like a hungry child."

Chinese Nympho Clitoral Cream, Ralph read from a clear glass jar full of purple fluid, and laughed. —Now this is a little item you aren't going to find on every store's shelf.

Wild Cherry–Flavored Peter Licker, Alice Ann read from a label on a red jar. —A sucker's delight, it says here. Yum, yum. I certainly wish I had had this tawdry treasure last night, when it might have come in handy.

What does that mean, anyway, Alice Ann? Ralph said.

Oh, Ralph, just wake up and smell the coffee, Alice Ann said. —But what's done is done, don't you agree?

What does that mean, anyway? Ralph said. —Why do you always have to talk in riddles?

So you'll just have to learn to live with what's over and done, just like I've had to do, Ralph, Alice Ann said. She picked up a tube and read from its label: "Lovers' Lubricant, delicious, cinnamon-flavored, fragrant, slippery, wet, and wild."

Hey, Jim said, this is all gag stuff. This was supposed to be a joke. Lindsay, do we have any Alka-Seltzer? I feel pukey and have this godawful taste in my mouth.

In the old days these tawdry items would have been worthless to Ralph and me, Alice Ann said. —Except for a cheap laugh. In the old days Ralph and I never had any difficulty in the fucking-each-other's-brains-out department. Even the tawdry fact that he was fucking you, Lindsay, didn't reflect upon our own wildly satisfying sex. All it reflected upon was Ralph's tawdry penchant for betrayal. Ralph has always felt perfectly comfortable with betrayal. Ralph has always had no conscience when it came to his pathetic, little leaning tower of penis.

Hon, please, Lindsay said.

You just had to start up, didn't you, Alice Ann! Ralph said.

Listen, Lindsay said, let's all call it a night.

Ralph was once my everything, Alice Ann said. —Just like the song says. I can actually remember when I was a person who had some pride. When I felt my life had some direction and meaning. But then Ralph went outside the marriage, and that meant that I was not good enough for him except in the wild abandoned sex department. We never needed any of this sort of tawdry crap in order to fuck each other's brains out, did we, Ralph? So, okay, Jim, we can, Ralph and I, use all the help we can get. So what about this Kamasutra Nipple Nectar, Lindsay? Do you recommend it? Does it work for you? Does it make Ralph kiss, nibble, lick, and suck you like a hungry child?

Oh, hon, Lindsay said, and reached across the table to put her hand on top of Alice Ann's. —We all need a good night's sleep, that's all.

You're right, Jim said, and yawned. —I think it's high time we all hit the old sack.

What I need to figure out, Alice Ann said, is exactly when my husband decided to hate me. I need to know when he decided to turn on me and cause me anguish and humiliation and to expose my pain to the world and then abandon me forever. And all the bitter, hard, sad things about my only marriage, which is the single greatest failure of my lifetime, have been laid bare for the world's amusement. That tragic rock has been rolled over again and again, and finally anyone I once thought I was or could again become is dead and buried. All my life's blood has been slowly drained from my body over the long reincarnations of my failed marriage. Well, I'm willing to try anything, Alice Ann said, and began unbuttoning the brocade front of her dress.

Here we go again! Ralph said. —You just have to give everybody another eyeful, right, Alice Ann?

Please, Alice Ann, Lindsay said.

Just shut up! Alice Ann said. She lifted her left breast free from her dress and opened the tiny glass jar of Kamasutra Nipple Nectar and began rubbing fingertips of the purple cream over her nipple. —So, Ralph, what do you think? Hungry? Do you want to kiss and lick and suck my nipple one last time, like the hungry piece-of-shit you have always been?

I think you've gone nuts, Ralph said. —That's my best opinion of that business.

Not doing the trick, huh? Alice Ann said. —Let's try something else. You love ketchup over everything, right, Ralph? Alice Ann said, and got up from the table and walked over to the refrigerator. She rummaged around inside and then turned and held up a bottle of ketchup. She undid the bottle top and began to methodically splash ketchup up and down the front of her dress.

Don't, Alice Ann, don't! Lindsay cried, and jumped up. She threw her arms around Alice Ann and held her for a moment, and then led Alice Ann back to the table. —Hon, your beautiful white dress, Lindsay said, and helped Alice Ann sit down. —We can get that out. We'll soak it overnight and it will be good as new.

Nothing is ever going to be as good as new or ever innocent again once it's ruined, Alice Ann said. —Is this enough for one night, Ralph? Will this keep you going for a while?

This has to end, Ralph said, and lit a cigarette. He emptied a bottle of champagne into a glass, half filling it, and tossed it down. —Once and for all, Alice Ann.

My life is over because of you, you miserable, ruthless, cold-hearted sonofabitch, Alice Ann said, and she tossed the nearly empty bottle of ketchup at Ralph's head. Ralph ducked back just in time, and the bottle smashed against the far wall. Lindsay clinched Alice Ann's forearms from across the table.

Enough! Lindsay cried. —Alice Ann, enough!

Put a stop to this madness, somebody! Ralph said. —Call the police, somebody. Somebody call them. This woman is crazy. We are dealing with a crazy person here, I'm telling you.

Jim, Lindsay said, Jim, do something.

Me? Jim said. —Why always me? Okay, Alice Ann, you behave yourself. You behave yourself, or you'll have to go to bed without your breakfast. Hey, what would you guys like for breakfast, anyway? How about a stack of waffles for my crazy friends?

Billy, Alice Ann said, wanted me to be sure to let you know, Ralph, just how guilty he felt about the blow job, and he hoped you wouldn't hold it against him.

What in the world did you just say, Alice Ann? Ralph said.

Blame me, Ralph, for Billy's world-class blow job, Alice Ann said. —It was I who insisted on sucking Billy's enormous boner until his old fat cheeks just about caved in. Now I suggest we put that business behind us and let bygones be bygones. I, for one, will drink to that, Alice Ann said, and picked up a half-filled glass of flat champagne and drank it down. She threw the empty glass at Ralph's head.

Ralph flinched just in time, taking the glass high on his shoulder. He jumped up from his chair, and Alice Ann shook free from Lindsay's grasp and jumped up also. Alice Ann grabbed a small knife from the cheeseboard and started around the table for Ralph. Ralph grabbed an empty wine bottle from the table and half swung, half threw it at Alice Ann, hitting her high on the side of her head, where it shattered and rained the room with flying green glass. Jim jumped at Ralph and tried to grab him in a hold as they tumbled over a chair onto the floor. Alice Ann ran from the room down the hallway. Lindsay stood there in the middle of the kitchen, mouth agape, clutching her throat, as she watched Jim and Ralph wrestle around on the floor, cursing, grunting, flailing arms and legs as they knocked over chairs and kicked the kitchen table, bottles, glasses, cups bouncing from it to smash on the floor. Finally they stopped rolling around and lay there, a tangle of arms and legs, gasping for air. Lindsay ran from the room after Alice Ann.

When he finally more or less caught his breath, Jim gasped, Okay, Ralph, have you had enough?

Me? Ralph gasped. —What about you? I've got you in a hold.

Are you crazy, Ralph? Jim croaked. —I've got you pinned.

That's news to me.

Just say *uncle*, Ralph, and I'll let you up.

You say *uncle*.

You say it first.

I don't see why I'm the one who has to say it first, Ralph said.

Okay, goddamn it, Ralph. Let's just both say it at the same time and get the fuck up off the floor.

Let's neither of us say it.

All right, Ralph, Jim said, and they both let their grips on each other loose, and they flopped back on the floor wheezing.

Finally, Jim pulled himself to his feet, staggered over to an overturned chair, righted it, and flopped down. Ralph crawled across the floor to another overturned chair, righted it, and pulled himself up.

Are you all right, Ralph? Jim said. —I didn't hurt you bad, did I? I was trying to go easy on you.

Hurt me? How about you? Did I hurt you is the question.

No, Ralph, you dickhead, you couldn't hurt me if you tried. The only person you hurt around here was your wife, Ralph. You've really done it this time, old boy.

I know, old Jim. God, I know, Ralph said, and buried his face in his hands. —What have I done, old Jim?

2

Jim saw the first splotch of blood on the runner rug in front of the bathroom door. There was a trail of splattered blood all the way down the staircase, and on the tiles of the entry, where perhaps Alice Ann had paused for a moment, there was a pool with a footprint in it. Out on the sidewalk Jim looked up and down the deserted street. The streetlights were hazy yellow and haloed in the fog, and fog crackled on the wires overhead, and from far off a car horn blared in alarm. The trail of blood led down the hill, and Jim started off in that direction just as he saw Lindsay and Alice Ann turn the corner down at Mason. Lindsay had an arm around Alice Ann's shoulders and a hand pressed against the side of Alice Ann's head, and they wove back and forth across the sidewalk as they stumbled up the hill. Jim ran down to them.

She's bleeding badly, Lindsay said, her voice surprisingly calm and steady. Lindsay took her bloody hand away from the jagged cut on the side of Alice Ann's head, just above her left ear, and blood bubbled from it. Jim whipped out a handkerchief and pressed it tightly against the cut.

Can you get her on up the hill? Lindsay said.

Yeah.

I'd better run up and call for help.

Call an ambulance.

Yeah, I'll call emergency. My God.

Throw some towels or something down the stairs, Jim said.

You're going to be fine, hon, Lindsay said, and patted Alice Ann on her arm, then ran up the hill.

Jim half-carried Alice Ann up the hill, and then helped her sit down beside him on the front steps. His handkerchief was soaked with blood, and blood ran down his arm and dripped off his elbow. He reached behind them for the pile of towels in the entry at the bottom of the stairs, then pressed one firmly against the cut. Blood spread through the white towel immediately, blossoming red and wet about Jim's fingers. Alice Ann, who had not said a word, put her head against Jim's shoulder. Her eyes were wide open and glassy, with a vague, faraway look in them, but her face was perfectly composed, serene even, and there was a slight smile on her pale lips. His fingers slippery with blood, Jim began with great difficulty to button the front of Alice Ann's dress, which was wet and red with blood.

I hope I've made Ralph happy one last time, Alice Ann said, her voice no more than a whisper. —I hope I've finally given him everything he needs.

Don't talk, sweetie, Jim said. —Ralph is grief-stricken.

Tell Ralph I did it all for him, Alice Ann whispered.

Don't, hon, Jim said. —Help is on its way.

I wonder how even Ralph will make something timeless out of this tawdry business, Alice Ann said. —I wonder if he can make even this shit sublime. Oh well, my work is done now. I give up. I've lost. I'm throwing in the towel. Now I simply want to rest in peace, Alice Ann said, and she shut her eyes.

Hold on, hon, Jim said, and pressed the towel even more tightly against the cut. —Help will be here any minute.

My only real regret, Alice Ann whispered, as she settled her head against Jim's chest and sighed, is that I didn't stab myself in the heart when I had that knife. That would at least have given my story a happy ending.

Bathed in the flashing red lights of the ambulance, Jim and Lindsay silently watched the paramedics quickly administer to

Alice Ann and then strap her onto a stretcher and roll her to the ambulance, where they maneuvered her into its back. Jim and Lindsay decided that she would follow the ambulance to the hospital and Jim would stay with Ralph, who, Lindsay had reported, was in pretty bad shape himself back in the kitchen. Without another word, Lindsay headed up the hill to where her car was parked. As Jim turned back toward the house, he caught a glimpse of their little Chinese landlady peeking from behind the curtains of her living-room window, and Jim smiled weakly and waved at her.

Rock Bottom

1

Jim found Ralph sitting at the table in darkness save for the flickering light from the little black-and-white television set. Ralph was fumbling with something on the table, and from their glowing embers in the ashtray Jim could see that Ralph had a couple of cigarettes going. Jim clicked on the overhead light and Ralph nearly fell over backward in his chair. Ralph dropped whatever he had been fooling with onto the floor. His eyes were wild-looking and his big frame was trembling. The floor was covered with broken glass, which glinted green in the bright light and crunched under Jim's boots.

Jesus, old Ralph, Jim said, and walked over and put his hands on Ralph's shaking shoulders. —Settle down, old dog. Everything is going to be all right, boy, Jim said, and rubbed Ralph's shoulders for a few moments. Jim bent down to pick up the can of Campbell's soup Ralph had dropped and placed it on the table.

A little soup, Ralph said, and patted the can. —I thought a little soup would be a good thing. You're out of chicken-and-noodles. But I like tomato soup, too, Ralph said, and began fumbling with the can opener. His hands were shaking.

Here you go, boy, Jim said, and opened the can for Ralph. —Zip, zip. Just call me the chef-of-the-future. Do you want me to heat this up for you, old dog?

No, that's okay, old Jim, Ralph said. —I've kinda got used to eating my soup this way. Right out of the old can. I can't tell you all the times in my life I've had to sort of eat on the run. Jim, just tell me right out, is Alice Ann going to die or something? Tell me the truth, old Jim.

Jesus, Ralph, no. No way. Calm down, boy. Just cool it, old dog. Alice Ann's going to be all right. She will.

Will they be coming for me?

What, Ralph?

Will they, you know, the authorities, be coming for me? Am I going to be put under arrest, Jim? Tell me the truth, Jim.

No, Ralph. Not unless I make a citizen's arrest, which ain't out of the question.

Nobody is coming for me, really?

No, Ralph, nobody. Jesus. Calm down, old dog. We told them it was some sort of dumb, freak accident. They were too busy trying to save Alice Ann's life to be much concerned about how it happened, anyway. Lindsay is at the hospital. She'll handle any questions.

I thought you said Alice Ann was going to be all right. You said that.

She is. She is. For somebody who lost about all the blood in her body, anyway.

Is she really going to be all right? Is she? Really? What did they say?

They said she had lost a lot of blood but that she was going to pull through all right. Except maybe for some serious brain damage due to loss of blood.

Oh, Jesus! Did they say that? Did they?

No, Ralph. No. I'm just jerking your string. I'm sorry, old dog.

Whew, Ralph said. —Whew. Jim, you don't happen to have any crackers around, do you? I like crackers with my soup. Especially some of those little, you know, animal crackers.

Animal crackers? Jesus, Ralph, you gotta be kidding, Jim said.

Jim took a broom from behind the kitchen door and began to sweep the kitchen floor. He swept the broken green glass into little separate piles all around the floor, and then swept the piles one by one into a dustpan, which he emptied into the trashcan under the kitchen sink. Jim dampened a fistful of paper towels and ran them over the grit of glass flakes on the kitchen counters. On top of the canisters next to the television set Jim came across the bottom of the wine bottle, like a large, smooth green coin of glass. If it had flown a mere inch to the left, the television screen would have been smashed to smithereens and Jim would have had to kill Ralph.

Old Jim, Ralph said, do you think it really happened?

What, old dog?

That business with Bill. What Alice Ann said.

You mean about her giving Bill a world-class blowjob until his fat, old cheeks near caved in?

Yes.

Nope.

Really, you think, old Jim?

Yeah, really. I, for one, didn't believe it for a second, old Ralph. And neither should you. Alice Ann was just pissed off and trying to drive you crazy as a bat, Ralph.

But why? I didn't do anything to her. Not recently, anyway. I've been trying to mind my p's and q's with her lately. A big flareup was the last thing in the world I wanted to happen on this trip. Maybe I should just turn myself in. Old Jim, who in the world am I, anyway? Who did that terrible thing here tonight? Who was that person going around doing terrible things and calling himself by my name? Is this it, then, Jim? Is this what it all comes down to, then? Is this that tomorrow I've been clinging to life to reach? Ralph said, and turned to look at the television screen as the station switched to commercials and the sound rose abruptly to a blare.

2

Lindsay did not return from the hospital until nearly nine o'clock. She found Jim sound asleep, with his head on the kitchen table, and Ralph staring wide-eyed at the television. Alice Ann is going to be okay, Ralph, Lindsay said to him, and Ralph merely looked at her and nodded. Do you have any cigarettes? Ralph said. —I smoked all mine up. Lindsay took a pack out of her purse and tossed them on the table before Ralph.

Lindsay took Alice Ann's blood-soaked dress out of the plastic bag a nurse had given her, and she put it in the kitchen sink to soak. Lindsay flopped down at the kitchen table, blind with fatigue, as heavy-hearted as she had ever been in her life. She took a cigarette from the pack in front of Ralph and lit it. Alice Ann, Lindsay told Ralph, who smoked and stared at the television, was going to be all right, but she had lost a lot of blood and the doctors wanted to hold her for observation for a day or so. As soon as she took a long, hot bath and napped, Lindsay planned to return to the hospital with Alice Ann's things. Alice Ann, Lindsay told Ralph, preferred that Ralph not visit her or call her right now. Ralph smoked and watched the television. I hadn't planned on it, Ralph said.

Later that morning, when Jim left the flat to go to the corner market, he found a sealed envelope slipped under the front door. He read the enclosed note as he walked down the hill. When he returned to the flat with a bag of booze and groceries, he found that Lindsay was up again and drinking coffee at the kitchen table with Ralph, who was sipping his third or fourth bourbon-and-water breakfast of the morning. When Jim placed the little box of animal crackers in front of Ralph, Ralph looked up at Jim with an expression of utter astonishment. Ralph immediately tore the little box open and plucked a cracker giraffe from it. Jim placed the note in front of Lindsay, who simply gazed at it for a time through the curling smoke of the cigarette dangling from her lips, before finally picking it up to read, and then read again, that eviction notice.

After work that Tuesday evening Lindsay went to pick up Alice Ann at the hospital, in order to drive her down to the little tract house she had rented in Cupertino after selling their home in Menlo Park to save Ralph's bacon. Alice Ann had looked somehow both awful and beautifully tragic to Lindsay, thinner and pale and yet dramatic for it, and Alice Ann (or somebody) had chopped off her long, lovely, blond hair. Because of the short, severe haircut, the bandage on the left side of Alice Ann's face looked like some fat, mushroomy growth. Lindsay had felt horribly sad and nervous and resisted an amazing urge to weep. Alice Ann was also nervous and edgy, with virtually nothing to say, and she chain-smoked incessantly as they drove down Route 280 south, while Lindsay chattered away a mile a minute. Out of the corner of her eye Lindsay kept glancing at Alice Ann's shaking hands. Lindsay told Alice Ann that she had soaked and bleached and washed the white dress several times, but that it was still somewhat discolored and would obviously need professional cleaning. Lindsay told Alice Ann that she had pressed the dress, or tried to, including its elaborately pleated front. Lindsay told Alice Ann the dress was in a box in the backseat. Lindsay chattered on about the various cleaning remedies she had tried as Alice Ann turned to retrieve the box. Alice Ann took the dress from the box and held it out in front of her to examine. Alice Ann crumpled the dress into her lap and lit a cigarette. When Lindsay glanced at Alice Ann she saw that although she was not making any sounds at all, tears were running down her face. After a time Alice Ann rolled down her window and flipped the stub of her cigarette into the wind. And then, without comment, Alice Ann tossed the dress out the window.

The little house Alice Ann had rented looked like a turd with windows, a squat brown stucco affair with a dirt yard in some subdivision of similar sad abodes. Several Mexican women were sitting in metal lawn chairs on the concrete porch of the house next door, and a group of plump brown-faced children ran about the yard. Lindsay declined Alice Ann's invitation to come in for a drink, saying she was dead tired and the traffic back up to the city would be bumper to bumper. They sat parked in front of the little brown house and listened to the car tick.

Alice Ann sat there and cried. Alice Ann's heaving, narrow shoulders felt amazingly frail to Lindsay, brittle, birdlike, as Lindsay held her and began to weep, too. God knows how long they blubbered like that, before Lindsay began to hiccup, and Alice

Ann drew back to look at Lindsay through streaming tears. Both of their noses were running, and when one of Lindsay's hiccups came out more like a burp with a juicy bubble on the end of it, they both started to laugh, and they laughed until they almost started to cry again. They sat there then, dabbing at each other's noses and faces with tissues Lindsay found in her purse, laughing again at intervals, until they both slumped back on the seat exhausted. Alice Ann lit a cigarette, and so did Lindsay. When they finished those cigarettes, they both lit another and smoked those, too, without much comment. The Mexican children were standing in a line along their front-yard fence watching wide-eyed, and the women on the porch kept giving Lindsay and Alice Ann furtive glances.

Presently Alice Ann reached up and turned the rearview mirror toward her. She tore the bandage off the side of her face with a single jerk. Squinting her eyes in the smoky air, Alice Ann gazed in the mirror, studying her face.

That fucker tried to launch my face like a ship, Alice Ann said, and laughed, as she ran her fingers lightly along the stitched wound high on her left jaw. —The face that launched a thousand fucking bottles, she said. She lit another cigarette, as did Lindsay.

When Lindsay finally said that she really should be heading back, that she would call Alice Ann in a couple of days and things would proceed from there, Alice Ann clutched both of Lindsay's hands in her own, and squeezed them tightly, almost painfully. Against all odds, Alice Ann told Lindsay, she and Lindsay had found one another in this lifetime. And as soon as she was rested enough and back on her feet, she and Lindsay would set forth again, launch their lives together again as sisters. Let Ralph enjoy his ill-gotten fame alone, let your own so-called husband have his little boner-breath slut, who was not fit to lick Lindsay's boots, for Alice Ann and Lindsay had each other now, and their sister hearts beat as one. They would make up the stories of their own lives from here on out, and live them purely for themselves. All their tomorrows were their own from here on out. They would find happiness, goddamn it, if it killed them, Alice Ann said, and laughed. Alice Ann's thin, pale face was radiant. Alice Ann kissed the backs of both of Lindsay's hands, and then she got out of the car. Alice Ann took her suitcase from the backseat and walked up the crumbly walk toward the little brown house, where her daughter appeared in the open doorway. Alice Ann's daughter pushed open the screen door and stood there puffing furiously on a cigarette. Hey, Mom, Alice Ann's daughter said, what in the fuck happened now, huh?

Alice Ann turned when she reached the door to smile and give Lindsay a little wave. Behind Alice Ann her daughter gave Lindsay the finger. Alice Ann blew Lindsay a little kiss and then disappeared inside the house, and that was the last time Lindsay would ever see Alice Ann. Lindsay and Jim would call Alice Ann for months, letting the phone ring off the wall, or leaving messages with one of the kids, which remained unanswered, until finally they let it go.

3

When Lindsay arrived back at the flat, she found the place ablaze with lights. She found Ralph sitting at the kitchen table as usual watching television, while he smoked and munched on hard spaghetti noodles he took from a box two at a time.

Ralph, Lindsay said, all you have to do is drop those noodles in boiling water. That's all there is to cooking spaghetti, you know, dear. You can boil water, can't you, Ralph?

Sure I can, Ralph said. —But this is the way I happen to like my spaghetti, real, what do you call it? *Al dente*. This is the way my old mom would serve up spaghetti when she was in a big hurry. Right out of the box, with maybe a jar of good old Chef Boyardee spaghetti sauce on the side to dip the noodles in, if she was feeling fancy.

Who turned every light in the house on? Lindsay said. —Where's Jim?

I did I guess, Ralph said. —I was getting a bad case of the willies. I heard some things, you know, noises. Strange noises. And the wind was blowing up outside. Those chimes drive me nuts, by the way. Binging and banging around. Jim's making a grocery-and-booze bolt. He's going to stir up some supper, he said. It's the last booze run I'll ever chip in on, by the way. I know I've said that before, but I mean it this time. I do. I've hit that rock bottom they tell you about, and I know it. I called Duffy's, that place, you know, north of town, where a drinking fellow can get on his feet. They give you hummers up at Duffy's, which is a little drink every so often, so a fellow can withdraw without going into convulsions and lapsing into a coma and dying from the DTs, if he's lucky. I'm going up there tomorrow, bright and early, if I can get a ride from somebody.

Here, hon, Lindsay said, and placed a set of car keys on the table before Ralph. —Alice Ann said you could keep the heap. Her word.

Well, Ralph said, and cupped the keys, I guess this is my fair share of our community property after eight thousand or so years of matrimony. Well, I'm not complaining. Water over the dam and all that. All's well that ends well, you know. Don't tell me anything about Alice Ann right now. Please don't, please.

She still loves you very much, Ralph. And you still love her. You know you do.

I can't not love her on some level, can I? Ralph said. —How could I not always love Alice Ann on some level? After all these centuries, these countless lifetimes. But I don't love her the way I love you now. And I won't ever be able to again. Not like I did.

You two will endure, Ralph, Lindsay said.

I can remember when our love for each other, Alice Ann's and mine, and I know how corny this will sound, but it was so sweet and childlike and unconditional that loving each other was no harder than loving yourself. But I just don't see how we can stay married to each other anymore. I don't really know how I'm going to live without her after all these years, but I don't see how we can live together without both of us going down the drain.

Those are among the most honest words you've ever uttered to me, Ralph. You owed me those words a long time ago.

This could be it, you know, Ralph said. —This could be our last chance, Lindsay.

We've been down that road, Ralph. But it's my fault. I

shouldn't have let things get out of hand again. Now I have to live with that mistake, too.

It's not your fault, Ralph said. —I know I'm just beating an old dead horse. Or old dead dog is more like it.

What I need to think about is Jim and me, that we, Jim and I, have to find a new place to live. I am utterly heartbroken about it. I feel undone right now, utterly. What will we do?

I'm not the one to ask, Ralph said. —That's a question for your husband.

What question? Jim said. He was standing in the doorway with two shopping bags in his arms. He walked into the room and deposited the bags on the kitchen counter.

About where we're going to live, Lindsay said. —I'm freezing in here, by the way. I've got goose bumps. Look at my arms.

Like somebody is walking over your grave? Jim said. —My old mountain granny used to say that about goose bumps.

I thought it was just me being cold, Ralph said. —Cold as a witch's, you know, bosom, as they say. I thought I was getting a bad case of the old shakes and shivers, which are my usual first symptoms of the raging willies.

Our little landlady probably turned the furnace off again. Letting us know how welcome we are here, Jim said, and he turned the stove's burners on and then lit the oven and left its door open. —I'll go build a roaring fire out front directly.

What are we going to do, Jim? Lindsay said. —We can't be out of here in a month.

Don't sweat it, baby, Jim said. —I'll take care of everything.

I don't blame her one bit for throwing us out.

You're right, I reckon, Jim said.

I hate to mention it, old Jim, Ralph said, but I'm about to faint from hunger. What did you get for supper, old boy? Something real quick and dirty, I hope.

Real quick and dirty and real American, Jim said. —Hot dogs.

Hot dogs! Ralph said. —I love hot hogs. Take me out to the ball game, that's my motto. Buy me some peanuts and popcorn and hot dogs. Hot dogs are the best cure known to man for the raging willies. Hey, old Jim, did you pick up any, you know, hooch?

Yeah, Ralph, I got some hooch. But only for hummers, Ralph. I'm starting you on the hummer regimen as of tonight.

I can't tell you how weary I am to the bone tonight, Lindsay said. —Jim, go ahead and fix Ralph something to eat. I'm going to go soak in a steaming bath for a while. Here in what used to be my home. God, but I always loved that huge old tub.

We're gonna wait for you, Jim said. —Ralph can contain his fat ass for a while.

I can wait, Ralph said.

Okay, guys, I won't be too long. I just want to lower what's left of this debris I call myself into that wonderful old tub for a while.

Take your time, babe, Jim said. —I'll get a fire going out front. Then I, for one, am going to repair to the deck for a spell. Check out that full, bloody moon. Have me a hummer or two.

Can I have a hummer or two, too, old Jim? Ralph said.

I'll study on it while I'm building the fire, Jim said.

I need a hummer bad, old Jim, Ralph said, and placed his hand over his heart. —My heart is going a mile a minute. That little devil is banging around in there like there's no tomorrow.

Lindsay stepped over and placed her own hand on Ralph's chest. —You're not kidding, Ralph. Maybe we should get you to an emergency room, hon. Jim, feel Ralph's heart.

No way, José, Jim said.

I'm all right, Ralph said. —This is nothing new. Sometimes it bangs away like this even in those rare moments when I'm not on the edge of hysteria, or in some blind state of panic. I'll tell you what's really scary, though. Those times when my old heart just stops beating altogether. It jerks me from sleep sometimes. Or from what passes as my sleep, anyway. My sleep is a joke. I haven't put together a good, solid hour of deep sleep since my early childhood. Back when instead of getting some good old regular childhood illness like the chickenpox or the measles or mumps or even polio, I came down with an acute case of the raging willies.

God only remembers why. Probably just the prospect of all those tomorrows stretching before me. And there's no such thing as a vaccination or cure for the raging willies. So I'll finally doze off. The next thing I know, I'm sitting bolt upright in bed with the sweats and shivers. Then I notice this deafening silence. Then it hits me. The sound that's missing is the sound of my own heart-beat.

Target Practice

Jim and Ralph stood on a rooftop deck in San Francisco's North Beach passing joints while they studied a fat full moon that moved palpably across a night sky hysterical with stars. They were waxing philosophical. They did not know that this would be the last time they would ever stand together on this deck overlooking the lights of North Beach and the dark Bay and a glowing Alcatraz Island beyond.

What Jim had been waxing philosophical about was how a vanished race of ancient Indians, people who were once alive on the curved surface of this planet not unlike he and Ralph, had looked up into the night sky in wondering dread and awe, and that hope that beat so humanly in their ancient Indian hearts, and when those ancient Indians considered that fat pie of a moon up yonder what they saw was not some mirror-image ancient Indian man in the moon. Rather, what ancient Indians saw in the moon were creatures from nature that were symbols of hope and renewal, like a great leaping blue trout. Now, there's the ultimate big one you can never really land but which can never get away either. Honest to God, old Ralph, ain't that just the most satisfactory fucken leaping blue trout in the moon you've ever seen in your miserable life?

Well, to tell you the truth, old Jim, Ralph said, I don't exactly see that blue Indian trout of hope in the moon you've been babbling about. To tell you the truth, I've always sort of seen something else in the moon, and not some man either.

Well, pray tell, Ralph, just what is it you see in the moon?

A goat.

A what?

A sort of goat, old Jim. Really. The shape of a goat.

A goat in the moon. Ralph sees a goat in the moon. Of course, Ralph does. Well, leave it to you, Ralph, to have as your personal vision of hope and renewal a smelly old goat.

Hey, there's nothing wrong with goats. I had me a goat once as a sort of pet when I was a boy. I loved that old goat, too. Bert was that goat's name. Bert the Goat is what I called him. Poor old Bert.

Why poor old Bert, Ralph?

Oh, poor old Bert the Goat got tangled up in his rope somehow one day, and somehow he fell over a big rock down in the field and hanged himself. It was a freak accident even for a goat. Bert was a real good old goat, but boy was he dumb. That didn't make any difference to me, though. My love for old Bert the Goat was unconditional.

And sweet and childlike?

You bet it was. Will you please pass that joint, please.

Ralph, I want you to tell me, your best pal since the untimely demise of Bert the Goat, the truth about something. Ralph, were you, being a typical little rural-boy type, and Bert the Goat ever, you know, an item? Ralph, truthfully now, did you ever get to know Bert, you know, biblically?

No! No way, José! Never! Not even once! I already told you, Bert was a good goat. Bert would have never gone for any hanky-panky like that. And if there's a goat heaven, old Bert is there right now.

Waiting for you, Ralph?

You bet he is. Old Bert the Goat would wait for me forever. Bert was a loyal type of goat. Jim, I just noticed you have your gun stuck in your belt.

Yes, I do, Ralph.

How come, old Jim?

Ralph, let me ask you something. Did you rat me out about Mary Mississippi to Lindsay?

Who? Mary who? What do you mean, old Jim?

When was the last time you screwed my wife, Ralph?

I never did that, Jim. You know, *screw*. We made love, but that was a long time ago.

Okay, Ralph, Jim said. —Think I'll get me some target practice, Jim said, and took the gun from behind his belt. Jim aimed his .38 at the moon and fired. At the explosion Ralph gasped and jumped and stumbled backward across the deck.

Missed, Jim said. —The goat moved.

That's against the law! Ralph gasped. —Shooting a gun like that in the city limits. You could get arrested or something.

Like I give a fuck, Ralph, Jim said, and pointed the .38 at Ralph.

Jim, what are you doing? You shouldn't ever point that thing at anybody! That thing could go off or something!

Like this? Jim said, and pulled the trigger.

Ow ow ow ow ow ow! Ralph howled as he staggered backward and tumbled over a chair onto the deck.

Goddamn it, Jim said, and lifted his .38 as though to inspect it. —Looks like I forgot to load it all up. Wouldn't you know.

That was an awful joke, old Jim, Ralph whimpered from where he sat on the deck. —I think I broke my arm. Really. In two, maybe three places.

What joke? Jim said. He stuck the .38 back behind his belt and fired up another joint as Ralph pulled himself to his feet. Ralph rubbed his arm as he rejoined Jim at the edge of the deck overlooking the Bay.

At that point in time Clint Eastwood was shooting a movie on Alcatraz Island based on a true-life book called *Escape from*

Alcatraz. As a gift to the city Clint Eastwood permitted the huge klieg lights he had erected to burn continuously so that Alcatraz Island glowed throughout the night through the fog like some enormous anchored ghost liner of lights, or some distant luminous island city of spirits. Something about that haunting, spooky sight unnerved Jim, but exactly what? That illuminated island honeycombed with cells, cells opening onto forgotten, undiscovered cells.

Would you mind sharing that number? Ralph said.

So you believe there is a goat heaven, Ralph? Here, goat-dick. Don't bogey it.

If there's any justice in this world, there's a goat heaven. I could use a hummer, too, old Jim.

And you put your faith in that?

Sure. You bet. Why not? I'll put my faith in a goat heaven any day of the week. Goat heaven is an endless field of sweet green grass with no big rocks anywhere. And there are no ropes in goat heaven either. And if I watch my p's and q's from here on out, you know, wash my old paws before supper and clean up my plate and say my prayers before bedtime and not play with my, you know, thing in the lonely dark I'm probably facing for the rest of my natural life, and if I get off the sauce, and stay off, well then, who knows, maybe old Bert the Goat and I will be together again someday up in goat heaven.

Isn't it pretty to think so, old Ralph? Jim said.

Living Memory

1

As the years passed by and their lives set off in different directions, Jim and Ralph would always attempt to tie one up on some pretext or other at least once or twice a year, usually for a trip together somewhere, when they would draw deeply from each other's memories and rehash half to death each shared event or disaster from the old days, and marvel time and again at all the dirty deeds they had gotten away with or for which they had come to forgive each other.

The final trip they took together began, fittingly enough, in San Francisco late one August. Jim had been on sabbatical leave that year from the Eastern university where he considered himself in deep disguise as a deputy professor. He had spent that year more or less bumming around, even hitching back and forth across country, perhaps in some final effort to recapture what he could of some romantic, rudderless, vagrant vision of himself. As Ralph had a new collection of stories out, he agreed to give a series of readings around the Bay Area to promote the book, as though at that point in his career any book of his needed promotion. The plan was to tie up in San Francisco, and Jim would carry Ralph's coat while he knocked off the readings, and then they would head East together, pretending that they were outlaw authors on the lam like in the old days, making the perfect clean getaway in Ralph's brand-new BMW. Ralph had standing-room-only crowds at each of his readings. He would read a few poems first, and then a story he had only recently completed based on the protracted death of Chckhov, which, as it turned out, was the last story Ralph ever wrote.

Ralph and Jim arrived in Iowa City early in the evening of their third day of cross-country driving. Although he had never lived there long, in many ways Iowa City felt like a hometown to Ralph, a sort of hometown of the spirit, for it was there that he felt as though his life had been released into significance as a writer, and where, for better or worse, he and Alice Ann had drifted firmly into that mythology that had carried their marriage forth for so many more years. They had been young and full of hope when they had first arrived in Iowa City, but while hunting for what they thought was the beginning of their real life together, they had merely figured out ways to inhabit their daydreams.

Ralph and Jim had taken a room at a large, new motel at the edge of Iowa City, and then Ralph suggested that they drive into town for dinner at a joint called the Mill, which Ralph described as being a big smoky barn of a bar and family-style restaurant popular with the young, hip faculty and students, and where Alice Ann had once waited tables in another lifetime. The grub at the Mill would be decent sturdy fare and plentiful and cheap, was what Ralph promised. At the Mill they would be able to get huge platters of spaghetti loaded down with fat meatballs, Ralph promised and, with any luck coming their way at all, laid. The joint would undoubtedly be packed with the current crop of young, hungry, would-be famous writers of tomorrow, bevies of horny writer-babes just clamoring to fuck their way to fame. Ralph had given a highly successful reading in Iowa City just a few months earlier, and because of the current critical and popular-press attention being given to his new book, Ralph was as hot as the old proverbial firecracker on the literary front. If he, old Running Dog Ralph Crawford, proclaimed high and low as the American Chekhov, could not get his load lightened in Iowa City, that hotbed of naked ambition and brazen, hungry heir-apparents, then he might as well pack up his pecker and go home to Momma, for what would be the worth then of fame for any man? Jim thought that this was a splendid idea. For surely simply being Ralph Crawford's sidekick meant that he, too, might get a shot at cheap romance in Iowa City.

Before they ate, though, Ralph wanted to drive around Iowa city for a spell and wax nostalgic. A light rain had come up as Ralph took Jim on a tour of a town transformed by nostalgia, where the wet night streets shone purely with the lights of the past. Ralph drove them out to a small trailer-park at the western edge of town, where out front there was a ramshackle motel and tiny restaurant, which appeared to be closed up. Off to the right among a strand of stunted pines were a half-dozen little frame cabins, also apparently boarded up and nearly overgrown with wild shrubbery and vines. When Ralph and Alice Ann had first come to Iowa City, they had rented one of those tiny cabins, number 6, for a couple of weeks while trying to arrange for student housing on campus. They had left their daughter with Ralph's mother in California until they got settled, so they were really alone together for the first time in ages, except for the fact that Alice Ann was pregnant again. But that didn't frighten them, for they were green and fearless in the face of the future. They felt as fixed and steady in their course as those stars which were as fat as fish in the vast Iowa night.

Sure, the facts of their lives didn't match the myth they had begun to make of their marriage, but those two weeks of pure, wondrous, abandoned six-and-seven-course sex in that shabby cabin fed the fantasy of their lives for years to come. There, deep in the heartland, they took new heart in themselves. They refound the freshness in themselves, and they were never more certain that they would offer each other solace and companionship forever, and that over the years their faithfulness to each other would become legendary, and that they would be able to submerge fully in their perfect passion forever. Night after night, Alice Ann would come into Ralph's arms an illusion, like the future, of untouched territory. My green, growing girl was just what Ralph would call Alice Ann, and press his face into her only slightly as yet bulging belly, as they lay on that old, violently creaky metal bed, night after night in the hot

Iowa dark, the steam rising from their wet, slick flesh, after having once again made the most amazing abandoned love of their lives. Even the cockroaches running across the nighttime linoleum sounded like creatures transporting themselves joyfully into new lives, and the faint, cross-fading voices on the old radio in the corner sounded like whispery calls of encouragement from that beyond we call the future.

Night after night Ralph and Alice Ann lay there in that hot dark getting sweetly sleepy together, wanting to fall asleep exactly as they wanted to die, at the same moment. Submerged in that lovely and pure isolation of love, they imagined an island called themselves, surrounded not by hot dark infinite fields of corn but by imaginary fish in a vast sea of perfectly still water, and any sound they heard outside their open windows they called a splash. But all that was when they were green and brave and beguiled by hope, back before the madness had set in. Ralph's last memory of those two weeks of true and isolated love was a perfect portent of the times ahead. He could see them still, late that last night, two phantoms in the rain, right over there in the gravel and red-dog beside the road, shouting at the top of their lungs, waving their arms crazily in the air, stalking up and down the roadside in the rain, accusing, accusing, Alice Ann's blue eyes turned green with anger and rage, green like those Iowa afternoon skies sometimes turned when storms were rolling in and tornado warnings crackled over the radio. Sooner or later, Ralph said to Jim, and popped the joint's roach into his mouth, everything that comes into your life leaves it. Just passes in and passes out. Every love story is finally left unfinished. And, finally, when the lovers are dead and gone, history, and everybody who ever knew them is history, then everything just passes at last from living memory and doesn't matter anymore, doesn't mean dick, in the land of the currently living.

2

Later that night in Iowa City, back in the motel room (just the two of them, old Ralph and Jim, for there was no romance in store for them that night, not that either of them was really serious about getting any in the first place, which if the truth be told had been simply old salty-dog talk), Ralph had put in a call to the woman he loved, and whom he would marry only weeks before he died. Jim put in a call to Lindsay, but the line was busy. Fuck, Jim had said to Ralph, I just hope Lindsay ain't gabbing with one of my girlfriends. Ralph said, How's the boy, by the way? Jim said, Boy's doing okay, I reckon. Rolf's a good kid. He's eating me out of house and home. His grades are real good. He's just this big goofy, dreamy, basically good kid. I tried to teach him how to hot-wire a car the other day, but he ain't got no mechanical abilities.

Ralph and Jim passed joints back and forth between their beds and lay there in the darkened room more or less watching television. At one point Jim said, So what do you hear from Alice Ann, by the way? Ralph said, I only mostly hear *about* her these days. From the kids mostly, on those occasions when they call to hit me up for cash. Alice Ann used the money I settled on her to buy the old farmhouse her mom and real dad had supposedly met at during a dance back in the Stone Age. Apparently she hired a bunch of hippie long-hairs who claimed they were master Zen carpenters to restore it so that she could establish some sort of karmic community center or something, something like that, some sort of Eastern Dumb-Nut Ideas Institute for those dropouts and drugheads and other blissed-out dopes who called themselves Zen-nicks, but the hippie board-bangers just generally ripped her off, sat around smoking dooby all day and digging their navels. So Alice Ann went belly up yet again, and now the last Ralph had heard she was back to slinging hash in some roadside truckers' diner in the Northwest somewhere, married to some mechanic or something; something like that, anyway. Who really knew. Who really knew anything at all.

Several weeks after Ralph's untimely death from lung cancer not a year after their last trip together, Jim returned home from campus one afternoon to find Lindsay working as usual in their back-yard garden she loved so. Who knew where Rolf was out running around. Probably at the library caressing the covers of books. Or sitting on a rock down by the river. The boy seemed to understand intuitively that every day it was both the same and a new river. The boy spent a great amount of time on his butt in the grass of hillsides considering the passage of clouds. Rolf was a big woolly-headed smart boy whose capacity for gentleness and empathy and foodstuffs astonished Jim daily.

Jim and Lindsay had bought a turn-of-the-century, yellow-brick barn of a house on a hillside in the Eastern city where Jim taught, which they called the Norman Bates Boardinghouse because it looked so spooky and haunted that neighborhood kids trembled deliciously when they skulked up the twisty, crumbly-concrete steps to trick-or-treat on Halloween. In the back-yard garden that day Lindsay was on her knees weeding among some delicate blue flowers. Jim pulled up a chair to the table on the back deck. It was the same round glass-topped table they had had on the deck back in their old North Beach days. On the table, beside a gin-and-tonic in which the ice had melted, lay a copy of Ralph's final collection of poems. Jim picked up Ralph's book of poems and thumbed through them, stopping here and there to read, while he sipped at Lindsay's watery leftover gin-and-tonic. At one point Lindsay stood up and stretched, while rubbing the base of her back. She spotted Jim and gave a little wave. For a few moments they simply gazed at each other across the garden. Finally Jim raised the glass as though making a toast, then polished its watery contents off. Jim said, How about I throw some dogs on the grill tonight? Lindsay said, That would be good. And then Lindsay knelt back down to weed among those delicate blue flowers whose name Jim couldn't recall on a bet.

What Jim had thought about as he watched his wife weed among those blue flowers was what if Alice Ann had been right all along and their lives were all locked in some crazy karmic conjunction. And in that ageless soup of seeds and ancient eggs they had, sure enough, shared countless incarnations jam-packed with lust and love and loss. And so maybe they could all carry forth the hope that they would, indeed, have other chances in other lifetimes to do better by one another.